Tried and Tested

Laura Kline and Jessica Mace

ISBN-10: 0692311688
ISBN-13: 978-0692311684

Edited by Jamie Morris.

Prologue

King Ethan Kidwell looked over at his wife, Brooke. She seemed a little more at ease than she had been in the past few months, and he was happy that she was adjusting to her role as the Queen of Raxx. As the daughter of a former President, it would seem natural that she would be used to the spotlight, but her father, the now Councilor of the International Council of Powers, Councilor Hathaway, had taken great care to allow her a somewhat private life away from the scrutiny of the public. Brooke looked up from the child she had been talking to, and smiled at Ethan. He knew that this particular event interested her. It was a ribbon cutting ceremony for the opening of a school for the deaf and blind, a routine, rather bore-some event for him. Brooke, though, had shown a considerable interest and even excitement over the event. As he had watched her throughout the day with various children, he knew that the topic of their own future children was sure to arise again. He had to admit, she did have a way with children, and he knew that she would be an excellent mother, but it was not something he felt he could deal with for now. He had never expected to be a King, and the responsibilities of the position were taking their toll on both of them.

Brooke walked over to Ethan and put her hand in his giving it a gentle squeeze of affection.

She leaned towards him and spoke, "His name is Bronson. He lost most of his vision in a car accident a few years ago. He says I am beautiful."

Ethan put his arm around her waist and replied, "Well, his vision must not be too bad. He's right."

Brooke smiled. She was proud of her husband, and she was happy to be here with him today. He turned towards her, gave her a quick kiss on her temple and then stepped up to the podium to give his short speech of dedication. Brooke was happy that the weather had held up for the day. According to the weather reports, a storm was headed their way, but so far there was only a faint breeze. As Brooke listened to the sound of Ethan's voice, her attention wandered to the children gathered at the base of the platform they were standing on. A translator signed for those who were deaf, and the excitement of the children over their new school was palpable.

Ethan's speech was over, and the Principal of the school stepped forward with the symbolic scissors that would be used to cut the ribbon. Brooke mused over the argument that had ensued earlier between the event organizer and security over the type of scissors that would be used. As always, safety was a primary concern, especially with the turbulent circumstances surrounding the country following the war with Aldrich. Additionally, many were still expressing their discontent that Ethan was the ruler in lieu of his sister, Nicole who was now married to the king of Lionel.

A rumble was heard in the distance, and Brooke looked out across the audience to the sky. It had suddenly grown darker, and the wind was picking up. As her eyes traveled back to Ethan and the ribbon, she felt an uneasy awareness of something being not quite right. When she had looked out at the horizon, the eyes of almost everyone in the audience were on Ethan and the Principal, but there were a set of eyes that seemed focused elsewhere. She felt a sudden dread and hesitantly scanned the audience more carefully this time. Her eyes locked with a man standing about fifty feet away directly behind the children who were gathered in front. He did not divert his glare, and as she stood, stunned by the temerity of his stare, his lips twisted into a sinister smile. Fear immediately coursed through her, but she felt paralyzed. She watched helplessly as the man lifted his hand with some kind of device clearly evident in its grip. Before she could react, an explosion rocked the entire platform she had been standing on throwing her to the ground.

The rest was a haze. She was vaguely aware of voices around her. A security guard was pulling her to her feet. Someone was yelling as they were being pulled away. She looked out towards the crowd again and was nauseated by the sight of bodies of children littering the lawn. She saw the little boy, Bronson, who she had been talking to earlier. He was still alive, but seemed trapped beneath a piece of shrapnel from the blast. She tried to move towards him but was yanked back by the strong arms of her security. She tried to wrestle free, and then she was free. Another explosion sent her flying through the air. She landed face down on a heap of the now destroyed platform. She felt a sharp pain in her side, and then all went black.

Chapter 1

It was an unusually busy Thursday afternoon at the Mattell Grill and Pub.

Todd Heart threw up his hands as one of the servers flew by throwing a dish in the already full sink and splashing Todd in the process.

"Come on, man!" Todd protested.

"Speed it up. There's more coming."

Todd was sick of dishes, but at least here he was free to make his own life and his own decisions. He was out from under what he considered the tyranny of the place he called home. This was not a life that most would choose, and he certainly could have many other choices, but for now, this gave him what he wanted - anonymity and a chance to make his own name. At the moment though, the dishes were getting the best of him. He took off the apron he was wearing and threw it down. He headed for the restroom. It was on the other side of the restaurant, and as he walked towards it, an image on the big screen in the corner of the bar area caught his attention.

He walked over to get a better view and rested his arms on the back of a high-backed bar stool. The image that had caught his attention was gone, replaced with the image of his country's Public Relations Advisor to the King, Noelle Rose.

Noelle was speaking, "King Daren and all of Lionel offers its support to the country of Raxx in its time of need. We have received word that King Kidwell, our own Queen's brother, escaped the blast with no injuries. Queen Kidwell is still in critical condition. . . "

Todd didn't hear anything more as Noelle Rose continued. The image had once again changed. He watched as the platform on which the King and Queen of Raxx were standing exploded sending shards of metal flying in all directions. He saw Ethan thrown to the ground by his security, their bodies jerking spasmodically as they blocked him from the blast. Then he saw the horror on Brooke's face as a piece of the debris pierced her side and then she fell to the ground limp and lifeless.

Todd's hands gripped the back of the chair tighter and he clenched his jaw as he fought against the images that were surfacing in his own mind. Images of a twisted black car with smoke and flames. Of his father kneeling in the midst of the wreckage cradling his mother in his arms. Weeks, months of news stories about his own personal tragedy being displayed for the world to see. Images that haunted him. Images that he was trying to run away from. Todd took a deep breath and gained control. He knew Ethan and Brooke well. Before taking on the role of King in Raxx, Ethan had been the Chief Advisor in Lionel. Ethan was tied by blood to Lionel as well - Queen Nicole was his sister and the rightful Queen of Raxx.   Todd sincerely hoped that Brooke was okay.

Todd became aware that he was no longer alone. Others in the restaurant had gathered to see to the newscast more clearly. The scene had returned to a reporter who was rehashing the events as they had happened. Suddenly, the reporter's story was interrupted with a shrill beeping noise indicating that there was a national emergency.

A voice that had been chosen for its reassuring quality came on, "The University of Lionel has been attacked. Emergency response teams have been deployed. If you have friends or family within the area, you are asked to please stay away so that the response teams can access the area. For the most current updates, visit the university website."

The broadcast was brief and lacked details, but the reporter quickly returned with additional information on the attack.

"From what we are hearing and seeing, there were two large blasts on the university campus. One was centered near the university library, and the other seems to have been centered in the women's dorm area," the reporter explained.

A picture of the mentioned dormitory appeared next to the reporter's head. The media had apparently been unable to obtain pictures of the blast areas yet as the picture showed no damage. Todd recognized the picture on the screen. It was the dormitory where his own sister was living. Fear gripped and immobilized him. He waited for the next words from the reporter's mouth. If his sister had been caught in the blast, it would be the news story of the year, and he would once again suffer paralyzing loss.

The reporter had continued with more details, but now she focused on the detail that most interested him, "We are just receiving word that the second blast collapsed the dormitory that Princess Kelly, King Daren's niece, was staying in. However, we have also just learned that Princess Kelly was pulled out of the university and taken home to the palace less than a week ago by her father, Commander Heart."

Todd breathed a sigh of relief while slamming the back of the chair he had been resting on earlier with his hand. Involuntarily he muttered a satisfied "yes" and then looked around self-consciously. He suddenly became aware that others in the room had a stake in this as well, but their outcomes may not be as favorable. Cynthia, one of the servers, was standing a few feet away. Her eyes were wide and her hands were shaking. He knew that she was a student at the university.

Todd moved closer to her and took her hands in his own. He then leaned down to her eye level.

"Cynthia. Look at me," Todd insisted.

The girls eyes were glued to the television, so Todd gently turned her away from it.

Again he commanded, "Look at me, Cynthia. It's going to be okay."

His confidence seemed to reassure her and she looked at him hopefully.

"Do you need to go?" he questioned.

She seemed uncertain, "I can't . . . my shift. . ."

"I'll take care of it."

She gave him a thankful nod and left. Todd looked around the room. Several customers seemed distraught. It was time for him to go home, to his real home at the palace, but for right now, he was needed here.

Chapter 2

The first report about Raxx had come at 1:00pm in the afternoon. King Daren of Lionel had been eating lunch when he was interrupted by his security with the news of the first of several terrible accounts that would follow. In addition to the attack on the university, it seemed that some type of poison had been released in a hotel in Macera killing over 100 guests and workers and sending countless others to the hospital. King Daren summoned his council, and they watched and worked for over an hour as more reports of explosions and similar attacks in several other public places flooded in.

Commander Christopher Heart was barking orders faster than his men could move to follow them. He had already deployed units to each of the attack sites. He was waiting to hear that the areas had been secured. In the meantime, he was determined that any further threats to his country would be annihilated.

He yelled to his secretary who was stationed outside his office door, "Lieutenant Bailey, tell Noelle to contact all stations. I want the roads cleared. Everyone should be in their homes within the next three hours. Anyone found in a public place will be brought in for questioning. Those who are farther away from home will be bussed to a secure location until further notice. That includes anyone staying in a hotel. They need to be ready to go within the hour."

Christopher picked up the phone that was nestled among several stacks of paper that had made an appearance on his desk over the last few hours and dialed the palace technical systems engineer. "Mr. Moulder, I want all satellite footage routed to both my office screens and my handheld. Inform me immediately if your team finds anything on the recordings. And Dawson, you better make damn well sure this palace is secured."

As soon as he put the phone down, it rang. He picked it up, had a brief conversation with the person on the other end and then headed for his second in command's office.

Captain West was standing talking on the phone himself when Christopher entered, but that did not deter the Commander.

Without waiting for him to finish his phone conversation, Christopher addressed Captain West, "The attack sites are secured. I am going to the hotel. We may have a lead there. Planes are grounded, a curfew has been set and General Ben Canaan is assembling teams to search homes. Follow protocol and take care of the rest of it."

The commander was gone before the Captain could respond with even a "yes, sir."

As Commander Heart exited through the service entrance doors of the palace, he was joined by five of his most trusted men. A helicopter waited for them, its blades whirring in a high-pitched urgency and picking up speed as they approached.

Within minutes, the Commander and his men arrived at the site of a hotel that had been attacked using poisonous gases. The hotel was in the province of Macera, but it was on the border of Hearthill where the palace was located. Lionel troops had secured the area for the Commander's arrival, but emergency crews were still working on the borders assisting those who were still struggling for life and preparing the bodies of those who had given in to the poison.

As Christopher approached the scene, all eyes, both military and non-military alike shifted to look at the legendary King's Commander. Christopher had successfully kept the small country of Lionel secure for nearly 20 years, and he was well known around the world for his military prowess. Over the years, Lionel had had its share of enemies, but every one of those enemies had come to fear and respect Lionel forces and their Commander.

The General who had been placed in charge of this area of operation approached the Commander and saluted.

Christopher addressed him, "Why are these injured still here?"

"Sir, we don't have enough ambulances to transport them all. We have to send them in rounds," the General explained.

Christopher's brow creased at the General's explanation. "Then get your men in those military trucks and get these people to a medical facility. General, are you sure you can handle this?"

The General seemed abashed by the Commander's reprimand and immediately sprang to action. To the surprise of the men around him, Christopher joined in helping move the injured onto the vehicles. The poison had shown no favoritism, and Christopher's anger towards this faceless enemy grew stronger as he watched the faces of both children and elderly in agony.

Once all the injured had been loaded, Christopher once again found the General. "Where are the containers?"

"We've set up a contamination area, and my men have been working on analyzing the residue that was left behind. It seems that the poison was introduced through the complimentary cookies that the hotel passes out during lunchtime. It is a form of a Botulinum Toxin. The vials we found contain small doses that were probably used for Botox injections. One of our researchers discovered that several dermatology clinics in Cashteh reported a series of thefts over a year ago. Among the items taken were several vials of Botox from each of the locations."

Christopher contemplated this information. Cashteh had once been one of Lionel's greatest nemeses, but since the former King had met his demise, and his niece had taken over, the two countries had become more ally than foe. Still, the winds of politics could swiftly shift and it would be foolish to rule out any possibility. One vial of the poison would be more than enough to poison the entire population of the hotel. If several vials were stolen, then perhaps more attacks were planned. Christopher briefly thought about his son, Todd, who had been absent for several months now. According to Christopher's resources, Todd was working at a restaurant. He immediately pushed the thought out of his mind.

"How was the poison introduced to the food?"

"Once we determined that the poison was in the cookies, they tested all the ingredients in the kitchen. Traces of the poison was found in the bottles of vanilla that would have been used."

"I want everyone who stepped foot in that kitchen over the past 3 days to be brought in and questioned."

"Sir, we've already accessed the camera footage and are bringing them in. We have also sent an alert to all food manufacturers and distributors to be wary."

"Good. Let's keep it at that. I've ordered a curfew. Most people should be eating at home tonight. Contact the shelters and set up testing of any food distributed there. Keep it under wraps though. There's no need to create panic. Make sure the distributors are provided with the means to test their products as well. A sampling should suffice for now."

"Yes, sir." The General saluted and set to work.

****

Around Lionel, the news had changed to a slightly more positive outlook as reports of thwarted attacks started trickling in. Commander Heart's quick actions and highly trained forces had prevented even more disaster. Daren and his council worked late into the night. No one seemed to know how or why this had happened. Christopher had returned with a possible lead on the origin of the poison, but even that proved to be a dead end. Finally, when nothing else could be ascertained, Daren sent his weary and worn council members away.

For the next two days, King Daren demanded answers, but none were to be found. Over 500 people had either been killed or injured in the attacks. The most personal connection was the attack on Lionel University where Daren himself had briefly attended, as well as most of his family members, the most recent being his niece Kelly. Her father had withdrawn her only days before. It appeared that the attackers thought she was still there as the explosion was centralized in the area she would normally have frequented. Tempers were flaring and everyone was on edge. The next day was Sunday, and Daren declared a day of rest and supplication to God for all. It seemed for now that the country was at least secure. Military personnel would remain stationed throughout Lionel with a heavy presence on the borders, and the curfew would remain in effect indefinitely. They would begin again on Monday, hopefully with a fresh outlook and some answers.

Chapter 3

Captain Chad West paced the entire length of his suite as he contemplated what he was about to do. With the country in turmoil and the many demands that would be made of him, he wondered if this was the right timing for his plans. However, he reasoned that there never seemed to be a right time and regardless of the circumstances, he wasn't going to back down on this decision.

Chad looked at his watch. The Sunday morning service would start in twenty-one minutes. It would last an hour and fifteen minutes, and then Chad would make his move. He wasn't sure how the king would react to his request. He decided to chance it anyway. At this point, he had nothing to lose.

Chad checked his appearance once more. His mother had taken great care to make sure his suit would be flawless, and he wondered if her motherly instincts had forewarned her that something was up. He smiled as he considered how childish it seemed that his mother did his laundry. Although his mother could be a little interfering at times as all mothers often are, he was grateful that she had been hired in the palace to oversee housekeeping. He could easily check in on her when he wanted to, and he was assured at all times that she was safe and happy. She definitely deserved to be. His father had shunned her as soon as he found out she was pregnant, and her family had disowned her. She had been forced to leave the country of her birth and travel to a new life and a new start. She chose a country where men were held responsible for their actions and were required to take responsibility for their decisions. In Lionel, she could be assured that a rich and powerful man would never be allowed to disgrace and humiliate her as she had been in Lavinia. As a single mother, she had worked hard to give Chad all the necessities of life, but most importantly she had instilled in him the values and principles that had made him into the courteous yet determined man of integrity and faith that he had become. He had asked her on several occasions to stop working and let him take care of her for a change, but she would have none of it. She said that an idle hand created an idle brain, and at only 44 years old, she was much too young for either. Everyone in the palace loved her as Chad knew they would, and she was content to work there. Chad remembered the pride on his mother's face when he told her that he had been selected to serve in the royal guard at the palace. Then he remembered the tears in her eyes as he took the oath that would make him the next in line to be the King's Commander, the highest honor he could achieve in his profession. He knew there would be tears in her eyes today as well when he stood and made his request of the King.

Chad left his room and made his way to the palace chapel. His mission overshadowed his usual outgoing and friendly nature. As he entered the chapel, his attention was focused on finding Ashley. He saw her near the front of the room talking to her uncle, Prince Brandon. He took a moment to just stand and gaze at her. Her long, wavy auburn hair contrasted beautifully with her blue eyes and pale skin. She was probably the smallest adult in the room with her petite frame, and Chad mused at how even that characteristic made her unique. She was smiling, and he was sure that she and Brandon were exchanging playful insults with one another. She could be childlike and free-spirited, but she could also walk into a room and demand the attention of the most respected government officials.

Ashley looked up and caught Chad staring at her. She smiled and indicated with her eyes for him to come to her. He obeyed.

As Chad walked toward her, Ashley became lost in thought. She remembered when things had first changed between them. She was almost seventeen, and she had known Chad for much of her life. They were at an ICP function. King Daren had graciously allowed her to go to the dinner celebrating the induction of the new Chief Councilor Hathaway to the International Council of Powers, a conglomeration of several countries that would come together to diplomatically resolve their differences. It was really a place for countries to make secret alliances, trade information, spy on one another and manipulate one another for their own selfish gains. Depending on who was in power, the ICP could either be a country's best ally or its worst enemy. Ashley had been inspired by the masses of people from different countries and cultures that were present, and it was probably then that she had decided to pursue a career in international relations.

After the dinner, she had been so entranced with all the events that she had not realized that everyone in her party had departed, and she had no idea how to get back to her room. She remembered how Chad had been uncharacteristically playful as he teased her about her lack of directional skills and refused to point her in the direction of her room. He had finally relented, and as they walked down the halls, she had suddenly become annoyed by the fact that he walked behind her and insisted on referring to her as Miss Heart and ma'am. She had complained, and he had reminded her of his duty to protect her, but as they walked on, he eventually made his way to her side.

She thought of how he had surprised her with his knowledge of paintings, history, and government, and how quickly her perception of him began to change. By the time they had reached her room, she was entranced by him. After making her night by finding her a Pepsi, Chad had noticed something in her hair. She tried unsuccessfully to remove it, and after several failed attempts she finally asked Chad to help her. As he stepped towards her to remove it, his hand brushed her cheek. He had frozen for a moment seeming almost statuesque. His eyes had filled with desire, he had moved closer, and before she knew it, their lips had met. She would never forget the look of complete trepidation on his face when he pulled away, shoved her into her room and then quickly excused himself for the night. When he found her in Prince Trevor Benson's room the next day, she remembered how she had so pointedly explained to Chad that Trevor had tried to take advantage of her, but that she had informed him that she was saving herself for marriage. She had then threatened Chad with telling her father about their kiss the night before if he felt the need to mention her situation with Trevor. Ashley had held that over Chad's head for months. She would never forget the day she blurted out in anger to her father that Chad had kissed her. Surprisingly, Chad was still alive. Even more surprisingly, Chad had finally mustered the courage to ask her father officially to date her. After many trials and tribulations, questions and misunderstandings, an on again, off again relationship and Prince Trevor's constant interference, she and Chad were finally together.

Ashley was brought back to the present by her sister Kelly, "Um, Ashley, everything okay? Are you here with us?"

Ashley just nudged her sister and looked up at Chad again. She knew it would be impossible to concentrate on the message given by Pastor Isaiah, and she also knew that the next hour and a half would seem like forever.

Just as Chad was about to reach Ashley, her father pulled him aside to speak with him. Christopher was the last person Chad wanted to speak with at that moment. He wanted to get to Ashley, and he didn't want Christopher becoming suspicious. Chad answered Christopher's questions noncommittally but enough to suffice. Then he finally reached Ashley's side.

Ashley looked up at Chad and whispered, "You haven't changed your mind, have you?"

Chad replied, "This should have happened almost a year ago. I think we have both waited long enough, don't you? Or are you thinking of backing out on me?"

Ashley simply smiled as her father and sister joined them. Chad hoped it was a smile of encouragement. As the service dragged on, Chad thought over again and again exactly what he would say once it was over. He couldn't be sure how the King would respond, but he hoped it would be positive. Then there was the matter of Commander Heart. Chad had a fairly good idea of what he would say, but then again, Ashley's father could be quite unpredictable at times. Just as he thought the service would never end, he heard Pastor Isaiah say, "Let's all stand for a closing prayer."

Chad was certain that his heart stopped. For a brief moment, his lungs failed him, and then he regained composure. Pastor Isaiah said "amen," and people started to head out. With an effort of resolve, Chad walked to the front of the palace chapel, seized the microphone and began, "Everyone, if you could please indulge me for a few moments, I have an important matter I would like to address."

Chad looked out at the sea of faces staring back at him. He took a deep breath and then addressed Ashley's uncle, "King Daren." He then looked at her father and continued, "Commander Heart, as you both know, Ashley and I have been engaged for quite some time now. We had hoped to be husband and wife by now, but circumstances have prevented that on numerous occasions. We love each other, and we want to be together sooner rather than later. So, I would like to ask you both for your permission to marry today with all our family and closest friends present."

Chad scanned the faces looking back at him; some were full of surprise, others seemed amused, and still others were smiling in encouragement. Chad looked at the faces of the two who mattered most and waited for their reply.

As soon as Chad had taken the stage, Christopher and Daren had looked at each other questioningly. It was clear that neither had any idea of what Chad was doing. That concerned them. However, as Chad poured over his request, both men relaxed somewhat.

Christopher nodded his approval for Daren, and Daren addressed Chad, "Captain West, I would be more than happy for you and Ashley to put this matter to rest. You have my permission and my blessing."

Chad didn't wait to hear from Christopher. He had seen the look of agreement pass between the King and his brother, and he breathed a sigh of relief.

"If everyone could give us a few moments to change our attire, we will proceed as soon as possible. Dawson, would you do me the honor of standing with me as my best man?"

Dawson Moulder, the palace technical systems engineer, smiled, "Of course. It would be an honor."

Ashley spoke up and addressed her sister, "Come on Kelly. I know you'll never forgive me if you aren't a part of this."

Kelly and Ashley hurried to the suite to get Ashley prepared for her wedding. Although she was old enough to have a room of her own, Ashley had not yet moved out of the suite she shared with her father, his wife Sarah, and two youngest half brothers. Kelly had been talking the whole way, but Ashley only heard bits and pieces. She felt as though she had been waiting forever for this day, and she was so happy and so proud of her soon to be husband for having the courage to pull this off.

As they entered Ashley's room, Kelly nearly screeched in surprise and indignation.

"You even have your dress laid out? I can't believe you didn't tell me any of this! I could have helped."

Ashley noted the hurt tone of her sister and replied, "Kelly, I wasn't trying to keep anything from you, but we both know you couldn't keep a secret from Dad if you wanted to. He reads you like a book, and as soon as he questioned you, you would've broken down and told him everything. It's not a bad thing, Kelly, but Chad and I didn't want to risk anyone finding out. I'm sorry. I need your help now."

Kelly seemed placated. Ashley sat down in front of the mirror and addressed Kelly.

"The first task is to tackle this mess of hair. Grab that magazine off the bed. I want my hair to look like page 27."

Ashley could have had any number of professional stylists at her disposal, but she knew her sister was just as adept as any of them and would enjoy the process. As she worked, Ashley watched Kelly in the mirror. Kelly's long, straight, blonde hair matched their father's and was a sharp contrast to Ashley's long, auburn waves. Ashley hoped that today's events would cheer her sister. Since coming home prematurely from the university due to homesickness, Kelly had not been herself. The attack on the university had left one of Kelly's friends severely injured, and Ashley knew Kelly felt guilty that the attack had purportedly been targeted at her. Kelly caught Ashley staring at her and smiled.

"How did you know you loved him?" Kelly questioned.

The question was out of character for Kelly, but in her wedding bliss, Ashley was oblivious.

"I don't know that there was any one defining moment, but it definitely started when I was seventeen at my first ICP meeting."

Ashley recounted how excited she had been at the opportunity to go to the International Council of Powers.

"I got lost," Ashley continued. "Everything was so new and exciting. I didn't realize everyone else from Lionel had left. I wasn't sure how to get back to my room."

"Were you scared?"

Ashley knew that her sister would have panicked in that situation.

"Maybe a little at first, but then Chad showed up."

"So, he rescued you, and you fell in love with him?" Kelly taunted.

Ashley smiled, "Eventually, yes."

Ashley had taken care that morning to do as much as possible to be ready. Once her hair was done, it only took a few minutes to freshen her makeup. She knew people were waiting for her and Chad to return. She stood up. Her dress was a simple mermaid style flaring slightly at the bottom. As she stood in front of the full length mirror, Kelly fussed making sure every fold of dress and strand of hair was perfectly in place. Once she was satisfied, Kelly stood back to look at her sister. Tears filled both girls' eyes.

Embracing each other, Kelly was the one to speak, "I'm so glad you're happy, Ashley."

Ashley pulled back to look at her sister, "Thank you, Kelly. We are totally going to do this for you some day. Ready?"

As they exchanged their vows, Ashley focused on every aspect of the man she was about to call husband: his dark brown waves of hair were combed neatly away from his tanned forehead, and his kind, blue eyes held the intense passion that she had come to know so well. He didn't tower above her as her father did, but rather stood at what she considered a perfect 5'11." Dawson and Kelly stood by as Pastor Isaiah reminded the couple of the sanctity of marriage. Not only would they be vowing a commitment to one another, but more importantly it was a commitment to God. In Lionel, this was a lifetime commitment. Dawson and Kelly would serve as accountability witnesses and would stand by their sides throughout the course of their marriage reminding them of their vows to each other. Chad and Ashley both breathed a sigh of relief when they heard Pastor Isaiah pronounce them man and wife. They knew they would need to cherish the next 12 hours because in the morning, Chad would be called upon by the King to assist in a plan of action to deal with the recent attacks. For now, Ashley would have to be content with the simple fact that Chad was finally hers.

Chapter 4

     As King Daren prepared for his council meeting, he hoped that his council members would be clear-headed and decisive. He knew that a possible war was on the horizon, but it exasperated him that he had no leads on who the war would be against. The palace was on lock-down until they had answers. He wanted answers. He wanted to take action, but going to war might just do them in. They were already stretching their resources with the enhanced security. Daren's mind wandered to the repugnant idea of borrowing from another country. Pastor Isaiah had recently reminded Daren of God's many promises to provide for his children. In particular, Daren's thoughts moved towards the promise, "And God will generously provide all you need. Then you will always have everything you need and plenty left over to share with others." Daren was waiting to see that happen. Lately, King Daren wondered if God had forsaken him. He had worked so hard to lead his country in truth and righteousness. Had he somehow failed? There were no answers – from God or anyone. Still, he knew he had to maintain his faith. He was King after all, and he would lead by example even if he didn't feel like it. Daren put on his game face and made his way to the conference room.

     As he entered, Daren made a mental note of the expressions and general attitudes of all present. Ian, his chief advisor, and Deanna, his financial advisor, were talking in low tones. Christopher and Alan, the palace hospitality advisor, were ignoring one another, and Lance, the foreign affairs advisor, had not yet arrived, as usual. Chad was sitting at the end of the table. Daren watched him looking over the notes for the meeting and mused that at least Chad was wise enough not to gloat over his enjoyment of the night before. Christopher may love Chad like a son, but he loved his daughter more, and the thought of any man with her might just be more than Christopher could handle in his current state.

     King Daren had been somewhat concerned that Captain West would be preoccupied with his recent marriage, but he seemed very focused. In fact, he seemed more attentive than he had in quite some time. For a brief moment, Daren regretted having made him wait so long to marry Ashley, but quickly diverted his thoughts. As King, he could not waste time on regrets. Besides, the delay had been more for the benefit of Ashley. Daren knew all too well the toll that the demands of being a Commander could take on a marriage. Ashley's own mother had sought the intimacy of another when his brother Christopher had denied her the attention she needed. Daren did not care to repeat that history with Chad and Ashley. Ashley needed to understand that Chad would often have to place the demands of King and country above the needs of his wife.

Lance arrived with seconds to spare, and Daren indicated for Pastor Isaiah to open with prayer.

Pastor Isaiah finished his prayer with, "In the name of our Lord, God and Savior, Jesus Christ, I pray. Amen."

Daren thanked Pastor Isaiah and waited for him to exit. As soon as the doors were secured, he turned to Ian, "Let's get started."

Ian addressed the council, "As everyone knows, we are here to develop a plan to deal with the recent attacks and prevent future attacks. . ."

Christopher interrupted, "Please explain, Mr. Garrett, how we are to deal with the attacks if we don't even know who attacked? Perhaps Mr. Sterling should enlighten us on this matter. Mr. Sterling, you are the foreign affairs advisor. I think we can rule out the possibility of an inside threat, so who is behind these attacks? Surely you have some insight into the matter?"

Daren could tell that this meeting was quickly going to become rather heated and have no benefit unless he intervened. The problem was that once Christopher was in a fervor, it was difficult to cool his ire. At the same time, Daren was also a bit incensed with the fact that Lance Sterling, his foreign affairs advisor had failed to provide any useful information. Daren knew that under normal circumstances, Lance had always been informed and could be relied upon to provide pertinent details. Weighing those two thoughts, Daren chose to remain silent and wait for Lance to respond.

Lance was hoping that Daren would step in to intervene, but when he glanced at the King, he saw that there was little hope of that. Daren had already expressed his irritation with him over this matter in private. Lance also knew that occasionally, Daren allowed his council members to suffer a little public discomfort as retribution over their inaction. Mentally, Lance reprimanded himself. He knew this was going to happen. Pulling himself together Lance opened his mouth to speak but was cut off by the King.

"Lance, we are all waiting. I spoke with you about this two days ago and made it clear that I expected answers at this meeting. What steps have you taken to obtain the information we need to act?"

Daren knew that in a way he had just given Lance an out. Lance obviously didn't have all the answers, but asking what steps he had taken would at least rule out several possibilities. The look of relief on Lance's face confirmed Daren's thoughts.

Lance answered, "Sir, I have spoken with Councilor Hathaway. He is, of course, just as eager to discover who is behind these attacks as we are. His daughter is a victim, and he wants justice. If we assume that the attacks in Raxx and those here are related, then we need to look at common enemies of both countries. Additionally, the attacks were quite personal, so specifically we should narrow down those enemies that have personal bones to pick with both King Kidwell and King Daren . . ."

Ian Garrett, the Chief Advisor to the King, interrupted, "Mr. Sterling, do you have any useful information, or do you plan to waste our time rehashing facts that we are all smart enough to decipher ourselves?"

"I have a list."

"The man does have a brain after all," muttered Christopher.

Purposefully ignoring Christopher, Lance hastily continued, "I have also been in contact with the enemies of those on the list to find out if they have any intelligence that could assist us. Unfortunately, our enemies' enemies are not cooperative."

This was going nowhere. Daren looked over the list that he could have created on his own in ten minutes time. He and his council were grasping at straws.

"Lance, have you spoken with Ethan? Does he have any insight into who might be behind this?" Daren questioned.

Before Lance could respond, the communications pad lit up indicating that someone was outside the conference room door. Christopher jumped to his feet as Daren hit the button to display a visual of the would be intruder. A video popped up on the LCD. Captain Tyler Woods, King Daren's personal security was at the door waiting.

Christopher pushed the audio, "Captain Woods, what is it?"

Captain Woods responded, "Commander Heart, sir, this is Captain Woods, clearance 13498293CharlieFoxtrotRomeo. I need to speak with the council, sir."

Daren nodded his approval to Christopher. Captain Woods had provided the code indicating that it was safe, so Christopher opened the door. Everyone in the room had tensed at Tyler's intrusion. Captain Woods would never interrupt a meeting unless there was an important, and usually dire reason. All eyes were on Captain Woods as he entered. His expression was stern, but that was normal for Tyler. Daren remained silent, so Christopher addressed Tyler.

"Captain Woods, I'm sure you have a good reason for interrupting us."

Woods addressed the king, "Yes, sir. King Daren, there has been a major earthquake in Pilnez."

Ian spoke up, "Clarify 'major,' Captain Woods."

"8.8 magnitude, sir."

At that, all eyes turned to the king. Daren simply stared at Tyler waiting for him to finish.

Tyler proceeded, "Sir, rescue units and disaster response teams have been deployed. The quake was in one of the more rural areas of

Pilnez, so the structural damage is not severe. There are several residential areas in the region that have been affected, sir. Information concerning fatalities and injuries is forthcoming, sir."

"Captain Woods, you are dismissed," Daren ordered. Alan noted that the king sounded exhausted.

Everyone sat in silence contemplating yet another disaster. Daren addressed Christopher, "Bring up the satellite photos of the area. We need a visual of what we are dealing with."

Christopher, relieved to have a mission, immediately went to work. As the rest of the council watched him, Daren took control.

"Ms. Rose, begin making plans for a press conference immediately following this meeting. Ian, get the numbers. Christopher, I know we are stretched on military, but the area needs to be secured. Lance, contact our allies. We have an arrangement with them for supplies in cases of emergency. Alan, find out who is organizing the relief efforts and make sure they have all the supplies they need. Work with Deanna to figure out funding for the supplies."

Deanna spoke up, "Sir, there is no funding."

At Deanna's comment, the entire council tensed and became silent. Daren's jaw and fists clenched as he thrust himself backward into his chair. He knew the country's financial situation. They had been working to lessen the burden and had been making progress, but now their state of affairs seemed dire.

"Figure it out, Deanna. That's your job." Daren knew he had just directed his frustration at Deanna and he immediately felt a slight tinge of regret. Pastor Isaiah's recent words to him flooded his mind: "And God will generously provide all you need. Then you will always have everything you need and plenty left over to share with others." The problem was that Daren felt forsaken by God right now.

Deanna had remained unshaken by the King's admonition, and she responded, "Sir, perhaps one of our allies could assist with fi . . ."

"No! That is not . . ."

Suddenly, something stopped Daren in mid speech. Everyone looked at the king to see his eyes glued to the monitor where Christopher had just pulled up the footage from the earthquake. In the before and after scenes, they could see that where beautiful homes with manicured lawns once stood, there was now a gaping hole. In certain areas, fires raged uncontrollably resulting from the aftershock, and all over, black clouds of smoke, dust and debris covered a 30 mile cavern. Daren pulled himself away from the devastating scenes, told Christopher to take it down and instructed his council to get to work.

He addressed them, "There will be time for mourning later. Right now lives are on the line, and our country is looking to us for direction. This meeting is adjourned."

Chad was one of the last to leave. He had desperately wanted to speak during the meeting, but it had been made clear that currently his role on the council was a silent one. He couldn't help but notice the sharp contrast between today's events and the much more cheerful ones of the day before. What should have been his time of joy was being overshadowed by gloom and despair. What was even more frustrating was the fact that he felt useless. Everyone else had been given a task, and he was determined to do his part as well. With a seemingly newly found confidence, Chad approached King Daren.

"Sir, may I please speak with you for a moment?"

Daren had no desire to talk to anyone, yet he acquiesced, "What is it, Captain West?"

"I realize that I am not an official member of the council, sir, but is there something I can do to assist?"

"Captain West, I am certain that Commander Heart will have his hands full in the coming months. Assist him with whatever he needs. You will be the Commander one day. This is a good time to learn some of the responsibilities of that position."

Chad was not satisfied with that response, but he knew better than to argue. He thanked King Daren for his time and made his way to Christopher's office.

Chapter 5

Christopher's head was about to explode. His country had been attacked and nothing was being done. Every single one of Daren's advisor's, including himself, had seemingly been rendered impotent when it came to taking action to avenge whoever had attacked them, and now, on top of it all, there was an earthquake to contend with. From the moment the attacks had taken place, Christopher had had his men training. They would be ready to deploy as soon as there was a target. If they could ever figure the hell out who the target was!

Lieutenant Bailey, Commander Heart's secretary could hear his pounding footsteps long before he ever arrived at his office. She glanced up as he entered and noted that he definitely had the look of a hungry, fierce beast on a mission. She also noticed that a few strands of his long, dirty blonde hair had come unsecured making him look even wilder than usual. His blue eyes held an intensity that few could reckon with. She felt a twinge of pity for anyone who might have to deal with his ferocity today.

Christopher stomped into his office, his head barely clearing the top of the office door, and tried to focus. He now had to figure out how he was going to find the resources and men to deal with any unrest created by the earthquake and keep them battle ready! It never stopped. Christopher reached to pick up the phone to call his top General, Caleb Ben Canaan, but the phone beeped before he could reach it. Lieutenant Bailey informed him that Captain Walters was waiting to see him. He knew he didn't have an appointment with her, and he briefly wondered what else had gone wrong. Irritated, he told Bailey to send her in.

The scowl on Commander Heart's face did not escape Teresa as she entered. She knew he had been on edge since the attacks, but she was not going to let that prevent her from insuring that palace security was on top of things. Nor was she going to let even her Commander reprimand one of the royal guard unfairly. She waited to be addressed.

"Captain Walters, I am quite busy. What is it?" growled Christopher.

Noting that his tone matched his scowl, Teresa braced herself for a fight and said, "Commander Heart, sir, I spoke with Lieutenant

Franklin as you asked. I have his account of what occurred, and I checked the cameras to confirm his story. I'm not sure, sir, what exactly it is that you want me to handle."

Christopher had nearly forgotten the incident with Franklin, and he had no desire to rehash it now. The truth was that he had overreacted, but he was never going to admit that, especially not now and not to Captain Walters. Instead, he hurled the problem back at her.

"Captain Walters, if I had wanted to waste my time handling the situation, I would have done so. I asked you to take care of it because I am somewhat busy with other matters at the time. However, if you can't handle it, then perhaps I should find someone who can."

Teresa was almost tempted to roll her eyes at his audacity, but she had known him for a very long time. There were few that could endure his diatribes, but she understood him well. She wondered if he even remembered what Franklin had done. She knew he wouldn't admit it if he didn't.

Teresa replied, "Sir, Lieutenant Franklin followed all the procedures he was supposed to. I have handled it, sir, in the sense that I have ruled out any errors on Franklin's part that I can see. So, if there is something more that I need to know in order to best handle this, then you. . ."

Teresa stopped mid-sentence. Christopher's attention had been diverted to the office door, and his expression was unreadable. Teresa turned and saw the reason for Christopher's sudden change.

Todd, Commander Heart's teenage son stood in the door with his fists on his hips and his legs spread. Looking ready for battle, he addressed the Commander, "When are we going to war?"

Christopher was immediately relieved to see his son, but he was also vigilant in addressing his son. Suddenly remembering that Teresa was still there, he quickly dismissed her.

Once she had departed, Christopher stood and gingerly addressed Todd, "We're not at this time, son."

Todd's expression morphed from frustration to confusion to annoyance, "What do you mean, we're not going? Someone attacked our country, father, and it's your responsibility to do something about that!"

Under normal circumstances, Christopher would have flared at Todd's accusatory tone and lack of respect, but his son had been gone for quite some time, and he had no desire to send him immediately retreating from the palace again, especially not when the country was in such turmoil and possible danger.

Trying to retain as calm a demeanor as he could muster, Christopher explained uselessly, "Todd, believe me, I have every intention of seeking retribution against those who have done this. As soon as we are ready, forces will be deployed."

Todd couldn't believe what he was hearing. His father was a lot of things, but cowardly was certainly not one of them. He was surprised his dad wasn't banging down someone's door right now and taking them out with an AK47.

Todd almost yelled, "Ready? What the heck does it take to be ready? Do you need them to blow up a few more buildings so that we can justify kicking their butts for this? Why are we waiting? This is stupid!"

Christopher could tell that no excuse would satisfy his son, and he wanted to keep communication open with him. He replied, "Todd, we don't know who attacked us. Once we know, you can be sure that immediate action will take place."

Christopher could immediately tell that his candor had not had the intended effect. Todd's entire body had almost seemed to ignite, and his face was aflame.

Todd's aggravation erupted and he moved towards his father, "What do you mean, we don't know who did this? How can you not know? Don't we have some of the best intelligence in the world? How long has it been, Dad?"

Todd waited for his father to respond, but then realized he wasn't going to.

Todd continued, "You seriously have no idea? How the heck can you possibly have NO idea who attacked the university that Kelly was attending just days before the attacks?"

Christopher knew that Todd was close to Kelly, his twin sister, so these attacks were even more personal to him.

Christopher started to speak but was cut off.

Todd nearly yelled, "What have you been doing dad? I mean, isn't it your job to keep our country safe?"

Todd's searing accusations destroyed any resolve that Christopher had to mend relations with his son. Feeling suddenly overwhelmed and completely incapable, Christopher stepped away from his chair and pointed to it while addressing Todd, "If you think you can do a better job, son, then go right ahead and do so!"

Christopher was rarely caught off guard, but Todd's next words nearly knocked him back into the chair that he had so glibly just offered.

Todd looked like a young, unruly lion ready to pounce on its prey, but his words held a slight twinge of pain, "Well, dad, I guess we'll never know how well I could do in that chair since Chad, who has no father to speak of, has already been named as the next Commander!"

Before Christopher could muster a reply, Todd stormed out of the office. Christopher sank into his chair, and he suddenly felt tired and aged. Christopher had, on several occasions, bemoaned the fact that his son seemed to share no interest in following in his father's footsteps. Todd had been undisciplined, rebellious and directionless. Christopher felt something like regret and sadness creep into his soul, and he vowed to himself that the events of the day would never be discussed with anyone. Shutting his door, he picked up the phone to make that call to

General Ben Canaan. He now had three disasters with which to contend: a war, an earthquake and his son.

        After speaking with King Daren, Chad had made his way to Commander Heart's office to find out where he was needed and how he could help. As he entered the outer area of the office, he greeted Lieutenant Bailey with a smile. That smile soon faded as he heard raised voices coming from the Commander's office. Chad listened intently. One voice obviously belonged to Commander Heart. It took him a moment to realize that the second belonged to Todd, Commander Heart's son, Ashley's brother. Chad felt a momentary twinge of anger towards Todd. Ashley had really wanted Todd to be present for their wedding, but he had run off months ago with no regard whatsoever for anyone but himself. Besides that, he had been nothing but trouble for Commander Heart over the past few years, and now, of all times, he actually had the audacity to argue with his father! It was probably over some trivial matter to top it all off. At first, Chad fought the urge to eavesdrop, but his curiosity got the best of him. He reasoned that it would put him in a better strategic position to deal with Commander Heart if he knew a little of what to expect when he went in. He knew that Lieutenant Bailey would know he was trying to overhear the conversation, but he also knew that her ears were just as tuned in as his. As Chad listened, his frustration with Todd grew to resentment. Todd was actually criticizing the Commander's ability to handle his job. What was worse was the fact that the Commander seemed to be letting him do it. When Chad heard Todd use the word "stupid' in reference to the Commander, Chad decided it would be better not to have an encounter with Todd at the moment and asked Lieutenant Bailey to inform the Commander that he would return shortly.

        Chad decided to make his way to see Ashley. It was nearing lunchtime anyway, and maybe he would be able to pull her away from Mr. Sterling for an early lunch. Chad decided to take the long route to Mr. Sterling's office. He needed to cool off a little after overhearing Todd's searing words. He forced himself to focus on the remarkable beauty of the palace décor. In his youth, Chad had made a point to learn a little about anything and everything he could. He wanted to be well rounded and able to fit into any situation. He knew he wanted to work in the palace one day, and he knew he wanted to be a member of the Royal Guard. His ambitions had not quite reached as far as Commander, but he could truly say that his dreams and goals had been more than realized. He looked at the paintings on the walls. King Daren had made a few changes to the palace when he took power, but overall, everyone would agree that King Daren's father, King Joseph, was a master at interior design. He had an eye for the natural beauty of Lionel, and in regard to this preference, had hired several renowned artists to capture that beauty in paintings that now adorned the palace halls. Mountains, rivers, streams, and forests came alive and helped to calm and focus Chad. The marble majesty of the floors and walls added to the sense of awe, and

Chad felt grateful once again to live in such a beautiful place. As he neared his destination, he offered up a silent prayer of thankfulness to God for His many blessings over the years, but especially for the woman he was hoping would join him for lunch, the woman he loved irrevocably, his wife. A contented smile crossed Chad's face at that thought. He was still wearing the smile when he encountered Jada, Mr. Sterling's blonde, porcelain faced secretary.

Jada was the first to speak, "good morning, Captain West. I will let Mr. Sterling know you are here."

"Thank you, Ms. Hyde."

Chad could have easily barged into just about anyone's office in the palace had he wanted to, and Commander Heart had certainly taken advantage of that aspect of his position over the years, but Chad's deep sense of propriety overcame his need to display his power. He waited patiently for Mr. Sterling to approve his entrance.

"You may go in, Captain West. By the way, congratulations, Sir." Chad smiled again and thanked Jada. As he entered the office, Chad mused that everything was just as he would expect it. Mr. Sterling sat at his desk with the usual smug, amused look that he wore in almost every situation. Ashley sat to his right using a corner of his desk for her own tasks. Chad also knew that the next words out of Mr. Sterling's mouth would be some sarcastic jab about Chad's real reasons for visiting the office.

"Ah, Captain West, what an unexpected and pleasant surprise. I am honored. To what do I owe the pleasure of our future Commander's visit?" Lance quipped.

Normally, Ashley would have teased Lance about not having enough clout to deserve a visit from such an important person, but she knew that Lance had been under fire for his lack of knowledge or intel about the recent attacks. In light of that fact, Ashley really was not sure if Chad was there for her or for Lance. She hoped it was not the latter. It had killed her that morning when Chad had been forced to leave so early to attend a council meeting. Such a sweet and wonderful night had been cut short by duty and service. All morning she had fought the urge to go and find him, so seeing him standing there right now was making her even more anxious. She knew he probably had a million things to attend to, but she still desperately wanted some of that attention. Now.

Chad addressed Mr. Sterling, "Good afternoon, sir. I was wondering if you would allow Mrs. West to join me for lunch."

Ashley's eyes lit up at the reference to her married name and she breathed an audible sigh of contentment drawing both men's attention. She immediately regretted her action knowing that Lance would miss no opportunity to exploit her obvious desires. He certainly didn't disappoint.

"Captain West, it is hardly 11:00am in the morning. For some unknown reason, Mrs. West here was quite late in her arrival to work this morning. She's barely been here an hour, and now you want to drag her away for what can hardly be considered a reasonable time for lunch? I'm not sure that I can spare her."

Chad noted the playful tone in Mr. Sterling's response and chose to allow Ashley to fight this battle. He thanked Mr. Sterling for his time and went out to wait for Ashley to join him. It didn't take long just as he knew it wouldn't. They walked stoically past Jada. Reaching the hallway, they gave each other a knowing look and made their way directly to their suite with all thoughts of lunch thrown to the wind.

Aware of the cameras that lined the hallways Chad and Ashley engaged in small talk as they hurried to their suite. As the door shut, Chad was prepared to talk to Ashley, but she immediately made her way into his arms, and he knew that conversation could wait for later.

After fully enjoying the benefits of marriage, Ashley lay satisfied in Chad's arms with her head resting on his chest. She knew that he would soon have to return to work, but she tried to concentrate on enjoying the comfort and delight of the moment. Their relationship from the start had been clouded by his devotion to his work, and she understood that even in marriage, this would never change. Rather than getting better, she knew that inevitably as he took on more and more responsibility, their time together would become more and more sparse. However, it would forever be these moments that made it all worth it; she could only hope and pray that Chad would be able to overcome the challenges that had turned her father into the workaholic that had eventually driven her mother to find comfort and fulfillment from another man.

Chad so much wanted to just lay there forever and take pleasure in his wife. He knew that no matter how much Ashley mattered to him though, his mind would always eventually gravitate back to his responsibility as the future Commander. He had actually considered giving it all up for Ashley at one point when she seemed upset that he had been named, but he understood now that if he had, he would have grown to resent her and their marriage for denying him that opportunity. They had both struggled with boundaries and expectations, but he really felt that she was trying to understand the balance he was trying to keep. He also knew that they needed to have a serious talk. He shifted and moved her so that he could see her face. He touched her cheek, and she nuzzled his hand.

Unsure of how to begin their next conversation, Chad went straight to the point, "Ashley, have you seen your brother?"

Chad's question caught Ashley off guard. She sat up slightly frustrated.

"Why are you asking me if I've seen my brother, Chad? What's wrong? What are you not telling me?"

Chad silently reprimanded himself for his brusqueness and quickly set to assuage Ashley's obvious concern, "No, nothing is wrong. I wasn't sure if you were aware that he has returned, but obviously you aren't. He was in your father's office earlier today, and I just wondered if he had stopped by to see you."

Ashley felt an immediate wave of relief. Todd was back. She suddenly felt a strong urge to seek him out and talk to him. She had been so disappointed that he missed the wedding, but at the same time, she understood his need to get away from here and try to figure out his life. She had done that herself, in a way, when she had gone away to Lionel University, but because she was the Commander's daughter, she had been under constant scrutiny. When Todd left, he managed to slip away free of security. Sons always had it easier, she thought. If she had done things the way Todd did, her father would have had every single policeman and soldier scouring the streets for her. She actually was surprised that her father hadn't done the same for Todd. At the same time, she realized that despite her father's seeming inattention to his children over the years, he truly did understand them all a little better than they realized. He had seen that chasing after Todd would only drive him further away. Now, Todd was back. She jumped up and started getting dressed.

Chad had watched her deep in thought. He knew that she and Todd shared a special bond and understanding that he would never comprehend. When Todd had left, Chad had been frustrated that he would cause more stress and frustration for his father. He was surprised that Ashley didn't feel the same. Once again he wondered what she was thinking now.

Chad waited for her to get dressed, admiring his wife, and then inquired, "Are you going to find him?"

"You know I have to get back to work, Chad," Ashley responded.

Chad was certainly not ready for their time together to end. In an ideal situation, they would be on their honeymoon right now. Recent events had precluded that possibility, and not knowing when things might turn around, they had both agreed that a honeymoon could wait. Marriage could not. He was enjoying marriage. Besides, no one had given him any responsibility, and he wondered if they were giving him a bit of a break because of his newlywed status. As soon as that thought crossed his mind, the phone rang.

"Yes, sir," Chad answered noting that it was Commander Heart who was calling.

"Where the hell are you?" Christopher thundered, "I expected you in my office over an hour ago!"

Chad had no recollection of Commander Heart mentioning that expectation, but he knew better than to argue.

"I'm on my way, sir," Chad responded while looking at Ashley disappointedly.

"My father?" Ashley inquired.

Chad nodded knowing she had probably heard her father's roar all the way across the room. He also noted that she seemed very anxious to leave. Maybe it was best that Commander Heart had called after all.

He knew Ashley would be making a detour to see Todd on her way back to work. Chad walked over to her and pulled her close. It felt good to know that she was his wife. He held her until he could feel her impatience and then reluctantly let go.

Ashley tried to excuse herself, "Chad, we can't give Lance too much to talk about. You know he will have all sorts of suggestions as to why I've been gone so long already. I'm prepared to endure his insinuations for at least the next few months as it is."

Chad grinned, "He's just jealous he's not giving anyone anything to talk about."

Ashley giggled at Chad's uncharacteristic remark. It was highly unusual for him to criticize or joke at the expense of another, especially one of King Daren's council members. Maybe this whole marriage thing was loosening him up a bit. Ashley blushed a little at the connotation of that possibility. She needed to leave. Now.

"Oh, by the way, you need to talk to Mr. Walters about our new suite when you have a chance. He needed some information from you. I've already talked to him about what I want," Ashley mentioned on her way out.

"Our what?" Chad questioned.

"Just talk to Mr. Walters," Ashley shrugged making her way out the door as quickly as possible. She knew Chad would make a ridiculous ordeal out of a simple living arrangement change, and she didn't want to deal with it right now. She would have to make sure that Mr. Walters contacted Chad soon so that she would never have to deal with it. Chad could be so uptight about the stupidest things.

Chad's mood had quickly changed from pleasantly satisfied to bothered and frustrated. The ever latent thought that he was not good enough for Ashley threatened to surface, but he quickly suppressed it. She was a princess, and a princess deserved a nicer suite than the one he had been living in this past decade. Besides, there were other more pertinent matters at hand, and it would be a waste of time and energy to grapple with this issue right now. Chad dressed and holstered his gun. Commander Heart would not appreciate waiting any longer than he already had. Chad made his way to the Commander's office.

As soon as Chad stepped into Christopher's office, the Commander started barking orders, "I've spoken with General Ben Canaan about the situation with the earthquake. Right now, I want you to focus your attention on taking care of that. I need to continue to focus on keeping our country safe from further attacks from unknown sources. Do you think you will be able to handle that, or do you plan on disappearing again?"

Chad had noted Christopher's obvious exasperation at the word "unknown." He knew it was infuriating to the Commander that they still didn't know who had attacked them. Chad was about to respond to Christopher when the phone rang. Chad decided to take a seat and look over the information that the Commander had shoved at him during his tirade. There was no way to anticipate how long the phone conversation might be.

Christopher wanted to throw the phone across the room. He briefly considered not answering. It would probably be someone else with more bad news anyway, and he had enough to handle as it was. Begrudgingly, he pushed the button for the speaker.

"Sir, General Ben Canaan is holding for you. He says it is a personal matter, sir," his secretary, Lieutenant Bailey, informed him.

Christopher picked up the line without responding to Bailey and addressed the General, "What is it, Caleb?"

He was met by the bear-like, gruff voice of a man that he had come to both respect and consider a life-long friend, "Commander, sir, you may already be aware of this, but Prince Todd just enlisted for the military. He is anxious to go to war, sir."

Christopher felt like someone had just punched him in the gut and then given him a bouquet of roses. He was pleased that his son was finally taking on some form of responsibility; however, he wasn't sure that his son was quite ready to run off to war, and he certainly did not want any more casualties within his own family to deal with.

Christopher decided to address another matter first.

"General Ben Canaan, Captain West is on his way to see you. He will be handling the security needs for the aftermath of the earthquake."

Christopher nodded for Chad to be dismissed from his office. Whatever he had to say about his son's impulsive decisions did not need to be said in the presence of Chad. There was already a slight rift between the two, and he did not want to give excuse for a greater one. There would come a day when the two of them would need to accept the fact that they were family and needed to work with each other and not against. He knew that Chad's discipline and austerity made it difficult for him to understand or accept Todd's more rebellious individuality.

Ben Canaan knew there must be a reason that the Commander had not directly responded to his information, so he waited patiently. When Christopher did respond, it was succinct.

"When?" Christopher solicited.

It was quickly becoming clear that the Commander had no prior knowledge of Todd's decision. This didn't surprise Caleb at all. It had only been a few months since Todd had left the palace, and just before that, Caleb had been placed in charge of overseeing Todd's weed pulling sentence. It probably would have offended most Generals to be asked to baby-sit the Commander's teenage son, but Caleb had considered it an honor that the Commander would entrust him with one of his most precious treasures. In all truth, Caleb had grown somewhat fond of Todd through the process, and they shared a respectful dislike of each other. Besides, his daughter, Becca, was certainly fond of Todd, and had finally found a friend in him. It was a friendship that Caleb planned to keep a very close watch on, but Becca had been happier since she started pulling weeds with Todd, so he allowed it to continue. She deserved some happiness, he reasoned. He just hoped that Todd valued the friendship as well, or else Becca was bound for heartbreak. He knew that if nothing else, Todd had appreciated the company.

General Ben Canaan answered the Commander's question, "This morning, sir. He must have registered at one of the recruiting offices on the outside. He happened to pick one that General Fleming oversees, and the General and I know each other pretty well. To get to the point, Fleming gave me a call as soon as Todd left."

"I want him under your command, Caleb," Christopher stated.

General Ben Canaan noted a hint of fatigue in the Commander's voice.

"Yes, sir. I'll see that it's done."

"Thank you, Caleb. Take care of him." Christopher ended the conversation.

Chapter 6

After the council meeting, King Daren had returned to his office. He felt powerless and at the mercy of both nature and an unknown enemy. Another King would have just executed a few council members for their seeming ineffectiveness, but Daren knew that his council was just as frustrated as he was with the situation. His council had been handpicked, and they were the best that could be found. Over the years, the council had changed and grown, but no matter what, they remained masters at solving problems. If his council had no answers, he had no idea where to turn. All he could do was wait, and that was the hardest thing of all for a King to do.

Daren sat at his desk. It was a dark mahogany with hand-carved designs adorning the front. The wood was unfinished giving the otherwise elegant design a bit of a rustic edge. There was a dark leather sofa placed directly in front of the desk. The floor was marble with rugs placed strategically to give it warmth and depth. There were windows on both sides of the desk but not behind the desk. A separate smaller desk and chairs were set up along the wall behind the couch, and four other chairs lined the walls beneath the windows. Aside from the dark color of the sofa and desks, the rest of the office was decorated in light neutral tones. Daren's phone beeped, and Shayla informed him that King Kidwell was on the phone. As Daren picked up the phone, he hoped that Ethan would have some kind of lead for him.

"Ethan, how is Brooke?" Daren inquired.

"She's still healing. The doctor says it will take some time. He also thinks that she's still in shock from the blast," Ethan answered.

"I hope, Ethan, that you are calling me because you have some useful information."

Ethan appreciated Daren's directness. He had no desire to discuss his wife's condition right now, but he appreciated the fact that Daren had asked. Ethan returned the candor.

"Prince Trevor Benson and Kendra arrived this afternoon. Trevor is asking that I allow Kendra to stay here in Raxx while he visits you. He claims to have some important information to share with you."

"Do you think he does?" There was a mixture of doubt and surprise in Daren's voice.

"I'm not sure, Daren. You never know with a Benson."

"What is he asking in return? Does his father know he's coming to see me?"

"Daren, you know that the Bensons do not consider me a legitimate ruler here in Raxx. Although Trevor will use me as a dumping ground for Kendra, he certainly won't share any information that he would consider valuable."

"No, the Bensons think they are the legitimate rulers of Raxx. If Lionel hadn't stepped in 13 years ago, they just might be. Be careful, Ethan. Warren Benson would gladly take over for you."

Ethan knew that Daren's comment was not meant to offend, but he also knew that Raxx owed a great debt of gratitude to Lionel for their help in the war with Raxx. If King Benson had had his way, he would be married to Nicole in lieu of Daren and would be ruling both Aldrich and Raxx. Ethan was grateful that his sister was with Daren, but he also would prefer that she had fulfilled her duty as Queen in Raxx.

Ethan responded, "Yes, I know. Do you want me to send him or not?"

"Send him. What do I have to lose? He comes on your plane with your security. Those are my conditions. If he refuses to abide by them, then he can stay in Raxx with you. Just watch that he doesn't take over. We don't want his father to be too proud of him."

"The way things are going right now, Daren, I might just hand over the throne willingly without a fight, but not to a Benson. Plus, he's Kendra's husband, so there's two strikes against him!"

"I appreciate the phone call. Let Lance know Trevor's decision."

"Daren, there's something else."

Daren was tempted to hang up the phone. Ethan's tone indicated that the "something else" was not good news, and Daren had had enough of bad news lately.

"What is it, Ethan?"

"Megan is here. She's been here for about three weeks now."

"What do you mean she's been there for three weeks? Where is Gavin?"

There was a pause before Ethan responded, "I suppose he's in Mikasa."

"That bastard," Daren growled in a barely audible tone, "Send Megan to me. You have enough to handle."

Daren's remark was uncharacteristic, but Ethan understood. Daren's sister, Megan, had been married to the King of Mikasa, Gavin Zeffrin, for years now, and their entire relationship had been tumultuous. Megan had just given birth to their second child, a son, only months ago. Megan had revealed little of why she left Mikasa to come to Raxx, but Ethan was sure it must be fairly serious if she had abandoned her newborn son. He knew Daren was dealing with issues of his own, but Ethan grabbed at the opportunity to get Megan off his hands.

"I will send her on the plane with Trevor, if that's okay with you. If Brooke was conscious, I am sure she would appreciate Megan's companionship, but she's not, and I think even Megan is feeling a bit uneasy."

Daren could only imagine how Megan had most likely reacted to Brooke's condition. The two had been friends since they were very young, and it was only because of Brooke that Megan would have felt comfortable running to Raxx in the first place.

Daren responded, "That's fine Ethan."

After hanging up with Ethan, Daren immediately called Lance. Hopefully Lance might actually have some insight into why Prince Trevor was visiting. Over twenty minutes later, Daren hung up the phone frustrated once again. It seemed that everywhere he turned was a dead end, and he was getting tired of it. Trevor's news better be good. In the meantime, there were some matters that could be taken care of. Daren walked out of his office.

He addressed his secretary, "Shayla, call the council members. I want a meeting at 7:00 in the morning."

It was the end of the day, and Daren intended to get some rest before the next day's events. He realized that sitting in his office with no information or leads was futile. Dinner with his family was in order.

Chapter 7

It was nearly 2am in the morning when Chad finally made his way to his suite. He was surprised to find the lights still on and his wife awake. She was standing on top of the kitchen counter on her tiptoes reaching to clean the tops of the cabinets. She was also wearing a very short, sexy light blue negligée. Chad instinctively started to look away, but then remembered that she was now his wife. Instead, he stood quietly enjoying the view.

"You could help," Ashley stated without turning around.

"I'm fairly certain we have people who do that for us," Chad stated.

"Well, they're obviously not doing a good job."

"I'll speak with my mother about that."

Ashley turned at that and gave Chad a disgusted look. "Are you going to help me down?"

Chad moved toward Ashley, put his arms around her legs, and then gently slid her to the ground. As he did so, the already short negligée slid up leaving his arms to embrace bare skin. He gently rubbed his hand on the soft skin of her back and heard her intake of breath as he did so. She moved closer and reached up to meet his lips. Chad again lifted her taking her towards their bedroom. They melted into each other as they enjoyed the bliss of the benefits of marriage. When they were both exhausted and lay totally relaxed, Chad laid on his side looking at his wife. "Are you going to tell me why you were dusting cabinets at 2 in the morning? Are you upset that I was so late?"

"Maybe. No. I know you have a lot going on. Everybody does. Did you know that Todd enlisted?"

At that news, Chad bristled. The last thing Commander Heart needed was to be concerned about Todd.

"I'm sure your father will put a stop to that." Chad tried to sound reassuring.

"I don't think that's a good idea."

"Ashley, what's not a good idea is Todd making your father worry more than he needs to right now. This is serious, Ashley. If we can ever find out who is behind this, it will most likely mean war. Todd isn't just going to be playing around on some training course pretending to be a soldier. If he joins, he will go to fight. I don't think Todd is quite ready for that."

"My father has been to war."

Chad was getting more frustrated by the minute. "Todd is not your father. He would probably end up getting several people killed because they'll be worried about protecting the Commander's son. I'm sure your father will not let him go through with this."

"It would probably be good for him. I'd go if I could."

Chad was incredulous. He rolled onto his back and shook his head. "Ashley, do you not understand what's at stake here? This is not a game! This is not just one of your brother's selfish schemes to gain attention. This is real."

"I work with Lance, Chad. I know what's going on. Why do you think I don't understand this?"

Ashley was becoming defensive, and Chad tried to temper his tone. "I'm not trying to . . . This isn't about you, Ashley. It's about your brother being self-absorbed and making another careless decision without thinking about the consequences."

"You don't understand him, Chad."

Chad didn't want to argue. The truth was that he didn't understand Todd one bit, but he did understand that all the headstrong prince had done for the last 4 or 5 years was cause trouble and stress for everyone he knew.

Chad tried a different approach, "Ashley, I'm sure your father will handle this. There's no need to worry about it."

"I'm not worried about it. You're the one who brought it up."

"I wasn't the one cleaning cabinets at 2am."

"Well, you didn't seem to mind."

"No, no I did not. It was nice to have some time with you. I'm sorry I don't have more."

Ashley leaned in and kissed her husband. "You should sleep. I love you."

"I love you," Chad smiled.

As Chad closed his eyes, Ashley spoke again, "I hope we get whoever is doing this soon."

Chad again turned to her. He didn't want to upset her, but the burden of the last few days was heavy. The entire nation had been weakened by the attacks. In the past, Lionel had always acted swiftly and effectively when threatened. The longer the enemy remained unknown, the weaker Lionel appeared.

"We have to," he simply stated.

"I know. The world is watching. Lance has talked a lot about how if Lionel appears weak, then the rest of the world sees God as weak."

"Daren has upheld his faith and he has done everything he can to ensure our country remains faithful. We just have to trust that God will remain faithful to us." Chad felt the uncertainty in his own voice as he said it, but he hoped that his words had reassured Ashley.

She snuggled close to him, and he held her in his arms as they fell into a restless sleep.

Chapter 8

Deanna was the first to reach the council meeting room the next morning. She keyed in her clearance as the security system scanned her profile to verify her identity. The scan was a feature of the upgraded security system that was in the process of being installed. Halfway through the scan, the door slid open, and she noted that Dawson must still be working out the kinks in the system following the security breach. Nonetheless, she still felt fairly safe and secure. She had worked in the palace for quite some time and remembered the days when technology was scarce, but Commander Heart's men had always been prepared and vigilant. As she sat down at the big, sturdy, cherry wood table, she took a few moments to relax. The room was not huge, but definitely had an air of authority and power to it. The chairs were upholstered in burgundy leather. They were designed to be both functional and aesthetic at the same time. Like most of the rest of the palace, the floors and uncovered portions of the walls were marble. A large, richly decorated rug had been placed beneath the table and chairs for soundproofing and added ambiance. The walls were adorned with LCD screens that displayed painted scenes from significant events in Lionel's history. One of the pictures on the screen across from her seat was currently displaying the scene depicting the coronation of King Lukas Heart, the first king of Lionel and the king who had ordained the country as one devoted to God.

She heard the door open and was happy to see the only fellow female council member, Noelle Rose. She smiled in greeting, but the smile was not returned. Noelle seemed deep in thought, and it was a scowl that crossed her forehead as she sat to Deanna's left. Seeing that there would be no conversation with the public relations advisor, Deanna returned to admiring the amenities of the room. The King would sit at the head of the table with his brother, Commander Heart on his right, and his Chief Advisor, Ian on his left. Slowly, other Council members came meandering in. It was still early, so no one was yet in a rush. Ian came in next and took his place next to her. Surprisingly, it was the King's foreign affairs advisor, Lance, who entered next and filled in the last seat on her side of the table. Alan came next and took his place directly across from Deanna. When Christopher grounded himself next to Alan,

Deanna mused at Alan's disgruntled look. Some things never changed. Alan, the ever level-headed, considerate hospitality advisor would forever be at odds with the hot-tempered, unyielding Commander. Chad had entered with Christopher and filled the chair on Alan's other side. It was unusual for the entire council to be present before the King's arrival, but she realized that they were all aware of their King's frustration and were eager to assuage the burdens that had been placed upon them all. Deanna had already talked to a couple of the other council members the night before, and she knew that all present hoped that an unplanned meeting meant news. Any news at this point would be better than oblivion. She also hoped that the King would be more accepting of the financial situation they were in.

When King Daren finally entered with Pastor Isaiah, all the council members stood. Once Pastor Isaiah had prayed for God's guidance and blessing, the council was seated and Pastor Isaiah exited the room.

Daren was surprised that his secretary, Shayla, had not yet arrived. He was not angry as he knew she would have a good reason, and she never purposefully missed Pastor Isaiah's opening prayer.

Daren had not had time to meet with his chief advisor, Ian, to go over the meeting's agenda, so Daren himself started, "First of all, I received a phone call from Ethan yesterday. Prince Trevor Benson is on his way here and supposedly has information he wishes to share."

At the mention of Trevor's name, Chad bristled. Questions raced through his mind. Had Trevor already received word of his and Ashley's marriage? Was that why he was coming? Chad could just imagine Trevor fabricating some conspiracy to connive his way into the palace and get to Ashley.

Daren continued, "I will speak with Trevor myself when he arrives. Lance, plan to be there. As far as the earthquake aftermath is concerned, I want someone I know overseeing the relief. I won't spare any of you at this time, so we need to delegate someone."

Christopher immediately spoke up, "Send Prince Brandon. He's practically useless around here. He might as well be good for something."

Lance quickly countered, "Is that really the best idea? I mean, what qualifications exactly does Prince Brandon have to recommend him for this big of a task. I, of course, have the utmost respect for Prince Brandon, but I am sure there are other responsibilities that he is better suited for. You don't resolve a disaster with another disaster."

"And what qualifies you, Lance, to determine if someone else can do a job well? Maybe we should take an in depth look at your benefit the past few months." Christopher shot back.

Lance was bordering on treason by speaking so critically of a member of the royal family. Daren also knew that his council remained on edge. They had always had disagreements. Daren had chosen each of his council members for many reasons including their individual unique insight, which meant they didn't always see eye to eye. However, he knew that the intense personal attacks and negativity were due to the tremendous stress they were all under right now. Daren put an immediate stop to Lance's rambling, "I will speak with Brandon. Christopher, he will need a security detail."

Christopher deferred to Chad, "Captain West, that will be your responsibility."

Normally, Chad's response would have been instantaneous, but he was still smoldering over the fact that Trevor would be arriving shortly.

Christopher wanted to strangle Chad. The dimwit was actually daydreaming during a council meeting. Christopher's voice thundered this time, and the other council members tensed in response.

"Captain West! Do you think you could spare us a bit of your attention for a few moments?"

Christopher's voice certainly broke Chad's reverie. He became keenly aware that all eyes were on him, and he also was aware that they were obviously waiting for his response. The problem was that he had no idea what had been asked.

Christopher noted Chad's look of confusion and repeated himself, "Captain West, you will make sure that Prince Brandon has appropriate security while he is in Pilnez."

"Yes, sir," Chad agreed.

Although Chad knew he would suffer Christopher's wrath later, he was thankful for the save. The Commander had recommended Chad, Chad was now his son-in-law, and Chad knew that Christopher's intercession had more to do with salvaging his own pride than it did with sparing Chad embarrassment.

King Daren spoke up, his tone impatient, "Christopher, give us an update on the attacks."

"All sites have been secured. Investigations at each site are under way. Right now, there are no leads" Christopher stated.

"Commander Heart, did you have prior knowledge of these attacks somehow?" The question had come from Alan Walters, and its effect was palpable.

The muscle in Christopher's jaw tightened as he addressed Alan, "What exactly are you suggesting, Alan?"

Alan knew that Christopher's temper was volatile, but he continued anyway. It was an issue that needed to be addressed, and he would not be intimidated by the Commander's brutish demeanor. "Commander, you pulled your daughter, Kelly, out of the university just days before these attacks. Now that the attacks have happened, I think it is a fair expectation that you provide a reason for the timing of your decision. I am sure that the thought has crossed the mind of every member of this council. It's not a matter of incrimination, but rather a matter of prevention. If you had sources that indicated the attacks were a possibility, then I think it is essential that you divulge that intelligence to the entire council at this point."

Deanna looked at Christopher in anticipation of the explosion that was inevitable. She was sure that the fact that the question had come from Alan made it even more volatile. Christopher's face was red, his hands gripped the sides of his chair, and he was nearly hovering over Alan who had a stubborn look of determination on his own face.

Christopher's reply was surprisingly restrained, but it was the kind of restraint a lioness exhibits just before it pounces on its prey. "No, I did not have prior knowledge of the attacks. I did not pull my daughter out because I thought there might be a threat. That is all you or anyone else in this room needs to know."

Christopher hovered above Alan for a moment, but then relaxed somewhat into his chair when Alan remained silent. He continued to eye Alan as though he was prey, but he seemed otherwise subdued for the moment.

Daren continued delegating responsibilities while Christopher simmered. Christopher continued to glare at Alan occasionally, but Alan kept his attention diverted. It wasn't just the question that Alan had asked that had set Christopher on edge; it was the implication behind it. Christopher was sure that every person in that room was questioning his ability to handle things. He should have had intelligence on the attacks. There was no way that this should have happened under his watch, but yet it did. It was his fault that the enemy had infiltrated his country and been able to do such horrendous things. He would have been less ashamed if he had withdrawn Kelly based on possible threats. As it was now, he looked completely incompetent. He was also sure that Alan was reveling in the fact that he could call him out on his incompetence for all to see!

Daren tried to move the council's attention away from Christopher for as long as possible, but they were nearing the end of their agenda, and the security system status needed to be discussed. Daren looked at Christopher and noted that he was still clenching his jaw in frustration. He knew his brother blamed himself for much of what had occurred, and Daren had found himself bewildered that all of this had happened so unexpectedly. It would be of no use to dwell on failure right now. Once this had passed, he would confront Christopher.

Daren addressed Christopher, "Commander, what is the status of the security system upgrade? Does Mr. Moulder have an estimated deadline?"

Deanna thought it was impossible for Christopher to look any more frustrated than he already did, but at Daren's question, Christopher's scowl deepened, and his face became a momentary crimson. She somewhat empathized with Christopher's frustration over the security system. She had been waiting on Dawson Moulder to give her the final numbers of the cost of the upgrade for weeks now. With the budget being so strained even before the earthquake and attacks, she dreaded the amount it would most likely cost in the end.

Christopher's face returned to a normal hue, and he answered Daren, "Mr. Moulder seems to continuously run into road blocks on this project. He hasn't yet provided a set date."

Daren's own patience was running thin, and he was tired of running in circles.

"Commander, get Mr. Moulder in here. I want a date." Daren ordered.

Christopher made the call. A low murmur permeated the room as the council waited for Mr. Moulder to arrive. It was Noelle's turn to be tense. Dawson had been spending every waking moment working, but she knew he was nowhere near having the system up and running. The little time they had had together recently was strained due to his long and stressful hours, and she was frustrated that it was taking so long. If she, his own wife, had no compassion, she could only imagine what King Daren and the rest of the council was feeling.

The door to the conference room opened, and Dawson Moulder strode into the room. Noelle's tension mounted, and she didn't even turn around when he approached the back of her chair and stood.

Dawson's stance was confident and one hand rested in his pocket as he addressed Christopher, "Commander Heart, you wanted to speak with me?"

There was an empty chair on Christopher's side of the table at the end, and Christopher motioned for Dawson to sit in it. Noelle still diverted her gaze even as Dawson moved into her line of sight. She knew that the next few moments would not be comfortable for him, but she also felt that he had it coming. She waited for Christopher to begin the interrogation, but it was Daren who spoke first.

"Mr. Moulder, I need to know when my palace is going to be secure," Daren blandly stated.

Dawson had situated himself into a relaxed position, but when the King addressed him, he sat forward in his chair. He addressed Daren directly, "Sir, I can assure you that the palace is secure. However, as I have informed Commander Heart, Mr. Ellison and I are working as quickly as we can on the upgrades. I originally estimated that each section would take approximately 2 to 3 weeks to complete, but that estimate has proven to be inaccurate. There have been some unforeseen problems at each step that are prolonging the process."

Ian noted the look of annoyance on Daren's face and interposed, "Mr. Moulder, we aren't interested in the details of the process. We are interested in exactly when the process will be completed. It is imperative now more than ever that this is done."

Obviously, the council members had no knowledge of technology or programming, Dawson thought as he tried to form a response that would be on their level of understanding, "I understand the concern, but just as you cannot anticipate every setback that comes your way, this system is no different. I can give you an estimated date, but it will be subject to change depending on the problems I encounter at each step."

Dawson's analogy threw salt on an already open wound, and Christopher lost all restraint. He was up out of his seat and was roaring, "Are you telling us, Mr. Moulder, that after all this time, you still have NO idea when this will be finished!?"

Dawson wasn't quite sure how the conversation had escalated to this point, but he was not going to allow the entire council to see him as incapable. He met the Commander's glare and stated calmly, "Commander, as I said, I can give an estimate, but it will be subject to change. I don't think it is reasonable to expect me to be able to foresee the future. Additionally, because of the sensitive nature of this project, I don't have the . . ."

Dawson's sentence was cut short as Christopher grabbed the front of his shirt and lifted him out of his chair. Before he could react to what was happening, the Commander violently slammed him against the side marble wall. His head banged against the bottom of one of the display screens so hard that it dismounted from the wall and hung dangling from the electrical cords. Christopher was yelling again, but his words were unintelligible to Dawson as he tried to recover from the shock and pain of the unexpected assault.

Everyone in the room sat stunned. Noelle feared for her husband's life, but no one dared utter a word lest they be the next victim of Christopher's wrath. Daren knew that there would be no reasoning with Christopher in his present state. He could easily intervene himself, but if Christopher blindly retaliated against him in any way, it would place both of them in a compromising situation in which Daren would have to reprimand Christopher for endangering his King. After seeing that Christopher was not backing down, Daren finally rose to bring his own security into the room to intervene. Normally, the council would rise when Daren stood, but they all remain seated apparently in shock or fear. Before Daren could reach the door, it opened and Shayla, his secretary, finally arrived.

Daren gave her a questioning look and then addressed his security, "Tyler, take care of this."

Christopher was still yelling, but his grip had loosened somewhat. Dawson took the chance to try to move away. Dawson's move gave Tyler a brief opportunity to place himself between Dawson and Christopher.

Dawson stood paralyzed while Christopher continued to rant.

Finally, Daren spoke up angrily, "Mr. Moulder! Get out. Christopher, sit down!"

Christopher gave Tyler a final push of frustration and then begrudgingly followed the King's order. Daren was still standing. As soon as everything was calm, Shayla, his secretary, who had also remained standing, addressed the King, "Sir, King Estrada of Lavinia is requesting permission to enter air space and land on the palace air strip. He claims to have an urgent matter to discuss with you."

"What is King Estrada doing here?" Daren questioned. There was exasperation in his voice.

Shayla answered, "I don't know sir. Do you want to allow him to land?"

Daren sighed. "Yes, but make sure he and his plane are cleared out before Prince Trevor arrives. Lance, any idea why Estrada would be visiting?" Daren questioned.

"He's rich, sir. Perhaps he wants to offer assistance for the disaster relief."

Daren was not amused. "It's apparent you don't have a clue about anything that is going on. Can you at least provide me with some useful information about King Estrada? What do we know?"

While the King and Mr. Sterling were talking, Ian busied himself with finding information on King Estrada. It was surprisingly difficult to find a picture of him anywhere, and the few Ian did find were obviously taken from a distance and not very defined. Ian projected the pictures so that Daren would at least have some reference before meeting with King Estrada. Lavinia was a small but affluent country that kept to itself for the most part, and apparently their King did the same.

Lance replied, "He's only been in power for approximately two years, sir. He never attends ICP meetings, and his representative usually abstains on votes. I am sure you remember that we traced the security breach during the gala a few months ago to a guest from his country, but she disappeared and no further leads were ever obtained."

Daren was distracted by some pictures that Ian had brought up on the display screens, and he stopped Lance. "That's enough, Mr. Sterling. Ian, what is that?"

"Those are pictures of King Estrada."

"They aren't very good. They are too far away."

"Yes sir, I can't seem to find anything else," Ian responded.

Daren had full confidence in Ian's research abilities, and he found it unusual that this King had managed to stay out of the limelight so effectively. He turned his attention back to Lance, "Have you ever met King Estrada?"

"No sir. As I said, he does not attend functions outside of his country."

"Well, then we will just have to find out for ourselves why the reclusive King of Lavinia has decided to grace us with his presence. Ian, I need to speak with you. Unless there is anything else that needs to be addressed, I think it best that we end this meeting."

Everyone started to rise, but Lance stopped them, "Just a moment. Sir, there is something I think we need to consider again. I know this was discussed previously, but are we absolutely sure that Mr. Moulder is innocent of any involvement with the security breach that happened during the gala?"

Daren's response was uncharacteristic and almost apathetic. "At this point, nothing would surprise me. Christopher?"

The Commander had seemed to recover from his previous outburst and was once more in control, "We can certainly question him again. He doesn't seem to be too concerned about upgrading the security in a timely manner, so perhaps there is an ulterior motive."

Daren agreed, "Do it, Commander. We need to follow all possible leads."

Chad was incredulous. Not only had Dawson proven his loyalty and commitment to King Daren and Lionel repeatedly, but Chad had personally witnessed the questioning that Dawson had undergone following the security breach. Dawson was a genius in the computer world, but he was not trained to withstand or evade the kind of intense interrogation he had been subjected to. Furthermore, Chad could not believe that Noelle remained silent on this. She should at least speak up for her husband. When she did not, Chad decided that someone needed to.

Risking a reprimand, Chad spoke his mind, "King Daren, Mr. Moulder has already been cleared of any involvement. I witnessed his interrogation, and his answers were honest and straightforward. I think further questioning is unnecessary and counter-productive. You want the security systems updated as soon as possible. Doing this will only cause a longer delay."

Knowing that Chad was most likely prejudiced by his friendship with Dawson, Daren addressed Chad directly, "Captain West, while your perspective is appreciated, we will proceed as planned."

Daren was taken aback when Chad continued, "Sir, both you and Commander Heart have even admitted that the intense circumstances that Mr. Moulder was put under leading up to the breach were unfair and nearly insufferable. However, even though he was expected to handle the security for both Lionel and Raxx, and travelled back and forth, exhausted and stretched to the limit, he still expressed genuine sorrow and responsibility over the fact that the security codes were obtained from him. I realize that you are angry with his . . ."

Chad was cut short by Ian. "Captain West, your role in these meetings unless otherwise specified is a silent one! You will, therefore, Captain, keep your unsolicited comments and opinions to yourself!"

Nothing more was said. Daren had risen during Chad's diatribe. Ian could tell that Daren was ticked. The King had reached his limit and this meeting had come to an end. Ian adjourned the meeting. King Daren was the first to leave.

Ian allowed some time to pass before going to King Daren's office. As chief advisor, he did not need permission to enter his King's office. He nodded in greeting to both Shayla and Captain Woods and then proceeded into the office. King Daren was sitting at his desk staring intensely at his computer. Ian stood and waited to be recognized.

Daren finally acknowledged him, "Ian, King Estrada's plane has landed. Go meet him. I will meet with him over dinner this evening at 7:00pm. Find out if he intends to remain here overnight and make arrangements if he does. Prince Trevor should arrive within the next half hour, and I will meet with him. That's all."

Ian could tell that Daren was in no mood for discussion so he acknowledged the king's order and exited. Approximately an hour later, Shayla informed Daren that Prince Trevor had arrived. He called Lance and instructed him to meet Prince Trevor and bring him to his office.

Chapter 9

Daren heard Lance speaking to his secretary, Shayla, and looked towards the doorway. He noted that his security, Lieutenant Woods, had tensed at the arrival of Prince Trevor, and Daren stood waiting for the two men to enter his office.

It had been two years since Daren had last seen Trevor, and as Trevor walked into the office, Daren noted a subdued yet stern defiance in his expression and body language. Daren wondered where that defiance was directed.

"Prince Trevor. Please have a seat," Daren offered.

Trevor's eyes had slowly wandered around the perimeter of Daren's office, and to Daren it almost seemed as if the Prince momentarily felt caged and was looking for a means of escape. At Daren's offer though, the Prince turned a steady and now controlled gaze to the King as he relaxed into the armchair in front of Daren's desk.

It was Trevor who now spoke, "King Daren, I would like to offer my condolences on your recent string of tragedies. I am sure your country's resources must be stretched to the limit at this point."

The comment irritated Daren and was a reminder of his country's current poor financial state. Daren was trying to suppress his disgust for Trevor's father and give Trevor the benefit of doubt. He was finding it very hard to do. Trevor may have been sincere in his comment, but had it come from Warren Benson, his father, it would have been a jab.

Daren finally chose not to acknowledge the comment at all. "Well, Trevor, I understand that you have information to share with me."

A contemplative look passed over Trevor's face as if he were struggling with something. Daren stole a glance at Lance and waited for Trevor's reply.

"I do. But first, I must insist that my presence here will remain undisclosed. As far as anyone knows, I am still in Raxx. My father threatened Kendra and I took her to Raxx for her own safety, but even she does not know I am here."

Kendra was Trevor's wife and was also the cousin of Queen Nicole, Daren's wife. Warren Benson had approved of Trevor's marriage to Kendra with hopes that it would give him a path to the throne of Raxx.

44

Daren chose to address the matter of Kendra first. "Marrying you was a death sentence for Kendra in the first place, Trevor. She is strong-willed, and it was inevitable that she and Warren would eventually come to odds. She chose to leave here and subsequently leave my protection. She is fortunate that Ethan is willing to shelter her."

Daren had paused, and Trevor remained silent.

Daren continued, "Trevor, I have no reason to disclose to anyone your presence here."

Trevor nodded in acceptance. "My father is working with Kann Zinn. Together, they have orchestrated the attacks on both Raxx and Lionel."

Daren was seldom shocked or caught off guard, but fire burned in his eyes as he glared at Trevor. How many times did Warren Benson and Kann Zinn have to be defeated? Daren wished he had killed both men long ago.

"How long have you known of this?" Daren demanded of Trevor.

Trevor's eyes momentarily narrowed at Daren's accusatory tone, but he answered without emotion. "Following the attacks, Kendra informed me of a meeting she was privy to between my father and Kann Zinn. My father thought he could exploit her to gain information about Lionel and Raxx. It seems she was convicted by the images of hundreds of dead bodies."

Daren shook his head. "I would think, Trevor, that Kendra would have grown accustomed to images of tortured and dead bodies while living in your father's palace. Isn't torture and death considered a common form of entertainment for him?"

A dark shadow passed over Trevor's face as Daren spoke. There was tinge of anger in his reply. "This is not about Kendra. My father has long wanted to see Lionel destroyed. And yes, I am quite certain my father reveled in the images of the dead and dying citizens of Lionel. You know who attacked you now. It is time for me to depart." Trevor stood to leave.

Daren was not ready for the conversation to end. He still did not entirely trust Trevor, and he needed more information. He also was not sure what he was going to do with Trevor quite yet.

"Sit down, Trevor. What is Zinn's stake in this?"

Trevor made no move to sit down, but he did answer the question. "Zinn has been in hiding in Cashteh. He's managed to amass a small army and thinks he can take out his sister - but only if Lionel is not involved. The attacks were meant to cripple Lionel to the point of pulling troops from other countries, including his country of Chiria. Once Lionel was out of the way, he could depose his sister."

"And what does your father gain from Zinn?"

"Access to Chiria's ports - another jibe at Lionel as you have refused him access to your ports, Daren." Trevor now decided to sit down. It seemed that the dark cloud that had descended on him had now dissolved with the turn of conversation. Daren wondered how much of his father's torture Trevor had endured these last two years as retribution for Trevor's defiance.

Another thought crossed Daren's mind. "Was Ethan intended to die in the blast in Raxx?"

Trevor gave a slight smile. "The event was rehearsed, Daren. The bomber knew exactly where Ethan would be standing."

Daren thought about that for a moment. The bomb had been centralized near the opposite side of the stage from Ethan. Daren had been looking down as he contemplated; his head now jerked up. "Brooke was the target?"

"That part of the plan was Zinn's idea. He still holds you and Councilor Hathaway, Queen Kissinger's father, responsible for turning the ICP against him the last time he tried to depose his sister. He wanted Hathaway to suffer."

"Killing Ethan would have left Raxx without a leader."

"Queen Nicole would still be alive, and I am sure that my father figured that once Lionel fell, Raxx would be open season. And as you pointed out, my father enjoys a more personal approach with his enemies. He hates Ethan almost as much as he hates you. Death by explosion would be much too merciful in my father's opinion."

Everything Trevor was saying made sense. Furthermore, if Benson had gained knowledge of Lionel's financial situation through the data that had been stolen over a year ago, he may have thought Lionel was weak enough to be defeated.

"Why are you sharing this with me, Trevor?"

Again, Trevor seemed conflicted. "I don't want or expect anything from you, Daren, if that is what you are thinking."

"I find that hard to believe," Daren quipped.

Again, Trevor stood. "As I said before, you have your information. Do with it what you will. I am done here."

Daren stood as well. He sought to temper Trevor's fury. "Trevor, thank you for the information. I'm just trying to decipher if the next king of Aldrich will be an enemy or an ally."

The comment seemed to make Trevor even more tense, but his anger at Daren dissipated. "I have never seen the sense in our countries being enemies, and I don't see that it has benefitted my country or its people in any way. My father lives for strife. I don't."

Daren hoped Trevor's words were sincere. "That's good to hear, Trevor. Perhaps some day soon our countries can be allies."

"Perhaps."

"Lance, do you have any questions for Prince Trevor before you escort him to his room?" Daren questioned.

Lance turned to Trevor, "Prince Trevor, if you don't mind, I would like to meet with you first thing in the morning. There are some things I will need to do based on the information you have provided, and I am sure that questions will arise."

Trevor gave a slight nod in agreement. Lance then escorted him out.

Chapter 10

Ashley was growing impatient. Lance had left over two hours ago to go meet with King Daren and Prince Trevor. No one had told her that Trevor was coming, and she couldn't wait to interrogate Lance when he returned. She tried to focus on the work that Lance had left for her, but her thoughts kept returning to Trevor. She had seen him at an ICP function a few months ago, but it had been the first time anyone had seen him since over a year ago when he had left Lionel and returned to his own country. He had had a haunted look about him when she saw him at the ICP headquarters, and she had felt a cold chill when Trevor informed her that his father told him every day that he would make a great king. Trevor's father, King Warren Benson, was guilty of countless horrendous atrocities, and she was sure that he was doing all he could to shape his son into a monster as well. Trevor was so much better than his father, and she hoped that he would be able to remain the man she had once loved.

Lance finally returned, and Ashley nearly assaulted him with questions. When he did not respond in his usual droll manner, she became concerned. His melancholy state made her even more anxious, and she tried unsuccessfully to practice self-restraint.

"Lance, is something wrong? Why is Trevor here? What does he want? You have to tell me what happened." Ashley nearly begged.

Lance still wasn't responding, so Ashley began again, "Lance! Please! You know I've been waiting . . . "

Lance finally interrupted, "Just give me a moment, Princess. It's quite a bit to take in, even for an intellectual like me. I'm also not sure how sensitive the information is."

"Lance, really?" Ashley rolled her eyes. She knew that Lance was not going to withhold information about Trevor from her. He was just goading her as usual, but she did sense an air of seriousness about his demeanor that was unusual. She was about to harass him even further, but he started talking.

"Princess, you know we've had no leads on the attacks. Well, Prince Trevor just provided us with a big one. He has intel that his father is working with Kann Zinn, and they are behind the attacks. King

Benson has apparently threatened Kendra, so Trevor took her to Raxx for her safety and then came here to share the information. We are in the process of confirming it."

It angered Ashley that King Benson had dared to attack her country, and she felt an intense admiration for Trevor for having the courage to go behind his father's back to share this information. She did not even want to try to imagine the horrendous things that King Benson would do to his son if he ever found out. It gave her a slight array of hope that Trevor might yet overcome his family's appalling legacy. She felt a sudden urge to see him. She had made her choice to be with Chad, but she would always love Trevor, and she was sure that Chad would understand if she simply thanked Trevor for the sacrifice he had just made.

She looked over at Lance and caught him staring at her with that assessing gaze he used when trying to ascertain someone's thoughts. It sometimes annoyed her that he was so good at figuring out what she was thinking, but it had also been quite endearing. She had come to value his insight, but right now, she did not care to discuss her thoughts with him.

"I think I'll leave for the day," she remarked. "There's not much else I can do right now."

Lance could see by the look on Ashley's face that she was determined to go. He was concerned about what she was most likely planning, but he also knew that she had made up her mind and no amount of discourse would dissuade her.

He dismissed her, "Very well, Princess. I shall see you bright and early tomorrow."

Ashley had considered asking Lance where she could find Trevor, but that would just have raised more suspicion on his part. Trevor was most likely in the guest quarters, so she headed that way. As she approached, she was relieved to see that Lieutenant Grant was on duty. Grant did his job well, but he didn't pry into your business like some of the royal guard members did. It was unlikely that he would report back to her father on her activities.

She approached him and questioned, "Lieutenant Grant, will you please tell me which room Prince Trevor Benson is staying in?"

He answered, "Yes, ma'am, he is staying in 542."

She thanked him and headed towards the room, but was stopped by Lieutenant Grant.

"Princess Ashley, he's not in there right now. I believe he was headed to the dining hall."

It slightly bothered her that her conversation with Trevor would be so public, but she headed towards the dining hall anyway. She could only imagine the gossip that would fill the palace if certain people saw her and Trevor talking. It didn't matter though. She wasn't doing anything wrong. She was simply thanking a friend for helping her country.

When she arrived at the dining hall, she saw Trevor sitting in a far corner. It was late in the day, so the dining hall was empty for the most part, but there were a few enjoying a late lunch. Ashley also noted with satisfaction that the royal dining area where he was sitting was empty. As Ashley approached Trevor, she noted that he seemed unaware of his surroundings. He rested his elbow on the arm of his chair, and his chin was supported by his thumb. He looked deep in thought. Ashley's nerves were suddenly on edge. She was contemplating not going through with this when he looked her way. His intense green eyes flashed recognition, and a slight smile escaped through his otherwise hardened face. He stood, and suddenly she felt slightly weak. She quickly mentally admonished herself for being so affected and regained her composure. She forced herself to walk towards him extending her hand for a handshake.

Trevor took her hand gently in his own, and did not release it. His height was a match for her father's, and it was both intimidating and stimulating. He had changed so much since the first time she met him. She had been only 14, and he was 15. He had been carefree and charming. He now had an almost ominous air about him that was frightening yet exhilarating. Every movement he made seemed slow and deliberate as if designed to elicit a specific response. When he spoke, his voice exuded a controlled potency.

"Ashley, what an unexpected but pleasant surprise. Would you care to join me?" Trevor asked.

Ashley was still trying to recover from the unexpected feelings that his presence caused. She continued to stare at him for several moments without replying. He simply stared back and patiently waited for her answer.

She finally formulated an answer, "Yes, thank you, but would it be okay if we sit in the royal dining area?"

Trevor flashed his half smile once more and motioned for her to lead the way. She made her way to an area of the room that was not visible to any would be onlookers. Trevor pulled out a chair for her and waited for her to be seated. He then stood looking down at her for a few moments before taking a seat himself.

Trevor did not speak, but simply stared at her with that unnerving intense look he had adopted. It made her uncomfortable and she sought to fill the silence.

"Trevor, thank you. I know the risk you took in coming here, but what you've done means so much."

Trevor waited a few moments to respond, and the suspense nearly drove Ashley insane.

His response was pointed, "You were in danger. I could help. It is what was necessary."

Again they sat in silence. The intensity in the air was palpable, and Ashley groped for just the right words to continue the conversation. To her relief, Alan arrived to take their order. Ashley certainly did not have much of an appetite, but she ordered food anyway. Trevor ordered as well. As Alan was about to leave, Ashley called him back.

"Mr. Walters, perhaps you could bring us a bottle of wine as well, please." Alan looked at her questioningly and somewhat accusingly she thought, so she tried to dismiss him quickly, "That will be all, Mr. Walters."

Once Alan departed, Ashley and Trevor engaged in brief chitchat about their lunch selections but then returned to an awkward silence. Ashley looked down at the table and absentmindedly toyed with the silverware. There were so many things she wanted to ask Trevor. She was looking down at the silverware and thinking about those questions when Trevor reached across and took her hand startling her.

She looked up at him and stammered, "How is Kendra?"

Trevor's expression did not change at all nor did he remove his hand as he answered, "Kendra is in Raxx. She is away from my father for the moment, so she is just fine, I am sure. I expected you to be enjoying a honeymoon."

Trevor's reference to her two-day-old marriage rattled Ashley, and she withdrew her hand from Trevor's.

"A lot has happened. Chad needs to be here right now. We can go away later. We do have the rest of our lives."

It irritated her that her answer sounded pathetic and defensive. It irritated her even more when Trevor seized on her seeming insecurity.

"Yes, Ashley, you do. I am sure this won't be the first time that his career is placed before his marriage. The marriage itself has been postponed many times as a result of his obligations, has it not?" Trevor paused, letting the question hang in the air. After a moment, he continued, "Well, let me offer you my congratulations. I know you have waited a long time. I hope you are not disappointed."

Ashley's emotions were all over the place. Alan arrived with the food and wine. He once more gave her a questioning look, and she knew it was because of the wine. Although members of the palace occasionally enjoyed a glass of wine, they seldom indulged, and she was no exception. As soon as he poured her a glass, Ashley took a long drink.

Ashley tried to change the subject to a less sensitive topic.

"I was surprised to see you at the last ICP meeting. It had been a while. Do you plan to attend on a regular basis?"

Trevor gave her a thoughtful look and questioned back, "Do you attend the meetings on a regular basis, Ashley?"

Ashley took another drink and replied, "Well, I am working with Mr. Sterling full-time now, and I plan to steal his job from him eventually, so yes, I will be attending regularly."

"Well, then I shall have to make it my priority to attend as often as possible as well."

Ashley reminded herself that she and Trevor had been and were still friends. It was not unusual for two friends to find opportunities to see each other.

Ashley asked another question, "Does your father plan for you to eventually take over?"

She watched as what could only be described as a mixture of both pain and hate briefly passed over Trevor's face. She wasn't sure if the cause had been the mention of his father or of his potential sovereignty. The look was gone in an instant, replaced by his placid, yet piercing stare.

"My father plans to live forever, but yes, I am the next in line."

"It is hard to imagine you following in your father's footsteps."

"Well, he is trying to shape me into the King he expects me to be."

The wine was taking its effect on Ashley, and she was feeling more at ease. "Trevor, do you remember how we first met?"

"I could never forget the first moment I met you Ashley. It will forever remain etched in my mind as one of the best days of my life." Trevor seemed momentarily lost in another place and time, and it was almost a full smile that crossed his face. When he focused his attention back on her, a look of haunted desire filled his eyes. Ashley found herself mesmerized by the look. Her head was swimming, and she felt light-headed. A feeling of overwhelming gratitude for what he had done overcame her, and she felt the need to express it.

"Trevor, I really am grateful to you for coming here and telling my uncle what you did. I'm so thankful that I met you in the music store. I'm sorry things didn't work out between us, but I truly do care about you and value our friendship. Just think, if I hadn't knocked over that display, we'd never be where we are now!"

Ashley's intoxication obviously amused Trevor, and he almost laughed as he responded to her outpouring, "And where is it exactly that we are now, Ashley?"

"Well, we are obviously good friends. We can hang out together and talk and just enjoy each other's company," Ashley gushed. She reached up and touched her face. It seemed really hot, and she looked at Trevor with a concerned look, "Is it warm in here? It feels like the air has stopped working."

Trevor seized on the moment, "Perhaps a little. Would you like to walk outside and get some fresh air?"

"Okay," Ashley responded with an unrestrained smile.

As they made their way to the courtyard, Ashley rambled about the air not working and how nice it was outside. She was thoroughly enjoying herself, and her laughter filled the hallway. They reached the courtyard, and Trevor opened the door for her to go through. She smiled up at him gratefully and he took her arm to steady her.

Ashley continued to talk nonstop, and Trevor just listened. He seemed unaffected by her loquaciousness. After they had walked for a while, Trevor stopped and turned towards her.

"Ashley, you have to know that I still love you. You are the one I want to be with. I would never neglect you. We have had a very enjoyable time together today. We could be doing this every day."

"But I'm married to Chad, and you have Kendra," countered Ashley.

"Kendra is not a concern, Ashley. One word from you Ashley, and Kendra is gone. And Chad, he does not appreciate you Ashley. You are a princess, and you deserve better. I can make you a queen."

Trevor's admiration was very flattering to Ashley, but even though she was inebriated, she struggled with the propriety of their conversation.

He tried a different angle, "Ashley, at least agree to meet with me again tonight. It is only when I am with you that I feel like myself. We can have dinner together or just spend time talking."

Trevor's voice had lost its sinister edge, and he really did sound more like himself. Ashley felt that her time with him was having a positive effect, and she didn't see what harm it would do to continue spending time with him.

She smiled in agreement, "A late dinner then."

They had been walking, but at Ashley's acquiescence to his request, Trevor once more stopped and turned to her. He was standing very close to her, and Ashley felt slightly elated. Her elation was cut short by the sound of Chad's voice.

"Prince Trevor, please excuse me, but I need to speak with my wife," Chad insisted as he reached Ashley's side.

It was Ashley who interjected, "I'll be there shortly, Chad. Trevor and I were just taking a walk. I think the air conditioning might be broken inside."

During this exchange, Trevor had made no move to distance himself from Ashley. Seeing them standing so closely had disturbed Chad, and at Ashley's response, Chad reached for her arm and pulled her towards him.

Chad now appealed to Ashley, "I am sure that Prince Trevor has had enough of your time for the day. He will surely understand if your husband takes you away."

Trevor now spoke, and his voice was filled with contempt, "Lieutenant West, Ashley and I were discussing international affairs. I don't expect you to understand the complexities involved. This is a matter of importance, and I am sure that King Daren would not appreciate your interruption. I do not believe that Ashley is in the habit of interrupting you when you are busy with work, which I understand is quite often."

It took every ounce of control Chad had to keep his tongue in check. It had been a long day, and a confrontation with Trevor Benson was the last thing he wanted. Chad knew that Trevor had purposefully put him at a disadvantage by making this a political affair. Trevor was a Prince, and that ultimately gave him power over Chad. However, Ashley was his wife, Princess or not, and he was not going to allow her to prance around the palace with her former fiancé! With that in mind, he risked ignoring Trevor and focused his attention solely on Ashley.

"Ashley, it has been a long day. I want some time with you before retiring for the night. You and Mr. Sterling can finish business with Prince Trevor in the morning."

Ashley smiled at Chad and replied, "Alright, my love, Trevor and I are meeting later for dinner anyway. I will just wait until you go to bed."

Had his wife gone crazy? He instinctively grasped her arm tighter and pulled her closer to him. The moment he did, he understood the reason for her insensibility. The smell of alcohol was potent.

His face was livid with anger as he addressed Trevor, "I do not think, Prince Trevor, that my wife is in a state of mind to discuss any matters of importance at this time. You will excuse us. She is done here."

At that Chad practically dragged Ashley away. The thought that there could be spectators watching this mayhem momentarily concerned him, but then he realized that any number of people had already seen too much. Ashley protested the entire way to their room, but Chad was unrelenting. He forced himself to remain calm and used the strategies he had learned in training to control his emotions.

Chad gently shoved Ashley into their suite and turned to shut the door. When he turned back towards her, she threw her arms around his neck and pressed her body up against him. These tactics would normally work, but under the circumstances, Chad was too irate with Ashley to be seduced. He also briefly wondered if she was sober enough to even know that she was no longer with Trevor. He pushed that thought out of his mind and unwound Ashley from himself. He guided her to the couch and forced her to sit down. She tried to pull him down with her, but he would not capitulate. He wanted more than anything to ask her what she was thinking, but he knew her answer would not be sensible in her current condition. He walked to the kitchen and poured her a glass of water. Taking it to her, he sat on the opposite end of the couch and instructed her to drink. He then picked up a book and busied himself with reading. Ashley finished her water and then moved closer to Chad.

"Why are you reading?"

Chad tried to ignore her question.

Ashley continued, "Chad, you said you wanted to spend time with me. If you are just going to read a book, then there's no need for me to be here."

Chad looked up, "Where do you want to be Ashley? With Trevor?"

Ashley smiled, "We were having a good time until you pulled me away, but I can spend time with you now. I don't want to watch you read a book though."

Realizing that Ashley was not going to leave him alone, Chad simply pulled her close allowing her to rest her head on his chest, "Rest Ashley. We will talk when you are sober."

Within minutes Ashley was asleep.

Chapter 11

King Daren had remained in his office following the meeting with Prince Trevor Benson. Daren now turned his thoughts towards his imminent meeting with King Estrada. He could not even imagine what the reclusive and somewhat peculiar King could possibly want. Estrada's country rarely got involved in other country's affairs, and King Estrada had certainly not been very accommodating when a security breach during an International gala at Lionel palace had been traced back to a guest from Lavinia, King Estrada's country.

As Daren was pondering King Estrada's visit, Lance arrived. Daren acknowledged Lance and then motioned for him to sit down.

"Queen Nicole will be joining us for dinner. We will wait for her to arrive. Have you spoken with Ian? Did Estrada share any information with him?" Daren questioned.

"Yes, sir. Mr. Garrett seemed quite intrigued with him. Apparently King Estrada is a talented pilot in addition to being a King. He flew his own plane and had no additional security or attendants upon his arrival," Lance answered.

Although Daren did find that information interesting and unusual, it didn't provide any further explanation as to the reason for Estrada's visit in the first place. Daren waited for Lance to continue hoping that he would have something more.

Lance sensed that the King was waiting for him to continue, and he was quite relieved at Queen Nicole's timely arrival. He immediately stood and greeted her.

"Queen Nicole, I understand we will have the pleasure of your company at dinner this evening." Lance stated.

Nicole gave Lance a compulsory smile and then approached Daren's desk. Daren rose. He put one arm around her waist and gave her a kiss.

"You look beautiful."

"Thank you. You didn't tell me that we would have to put up with Mr. Sterling all evening." Nicole responded.

"Yes, well let's hope that he proves himself to be valuable. Let's go." Daren ordered.

As they walked, Nicole studied her husband. The financial stresses of the last few years and especially the added stress of the last week were taking their toll. She knew he had not had much sleep, and the red surrounding his normally deep blue eyes was a telltale sign. Earlier, he had briefly shared with her the information that Prince Trevor gave him, and she knew that he must feel that the weight of the world was on his shoulders. Despite it all, he still maintained an aura of power and self-control. He stood tall, and his blonde, shoulder length hair fell in wisps enunciating his square-jawed face. His hairstyle gave him a somewhat wild, yet purposeful look.

Nicole glanced back at Lance. He too seemed deep in thought. She knew that Daren's earlier comment about Lance's benefit had deeper implications. Lance was originally from her home country of Raxx and had served her mother, the previous Queen of Raxx, before her untimely death. Nicole had recommended Lance to Daren long ago, and she had full confidence in his abilities.

The walk to the dining hall had been a silent one. As they neared the entrance to the royal dining area, Daren ushered Nicole through, and she was the first to get a glimpse of King Estrada. The incredibly handsome King rose from his chair and moved toward the party of three. He went directly to Nicole. When she offered her hand, he took it, and looking into her eyes as he did so, he raised it to his lips and kissed it. Nicole felt somewhat foolish as she felt a slight blush taint her cheeks.

Estrada spoke, and his voice was like velvet, smooth and serene, "Queen Nicole, it is a pleasure."

King Estrada had to be at least ten years her junior, but his looks and demeanor had a breathtaking effect on Nicole. She had never met a man who made such a striking first impression. She knew that he kept mostly to himself, and she wondered if he knew the effect that he had. If he did, she had to admire him for not using it to his advantage. Not daring to look at Daren, she glanced at Lance. He, too, seemed to be taken with Estrada. They were shaking hands, and Lance seemed to be at a loss for words. She finally looked at Daren. His full attention was on King Estrada, and she was grateful that it was not on her. Daren guided them to a table. The three men waited for her to sit down first.

Eager to get this over with, Daren began, "King Estrada, your arrival was quite an unexpected visit. I understand that you have some information that you wish to share."

Mr. Walters was expecting them and had already prepared the menu. Before King Estrada could speak, Mr. Walters started pouring each of them a glass of red wine. Alan started to speak, but Daren waved him away and turned his attention back to Estrada awaiting his response.

King Estrada studied the wine at length before taking a sip. When he finally did so, a brief look of euphoria passed over his countenance.

He looked at Daren earnestly, "This is a most excellent vintage. Is it from a native vineyard? I do not recognize it."

Lance noted the look of impatience on Daren's face and interceded, "Yes, King Estrada, it is from the province of Cousineau. Unfortunately, the recent earthquake and aftershocks affected much of the region."

"Ah, yes, such a great tragedy. My condolences, King Daren, for your losses."

Alan arrived once more with the salad and appetizers. When he left, Estrada continued.

"King Daren, I must first thank you for taking the time to speak with me on such short notice. I came because I owe you a sincere apology for my seeming apathy towards your prior request. I hope you understand, King Daren, that my lack of action was assuredly not a representation of my respect or admiration for you and your country. I certainly did not fully understand the urgency of the matter until the attacks on your country occurred."

Daren had no desire to waste his time listening to this King's interminable excuses. Surely he understood that Daren had more important matters at hand. No longer concerned with propriety, Daren interrupted.

"King Estrada, it was unnecessary for you to travel here to offer your apology. I do not make frivolous requests of other Kings, and your indifference to our plight was disconcerting. However, seeing that our countries have had no other misunderstandings, I accept your apology. I hope that in the future, should something similar arise, I can count on your cooperation."

King Estrada seemed genuinely affected by Daren's brusque response and continued in an almost subservient manner, "King Daren, I assure you that I understand how valuable your time is. Please forgive me if I implied differently. When the attacks on your country occurred, I mourned for you, and I also feared that my inaction could have played a part. I immediately did what I should have when you contacted me months ago. Upon investigation, I discovered that the woman who was escorted by my country's representative to the gala was hired through an escort service that is often used by members of Lavinia's political hierarchy. It was also discovered that a rather large sum of money was deposited by the company close to the gala. After interrogation, the owners of the company admitted to accepting a bribe from the woman to ensure that she would be the one to escort our representative. Unfortunately, she appeared close to the gala and disappeared immediately afterwards. The company normally keeps records and photographs of their employees, but her payoff was large enough that no questions were asked. I have made sure that the company will no longer function, and the owners will be punished for their part in this. I sincerely wish that I could offer more assistance. The picture you provided of her has been widely circulated, and if she is still in my country, I assure you she will be found and turned over to you immediately. I do not desire to make an enemy, King Daren. I accept full responsibility for this incident, and stand ready to make it up to you in any way you see fitting."

As he spoke, Lance noted that King Estrada had an almost entrancing quality to his voice. Lance knew that Daren would expect him to provide a full behavioral analysis on Estrada following the meeting. The problem was that Lance was having difficulty analyzing him. Estrada was the King of perhaps the wealthiest country in the land, yet everything about his demeanor indicated that he was servile to Daren. His earnestness was exaggerated, yet he seemed sincere. There was absolutely no reason that Lance could imagine for him to admit his shortcomings to Daren. If he had never again contacted Daren, there would have been no repercussions. Lavinia certainly didn't need Lionel's help either. All in all, this man was an enigma.

Estrada's pace was slow, and he had continued talking as Alan brought their dinner and they started eating. Daren did not have much of an appetite, and he noted that Nicole's food remained untouched as well. Daren had also found his mind wandering while Estrada droned on, and he remembered that he still needed to speak with his sister, Megan, before the night was over. When Estrada finally finished talking, Daren hoped that he would eat faster than he had spoken. Daren noticed Alan checking on their table from a distance. When Alan started their way, Daren stayed him with a look. He knew that Alan would be concerned that the dinner was disagreeable. Daren made a mental note to ask Alan to send his leftovers to his room to assuage his concerns. When Daren looked back, King Estrada was staring at him intently as if awaiting a response.

Daren made an obligatory reply, "King Estrada, let's just put this behind us. The only request I will make of you is that you remain our ally."

Lance found Daren's choice of words slightly amusing. Lavinia had always been neutral where Lionel was concerned, neither ally nor enemy. He also was somewhat vexed that King Daren did not ask more of King Estrada. Lionel was certainly in need of financial assistance, and Lavinia had more than enough to spare. King Estrada seemed aware of Daren's restlessness and finished his meal prematurely.

As they stood to leave, Nicole noticed that Daren seemed irresolute when he addressed Estrada, "King Estrada, I hope you will enjoy the remainder of your stay. You understand that I have many matters to attend to."

To Daren's relief, Nicole offered her assistance, "Daren, if you don't mind, I can show King Estrada around."

"Absolutely. Queen Nicole can give you a tour."

Estrada replied, "Thank you, King Daren. Queen Nicole, I am honored."

Lance found it unusual for Daren to agree to Nicole escorting Estrada around the palace, but he knew his king was overwhelmed. Daren swiftly departed while Estrada and Queen Nicole headed in the opposite direction. When Lance looked back at them, he was surprised to see Estrada offer his arm to Queen Nicole. He was even more surprised when she accepted.

Chapter 12

Daren made his way to Megan's room. This entire day had been taxing, and he was sure that his meeting with Megan would be no different. She was married to the King of Mikasa, Gavin Zeffrin, and their marriage had been a turbulent one. Daren did not condone divorce, but he sometimes thought it might be easier if she would just leave Gavin once and for all. King Zeffrin had certainly given her reason to on more than one occasion. Whatever had occurred this time must have been quite significant for Megan to leave her newborn son behind.

As soon as Megan's door opened, she threw herself at Daren and clung to him. He held her and allowed her to cry. Following their father and mother's death when he was only seventeen and she twelve, Daren had practically raised Megan. He had doted on her; she nearly worshipped him, and he knew that their closeness had been a part of the strain on her marriage. Once she was calm, Daren pushed her away from him and led her to the couch in her suite. He then took the chair across from her.

"Megan, what happened? Why were you in Raxx?" Daren asked.

She looked like she was about to cry again, and Daren waited as patiently as he could. She regained control and answered, "I had to get away from him. He wouldn't listen to anything I said."

Daren was utterly exhausted, and getting information out of Megan was excruciating. After hearing what Trevor had to say, he needed to know what this was about and whether or not it related to Benson. Not too long ago, Gavin had been angry with Daren and had considered an alliance with Benson. They had worked things out, but Gavin was unpredictable, and any number of things could have occurred since.

"Megan, are you leaving him? Do you plan to stay here?" Daren asked.

"No. I don't know. I just need some time to think."

"Well, according to Ethan, you've been thinking for the past three weeks in Raxx. Megan, I assume there's more that you are not telling me. You have a daughter and a newborn son in Mikasa. I'm sure they are missing their mother. And I am sure that you have a better reason for leaving than Gavin's lack of attention to you."

"I know. I just don't know what to do."

Daren was getting frustrated. "Megan, you need to tell me why you are here."

His tone must have expressed his mood because Megan again burst into tears.

Talking to Megan was going nowhere. Daren sensed that Megan probably wanted to go back, but she most likely was afraid that Gavin would not welcome her back. He decided he would make a call to Gavin to hear his side of things. He was sure that Gavin would be just as vague on the details, but at least he could get a sense of where this was going and whether it was just a domestic dispute or more.

He gently lifted Megan's chin, "Go to bed. You have some important decisions to make. We will talk about this later."

Daren kissed Megan on the forehead and left. He would call Gavin from his suite. He didn't care that the hour was late. Daren entered his suite and noted how quiet it was. His children had probably gone to bed hours earlier and would be sleeping soundly by now. He went into each of their rooms to check on them. His son, Noah, had managed to kick his covers to the end of his bed. His arms and legs were long for a twelve year old, and one leg hung off the side. The rest of his limbs were askew filling as much of the large bed as possible. Daren gently lifted the fugitive leg and placed it back on the bed. He then pulled the covers over Noah. He sat on the edge of the bed and studied his son's face. It was peaceful and void of anxiety. He lifted a prayer to God that Noah's life and eventual reign would be one of peace and safety. He also prayed for God's guidance and wisdom in raising his son to be a Godly and just king.

Next, Daren made his way to Kiley's room. Unlike her twin brother, Kiley was nearly rolled into a ball in the middle of her bed. Her long, blonde, wavy hair trailed behind her, and she looked like she was sheltering herself from something or someone. She had always been the more troublesome of the two, but lately sheer rebellion had reared its ugly head. Although she was still young, Daren was concerned for his oldest daughter. She was so strong-willed, and he struggled with disciplining her without destroying her spirit. Daren also said a prayer for Kiley, but whereas he knew exactly what to pray for Noah, he struggled with his prayer for Kiley. Her future was so uncertain, and he could only hope that she would use her stubborn determination for good.

Lastly, Daren went to Emma's room. Emma was only eight, and she was Daren's baby. Unlike her brother and sister, Emma had dark hair and olive skin. When she was first born, Daren had secretly had a DNA test done to ensure that she was his. He felt almost ridiculous now for having done so. Nicole had never given him real reason to doubt her fidelity, and Emma was certainly his in every way. As he sat on the edge of her bed, Emma stirred slightly. Her eyes opened in a sleepy haze, and he brushed the stray hairs out of her eyes. Leaning down, he kissed her on her cheek. She lifted her arms for him to hold her, and he did.

With his chin on her head, he prayed for his baby, "Father, thank you for this beautiful and angelic reminder of your many blessings. Forgive me for my doubt and uncertainty. Please continue to place your hedge of protection around my family. God, please let Emma's heart remain as soft and cheerful as it is now. Amen."

He disentangled himself from Emma and went into the office of the suite to make his phone call. His visit to his children had calmed him somewhat, and he lifted one last prayer to God for wisdom in dealing with Gavin. The phone rang several times and was then redirected. Daren hung up and called again. This time, Gavin picked up on the second ring.

"Daren?" Gavin sounded irritated as usual.

Daren went straight to the point, "Gavin, Megan is here."

"Should that surprise me, Daren? It's not unusual for her to go running to you." Gavin hissed.

"Gavin, I'm calling to let you know. How are Hailey and Silas doing?" Daren questioned.

"I'm sure they would be better if they had their mother." Gavin responded.

Gavin's response let Daren know at least part of what he needed to know. Gavin wanted her back.

"Perhaps you should call her," Daren suggested.

There was silence from the other end.

Daren continued, "Gavin, Megan is ready to return, but she needs to hear from you that she is welcome."

It angered Daren that he had to pander to Gavin to get him to call Megan. Megan certainly deserved better, but his goal was to get this worked out as quickly as possible.

Gavin finally answered, "I will speak with her."

Daren decided that further conversation with Gavin could wait. It was late and neither of them would be in the best state of mind to address the Benson issue. "She will be happy to hear from you."

"Good night, Daren."

"Gavin."

When Daren went to his room, he was surprised to find that Nicole was not there. He then remembered that she had agreed to escort Estrada on a tour of the palace. He felt a momentary pang of pity for her knowing she would have to listen to King Estrada's droning voice. He headed toward the door of his suite to order his security to have her return, but she came through the door before he reached it. She had an odd look on her face, and he imagined that the eccentric King had baffled her. He had no desire to hear about it.

"It's been a long day. Get changed and come to bed." Daren ordered.

Nicole wanted to talk with Daren about Estrada, but she could tell that he was in no mood to talk. She quickly changed and slipped into bed next to her husband. Daren kissed her, put his arm around her and fell into a restless sleep.

Chapter 13

Ashley had been sleeping on Chad's shoulder for nearly two hours. Chad tried to move her off of him so that he could go to the bathroom. When he did, she awoke. At first she seemed disoriented, but then her confusion turned to panic.

"Chad, what time is it? How long was I asleep?" she cried.

"It's ten o'clock," Chad answered, "I'll be right back and then we can talk."

When Chad emerged from the bathroom, he was surprised to find Ashley in their bedroom changing her attire. At first he thought she was getting ready for bed, but when she donned a very alluring dress, he questioned her.

"Ashley, what are you doing?"

"I thought I told you. I agreed to meet Trevor for a late dinner. Hopefully it's not too late," Ashley explained. "Will you get me something for my head, please? It's killing me."

Chad stood completely dumb-founded. He could somewhat understand Ashley's previous behavior due to the influence of alcohol. The fact that she was still planning on meeting Trevor for dinner now that she was sober was beyond him. Ashley had always had a mind of her own, but her actions right now were disrespectful and vindictive towards him, and he wasn't aware of anything he had done to instigate this treatment.

As she continued to primp, Chad confronted her, "Ashley, you surely aren't serious about going to meet him."

"Chad, he's only here tonight. He's leaving tomorrow. I haven't seen him in such a long time. I actually got him to smile today. I don't understand why this is bothering you so much. It's not like . . ."

Chad interrupted, "You don't understand why this bothers me? Seriously?"

Ashley continued, "Chad, listen. Think about all he goes through with his father and how horrible it must be."

Chad was fuming now, "I am sure that he shared quite a sob story with you, Ashley, and perhaps some of it was true, but I don't care.

It bothers me because he is your ex-fiancé, Ashley. He is still in love with you!"

"Chad, don't you think you sound a little paranoid? It's just dinner between two friends. Nothing more. You have nothing to worry about."

Chad was tempted to make a call to Dawson and have him secure their suite so that Ashley couldn't leave. He knew that the end result of that action would not be favorable though, so he resisted the urge. Ashley's love and devotion to him had to be by choice and not force. He decided to use another strategy.

"Ashley, I do not want you to meet with Trevor tonight. I love you, but you embarrassed both yourself and me with your actions earlier today, and if you meet with him tonight, it will be in complete and total disregard of my wishes and feelings. You married me only two days ago. I am sorry that our first few days of marriage have been so disappointing to you that you feel the need to seek the attention of your ex." Ashley rolled her eyes at the last comment. Her dismissal of his feelings hurt Chad, and he responded to her with surrender, "However, it is your decision. I can tell you this though, if you go to meet him tonight, things will change between us."

Ashley shook her head and gave Chad a look of disdain, "Chad, I think you are blowing this totally out of proportion. It has nothing to do with you or with us."

"You are wrong, Ashley. This has everything to do with us, and your total disregard for my perspective on this is a telltale sign."

With those words, Chad stormed out of the suite with Ashley's voice in the background.

"A telltale sign of what? What are you trying to say? You're just being stupid! Don't walk away from me!" Ashley yelled.

Chad tried to convince himself that Ashley was right, and that he was making a big deal about nothing. But, her choice of the emerald green dress that highlighted her blue eyes and auburn hair indicated otherwise. He did know that Ashley had a big heart and her desire to help Trevor was genuine. He was also sure that Trevor knew that about Ashley and would have no trouble using it to his advantage. Chad didn't necessarily hate Trevor, but Trevor certainly hated Chad. Ashley had practically dumped Trevor for Chad.

Chad made his way outside and walked away from the lights of the palace. It was a clear night, and the stars were abundant. Seeing the stars always made Chad aware of the vastness of the universe and subsequently of his own insignificance in comparison to it. He recalled the question from King David in Psalms 144 that says, "I wonder why you care, God-why do you bother with us at all? All we are is a puff of air; we're like shadows in a campfire." Chad had often felt humbled that such a great God had paid him any attention at all, and even through this trial, Chad had to remember how greatly God had blessed him. He was also aware of the verse that says, "the Lord gives and the Lord takes away. Blessed be the name of the Lord." At that thought, Chad sent a silent plea to God for his favor. He also asked for wisdom.

Looking at the stars was having a disconcerting effect, so Chad decided to focus his attention in a less overpowering direction. He crouched to the ground and pulled a blade of grass. He hoped that no one had grown concerned. Still in his fatigues, he knew he blended into his surroundings away from the light. It would seem that he had disappeared to anyone who happened to be paying attention. That brought his thoughts back to a previous inclination he had so far avoided. There was a part of him that didn't want to know if Ashley had chosen to go to Trevor. He could simply stay away for the night, avoid cameras, and tell himself what he wanted. The other part of him wanted to watch every move they made. The two choices warred in his head, but his curiosity overpowered his fear. He stood up, made his way to the Commander's office and switched on the camera feeds. Once Dawson finished updating the system, they would be able to pinpoint the exact location of anyone in the palace using biometrical sensors, but for now Chad would have to rely on good, old-fashioned surveillance strategies. He searched through each camera feed for Ashley's profile. When he was unable to locate her, he found the camera feed from outside their room and started it at the time he had left. He fast-forwarded waiting apprehensively to see the figure of his wife in her green dress emerge. She never did. Chad ran through the feed again to make sure he hadn't missed anything. He wanted to breathe a sigh of relief, but he needed to see Ashley first. Maybe she was waiting for him to return so that she could say goodbye before taking off with Trevor. Chad chastised himself for such thoughts, but her behavior with Trevor earlier had taken its toll.

When he reached their room, he took a deep breath before opening the door. It was quite possible that he would be hit with a hurricane named Ashley.

As he entered, he found her sitting on the couch, dressed for bed working on her laptop. She looked up at him, and her expression was unreadable. They stared at each other for a few moments before she spoke.

"I didn't go." She waited. When he did not reply, she continued, "I'm sure you already know that."

Chad still remained silent, and it was driving Ashley crazy.

She spoke again, "Where have you been?"

Chad didn't answer. Instead he strode across the room, moved her laptop to the side and pulled her to her feet. Once she was standing, Chad put his arms around her and pulled her close.

Then he answered, "I took a walk."

She pulled away and looked at him, "A walk to another country?"

Chad smiled at her wit, "No, I was afraid that's what you might do."

Ashley smirked and rolled her eyes. She could tell that this could go down a dark path if she let it, so she took control.

"Chad, I love you. I mean, I sorta married you two days ago. I don't think I would have changed my mind quite yet. Give it a few years at least!"

Ashley smiled her full smile after her comment, and it was Chad's reassurance that she truly loved him. Chad smiled back at Ashley and gathered her into his arms. His love for her was intense. He knew that if he ever lost her, it would be his undoing. After they had embraced for a few moments, Ashley wriggled loose and grabbed her laptop.

"While you were off brooding, I took some time to pick out a color scheme for our new suite. Look," she demanded.

Chad sighed and sat down. His country was on the brink of war. He was second in command of its military forces, and he was spending time looking at color schemes. He tried to focus but found himself dozing off repeatedly.

Ashley prattled on for several minutes not realizing she had lost Chad to exhaustion. When she finally did look over at him, his head was laying at a right angle to his body, and he looked drained. She briefly regretted keeping him up so late when she knew that tomorrow would be a challenging day.

She awakened him, and his first impulse was an apology.

"Ashley, I'm sorry. I think I missed a few. Go back, and I'll tell you the last I remember."

Chad's thoughtfulness warmed her heart. She responded, "No, I know you are tired. Let's go to bed."

Chapter 14

Even though his country was about to go to war, Daren felt more at peace than he had in days. The enemy was no longer an unknown force. The council had met early that morning, war had been declared against Aldrich, and military forces were already in preparation for deployment. Daren decided to take care of the next crisis on his list - his sister.

He picked up his phone and spoke to his secretary, "Shayla, contact Megan and tell her to come to my office."

Daren busied himself with signatures on various requests while he waited for Megan. Many of the requests that passed over his desk were for funding. He was still concerned about the financial situation in Lionel, and he briefly wondered if perhaps he should put his pride aside and request assistance from King Estrada. The enigmatic king was still in the palace; he was scheduled to leave that afternoon.

Daren picked up his phone again, "Shayla, as soon as Megan leaves, I want to speak with Deanna, Lance and Ian."

Shayla informed him that Megan had arrived, and he ordered her to send Megan in. Megan entered and took a seat on the sofa facing Daren's desk. Daren felt a momentary pang of nostalgia as he remembered Megan as a young child sitting in that same exact spot shortly after their father had passed and Daren had become King at the young age of 17. She had asked him if he would still have time for her now that he was the King. He vowed that he would always have time for her, and in the years that followed, his office had remained open to his sister anytime she needed him. Now was no different. She had the same sad look on her face that she had had that day, and it burdened him that his sister was hurting.

Daren was direct, "Megan, Gavin wants you to go back to Mikasa. Is there any reason why you shouldn't go back?"

Megan was slow to answer, and that fact worried Daren.

"We just had some disagreements. I shouldn't have left, and once I did, I wasn't sure if he would let me come back. Are you sure he wants me to return?" There was doubt in her voice.

"I spoke with him last night. He made it clear. Megan, if he is mistreating you . . . " Daren started.

"No, no. It's nothing like that. He is just stressed, and I sometimes don't know how to handle things when he is on edge." Megan countered.

Daren didn't like her answer. He wondered why Gavin was on edge. He was hoping for more from Megan, but she remained vague. He would be making another phone call to Gavin before he allowed her to go back to him.

"Well, if you are ready to return, then I will speak with Gavin."

"Thank you, Daren."

Megan stood to leave. Daren stood and walked over to her. He put his arm around her and kissed her on her temple. She still seemed like a fragile little child to him. He quickly dismissed that thought and walked her to the door. Ian, Deanna and Lance were waiting outside. He ushered Megan out and ordered his three advisors to come in. For the next three hours they poured over the budget. In the end, the peace Daren had felt that morning had flown away leaving a heavy weight of despair. Much money had been embezzled several years ago, and Lionel was still in the process of recovering from that. Now, the earthquake, joined with the attacks and now a war had nearly depleted Lionel's resources. Daren would speak with Pastor Isaiah before he sought the assistance of Estrada, but he couldn't imagine where else he could turn. Perhaps God had sent Estrada just in time, but the thought of borrowing from another country and going into debt seemed somehow wrong.

Chapter 15

Chad watched General Ben Canaan's men move in synchronized symmetry. The General was intent watching their every move and taking notes as they drilled. Chad recalled his early days of training and noted the subtle differences that were unique to Ben Canaan's methods and tactics. Because of his knowledge and expertise of Aldrich, General Ben Canaan and his men would be going into the heart of the conflict, possibly even all the way to the palace. Chad wondered how Caleb felt about this mission. Caleb had been a high-ranking member of Aldrich's military, but when the king of Aldrich, Warren Benson, brutally raped and murdered Caleb's wife, the General had fled the country with his daughter Becca, who was then only 8 years old. The General's tragedy guided him back to his home country of Lionel where he had rejoined Lionel's military and quickly earned the appreciation and respect of Commander Heart. If all went as planned with this war, King Warren Benson would be dead, and General Ben Canaan would hopefully have closure.

Chad noted that three of Ben Canaan's men were standing apart from the others. They were probably the ones who had been chosen to stay behind and assist with domestic security in the aftermath of the earthquake and homeland attacks. They were the reason Chad was waiting to speak with the General. Chad made his way toward them. The General saw him and motioned for Chad to wait. Ben Canaan growled orders at one of his men and then broke away to join Chad.

General Ben Canaan saluted and then addressed Chad, "Commander West, these are three of my best men. They aren't overly thrilled about staying back, but they are reliable and will get the job done."

Chad already knew that any soldier would be chomping at the bits to go to war, especially in these circumstances.

"Thank you, General. Their service here in securing Lionel internally will be just as valuable as . . ."

Chad ceased his discourse when he realized that something behind him had caught the General's attention. Ben Canaan's brow was creased with either concern or frustration. Chad turned to see the source of the General's consternation. Becca, the General's 16-year-old daughter, was making her way down the hill towards them. She wasn't stopping, and she seemed distressed. Her normally calm and compliant manner was replaced with uneasy restlessness. Her pace was rushed and her brow furrowed in concern. When she reached the two of them, she blurted out, "Daddy, I need to talk to you."

Chad had not had much interaction with Becca, but he knew Ben Canaan fairly well, and he was sure that it was not commonplace or acceptable to the General for his daughter to interrupt when he was working. The austere expression on Caleb's face as he turned towards his daughter was further evidence of the rarity of this occasion. With that in mind, Chad started to excuse himself to allow the General and Becca to talk.

General Ben Canaan stopped him, "Commander West, just a moment, please. This will not take long."

Becca seemed to break into hysteria, "Daddy, you can't let him do this! You have to stop it! He can't go to war!"

General Ben Canaan put his hand on Becca's shoulder and spoke sternly yet calmly, "Becca, I am working. We will talk about this later. You need to go back to the palace."

His words did not deter Becca at all. She continued, "Daddy, no! Don't let him go! How can you let him do this?"

As Chad had hardly ever heard more than three words from Becca at a time, and then only in a soft spoken and shy tone, he was surprised at her tenacity now.

Becca continued, "How can Commander Heart send his own son to war? Please, daddy. He'll be killed."

Todd. This was about Todd. Chad could not believe it. The girl was obviously enamored with the young prince, and her emotional attachment to him was overcoming reason. Chad actually felt a momentary pang of pity for the General. He could tell that the General was slightly embarrassed by his daughter's behavior and more than slightly frustrated at her untimely disruption. Chad had to admit that he agreed with Becca that Todd shouldn't be going to war, but Chad's reasons were very different. Babysitting Todd during the mission would be a constant distraction to the General.

General Ben Canaan now took Becca by both shoulders. His voice was uncompromising, "Rebecca Ben Canaan, I am at work. Do you need to join my men in training? You are plainly in need of a little discipline."

Becca seemed daunted by her father's gruffness and remained silent. The General again addressed his daughter, "Becca, answer me."

Becca's tone was back to its usual passive acquiescence when she finally replied, "No, sir."

"Then go back to the palace. We will talk when I am off work."

As Becca trailed off, the General turned his attention back to Chad, "Forgive me, Captain. I am not quite sure what has come over my daughter. Her behavior is certainly not customary nor acceptable."

The thought that he never wanted to deal with a teenage daughter momentarily crossed Chad's mind. He and the General continued their discussion about internal security. They then discussed the war. Chad considered questioning the General about Todd himself, but then thought better of it. Commander Heart must be aware that Todd would be on the front lines if he were to remain with Ben Canaan. Chad did not understand Commander Heart's decision, but it was not his place to question it. As Chad walked back towards the palace, General Ben Canaan rejoined his men. Chad searched for Todd from a distance and found him. The prince was unloading an AK47 at various targets through a training run. He only hoped that the headstrong prince would be wise enough to stay out of the way.

****

While General Ben Canaan was speaking with Chad, his soldiers were enjoying a brief reprieve from their training.

"Here's what I don't get, Prince Trevor is still here at the palace, and we are going to war with his country. He's obviously enjoying his stay while he's here, and from what I hear Princess Ashley is enjoying his stay as well." The comment had come from one of the soldiers.

"What do you mean?" Lieutenant Newberry questioned.

"You haven't heard?" The first soldier responded.

"Newberry never knows what's going on," another soldier added.

"Prince Trevor and Princess Ashley had lunch the other day and the Princess got a little happy if you know what I mean," the first soldier explained.

"Happy?" Newberry sounded confused.

"A little too much wine."

A very concerned look spread across Newberry's face, "Surely, they didn't...."

"No, word is Commander West put a stop to it."

Newberry was incredulous, "You're crazy, man. You're making this stuff up. Where are you hearing all of this crap?"

"Lt. Franklin."

"What does Lt. Franklin know?"

"He was manning the cameras."

"That's crazy."

As the men had been talking Todd had moved closer to hear what was going on. Todd's instinct was to tear off their heads for talking that way about his sister, but since he was going to war with them in a few days, he thought he would keep his cool. They had subtly made it known that his presence was not appreciated. Every time he had approached one of the men, they had either outright ignored him or suddenly found something to occupy them. He had also heard mumbles about the "spoiled prince" playing soldier. For the next few hours Todd threw himself into the training exercises but with every passing hour his anger for Trevor compounded.

When the day ended, he didn't bother to get cleaned up. He grabbed his bag and headed for the guest suites. Lt. Peters was on duty. Todd demanded to know which suite Prince Trevor was staying in. He continued down the hallway and pressed on the door pager until the door slid open.

"How dare you!" Todd purged as he slammed Trevor against the wall and with one swing knocked Trevor to the ground. "She's married now and she's off limits to you!"

Trevor was completely caught off guard by Todd's onslaught and it took him a moment to process what had just happened. Trevor checked to make sure Todd wasn't coming after him. When he was confident that he wouldn't be blindsided again, he made an effort to stand up. "I haven't done anything to your sister."

"You got her drunk!"

"Ashley ordered the wine. She's an adult. I didn't force her to do anything." Trevor's tone was smug.

In that moment Todd swung straight for Trevor's gut, forcing his back up against the wall. "You had no problem taking advantage of her state and destroying her reputation. You're an ass!"

Trevor grabbed Todd's shirt pushing him back through the door and into the hallway with as much force as possible. Todd fell backwards as Trevor released him.

Todd's audacity had provoked Trevor and he shot back, "I can promise you, Todd, I didn't do anything your sister didn't want. I think you need to leave; I'm quite certain King Daren would not appreciate you doing this."

Trevor tried to back into the room, but before he could grab hold of the door to close it, Todd grabbed Trevor and heaved him back into the hallway causing him to crash into a table. The vase of flowers hit the floor splintering into tiny bits of glass. Before Trevor could recover, Todd had him pinned to the floor. Trevor could feel the bits of glass pressing through his shirt.

"Leave my sister alone!" Todd warned.

Todd raised his fists to send the message home but was stalled by hands grabbing him from behind. Todd spun around to face his captors. Lt. Franklin and Lt. Peters were the ones that had grabbed him, but Todd's attention was focused on Chad who standing beyond them.

Todd glared at Chad and warned, "If they touch me again, it's not going to be pretty!"

Chad directed orders at the two Lieutenants, "Leave him be. Get Prince Trevor to his suite and call for Dr. Xavier."

"You should be the one doing this!" Todd yelled at Chad.

"Todd, you don't know or understand everything that is going on. It's not that simple." Chad countered.

"My fist smashing his face is simple." Todd responded in an annoyed tone.

"Todd, he is a Prince, and he is here as an ally. You need to get out of here."

"I don't give a shit what he is and you …."

"Todd, that's enough. Go to my office now." It was Commander Heart who now spoke. He had appeared just behind Chad.

"Seriously? I don't think so." Todd turned towards Trevor's door.

Christopher could tell that his son was enraged and in no condition to reason. Chad's presence made the situation even more volatile. With that in mind Christopher addressed Chad, "Commander West, you're dismissed. I'll take it from here."

Chad was more than happy to walk away from this one. He might say something he would regret if he stayed. Christopher closed the distance between himself and Todd who was yelling at Lt. Franklin to open the door. Christopher dismissed Lt. Franklin.

"Todd this is over."

Todd gave an audible sigh of exasperation. "Whatever. Maybe she should have married him. I don't understand why no one else sees this as a big deal. She's married but getting drunk…"

"That's enough! You said your piece and made your opinions known, now go."

As Christopher finished his words, Trevor's door slid open.

"I want to speak with King Daren now." Trevor demanded.

Todd was on the verge of departure but at Trevor's words he bristled again. "Yeah Dad, call King Daren down here, let's see what he has to say about this. I'm sure he'll be just fine with the Prince of Aldrich getting drunk with his married niece and parading her around the palace. That will fit in just great with his exalted sense of morality!"

Christopher ignored Todd, "Prince Trevor please step back into your room, I will see if King Daren can speak with you, but in the meantime it would be in your best interest to stay in your room."

Trevor paused momentarily and then to Christopher's relief retreated to his room. He then turned back to Todd. "Listen son, if you know what's best for you, you will get out of here right now. I will do what I can to repair the damage that you just did. Focus your energies on training and if you're lucky just maybe you won't get kicked out of the military for this."

Todd gave another exasperated sigh, muttered "whatever" and walked off. Christopher then took a deep breath and pressed on the pager of Trevor's door.

Dr. Xavier answered the door. He had arrived shortly after the commander and immediately been directed to the suite by the lieutenants. Christopher pushed his way past him and into the room.

Trevor was lounging on the sofa, and despite his numerous injuries still retained an air of regality. Christopher had received word of the incident involving Ashley, and he understood why Todd was so angry. In fact, he had viewed the security footage himself and knew that Ashley had played an equal part in the affair. In deference to Trevor Christopher waited allowing him to speak first

"I trust King Daren is on his way."

"Prince Trevor, I was hoping that you and I could talk about this first."

Trevor sat up and leaned forward, his gaze was both serene and volatile at the same time. "Commander Heart, I am the crowned Prince of Aldrich. I came here as a friend and ally, risking my own safety, to give your King and Country invaluable information. The thanks I receive is an unmitigated verbal and physical assault from your son. I demand retribution."

As Trevor spoke, Christopher noted the changes in him. His boyish innocence was gone, and every move he made seemed calculated and stiff. Christopher knew that his father had most likely punished Trevor for his previous disloyalty and was now molding him into his likeness. Christopher only hoped that unlike his father Trevor still retained some humanity.

Christopher now appealed to that nature. "Prince Trevor, I apologize for my son's behavior. Our country has been violently attacked and we are all on edge. My son, Ashley's brother, will be going off to war in a few days time. Todd loves his sister dearly and your time with her the other day has created a bit of a scandal in the palace. You have sisters Trevor, and I am sure that you would do everything possible to defend their honor. My son was doing the same. He is young and impulsive. You look as though you fared well in the fight. Surely, this is just a misunderstanding and disagreement between two grown men that need go no further.

Trevor seemed to be listening intently to Christopher, and Christopher hoped that was a good sign. When Christopher finished his appeal, he waited for Trevor to respond. Trevor's indulgent gaze was unsettling, but it did not unnerve the formidable Commander. He had given Trevor the upper hand in an effort to save his son, but he would not yield any further. If the speech he had just given did not affect the prince, then he would simply have to formulate a new strategy.

Trevor finally spoke, "Commander Heart. I consider Ashley a dear friend. I assure you I had no intention of showing her any disrespect. I regret that your son perceived our time together in such a manner. I will excuse his actions this time. I do hope, that in the future, we can reason through our differences."

Christopher thanked the prince for his consideration and exited the suite. He would have to inform Daren of what had happened, and he would encourage the King to send Trevor home immediately. Christopher was concerned that Daren would demand Todd be disciplined for his actions, but there was also a chance that Daren would show understanding of the circumstances.

Christopher made his way to Daren's office. He had a headache, but he wanted to be the one who told the King what had just happened. As he walked, the walls in front of him seemed to be moving. He blinked to clear his head and looked again. The walls were solid. As his footsteps echoed on the marble floor that matched the marble on the walls, he attributed the mirage to fatigue. Ian, Ms. Troy and Mr. Sterling were headed down the hallway towards him away from the direction of Daren's office. Christopher wondered what they had been doing and why he wasn't a part of it. He stopped Ian.

"Mr. Garrett. Is there something I should know about?" Christopher questioned.

"Nothing that would interest you, Commander. We are trying to figure out how to pay for this war." Ian answered.

"Paperwork. Budgets. Yes, I think I'll stick with guns and battle. Is King Daren still in his office?"

"Yes."

Without any further acknowledgement of Ian, Christopher resumed his trek to Daren's office. If they had just been meeting regarding Lionel's finances, then Daren was unlikely to be in the best of moods. He hoped that Daren would not be tightfisted where the war was concerned. He marched past Shayla's desk and straight into the King's office. He did not wait for Daren to greet him, but sat down facing his brother. He took a moment to assess Daren's current disposition as he waited for Daren to speak first.

"What is it, Christopher?"

Christopher knew that Daren would appreciate a direct approach. "I am sure that you have heard about Trevor and Ashley's lunch rendezvous a couple of days ago. Apparently Todd just heard. He went after Trevor."

"Is he still alive?"

"Trevor is a little worse for the wear, but he survived."

"No, I meant your son." Daren retorted.

"My son can handle himself." Christopher was slightly offended by Daren's implication.

"So, Prince Trevor brings us critical information that we may never have known otherwise. Your daughter, who has been married less than a week, goes on a little tryst with him causing the entire palace to buzz with rumors. And now, your son sends Trevor home with a black eye. Our plan is to take out his father, and now I'm not sure if we just made an ally or an enemy of the future king of Aldrich."

"Daren, Todd was simply defending his sister's honor. Trevor is not completely innocent in all of this. He's still simmering over losing Ashley. I spoke with him after the fight. I believe he is still an ally."

Daren had been sitting back in his chair, but now he leaned forward as he spoke, "I hope you are right. I am sending Trevor back to Aldrich in the morning. You know there are many in Aldrich who would consider Trevor a traitor if they knew he was here divulging information. He needs as little opposition as possible when he takes the throne. What are you doing about your son?"

"He is leaving with Ben Canaan for Aldrich tomorrow."

Christopher waited for Daren to respond, but he sat silently, still leaning forward, engaged and calculating. Christopher hated it when he or a member of his family created unnecessary drama for Daren, especially when it affected Daren's role as king. He should be making Daren's job easier, not complicating it further. But then it seemed that everything in Christopher's life lately had been screwed up. He wished Daren would yell at him. Christopher could more than handle some good verbal combat, and he and Daren had certainly had their battles over the years. His headache was worsening, and when Daren still made no reply, Christopher continued.

"Daren, Todd is seventeen. He doesn't know why Trevor is here or what he did. He joined the military less than a week ago, and he's going off to war to defend Lionel. He shouldn't have attacked Trevor, but he is under an extreme amount of stress right now. I think he deserves a bit of a break." Christopher was having difficulty discerning Daren's thoughts, and he was concerned that Daren might demand Todd be reprimanded in an effort to make a statement to Trevor.

"An extreme amount of stress? He's been off doing whatever the hell he wants, Christopher. No one forced him to join the military. He's making big boy decisions, and he's going to have to deal with big boy consequences," Daren countered.

"You are right, Daren. No one forced him to join the military. He came in here infuriated over the fact that someone had dared to attack his country! He then joined the military to avenge those attacks. He is voluntarily fighting for this country and for you, Daren. My son has little training or experience, and he is putting his life on the line. I think the possibility of death is a 'big boy' consequence, don't you?" Christopher was nearly raging at this point.

It was obvious to Daren that Christopher was very concerned about Todd's safety and lack of discernment. He knew Christopher was baiting him into a confrontation, but he took a more diplomatic route.

"Do you want me to pull him out?" Daren questioned.

"Don't give me that option, Daren!"

Daren had offered in an effort to ease Christopher's distress, but the offer seemed to have had the opposite effect. Daren looked at Christopher questioningly and waited.

Christopher continued, "What am I supposed to say, Daren? If I say yes, Todd will resent you and me for it. He will run off again, and I may never see him again. If I say no, and he ends up dead, I will never forgive myself for sending him to his demise. Do not put that burden on me, Daren! I think I have enough to deal with as it is."

"Well, Christopher, we all have a lot to deal with right now. It's the life we live."

"Right, Daren, I forgot. The burden of kingship rests on your shoulders, and no one else could possibly have any difficulties that even begin to compare." Christopher leaned forward to emphasize his next words. "Your family is intact. Your children haven't lost their mother. Not only is my country under attack, Daren, but my entire life seems to be one battle after another. There is no area of peace for me."

Daren leaned back into a relaxed position. He calmly addressed his obviously distressed brother, "Well, Christopher, Lionel law states that if you join, you serve. Todd has joined, and he will serve. Let him work out his frustrations in combat. He's your son and my nephew. He won't go down easily. This may do him some good." Daren paused and then continued, "Christopher, I know you have suffered. Right now, I need you as my Commander. We all need your formidable strength."

Christopher did not immediately respond. He seemed to be taking in all that Daren had said, and when he did respond it was with renewed vigor and more characteristic of his usual demeanor.

"I have a lot of work to do, Daren. We are going to war tomorrow. Are we done here?"

Slightly amused, Daren dismissed his brother. He then raised a silent prayer to God for protection of all his military forces but especially of his nephew.

Chapter 16

Todd had no desire to talk to anyone. With that in mind, he made his way away from the more populated areas of the palace. He needed to take a walk. Maybe it would calm him down. However, with each step his annoyance with both Chad and his father increased. He seemed to be the only one in the palace that still had any sense. Since when did they cater to a Benson? Both of them should have joined in and helped him beat the presumptuous prince of Aldrich to a pulp. It didn't make sense that Trevor was there in the first place. They were going to war with his country in the morning, and everyone was treating Trevor like he was a guest of honor. It was just plain stupid. Trevor should be in chains, not fraternizing with his sister in front of the entire palace for all to see. All of this was just ridiculous. If he was married, and his wife was hanging out with her ex-fiancé, there would be one less man on the earth when he was done.

As Todd rounded the next corner, he heard noise coming from an alcove that led into the ballroom. He stopped and listened. Whoever they were, they were obviously having a good time. Todd momentarily forgot his rage and mused that even in such a controlled environment, people still found a way to gain a little privacy. He heard the girl laugh followed by whispers. Then there were some other sounds that indicated the couples' mouths were now occupied with each other. Curiosity got the best of him, and he decided to see who the clandestine couple was. The man had his back to Todd. His hands were exploring beneath the girl's shirt as she was backed against the wall. They were so deep into their kiss that neither one noticed Todd at first. It took Todd a moment to realize that he knew both people involved, and he knew one extremely well. His rage returned and he grabbed the man by both shoulders throwing him to the other side of the alcove. He then turned his full attention on Kelly, his sister. Her face was flushed, and she had a look of sheer terror.

"You let this creep touch you?! . . . What the hell are you thinking, Kelly? . . . He's a piece of scum. How stupid are you?" Todd fumed.

Lieutenant Newberry recovered from the ambush and interceded, "Prince Todd, I meant no disrespect to Kelly."

Todd turned on Newberry, "It's PRINCESS Kelly. Keep your hands off of her you bastard!" When Newberry made no move to exit, Todd yelled, "Get out of here!"

Newberry looked at Kelly who nodded for him to go. As soon as Newberry was gone, Todd went on a rampage.

"You want that low-life for your future? You know Dad is going to kill him as soon as I tell him."

`Kelly's face went white. "Todd, please, you can't tell dad. We didn't do anything wrong. Eric is leaving in the morning. We were just saying goodbye. Please, Todd. Don't do this. He won't even be an issue after tomorrow. Todd, I'm begging you."

"Only a piece of shit would sneak around here like that with you. How do you even know him? If he had any respect for you at all, he would date you the right way instead of sneaking around like a sleazy snake."

"Todd, you know Dad would never give his permission for us to date."

"Well, I'm sure there's a good reason for that. Creeper."

"Eric is a good guy, Todd. He was my security escort when I went to see my friend at the hospital after the attacks. I was really upset. No one here seemed to notice or care. Eric did. He listened. He helped me. He was a friend and then it just led into more. He's not a bad person, and he's certainly not a piece of crap."

"Yeah, he listened for a really long time before he started making moves, didn't he? It's been what, Kelly, almost two full weeks since the attacks? I can tell he really cares about your . . . feelings. I thought better of you than this."

"You're one to lecture me, Todd! You ran off, and we didn't hear from you for months. At least Eric was here when I needed him. You were off doing who knows what caring about no one but yourself!"

"Shut up. This isn't about me, and I can assure you Kelly, I wasn't doing THAT!"

"Doing what? What exactly are you accusing me of, Todd? We were kissing. That's all. You saw us."

"Yeah, I saw. I saw where his hands were too. You've known him less than two weeks Kelly, and he's doing that? You really think he respects you? You know what, forget Dad. I'll rip his head off myself!"

"Todd, stop it. You ran off and lived your life. Let me live mine! The last two weeks have been some of the best of my life. It all ends for me tomorrow anyway. If you care about me at all, you will let this go. Please, Todd. He's leaving tomorrow."

"And when he comes back?"

"Then, if he still wants to see me, I will tell him he has to ask dad. I promise. Okay?"

Todd gave an exasperated humph, "You've more than said your goodbyes. You don't see him until after we get back and he talks to dad. Understand?"

"Yes. Thank you for understanding. Todd, are you really going tomorrow?"

"I don't understand, and yes, I'm going tomorrow. Got it?"

"I'm sure dad could make it so you don't have to go."

"I'm not having this conversation. I'm going."

"But Todd, you're not trained for . . . "

"Look, drop it, or I'm going to go tell dad about Newberry right now."

Todd's threat silenced Kelly. She gave him one last hopeful look and then quickly departed. Todd checked around to make sure Newberry had cleared the premises completely, and then he continued his sojourn. He now had even more to think about. He knew he had been harsh with Kelly, but she had only been back from the university less than two weeks. If things were moving that quickly with Newberry, they were bound to go farther in no time at all. He couldn't believe Newberry was brazen enough to mess around with the Commander's daughter. By law, he and Kelly would be required to marry if things went too far, but knowing his father, Newberry wouldn't be around to marry Kelly if they did.

Chapter 17

Christopher was making his way to Captain Teresa Walters's office. To his disgust, Alan Walters rounded the corner heading in the same direction.

Alan addressed Christopher, "Good morning, Commander."

Christopher grunted in reply. His headache had steadily grown worse since yesterday, and it was becoming almost unbearable. He had no desire to chitchat with Alan. He was having trouble enough concentrating on more important things with this pounding headache.

Christopher noticed that Alan was studying him as they walked. "Is there a problem, Mr. Walters?"

"Are you feeling well, Commander?" Alan's inquiry was sincere, but its sincerity was lost on Christopher.

"I'm just fine. Are you hoping I'll suddenly fall ill, Alan? I can assure it would not free up any more of your wife's time. In fact, she would have to take over much of my mess that I deal with. I handle it. No one else wants to go. I can't think about the war. . . Ah, my head. Where's her office?"

Christopher looked at Alan, but Alan's face was fuzzy. Alan was saying something to him, but the idiot wasn't making sense.

"Commander Heart! Commander? What's wrong?"

Christopher seemed delirious. He was swaying. Alan moved to steady him, but the Commander's hulking form was too much for Alan to support. As Christopher went tumbling to the floor, Alan tried to break his fall as much as possible. Once Christopher was safely resting on the ground, Alan ran to Teresa's office for help. As soon as he barged through the door, Teresa knew there was something wrong.

"Alan? What is it?" she asked.

"It's Commander Heart. He just collapsed. He seems to be unconscious." Alan gasped.

Teresa immediately set to action. She picked up the phone. "I need a doctor up here now. Commander Heart has collapsed." She then picked up her radio and called for security.

While making her way into the hallway where Christopher was laying, Teresa questioned Alan about what had occurred. Although he had told her every detail, Teresa was not prepared for the sight of the Commander. His body nearly filled the hallway, but despite his immense stature, he looked vulnerable and fragile. Teresa, who was normally prepared for anything, felt helpless. She stood paralyzed just staring at her Commander. Other security arrived, and they too stood confounded. She expected Christopher to awaken any moment and start roaring at everyone present about standing around doing nothing. He didn't. He remained unconscious. Dr. Xavier finally arrived.

Feeling helpless to do anything else, Teresa yelled at the doctor, "What took you so long?"

Ignoring Teresa, the doctor checked the Commander's vital signs and then finally looked up at Teresa, "We need to move him to the clinic. Get your men to transport him. I have to run tests, and I can't do it here."

Happy to have a purpose, Teresa set to work giving orders. Alan interrupted her, and she swung on him with a look of ferocity. He looked at her with concern and gently touched her face. Then he spoke, "Teresa, it's going to be okay. You handle things here. I'm going to your office to contact King Daren. I love you."

Alan picked up the phone. He was worried about the Commander, but he was even more concerned about the effect this would have on his King. How much could one man take, he wondered? Shayla picked up and Alan asked to be connected to Daren. With no hesitation, he was.

"Alan, what is it?"

"King Daren, I am calling from Teresa's office. I was on my way here when I ran into Commander Heart. As we were walking, the Commander started babbling incoherently and then collapsed. He is being transported to the clinic as we speak."

There was no response.

Alan continued, "Sir, tell me what you need me to do."

Daren answered, "I'm heading down there. Notify Sarah. Let's keep this quiet until I know what's going on. Continue as normal."

King Daren put his pen down, took a deep breath and then quickly made his way toward the clinic. He could not imagine his brother being sick. Christopher's immune system was as tough as he was and Christopher did not get sick. As he was walking, he radioed Commander West.

"This is . . ." Chad began, but was cut short.

"Chad, Commander Heart has collapsed and is in the clinic. I am on my way to find out more information. What time are the men deploying this afternoon?"

"At 4:15, sir."

"Ok, continue as planned unless otherwise notified."

Daren arrived at the clinic just moments after they had managed to get Christopher down there. The security guards who had assisted were still there. As soon as Daren walked in the room, everyone but Dr. Xavier stopped what they were doing and turned their attention to him.

Daren looked at Teresa and spoke, "Captain Walters, until we know what has happened here, no one else needs to know about this. Get your men out of here and make sure they understand that." With the entire country already on edge, Daren knew that news of Christopher's condition would cause even more panic. Although Daren was the King, Christopher represented their sense of security.

"Yes, sir."

Teresa followed the King's orders and departed as well. She hoped that Alan was still in her office. She needed his comforting presence right now.

Daren looked to the doctor. "Dr. Xavier, what is this?"

Xavier gave a nonplussed reply, "I will need to run several tests. This may take a while. It all depends on what is wrong and which test reveals the problem. I could know within minutes, or it could be hours."

"Is this minor? Is it major? What is this? Give me something. We are deploying men for war in a matter of hours, and my Commander is non-responsive." Daren declared.

"King Daren, anything I tell you at this point would only be speculation. Only the test results will give a clear answer," Dr. Xavier droned.

Seeing that he was getting nowhere with the doctor, Daren mentally made a decision. He would wait two hours to see if the tests revealed anything. If there were still no answers within that time frame, and Christopher was still unconscious, he would move Chad into Christopher's position temporarily. Daren had purposefully avoided looking at Christopher as he talked with the doctor. Now taking a deep breath, Daren walked to his brother's side. Christopher was pale. An occasional moan would escape his lips and then his face would contort in what looked like extreme agony. Daren angrily looked to the doctor.

"Is he in pain? I thought he was unconscious. What's happening here?" Daren demanded.

"It is a state of unconsciousness, but he still seems vulnerable to pain. He's non-responsive to anything else though." the doctor blandly explained.

"Well, do something about it." Daren ordered.

"Sir, you run this country. I run this clinic. You hired me because I am the best. I know what I am doing."

Daren knew the doctor was right, but he felt completely powerless at the moment. He looked up to see Sarah coming through the door. After acknowledging her with a nod, he reached down and grabbed Christopher's calf. Giving it a squeeze of what he hoped would be reassurance to Christopher, he spoke to his brother, "This is not the time for a vacation, Christopher. You get over this immediately. That's an order."

With that, Daren turned and moved towards the door. He let Sarah through first. She had a look of concern on her face, but there was a serenity about her as well. He nodded in greeting and then walked out. Outside the clinic, Daren paused to regain his composure. He would need to retain a sense of stability within the palace and with the military. Before he walked away, he glanced back towards Christopher. Sarah was by his side. She was caressing Christopher's huge paw with her small, delicate hands. Her head was bowed in prayer. When they had first been married, Daren was concerned that Christopher's brutish demeanor would overpower Sarah's meek and sensitive nature. As the years had passed however, it seemed that Sarah had proven she was indeed the stronger of the two. She had weathered Christopher's tantrums and rages with patience, understanding and prayer. And even now when their warrior was seemingly defeated, her delicate strength and relentless faith continued giving even the King a sense of peace and surety.

Chapter 18

Todd double-checked his combat pack to make sure he had everything. He felt a rush of euphoria at the prospect of battle. The last few weeks had been a pointless waste of time. The sooner they made it into Aldrich and took out the bastard who had attacked his country, the better. It was an unusually hot summer day, and even the trees around him seemed to sag with exhaustion from the stagnant air. For Todd though, the heat coursed through his body making his blood boil with thoughts of revenge. He couldn't wait to head out. Todd heard Becca's voice behind him. She was talking to her father. He turned her way.

"Hey, weed girl!" he called.

Becca had been very aware of Todd's presence, and when he acknowledged her, she smiled shyly and waved at him.

"Weed girl, come here." Todd demanded.

Momentarily forgetting her father, Becca made her way to Todd without hesitation. Becca liked that Todd had a nickname for her, even if it wasn't the most flattering. He had started calling her that when she had volunteered to help him pull weeds, a punishment inflicted on him by his father for his recent bouts of rebellion. Weed pulling had become her favorite time of day, but since Todd had run off, she had missed him terribly.

Todd pulled on Becca's ringlets as he talked to her. "You going to miss me?" he questioned.

Becca smiled her shy smile once more and replied simply, "Yes."

"It doesn't look like you've been keeping these weeds under control while I was gone." Todd teased.

A look of genuine concern spread over Becca's face. "I've been studying more. I'm still struggling in chemistry," she explained.

Todd was amused at her reply and seized on her consternation, "So, you have an A- in a class. You should be ashamed. You're slacking off Becca. Bad grades, out of control weeds. What's happened to you?"

She started to respond but was stalled by the look of utter frustration that had suddenly passed over Todd's face. She was relieved that his attention was focused beyond her, and she turned to see what had caused his irritation. Captain West had arrived. She took another look at

Todd and timidly retreated when she saw that all the men had stopped what they were doing and were standing at attention.

Chad addressed the men, "Good afternoon. I know that all of you are expecting to deploy in a matter of minutes, but there has been a change of plans. Commander Heart has fallen ill. Until he is able to resume his position, King Daren has temporarily placed me in the position of Commander. Due to this unexpected chain of events, deployment is being postponed to tomorrow at 1400 hours. Everything will then go forward as planned. This will be the only delay. Enjoy the rest of your day, and I will see you back here at 1100 hours tomorrow. At ease." Chad turned his attention to Caleb, "General Ben Canaan, I need to speak with you."

Todd immediately made his way to Chad before Ben Canaan could. His tone was almost accusatory when he addressed Chad, "What's going on? Where's my dad?"

Chad was a bit taken back that Todd seemed ignorant of his father's condition. He had assumed that someone would have notified all of the Commander's family. However, Ashley had only learned of it after he had told her. Chad was genuinely concerned for Commander Heart, and he did feel compassion for Todd.

"I did not realize that you were unaware of what has happened, Todd. Your father collapsed earlier today. He's in the clinic."

"Wow, nice of you guys to let me know my father is sick. I am his son. Apparently his family isn't important, just his job. I'm sure you were more than happy to step in and help out, right? Don't get too comfortable. I'm willing to bet that this time tomorrow, my dad will be back in charge."

Chad decided to ignore Todd's insubordination. He understood his frustration. He wondered as well why no one had informed Todd of Christopher's condition. The only reasonable answer was that either everyone assumed someone else had told him or they had simply forgotten he was there as he had been absent for several months now. Chad wondered if Todd would decide not to go to war under the circumstances. Chad would be more than happy to give Todd a leave of absence. Chad felt it best to simply try to mollify Todd.

"I hope Commander Heart is able to resume his position as early as tomorrow. In the meantime, I am sure you will want to go see him."

Feeling he had dismissed Todd, Chad turned his attention to General Ben Canaan to discuss the change in plans. Todd wasn't ready for the conversation to end, but Ben Canaan's presence dissuaded him. Todd decided to grab his combat pack and head down to see his father. They were probably delaying deployment because his dad would be fine and back in charge tomorrow anyway. Out of the corner of his eye, Todd saw his sister Kelly. He assumed she was coming to see him, but she stopped before she reached him. She was cleverly talking to a few of the guys who were preparing for deployment, but the majority of her attention was focused on Newberry. Todd felt what could only be described as pure hatred for Newberry. His sister was a princess, and she might as well be throwing herself at this piece of scum. Todd promptly dropped his bag and headed over to where his sister and Newberry were.

He addressed Kelly, "What are you doing here?"

Kelly obviously hadn't noticed that Todd was there, and when he walked up, fear flashed in her eyes.

When she didn't respond, Todd continued, "Get out of here. There's no reason for you to be here."

Kelly didn't argue and promptly started to walk away. Newberry's combat pack was lying on the ground. Todd picked it up and chucked it at Newberry catching him off guard. Newberry caught it, but he was obviously angered.

Todd then addressed all the men, "My sister is off limits. Leave her alone."

Todd's intention was to leave it at that, but indignation overcame him. Before he even realized it, his hand had collided with Newberry's jaw. He felt a sudden release of tension. He had made his point and was walking away now. Newberry recovered quickly and was ready for a fight. He sent his combat pack crashing into Todd's back. Todd swung around, ready for battle. Within moments, both men were on the ground rolling and punching. There was shouting in the distance, but all of Todd's efforts were focused on pummeling Newberry. Someone's hands grasped Todd from behind pulling him off of Newberry. As soon as he was up, Todd wheeled on his obstructer. It was Chad. Todd's temper flared even more. How dare that bastard touch him! Todd let loose. He lunged for Chad's throat in an attempt to choke the life out of him. Chad easily avoided Todd's assault making Todd even more enraged. Chad was yelling at Todd, but his words didn't register. Todd swung repeatedly at Chad sometimes hitting his mark. Chad was now fighting back, and Todd gained pleasure from that fact. Todd's assault intensified, and Chad matched him blow for blow.

As the brawl continued, all the men stood dumbfounded. Kelly watched from a distance, wise enough not to interfere. King Daren had arrived with the intent of showing his support for Chad and hopefully allaying any concerns the men might have. At first he thought that they were engaged in some kind of training exercise, but when he saw who was involved, he knew otherwise. Hoping the skirmish would end on its own, Daren just waited patiently. When the blows showed no sign of slowing after several minutes, Daren decided to intervene.

Daren had positioned himself next to General Ben Canaan, and he now turned to the General and spoke, "General, put a stop to this."

Caleb followed the King's orders without delay. He ordered four of his stronger men to restrain both Chad and Todd. As soon as the two were pulled apart, Chad angrily addressed the men holding him, "Release me now!" When the men hesitated and looked at Ben Canaan, Chad shouted, "I am your Commander, and that is an order!"

The men promptly released him. Todd was still being held, but he was like a bull waiting for the gates to open. Chad looked at Todd and spoke to the men holding him, "Put restraints on him, now, and don't let go of him."

Chad then took a deep breath and stepped away to clear his head and regain control. He had not been prepared for this onslaught, and he still was unsure of what exactly had started it. Todd had a lot to answer for, and he had just reinforced Chad's concerns about him going into war. Todd definitely had the physical strength for it, but his impulsiveness was out of control. What Todd just did was grounds for dismissal from the military all together.

Daren realized that Chad had not seen him, and he gave his new Commander a moment before addressing him. When Chad headed back their way, his attention was focused solely on Todd, and he had a look of resolve on his face. Daren decided to let this play out a little further before interfering.

Todd had been restrained as ordered, and he was seething. Chad's words were direct and firm, "Lieutenant Heart, you have just violated the oath you took as a member of Lionel's Royal Guard. Your actions are not representative of the behavior expected and required of such an estimable position. You have dishonored yourself through your blatant insubordination, and there is no room for such conduct in this military." Chad was on the verge of dismissing Todd from the military altogether, but decided to give Todd one last opportunity to answer for himself. "Lieutenant, do you have anything to say regarding your actions?"

"I would've won. Take these off, and . . ." Todd began.

Daren was certain that the next words out of Todd's mouth would not help his current situation.

Daren intervened, "Todd, that's enough. Commander West, I need a word with you."

Every muscle in Chad's body tensed the moment he heard King Daren's voice. Chad felt foolish for not realizing that the King was present. He felt like even more of an idiot for letting himself get drawn into a fight with Todd in the King's presence. He had been the commander for less than 24 hours, and he had already screwed things up. King Daren had drawn him away from everyone to speak with him privately. Chad was already formulating his defense in his head, but the king's words to him caught him by surprise.

"Chad, everything that you said was correct, and what Todd did was deplorable. But, this rage is exactly what we need on the battlefield."

Chad was in disbelief. He was relieved that the King wasn't reprimanding him, but equally vexed that he was supporting Todd's behavior. He did not want to challenge Daren's thoughts, but Chad was the Commander, and he did not feel that Todd's behavior was acceptable anywhere, least of all on the battlefield. Chad felt that he could not stay silent on this matter. King Daren would do what he wished in the end, but Chad would have his say.

"Sir, with all due respect, I disagree with you. If Todd takes that rage to the battlefield, he will be impulsive and unpredictable. He could easily get himself and others killed. He obviously is not able to think before he acts, and discipline is critical when someone is in the midst of turmoil and chaos."

"This war gives him a mission. It gives him a focus, and I would ask that you take into consideration the recent circumstances that directly affect Todd."

"That is what I am concerned about, sir. He already lacks self-control, and Commander Heart's illness will only add to Todd's instability. It will make it more difficult for him to focus. I will do whatever you command, sir, but I do not recommend that Todd goes to war in his current state."

Rather than continue the private discussion with Chad, Daren walked away and back towards the group of men who were still gathered around Todd. Chad followed. When they reached the group, Daren walked to where Todd was restrained. The men holding him had cuffed his hands behind him, and they had positioned Todd so that he was kneeling on the grass making him easier to control.

Daren first addressed the men, "Release him."

Todd immediately got to his feet while rubbing his wrists where he had been restrained. He seemed somewhat placated, and Daren felt confident he wouldn't attack. Daren spoke directly to Todd, "Lieutenant Heart, Commander West is your superior. Regardless of your personal feelings towards him, you must respect that. Your actions are grounds for dismissal from the military. Commander West will make that decision, and I will support whatever he decides. Get control of yourself, Lieutenant."

Daren waited just a moment to make sure that Todd was subdued before making his exit. He would speak with Chad later.

Chad cautiously approached Todd. He didn't trust him not to throw another tantrum. Todd remained silent. He was obviously still angry, but Daren's words seemed to have had a humbling effect.

"Lieutenant Heart, I am going to take some time to consider what happened here today. I will inform you of my decision tomorrow morning. You are dismissed."

Todd was still considering giving Chad a piece of his mind but thought better of it. He would just go tell his dad. He turned away and headed up the hill towards the palace. Kelly was still standing in the same place. Her face was pale and she looked like she was going to burst into tears at any moment. Todd grabbed her arm and dragged her with him.

Kelly was both frightened at and angered by what Todd had just done. She started to protest but was cut short by Todd, "Just shut up ugly." Not wanting to provoke him she did as she was told. Todd would never admit it but having his twin sister with him as they went to see his father was comforting. Todd couldn't wait to talk to his father. He knew his uncle was being ridiculous about his father's condition.

Todd barged into the clinic still pulling Kelly along with him. He saw his dad laying in one of the beds and went straight for him. Christopher was in an enclosed room, and when Todd tried to open the door, it was locked. Todd immediately located the doctor and marched over to him, "Unlock the door."

"He's under quarantine. You can't go in." Dr. Xavier explained and then returned to his computer work.

It was Kelly who spoke up next, "What's wrong with him? Why's he under quarantine? Is he going to be ok?"

Dr. Xavier responded, "It's bacterial meningitis and we'll know whether or not he'll recover in a few days."

"I'm going to see my dad." Todd stated. He headed back towards the door determined to get through it one way or another. Dr. Xavier stood up and followed Todd, "Prince Todd, if you open that door you could expose yourself and I'll have to add another bed to that room."

"I live with him so I'm pretty sure I'm already exposed." Todd argued.

"If you insist on going in there then put these on." Dr. Xavier handed Todd a gown and respirator. Todd felt like a clown but was insistent to see his father. Todd entered the room, and as the door shut behind him, he suddenly had a lonely, empty feeling. He shrugged it off and looked out at the doctor, "how long has he been asleep?"

"He's not asleep; he's been unconscious since he collapsed."

As he said those words Kelly began to tremble and her knees grew weak. The doctor noticed and guided her to the chair. Todd saw that his sister was upset, but he was struggling with his own emotions of helplessness and anger. His mother had already been taken from him. Was God trying to prove some kind of point? He had heard Pastor Isaiah say that it's when someone loses everything and they have no hope left that they finally turn to God. Well, if that is what God was expecting here...it was not going to happen. Todd could not stand how weak his father looked. Christopher moaned in pain, and in that moment Todd decided that no one was going to stop him from deploying. He was not going to sit around and watch his father in this condition. Even if he had to grovel to Chad, he was going to war.

Todd heard Kelly crying outside of the room. There was nothing he could do for his father, so he would take care of his sister.

As soon as Todd came out of the room, Kelly clung to him burrowing her head into his shoulder. She mumbled, "Are we going to lose him too?"

"Everything's going to be okay," assured Todd.

Chapter 19

By the time Chad reached his suite, Ashley had gone to bed. He tried not to disturb her as he readied himself for bed. When he laid down, she rolled over and snuggled against him. He stroked her hair while they just laid in each others' arms without speaking for several minutes. She had stopped by her father's office earlier in the day to see him. The moment she had walked in and seen him sitting in her father's chair, she had burst into tears. The outburst was short-lived, and Chad knew that Ashley was trying very hard to be strong. He appreciated her so much for that. Neither of them had expected him to take even a temporary position as Commander within a few weeks of their marriage.

Ashley turned her head up and towards Chad. "How did the men take the news about my father?"

Chad wasn't sure how to answer. He didn't want to upset Ashley further. The men were soldiers, and they would fulfill their duty regardless of who was in charge. He was sure that they felt a sadness over the situation, but right now their minds were on the war. There was no room for sentimentality. He certainly wasn't going to tell her about Todd. She wouldn't sleep if he did.

He gave a vague response, "It's difficult for all of us Ashley. We all see your father as an impenetrable fortress. His condition is hard to accept. I think most of us are just focusing on what comes next. Get some sleep. I love you."

Ashley seemed content with his answer. She snuggled back down into the crook of his arm and fell asleep. Chad slept very little. In the dark of the room, he had managed to hide the wounds from his skirmish with Todd from Ashley. If he had let her know that her position on his arm was killing him, there would have been endless questions and concern. So, he sucked it up and tried to focus on other things rather than the pain. Even after he was finally able to gently move Ashley away, his shoulder still ached. It was the shoulder that he had taken a bullet while protecting Ethan Kidwell many years before Ethan had become the King of Raxx. He hoped that the pain was temporary and would subside in a few days. Even if it didn't, he would just deal with it. There was no time for complaints right now. Thoughts of Todd and what he should do also kept Chad awake. When his alarm went off to begin the next day, Chad was still unsure of what course to take. He quickly turned off the alarm and headed for the bathroom before Ashley could see him. He knew she did not have to be to work for at least two more hours, and she would go back to sleep while he was showering.

****

Shayla paged Daren. He pushed the speaker button and questioned, "Is it time?"

Shayla responded, "No, sir. You still have about 45 minutes. King Zeffrin is on the phone."

Daren picked up the phone, "Gavin?"

"I'm coming to get Megan," Gavin declared.

This would play perfectly into Daren's search for information. As Daren was contemplating an answer, Gavin continued.

"It's been long enough. I'm on my way," Gavin insisted.

"Well, you are always welcome. Have you talked with Megan yet?" Daren's tone was accusatory.

"We spoke this morning. I'll be there this afternoon."

"Come on ahead, Gavin. We've had a little bit of sickness going around, but you are more than welcome." Daren knew that if he was too welcoming, Gavin would become suspicious.

"Well, I'm coming."

"Well, that's settled. You are coming. We can talk more when you get here."

With that, the phone clicked, and Daren knew the conversation was over. If he could find out for certain that Gavin was not a part of this, he would consider seeking Gavin's support for the war. There was sure to be some opposition within the ICP to Daren declaring war on Aldrich, and Daren could use all the allied support he could get. He might even call in that favor from King Estrada if the need arose.

Daren busied himself with affairs of state while he waited on Shayla to inform him it was time to go out to the drilling grounds. He had intended yesterday to provide his support to Chad as the new Commander and to encourage the men as they prepared for deployment. His plans had been impeded, and he was going to try again.

As he approached the grounds, most of the men seemed to be just waiting. They were talking and laughing. Aside from their uniforms and the weapons they carried, no one would know they were about to engage in a war. Daren kept his distance at first taking it all in. He had a great respect and appreciation for these men who were willing to lay down their lives for their country. He scanned the various groups looking for Todd. He still didn't know what Chad had decided. He found Todd. He was sitting on his combat pack near the edge alone. He seemed deep in thought.

Daren had made his way down to the drilling grounds from the east side of the palace where his office was located. General Ben Canaan and Chad were now making their way towards the grounds from the west side. Daren walked their way. Chad saw him and paused in his trek. Daren indicated for Chad to continue on his course. As the three men approached, all of the men stood at attention. General Ben Canaan addressed them.

"Gentlemen, we will be heading out at 1400 hours as planned. Make sure everything is ready to go. Vehicles should be loaded and ready to pull out not a second later. Is that clear?"

Over 100 hundred men answered "Yes, sir," in unison.

Chad now stepped forward and addressed the men. "You all have your orders. Nothing has changed as far as plans are concerned. General Ben Canaan will be reporting to me, and I will relay to him any necessary information as you progress. I know that Commander Heart has full confidence in each and every one of you, as do I. We will make King Benson pay for what he has done." Chad had paused and seemed to be looking for someone. He found his mark. Addressing Todd, he continued, "Lieutenant Heart, come forward."

Todd was prepared to argue his case with Chad. He had thought about it all night, and he was confident that he could win him over with a perfect mixture of remorse, distress and devotion to the cause.

"Commander West, I would like to . . ." Todd began.

"Lieutenant Heart, you will observe protocol. I have not given you permission to speak." Chad waited just daring Todd to defy him. Chad was surprised when he did not.

Chad continued, "Lieutenant, you should not be wearing that uniform after what you did yesterday, and I am not confident that letting you go off to war when you are making such reckless decisions is a wise idea."

Chad paused, and he could tell that Todd was dying to speak. A part of Chad wanted Todd to repeat his behavior of yesterday so that an easy decision could be made, and he was very surprised when Todd made no move. Chad considered giving Todd the opportunity to bury himself, but thought better of it.

"Lieutenant, if you so much as look at someone the wrong way while you are out there, General Ben Canaan has been instructed to send you back immediately. There will be no more chances, Lieutenant, and I hope you understand that you are being shown an inordinate amount of clemency following your actions. Do you understand?"

Chad's words shocked Todd, and he made an effort not to smile at the fact that he wouldn't have to grovel to get what he wanted. He would have to find a way to earn the respect of his peers after this, but he was up to the challenge. Todd looked Chad in the eye and responded, "Yes sir, Commander West."

Chad returned Todd's gaze trying to appraise his sincerity. Perhaps the threat of being kicked out had really had an effect on the spoiled prince. Chad dismissed him, and Todd rejoined the ranks. Chad glanced at Newberry. He still was unsure of what had started the conflict between him and Todd. Unfortunately, there would be no time to question him or research it. It would have to be Ben Canaan's problem.

King Daren now began his speech to his men, "You are one of many units that will be deployed today. Your combined efforts will not only avenge our country of the wrongs that have been committed, but they will also serve to free a nation from the clutches of a sinister leader who has been a plague to many. Those of us who remain behind will keep you in our prayers. I thank God personally every day for each of you because I know that without your devotion and service, Lionel would not exist. Thank you."

Pastor Isaiah had been making his way among the men talking with them and encouraging them. He was now standing on the sidelines. Daren motioned for him to come forward. Each man bowed his head as Pastor Isaiah prayed for God's blessing and protection. Afterwards Daren remained with the men until all of them had boarded the transport aircraft. He and Chad then silently made their way back to the palace.

****
**

Daren had returned to his office after leaving the troops. It had only been three hours before Shayla informed him that King Zeffrin was requesting permission to land. Gavin should have had more than enough time to deplane and settle in. Daren expected him to arrive at his office any moment now. Daren had not met King Zeffrin as he arrived, and a meeting in Daren's office gave Daren the upper hand.

Shayla came to the door and announced Gavin's arrival. Daren stood and waited for him to enter. Gavin walked in followed by Megan. Daren stepped forward and extended his hand to Gavin.

"Gavin, please have a seat," Daren offered.

As Gavin moved out of the way, Daren stepped toward Megan and gave her a hug.

Daren then addressed Megan, "Gavin and I have some business matters to discuss. I'll have someone notify you when we're done."

Megan looked toward Gavin who shook his head in agreement. She left. Daren understood that Gavin was Megan's husband, but it still bothered him that she practically cowered in his presence. She had been raised a princess and was now a queen. She was his sister, and she should cower to no one. Daren set aside his feelings about Megan and focused on the matter at hand. As he turned toward Gavin, he saw that he was still standing. Gavin had the advantage of being taller than Daren, and he was obviously not going to give up that advantage by sitting while Daren was still standing. Gavin was taller, but had more of slender frame than Daren. His upper torso showed signs that Gavin worked out regularly, but his physique was more that of a runner than of a body builder. Gavin's hair was close cut and solid black in color off-setting his sky blue eyes. He had the look of a businessman and wore a constant almost sinister smirk which Daren was sure intimidated most people. Daren took his seat and Gavin followed.

Daren needed to find out where Gavin stood concerning Benson. "Gavin, as we go forward, I would like to have your support."

"I don't see the need to get involved in this, Daren. It's your concern, not mine."

Daren could see that Gavin was not going to make this easy.

"You know that King Benson is a potential threat to both of us. These attacks make Lionel appear weak. I would not be surprised if Benson doesn't use that to his advantage."

"Aldrich has never been a threat to Mikasa," Gavin quipped.

Daren didn't like the way this conversation was going. Gavin seemed a bit too supportive of Benson.

"Yes, well we both know that Benson has always been the one to strike the first blow. He's struck both Raxx and Lionel. There's no guarantee that Mikasa won't be next."

"You must be desperate, Daren, if you are begging for my support."

Despite the fury he felt at Gavin's accusation, Daren remained composed as he answered, "I wouldn't consider asking an ally for support a form of desperation. As I said, this benefits both of us. I'm sure I will find a way to compensate you for your support once this is over."

"I don't need charity, Daren."

Daren did not immediately respond, and the room grew silent.

"Gavin, I'm not completely clear on where you stand on this."

"As far as the ICP goes, Daren, I plan to remain neutral on this issue."

"And as far as Benson goes?"

Gavin huffed. "What is that supposed to mean, Daren?"

"As I said, I need some clarity on where you stand."

Gavin lifted his chin as he responded, "As far as I am concerned, Daren, Benson can go to hell."

Daren was relieved. He had hoped for more support from Gavin, but as a voting member, his neutrality would help somewhat if anyone rose to oppose him.

"That's good to hear." Now that Daren had better idea of where Gavin stood in regards to Benson, he decided to address another topic of concern that Gavin may be able to assist in. "Gavin, have you spoken with Queen Alyssa recently?"

"I have."

"Do you have any reason to suspect that she harbors resentment towards me or Lionel?"

"Why would she?"

"We were indirectly responsible for her uncle's death."

"I gave that order, Daren, and she has thanked me for it upon several occasions."

Daren decided to risk a little trust in Gavin. "I have intel that Zinn may be hiding out in Cashteh. As Alyssa is the Queen, I am concerned about her allegiance."

"Unfortunately, Alyssa does not have a very firm hold on what happens in her country. I doubt she knows he is there. You have no need to be concerned about Alyssa."

Gavin's candidness on this subject was unusual, but Daren appreciated it. Gavin and Alyssa had both been victims of a difficult childhood in each of their countries. They were close to the same age and no doubt found a kindred bond in their shared experiences.

Daren stood to end the conversation. Gavin quickly rose as well.

As they walked out of the office together, Daren addressed Shayla.

"Shayla, please arrange for Megan to meet Gavin at his plane. They are ready to depart."

Daren noted that the vein in Gavin's neck pulsed just a little at his order. Daren nodded a goodbye to Gavin and returned to his office.

Daren had been receiving daily updates from Christopher regarding the progress of the cleanup and relief from the earthquake. Now that Christopher was incapacitated and Chad was in charge, Daren had heard nothing. He picked up the phone to call his brother, Prince Brandon.

Daren was pleased when Brandon answered on the second ring.

"Yeah," was Brandon's response.

Daren sighed. "Brandon, I need an update."

"Daren?"

"Yes, Brandon."

"Short on help?"

"Brandon, just give me an update," Daren ordered.

"Yes, sir." Brandon's response was filled with sarcasm. "Everyone is ready to get started. We still need supplies."

"We worked out the funding three days ago. Did Deanna not send you the budget?"

"Yes, but the supplies have to be delivered."

"Brandon, this is serious. When is the delivery expected? What is taking so long?"

"The trucks are en route, but the roads are so torn up that it is taking longer than expected." Daren noted with satisfaction that Brandon's voice had lost its blithe tone.

Daren briefly considered suggesting that Brandon requisition helicopters to bring in the supplies, but he then remembered that the budget would not allow for that extravagance. Daren slammed his fist on his desk.

"Have any more injuries or deaths been reported?"

"No, still no deaths, and injuries are minimal."

"That's good." Daren was grateful for any good news right now. "Brandon, I am sure you are aware of the situation with Christopher. Until he is recovered, I want you to contact me daily with updates. Is there anything else you need?"

There was a tinge of surprise in Brandon's voice as he answered his brother, "Nope. Got it under control."

"Goodbye Brandon. Take care."

"Um, yeah. You too." Brandon sounded unsure.

Daren hung up. His entire world was falling apart, but he had to admit that even the least likely of people had stepped up during Lionel's hour of need. Despite the despair he was still feeling, the weary king raised a quick prayer of thanks to God for small blessings.

Chapter 20

General Ben Canaan's unit had traveled to the border of Lionel and Raxx. They would remain at the base in Raxx until it was time to attack. Todd had just gotten his cot set up in the bunker when General Ben Canaan plodded in. His presence immediately irritated Todd. He didn't need a babysitter. Nevertheless, Todd stood at attention and waited for the General to speak.

"Lt. Heart, I'll be taking a bit of a detour and you're coming with me." Ben Canaan growled.

"Why do I get such a privilege, Sir?"

Caleb noted the tone of sarcasm in Todd's response but chose to ignore it. Despite Todd's foolhardy behavior with Chad, the General had gained a newfound respect for Todd when he chose to fight for his country.

"Take only what you need. We will be back tomorrow morning."

"Yes, sir."

Todd grabbed his combat pack and exited the barracks. He heard jets fly over and lifted his eyes up to the sky. The sun was bright and hot. Instinctively, Todd took a drink of water from his canteen. The base was bustling with soldiers moving to and fro making last minute preparations to march into Aldrich in two days time. Sport utility trucks crowded the main road leading through the base. There were a few tanks lined up on the outskirts. Todd was anxious to get moving. He wasn't sure where the General was going, but at least it might provide a distraction. The other soldiers had still not warmed up to him, and it was becoming annoying.

He scanned the area and found General Ben Canaan standing near one of the sport utility trucks. He was speaking with another General. Todd walked his way, made sure the General saw him and then waited a respectful distance for Ben Canaan to finish his conversation.

Ben Canaan called to Todd, "Let's go. Get in."

Todd threw his bag into the back of the sport utility truck and seated himself in the passenger seat. He briefly entertained the thought of taking the driver's seat but thought better of it. A ride with Ben

Canaan driving was sure to take forever, and Todd had no desire to be trapped in a vehicle with the General for any longer than was necessary. Before the General got in, Todd took the liberty of turning on the radio and changing the station to one of his preference. If he was lucky, the music might at least provide an escape. General Ben Canaan got in and slammed the door. His hulking figure made the sport utility truck seem uncomfortably cozy. He started the engine. As he pulled out, the tires squealed on the pavement and Todd involuntarily grabbed onto the bar that was across the dash of the vehicle. A slight grin crept its way across his face as he noted that the General might just have a little more spunk than he thought. The grin faded when the General reached to turn off the music.

After about fifteen minutes of silence, Todd dared a question, "So, where are we going, Sir?"

"I'm going to see an old friend. A retired General. I'm going to run a few things past him before we head into Aldrich. He is a brilliant strategist." Ben Canaan explained.

This actually interested Todd, and he was suddenly pleased that the General had brought him along. He wondered if it was someone he had met before.

"What's his name, Sir?"

"General Perelli. I'm sure you've heard your father speak of him. He was injured in the conflict with Aldrich and Raxx about fifteen years ago. Because of his expertise, the Commander requested that he remain active despite his injuries. He did until about two years ago when he retired."

"How much further is it?" Todd regretted his question almost instantly. He felt like a child asking if they were there yet.

"We should arrive in approximately twenty minutes," the General answered.

Nothing more was said the remainder of the trip. They finally arrived at the General's house. It was set back off the road, and was surrounded by trees. The house was made of wood with a concrete foundation with a garage located to the side of the house. Todd noted that there was a basketball goal set up at the end of the driveway, and he wondered if the General had a son. If the son was home, maybe he and Todd could shoot some hoops while he waited for Ben Canaan. To Todd's disappointment, Ben Canaan parked the vehicle under the goal making its use impossible.

Before they could reach the front door, it opened, and a woman in her mid-fifties with medium brown hair ran out and threw her arms around Ben Canaan. The scene was rather awkward for Todd, and he hoped he could escape her enthusiastic display of affection.

She addressed Ben Canaan, "Caleb! What a pleasant surprise. I am so glad you came. Perelli will be happy to see you." Turning her attention to Todd she continued, "and who is this handsome young man you've brought with you?"

"This is Todd Heart, Commander Heart's son. He is a part of my unit." General Ben Canaan explained.

"Oh my. Well, it is a pleasure to meet you. We have a great admiration for your father. Come in. I'll get you both something to drink. Dinner will be ready shortly. You will be joining us. Perelli is in the den watching TV. You know where to go, Caleb."

Todd followed Ben Canaan to the den. He had stayed in an apartment during his sojourn outside the palace, but it was foreign and unusual for him to be in someone's home. The smell of roasted potatoes seemed to permeate every room in the house and Todd wondered what it would be like to live with the constant smell of food everywhere you went. His stomach growled, and he was happy that Mrs. Perelli was insisting on dinner.

As they entered the den, the first thing Todd noticed was a huge table taking up most of the room. Across it were charts, maps and other papers. A large Lionel flag took up much of the wall on one side, and beneath the flag were two chairs side by side. General Perelli occupied one of the chairs. Without looking up, the General spoke as Caleb and Todd entered the room.

"I see you conveniently coordinated your arrival with dinner time."

General Ben Canaan gave an uncharacteristic grin and replied, "You know I wouldn't miss one of your wife's home-cooked meals. General, this is Lieutenant Todd Heart. He's the Commander's boy. He enlisted immediately after the attacks. He wants to help defend his country."

General Perelli now made an effort to stand. It was a slow and seemingly painstaking process in which he used a cane to support and pull himself up. When he was in a standing position, Todd could see that his right leg seemed to be disfigured. The General limped towards him and extended his hand. Todd shook it.

Addressing Todd the General spoke, "It is an honor, Lieutenant. You are to be commended for your loyalty and bravery. Welcome to my home. It's not a palace, but it's my castle and you are most welcome."

"Thank you, Sir. The honor is mine." Todd felt an immediate respect for the General, and he was grateful that General Ben Canaan had spoken highly of him to this man.

"Please, have a seat." The General offered.

Ben Canaan took the chair next to Perelli, and Todd sat on a sofa that was adjacent to the chairs. As the two Generals talked and reminisced, Todd tried to discreetly look at the documents on the table, but they were too far away. He was more than relieved when Mrs. Perelli called them all to dinner.

As they entered the dining room, Todd noted that there were five place settings. He wondered who the fifth setting was for, but his thoughts were quickly diverted to the feast that was laid out on the table. Granted, he was used to good food, but for some reason, this food looked especially appetizing. They all sat and General Perelli prayed for God's blessing for the meal. The food tasted just as good as it looked, and Todd calculated that it was certainly worth the drive here with Ben Canaan and the long hours of listening to the two Generals drone on about the past. When they were halfway through the meal, Todd heard the front door open and close.

"That'll be Hannah coming home from work," Perelli explained. He then called to the visitor, "Hannah, come on in here. We are eating dinner, and we have some guests."

Todd heard some shuffling in the other room, and then the visitor bounced into the dining room. As soon as she saw Ben Canaan, she mimicked her mother's earlier reaction grabbing him around the neck and squealing with delight. She took the gesture one step further by planting a big kiss on the General's cheek.

She started to say something to Ben Canaan but stopped when she saw Todd. A huge smile lit her face, and she addressed Todd, "Who are you?"

Before Todd could answer, General Perelli spoke up, "Hannah, this is Lieutenant Heart. He's here with General Ben Canaan."

Hannah bounced over to Todd and offered her hand. Todd stood and took it. Her hand was soft, and he had a desire to hold onto it. She was pretty, really pretty. He was liking this side trip more and more.

"Hello Lieutenant Heart."

She made her way to her seat. When no one offered to introduce her, Todd questioned her, "Who are you?"

General Ben Canaan shot Todd a look as Hannah apologized, "I'm sorry. I thought you already knew. I'm Hannah Perelli. Sorry I wasn't here sooner. Apparently, a lot of people had pretzel cravings today. We ran out three times, and I stayed a little bit later to make up some batches for tomorrow. I'm not quite sure why they were so popular today, but I guess it's good business. Keeps money in my pocket. So, General Ben Canaan, what are you and father up to now?"

"Your father and I are just visiting. It's been a while."

"And you dragged this poor lieutenant along with you!? He'll be bored to death. I'm warning you, lieutenant, they will ramble on for hours. And then just when you think they've talked about everything they possibly can, they will start over on the same stories. The funniest part is that the stories change just a little bit each time. First time around, they are surrounded by 10 enemy soldiers. Next it's 25. I can't even begin to tell you how many times they've 'barely escaped death!'"

Hannah added a foreboding tone to her last few words. Todd was finding her to be quite amusing and a little intriguing.

Mrs. Perelli spoke up, "Hannah, perhaps you can entertain Lieutenant Heart for a little while if that's okay with General Ben Canaan."

Hannah looked to Caleb for approval.

Ben Canaan responded, "Just remain on the premises in case we get called back."

Hannah looked to Todd now, "Well, do you want to hang out for a while? Do you play basketball? If General Ben Canaan will move that beast out of the driveway, we can shoot a few hoops. What do you say?"

Todd was ecstatic, but he didn't want it to show. He gave a nonplussed reply, "Sure."

Hannah looked to her father, "May I be excused?"

"Yes, you may. Don't stay out there too late. You have classes in the morning."

"Yes sir."

"Did you practice your music today?"

"Daddy, it won't kill me to miss one day of practicing. Besides, we have guests, and it would be rude to shut myself in my room and ignore them."

"You know it's all about discipline, Hannah. You get out of a routine, and . . ."

Mrs. Perelli interceded, "Perelli, give your daughter a break. I am sure she won't suffer from not practicing one night."

"Thank you, mom," Hannah responded. "Lieutenant Heart, are you ready to lose?"

Todd rolled his eyes and stood. Ben Canaan threw him the keys to the sport utility truck. Todd waited until they were outside and away from prying ears to respond to Hannah.

"You play basketball?" There was a purposeful hint of disbelief in his tone.

Hannah merely smiled and responded, "Move that beast out of the way, and I'll show you how well I can play."

"Whatever, pretzel girl."

Todd got into the sport utility truck and started it. He hadn't driven one before, but he liked the feel. It was powerful. He would find a way to convince Ben Canaan to let him drive back. He backed it up and got out. A basketball had magically appeared in Hannah's hands, and she was dribbling it as she waited. Todd casually sauntered over to her intending to grab the ball from her unexpectedly. When he reached for it, she easily evaded his steal.

"Oh, watch out, pretzel girl knows how to play basketball." Todd teased.

"Yes she does, and exactly how did I earn the name pretzel girl?"

"You make pretzels, don't you? Did you have to go to school to learn how to make pretzels? Is there a pretzel class?"

"Ha ha. Funny. No, I didn't go to school to learn how to make pretzels, but I make some darn good ones. I'm really good at the parmesan, cinnamon and basil tomato ones. However, my friend Stacey is the best. She can make almost all of them really well. We have fifty flavors. A lot of them are made to order, but then it takes longer. Not too many people order the jalapeno ranch. I think we might discontinue it.

My favorite is the bacon cheddar pretzel, but I try not to eat too many of them. They aren't exactly the healthiest food. We do have some whole-wheat selections that are a little better for you. What's your favorite pretzel?"

Todd never knew that someone could talk so much about pretzels. He answered her, "Seriously? I live in a palace."

"Oh my gosh. You're just like my father! Every man's home is his castle. Well, my dad eats pretzels. What, are you just too good for pretzels? You've obviously never tried my pretzels. I bet you would love the cheddar bacon pretzel. I might have some in the freezer. My dad likes them, so I bring them home occasionally."

"Wow."

"What?"

"You're really into your pretzels. If I'm going to eat a pretzel, it has to be a fresh one. And I really do live in the palace." As they had been talking, they took turns shooting. Hannah now had the ball and was aiming for a three pointer. She made it.

Todd recognized her success, "Pretzel girl scores!"

"Of course I scored, and there's more where that came from." Suddenly Todd's comment sunk in. "You live in the palace? Oh my gosh! Your last name is Heart! Are you related to the King?"

"Just a little bit." Todd's tone was sarcastic.

"This is so cool! How are you related?"

"My dad is Commander Heart."

"Oh my gosh! Are you serious? I am playing basketball with a prince? And beating him badly? Go pretzel girl."

"Don't get all wound up. I'm letting you win, pretzel girl."

Todd and Hannah continued to banter while playing basketball. Neither one was really keeping score, but they were certainly enjoying each other's company. Over an hour had passed before they decided to take a break.

Hannah directed Todd, "Wait here. I'll be right back."

She then proceeded into the house. When she returned, she was holding two big glasses of sweet tea. Todd gladly accepted the drink and finished it off in one gulp. When he looked at Hannah, her eyes were big.

Feeling self-conscious Todd questioned her, "What?"

"I've just never seen someone drink that much that fast. I take it you like my mom's tea? She makes sun tea. She puts the bags in the water and then sits the glass pitcher out in the sun for it to steep. She also only buys a certain kind of tea. I think it's really good. Most people really like it. Do you want another glass?"

"Sure." Apparently it wasn't just pretzels that Hannah had a lot to say about. That was fine with Todd. It meant he didn't have to talk much.

She left and returned once more with another glass of tea. It took her a bit longer this time, and Todd noted that she had brushed her hair and probably fixed her make-up. There was also a hint of perfume.

"There's a stream running behind the house. It's cooler down there. Would you like to go sit for a while and cool off?" Hannah suggested.

"Sure."

As they walked together, Todd decided to question her about her practicing.

"So, what are you supposed to be practicing right now?"

"The violin. I play in the orchestra at school and at church on Sundays."

"Are you any good?"

"Of course. Good enough to be offered a college scholarship. I don't know if I'm going to go to that college though. I know I have to decide soon. This is my senior year. I've narrowed it down to about three choices. The other two colleges are offering scholarships for my academics. One of them has a really good program in Public Administration. Dad thinks I should choose that one, but the one offering the music scholarship has an amazing music program. It's so hard to choose. They all have nice campuses, and they are all offering two years full scholarship. I mentioned taking a year off from school to decide, and my dad just about blew a gasket. That reminds me, I do need to finish up some things tonight for the college fair tomorrow. I'm on the student council, and we are hosting the fair."

Todd just stood staring at Hannah in amazement. She took his failure to respond as an opportunity to continue.

"We can sit on that log down there. I was sitting there one day doing homework, and a little black snake decided to sneak up on me. He's no longer a part of this world. I don't usually mind snakes as long as they leave me alone, but he was just asking for it."

When Hannah paused, Todd took the opportunity to jump in, "You make pretzels. Play basketball. Play the violin. Have really good grades. Are a part of student council. And kill snakes? Is there anything you don't do?"

As they sat down on the log, Hannah spewed out a list of things she did and didn't do. Todd thought she was never going to stop.

He interrupted her, "Don't you need to take a breath?"

His comment caught her off guard, and she stopped talking momentarily. Todd took the opportunity to lean in and kiss her. It was quick, and he pulled back to see her reaction. She looked at him, smiled and leaned in for more. Afterwards, Todd decided that he would find a way to see her again once this war was over. It was getting late, and Todd knew he would need as much rest as he could get before they headed out. He stood and offered his hand to Hannah. She gladly took it, and they walked hand in hand back to the house. As soon as they reached the front door, Hannah let go. Todd was sure that her father was the reason.

As they entered the house, Hannah told Todd good night and headed to her room. Todd heard the voices of the two generals coming from the den and decided to see what they were up to. He could always excuse himself to bed if they were still reminiscing. As he walked in, both men were hovering over the table looking at a map and some of the other documents. As Todd drew nearer, he saw that it was a map of Aldrich and the two Generals were discussing strategy. In the tidal wave of Hannah, Todd had forgotten Ben Canaan's initial reason for coming here. He now wished he had returned sooner. Todd tried to make himself inconspicuous as he listened to the two men discuss strategy. At one point Ben Canaan looked up at him, but he did not tell him to leave. Todd learned that if needed, Ben Canaan would have nearly 75,000 troops at his disposal if needed. He listened intently as the men discussed their options.

General Perelli was speaking. "You say Benson is not aware of an imminent threat? Are you sure?"

"Prince Trevor claims his father was unaware of his visit to Lionel. We also have sources in Aldrich who have reported that no military or other unusual movement has taken place. According to them, it is business as usual. Benson seems pretty smug right now."

"Then you have two advantages - the element of surprise and a firsthand knowledge of the layout of the palace. I agree that a direct assault at the heart is your best move." There was fervor in Perelli's tone and Todd could tell that this was his passion.

"Alright then, here's a layout of the palace. Let's go over options."

The two men detailed over a dozen options before settling on four viable paths. Every one of them required a small team of special forces going directly into the palace with Ben Canaan at the lead. This frontline of troops would be flown close to the capital of Aldrich and dropped. They would then have a two-day hike to reach the palace. The sport utility trucks and other military vehicles would be deployed to the border of Aldrich drawing attention there.

Perelli now gave Ben Canaan a concerned look. "How are you dealing with all of this?"

Todd thought it was an odd question. This was what Ben Canaan lived for. He looked at Ben Canaan to see his reaction. The General seemed contemplative.

It took a few moments for Ben Canaan to respond. "I swore I would never set foot in that country again unless it was to kill Warren Benson."

"Does King Daren want him dead or alive?"

"Our objective is clear. Take him out. I think we have all had enough of Benson's antics. No one would argue that this world will be a better place without that bastard." Caleb's voice had an edge to it, and Todd noted the pain that flashed in his eyes as he spoke of Benson. The hatred was palpable and Todd found himself wrapped up in it.

Todd allowed himself to remember the horrible stories he had heard about Warren Benson. The countless women he had raped, mutilated and then murdered. The men who had been put on display and tortured as both warning and entertainment. The laws he had implemented that oppressed all of his subjects and gave him complete dictatorial rule over their lives. His open defiance of God and all who believed in Him. Todd felt a tinge of guilt at the last thought but quickly brushed it off. A passion of rage filled him as he truly understood for the first time what this meant for the General, Lionel and even the people of Aldrich who had suffered under this tyrant.

All these thoughts had rushed through his mind in seconds and he now focused once more on the conversation.

"What about Trevor? Is he in Aldrich now?" Perelli was asking.

"He will be."

"What will his fate be?"

"Daren hopes for an ally."

Perelli grunted. "From a Benson?"

"He is to be spared."

Todd was conflicted by this news. He honestly hadn't even considered the possibility that Trevor would be at the palace when they attacked, and he wasn't sure how he felt about sparing his life. It made no sense to him, but he made an uncharacteristic decision to try to reason it through. There must be a reason that he didn't fully comprehend just yet.

Before Todd realized it, over two hours had passed, and he had learned more in those two hours than in 18 years of life. A cloud of disappointment had settled over him as he realized that he most likely would not be a part of the central action.

Ben Canaan addressed him, "Get some rest, soldier. We leave in six hours."

"Yes, sir."

Chapter 21

Two days had passed since Todd and the General had visited Perelli, and the troops were loaded and on their way to the capital of Aldrich. To Todd's surprise, General Ben Canaan had informed him after leaving Perelli's that Todd was not to leave his side. Todd was going into the fray. If all went well, there would be civilian cars waiting for them to drive into the capital from several different points of entry. They would be dropped in the middle of the night onto uninhabited land. Anyone who happened to see them would have to be eliminated immediately.

Todd looked across the cabin of the plane and saw Newberry. They had purposefully ignored each other up to this point, but chances were they might have to work together in the next 72 hours. Ben Canaan announced that they were within range. For Todd, this meant that revenge was within sight. All the men stood and proceeded to triple check their gear. They then all moved to the rear of the plane and waited for the doors to open to begin the airdrop. As they did, Todd felt a rush of adrenaline. It was beginning.

Todd watched as rows of men in front of him took the plunge. It was finally his turn. Ben Canaan counted down, and then without hesitation, Todd stepped off the platform. The first few seconds felt like the downward plunge on a roller coaster. His stomach lifted up into his throat. He then turned over and over in the air becoming disoriented. The darkness made the sensation even stronger. He released the stabilizer shoot after about 15 seconds and it leveled him out so he was no longer spinning. The force of the wind pushed against his body making his face and arms flap in the wind. He was falling at 120 miles an hour. He pulled the parachute opening the canopy. For a brief moment he was jerked backwards but then the force of the wind slowed, and he was floating in air. Using the cords, he guided himself to land. As he neared the ground, he slowed himself down by pulling the cords into his thighs. As the ground came rushing towards him, he pulled the cords in closer to slow himself even more and gently touch down.

In the moonlight Todd could see a few of the others not far off. He made his way towards them, and then they all headed silently to the rendezvous point. They waited half an hour for everyone to arrive.

When all were accounted for, the troops changed into civilian clothing and made their way in eight different directions to where there would be cars waiting for them. To anyone who happened to notice, they would look like groups of college students on a road trip with an occasional old guy thrown in. Todd was pushed into the middle of one of the back seats between Newberry and another soldier. Ben Canaan rode in another car in the same position. They were the two most likely to be recognized, so they took the most inconspicuous positions.

Every movement and sound Newberry made grated on Todd's nerves. When Newberry tapped his fingers on his knee, Todd wanted to grab his hand and rip his fingers off. When Newberry cleared his throat, Todd gritted his teeth. Then Newberry started burrowing through his bag. In the process, he jabbed Todd in the ribs several times, and it took every ounce of Todd's resolve not to deck him. Newberry finally found what he was looking for and settled back into his seat. Todd was momentarily mollified while Newberry sat with a penlight quietly reading some papers he had pulled out. With Newberry no longer irritating him and holding his attention, boredom set in for Todd. He decided to take a look at what was so interesting to Newberry. Todd made no attempt to disguise his interest, and when he looked over, Newberry immediately tried to conceal the contents. It was too late however. Todd had already seen Kelly's name at the top of the papers. Without hesitation, Todd grabbed the papers from Newberry.

"Give those back," Newberry demanded.

Newberry tried to lunge for the papers, but Todd held them away from him and across the other soldier who was on his other side. The soldier squirmed to move as close as he could to the window, but the closeness of the quarters prevented a reprieve. The scene that followed was rather amusing. Elbows jabbed ribs, and arms were flying to little avail. At one point, Newberry was practically stretched across Todd trying to reach for the papers. The driver whose seat had been pounded from behind more than once had had enough. He swerved to the side of the road and abruptly stopped throwing everyone forward and then back.

The driver yelled, "That's it. Get out!"

Newberry didn't dare argue, and he opened the door. As he started to get out and stand, Todd took the opportunity to shove him to the ground. By the time Todd crawled out of the car though, Newberry was on his feet. The other soldier leaned across and pulled the door shut. The driver then took off down the road and stopped a distance away.

"I don't want to fight you," Newberry yelled, "just give me back my stuff!"

Todd had held onto the papers and now took an opportunity to scrutinize them more closely. Newberry lunged at him, and Todd blocked him with a hand to his sternum. Newberry tried a few more times, and each time Todd prevented his assault.

"Try that again, and you won't be getting back up!" Todd warned.

Newberry finally acquiesced. When Todd was confident that Newberry was nullified, he read the papers. They were letters to Kelly. They had only been gone three days, and there were already seven letters. At first Todd was angered.

"What part of 'stay away from my sister' don't you understand, creep?" Todd continued to read. "'I love you.' Seriously? You've only known her a few weeks, and you're telling her that you love her? "

"I do."

"That's crap. How is that even possible?" Todd was disgusted, and he didn't want to hear any more. He threw the letters at Newberry and started walking towards the car.

Some of the letters fell to the ground, and Newberry carefully picked them up and shook the dirt off. He then followed Todd to the car. By the time Newberry had reached the car, Todd had already taken his place in the middle. The driver spoke up.

"Newberry, up front. Sanders get in the back."

Sanders didn't seem too happy about the arrangement, but he got out and squeezed in next to Todd. He gave a stern look of warning to Todd and then shut the door. They started off once more.

****

As they neared the capital, the tension in the car was palpable. The success of their mission was dependent on the element of surprise, and one wrong move could ruin it all. Each team gathered at a predetermined rendezvous point. Todd was reunited with Ben Canaan. His team was in an alley between two tall buildings whose color resembled rusty pipes. All of the buildings they had passed were of that same dirty, used color suggesting years of neglect giving the city a vacant feeling that left the team feeling unsettled. It was around 4 in the morning, and the streets were quiet except for the occasional passing car. Not much was said. At 5am they would all change into their gear and then make their way quietly to the palace. A police car passed by, and the tension mounted as they waited to see if he had spotted them. A few minutes later, the car returned. The officer got out and walked towards them with a flashlight in one hand and his other hand on his gun. Caleb motioned for the men to stand down. He then grabbed Todd and pulled him over to the officer.

With slurred speech, Ben Canaan addressed the officer, "Good evening. My son here just turned 18. He's looking for an opportunity to get laid. Any suggestions? What do you say son? Two girls or three? Maybe we could go all out with 18? One for each year."

Ben Canaan slapped Todd on the back rather hard. They waited for the officer to respond.

The officer had a disturbing grin on his face as he replied, "There's a place down the street about two blocks. But if you want really good service, you might want to head over to 8th. They have former palace girls there. Well trained. A little pricey though."

Caleb responded, "My boy's 18. Only the best for him tonight."

"Well, whatever you're going to do, make it soon. Clear out of here."

"Yes sir. Thanks for the help."

Paralyzed by the conversation, Todd didn't speak a word. He had heard rumors of the depravity in Aldrich but seeing it was revolting.

The officer gave Todd a wink, "Enjoy." He then departed.

The next half hour creeped by slowly. At exactly 5am, without a word, every soldier started gearing up. The next half hour would be crucial. Anyone who saw them now would have to be eliminated.

It was time to move in. From this moment on non-verbal signals would be the form of communication until they infiltrated the palace. Some would stay behind to create a distraction if it was necessary. Other teams would be moving in at other points of entry to the palace. If all went well, they would take out palace security one by one moving deeper into the palace until they found King Benson.

Ben Canaan glanced back at Todd. "Stay close," he ordered.

For Todd to be included on a mission such as this with so little training was very unusual. However, over the years, Todd had paid more attention than his father realized. He followed behind Ben Canaan. Soldiers ahead were using silencers and knives to dispense of obstacles as they went along. Suddenly gunfire was heard from another area of the palace. They had been discovered.

Through his earpiece, Todd heard someone say "Smoley's down! Smoley's down."

At that, Ben Canaan ordered the men to move at a faster pace. They made their way down the hall taking out security as they went. They reached a large rotunda where four more hallways branched off. Up ahead, team members positioned themselves next to the hallway entrances waiting for the ambush from palace security. As enemy forces moved in, Lionel troops took them out one by one as they reached the entrance to the rotunda. But as more and more came pouring through, the rotunda filled with both Lionel and Aldrich forces. Some shots were fired but abruptly stopped. The proximity of the rotunda made it difficult to pinpoint targets, and neither side was willing to risk hitting one of their own. The men then engaged in hand-to-hand combat using knives in lieu of guns. General Ben Canaan moved in and joined in the fighting. Todd saw that one of their team members was at a disadvantage and moved to assist. He moved in from behind the enemy soldier ready to strike. The enemy saw him and turned blocking his attack. It gave the other soldier the advantage, and he stabbed the enemy in the side taking him down. Todd looked towards the other hallways to see if more Aldrich forces were coming. Movement at the end of the hallway to the right caught his attention. To his amazement, King Benson was being moved down the hall surrounded by guards. Todd's blood began to boil.

He looked Ben Canaan's way, but saw that he was preoccupied. With fierce determination, Todd left the team behind and headed for Benson.

King Benson and his escort were moving quickly. Afraid that they might be headed towards an escape route, Todd had to act. He pulled out a can of tear gas. The ceilings were high giving him plenty of room to lob the can. He threw it as hard as he could over the heads of Benson and his men. It landed in front of them blocking the path. Unfortunately, Todd had thrown it too hard, and it was not close enough to disable any of the security forces. They all turned towards him.

Someone was yelling, "Get him to the throne room!"

Three of the men separated from the group with Benson in tow. The others took up positions of defense. They started firing in Todd's direction. Todd moved behind a column and waited. Todd heard someone behind him yell, "Go on three! I'll cover."

Todd looked back to see the soldier who he had helped earlier. He nodded in agreement and took a deep breath as the soldier counted. Gunfire erupted all around him as he rushed to the next alcove. He and the other soldier then took turns covering each other as they moved forward. When they had almost reached the enemy line, a barrage of shots came from behind. Todd looked back to see Ben Canaan and others moving in. The door that they had taken Benson through was just on the other side of the hallway from Todd, but he would easily be caught in the crossfire if he moved in that direction. Time was crucial. Todd had to make a decision. One of the enemy soldiers closer to him was reloading. Todd darted out from the alcove he was in and dove at the soldier taking him to the ground. As he and the enemy wrestled for control, he could only hope that Lionel forces had seen him. Finally, he had the man in a chokehold. He pulled him up turning him towards the Aldrich forces hoping that Lionel forces would not shoot him in the back. The man was struggling making it difficult for Todd to move him. The gunfire from behind had stopped, but the Aldrich forces were still firing. His shield's body went limp and Todd realized that they had taken out their own man. Trying to keep his own body covered by the corpse was proving a difficult endeavor. His path across the hallway was unwieldy and slow. Each shot that hit the body of his shield belabored his progress even more. By the time he reached the doorway, he was covered in blood. He dropped the body and took cover. Lionel forces resumed their barrage.

Todd's adrenaline was rushing, but he took a moment for inspection. His body armor had taken several shots, but it seemed that none had broken through. The blood covering him was all from the other man.

Todd looked around him and realized that the doorway he had gone through was merely a small rotunda leading into another larger room. The doors of the larger room were very ornate and were closed. Todd checked the handle. The doors were locked. He knew that he should probably wait for backup, but he didn't want to risk losing

Benson. He took another deep breath and aimed his gun at the door. He fired a shot at the lock and then kicked in the doors. Shots came from two directions. Todd dropped to one knee, shot one shooter and then rolled behind a column that was a few feet away. He lowered himself to the ground and looked around the column. It took a moment for the second shooter to see him, and Todd had a chance to evaluate his surroundings. They were in the throne room. It was a rather large room with columns creating a pathway up to the throne. The other shooter had also taken refuge behind one of the towering columns. There was a door at the other end of the room behind the throne, and that is where Benson was most likely headed. There were only two men left guarding him though, so he was immobilized as long as Todd kept Benson's security occupied. He needed to reload, and as he reached for the magazine, he remembered that he still had a grenade. He pulled it out, removed the pin and threw it in the direction of the shooter blocking his path. At the same time, he jumped out from behind the column hoping to take advantage of the diversion the explosion would cause for the other guard. The body of the shooter went flying through the air along with shards of white column mingled with blood spraying the area. The third guard fired in Todd's direction, but his focus was on getting the king to safety. His lack of attention to Todd was his demise. Taking advantage of the moment, Todd stepped from behind the column, ran to position himself closer to the guard, took aim, and fired at the guard's head. The first shot missed, the second found its mark bringing the guard to the ground.

King Benson and his guard had been heading towards a partially concealed door behind the throne, and Benson now continued in that direction. Todd didn't know if Benson was carrying a weapon, so he advanced on him using the columns as a shield. Benson reached the door but then stopped abruptly. At first Todd wondered why he stopped, but then Todd heard gunfire coming from that direction as well. They were blocked from both directions, and Benson had nowhere to run. Benson turned back in Todd's direction. Todd had managed to close the distance between them and was now standing just ten feet away still using the column as a shield. Benson started for the gun that was laying on the floor next to the dead guard. Before he could reach it, Todd shot him in the knee bringing him to the ground. When he was sure that Benson was completely unarmed, Todd walked to where Benson was and stood in front of the king who had been brought to his knees.

"That was for my country," Todd declared.

"I surrender. I am unarmed." Benson pleaded.

The sound of Benson's voice enraged Todd. How dare he expect mercy after the countless atrocities he had committed. Todd aimed at Benson's other leg and pulled the trigger.

"That was for Becca and her father, General Ben Canaan."

"Enough!" Benson yelled. "I am the King of Aldrich! You cannot . . . "

Todd cut him off, "Shut up! And this . . . this is for King Daren!"

There was terror in Benson's eyes as Todd raised his rifle higher and aimed at Benson's head. Without flinching Todd pulled the trigger ending Benson's life. Todd took a moment to look at the now dead King laying in a pool of blood. How many lives had been ruined or lost as a result of this evil man? Todd couldn't believe that no one had taken him out years ago.

Todd knew that if he headed back the way he came, he risked running straight into the guards who had positioned themselves outside the door. It somewhat surprised him that none of them had followed him into the throne room. Ben Canaan and his men must be doing a good job of staving them off. Todd decided to take his chances with the other door. The gunfire from that direction was getting closer, but it still sounded far enough off not to be an immediate threat. As he headed for the door, a movement within an alcove to the side of the throne caught his attention. He raised his gun in immediate response. The figure stepped forward with his hands lifted in surrender. Trevor. Todd instantly felt compelled to blow him away, but Ben Canaan's words echoed in his head. Daren wanted him alive. Still, nothing good had ever come from a Benson, and Trevor's recent actions with his sister were proof enough for Todd of Trevor's depravity. Still, Todd hesitated. He had seen Ashley the morning they deployed, and her parting words were haunting him.

Todd looked Trevor in the eye and demanded, "Get on the floor. On your knees."

Rather than follow Todd's command, Trevor took a few slow, but deliberate steps toward Todd. The action along with Trevor's intent gaze unsettled Todd.

"Stop moving and get down, I said."

Trevor did stop moving, but he stood in defiance. "You've killed my father, Todd. Are you going to kill me as well? Do what you must, but if I die, I will not kneel beforehand. I have no weapon, but I do have my dignity."

Todd's finger twitched on the trigger. One shot would rid the world of that smug look forever. One shot would cause his sister to hate him forever and defy his King's orders. If someone else had found and killed Trevor, then Todd could have simply explained that he couldn't do anything to stop them. But he was in control here. Trevor's life was in his hands.   Ashley's plea echoed in his head, "Don't let them kill him."

Todd closed the short distance between himself and Trevor and then struck him in the head with the hilt of his rifle. While Trevor was disoriented from the hit, Todd kicked his feet out from under him bringing him to the ground, slamming his back into the hard floor. A groan escaped Trevor's lips as he tried to stand.

"Stay down!" Todd yelled.

Trevor continued moving and made it into a kneeling position. Before he could stand, Todd moved in and placed the barrel of his revolver against Trevor's head.

"I said stay down!" Todd's emotions were a mixture of anger, fear and even admiration. He wasn't sure if Trevor was trying to lure him into a trap or possibly delay Todd's actions until someone arrived. He also felt a sort of regard for Trevor's dauntlessness.

Trevor looked up at Todd. His eyes still held a smug confidence. "Does this make you feel powerful? You want to kill me? Do it! Just remember, you are here because of me. King Daren could have killed me when I was in Lionel. Does he want me dead?"

As Trevor spoke, Todd pressed harder into Trevor's temple with the revolver. He didn't like the feeling of having Trevor in his head. With the gun to his head, Trevor closed his eyes and took a deep breath. Just then the doors to the throne room burst open, and Ben Canaan came into the room. As soon as he saw Todd, he yelled orders to his men to stay back. The General made his way towards Todd and Trevor. Todd waited for the General's arrival never taking his eyes off Trevor until the General was only a few feet away. Keeping one eye on Trevor, Todd looked towards Ben Canaan. Todd expected the General to start barking orders, but he remained silent, his brow creased in either worry or alarm. Todd looked back at Trevor.

Ben Canaan spoke, but his normally gruff voice sounded more like a plea, "Todd."

Moments passed in silence. Todd wrestled with what to do. Finally, Todd leaned in closer to Trevor still pressing the gun against his head.

Quietly, Todd addressed the would be king, "You can thank Ashley for this."

At that, Todd stepped away and uncocked his revolver. Ben Canaan quickly moved in and assisted Trevor in standing. He then motioned for his men to move into the room.

Ben Canaan addressed Trevor, "King Benson, there is no need for any more bloodshed today. Order your men to stand down, your Majesty."

Todd had turned his back and was walking away from Ben Canaan and Trevor, but at the words, "Your Majesty," he turned to look at Trevor. The smugness had faded from Trevor's demeanor, and for a very brief moment was replaced with what could only be described as despair. Todd wondered if the full burden of responsibility had just set in for Trevor. Trevor quickly recovered however and made his way to the other door escorted by Caleb's men.

General Ben Canaan ordered his men to make sure the area was secured and then to attend to the wounded and fallen. Todd joined a group who were headed back out to the hallway he had come from earlier. In the heat of battle, it was easy to stay focused on the mission, driven forward by adrenaline and zeal. The battle lust was gone now, and the reality of what they had just accomplished was setting in. A keen awareness of the consequences of victory gnawed its way into Todd's consciousness as he stood surveying the carnage. Both Lionel and Aldrich forces lay slain. Some were only wounded, and some were still in the throes of death. Spent cartridges and stray bullets littered the floor, and the smell of sulfur was still pungent in the air. He and the other men made their way through the hall helping the injured, both allies and enemies. Todd heard a weak voice call his name, and he surveyed the area for the source. He saw Newberry slumped against a sidewall with another soldier kneeling by his side. Newberry's face was contorted with pain. Todd made his way to him.

Todd looked at the soldier who was kneeling. "We need to get him out of here."

The soldier looked up at Todd and shook his head. The gesture angered Todd and he moved toward Newberry.

"I'm getting you out of here. Let's go," Todd ordered as he reached to help Newberry up.

The other soldier grabbed Todd pulling him back and away from Newberry.

"Get your hands off of me," Todd yelled. "He needs medical attention!"

"Sir, he's not going to make it. Let him be at peace."

"How do you know? Are you a doctor?" Todd retorted.

Newberry spoke up, "Prince Todd, please, I need. . ."

Todd could barely hear Newberry. He shoved the soldier out of the way and then knelt down next to Newberry. As he did so, Newberry coughed, and blood poured out of his mouth. Todd then realized that the other soldier had been right. The only thing he could do for Newberry was stay with him until he faded away.

Newberry gasped for air and tried to sit up. Todd moved closer and tried to position him so that he was more comfortable.

As he did, Newberry mumbled, "I need you to do something. Please."

Todd nodded and waited for Newberry to continue.

"Tell her. Tell Kelly I love her. Please," Newberry pleaded.

All the hatred that Todd had felt towards Newberry at his advances towards Kelly dissipated. Unable to find words to say, Todd merely nodded in agreement to Newberry's request. The action seemed to relieve Newberry. His eyes closed and his face relaxed. His body shook involuntarily one last time, and then he took his last breath.

Todd had never experienced this closely the death of someone he knew before, and it gave him a feeling of powerlessness. Todd thought about his mother and how his father had held her after the accident. She had died in his arms. The thought grieved Todd, and he wondered how his father was doing. Suddenly, Todd felt the need to get out of the palace. He felt as though he was suffocating, and he needed air. He looked down. His body was still covered in caked blood from the soldier he had used as a shield. Scenes were playing in his head: some he had never even experienced. A hallway with bullets flying and soldiers falling to their deaths. Killing Benson. Sparing Trevor. His father holding his mother as she died. Newberry dying. Kelly screaming and crying. Todd felt like he was going mad. He started wandering looking for an exit. He was about to leave the hallway when he heard Ben Canaan's gruff voice behind him.

"Lieutenant Heart, where are you going, son?" Caleb questioned.

Todd just turned and looked at the General.

Caleb continued, "Come with me, Lieutenant. Stay close. You made enemies today. Word will spread fast. My job now is to get you home alive."

Todd didn't argue. He followed Ben Canaan back into the throne room. The general ordered his men to provide an escort. They moved in and surrounded the General and Todd. They then all moved as one through the palace. In less than an hour, the entire palace raid team had cleared out and had been replaced by a second wave of men who would assist with the transfer of power to Trevor.

Chapter 22

Some of the troops had been airlifted out of Aldrich. Ben Canaan, however, had felt that air transport proved a greater risk than ground at this point, and he and Todd had loaded into an armored vehicle with four other soldiers. The vehicle had three rows. Ben Canaan sat in the front passenger seat. Todd was in the middle with one other soldier, and the other two took the back row. The ride back would be much more comfortable than the ride coming. Todd felt a momentary pang of guilt at the thought. Newberry had been with him on the way here. Once they were out of the city, Todd relaxed a bit. They still had several hours drive before reaching the border and returning to the military base. The men were silent and images were still racing through Todd's head. Wanting to clear his mind, he decided to write Becca. The vehicle was equipped with tablets that could be used while in transit. Todd grabbed one and started typing.

A slight smile escaped as Todd addressed the e-mail. Thoughts of Becca, his "weed girl" brought him solace and sent a feeling of peace coursing through his body. He decided to begin with that epithet. He would not share the carnage of the day with her, but he would let her know that her father was safe, the battle was won and they would be home soon. He tried to think of what else he could include in the letter. So much of this trip had been filled with violence and tragedy. Hannah. He would tell her about Hannah. His smile widened as he described "pretzel girl," and wrote about their basketball game. He thought that Becca would like Hannah, and he wondered if they would ever have a chance to meet. He ended the letter and hit send. The events of the day were catching up with him. He leaned back and soon fell into a fitful sleep.

Very early the next morning, the convoy crossed the border into Lionel. Travel to base would take less than an hour from this point. Todd had been awake for several hours now. He looked at the men around him. As far as he knew, they had not slept at all. Yet, although they looked weary, they remained alert. It finally dawned on Todd that their unceasing vigilance was due to him. They rolled into the base and unloaded. General Ben Canaan then ordered the men to rest. Debriefing would begin in six hours.

Todd went to the barracks and laid down on a bunk. Sleep was elusive. He had never been through debriefing before, but he knew that they would want as much detail as possible. With that in mind, Todd replayed the previous days events over and over in his mind trying to remember what he could. He wondered if he would be praised or reprimanded for his actions. Had he not acted when he saw Benson, there was a good chance that he would have escaped, and the mission would be a failure. Todd decided that he might have to convince his inquisitors of that certainty.

****

Todd emerged from debriefing feeling somewhat reassured in his actions. There had been many questions, but at the same time, there was an underlying tone of respect and possibly even admiration from his questioners. No one had accused him of reckless behavior or poor decision-making. It was a new feeling for Todd, and he liked it.

Todd wasn't sure where to go. There would be more debriefing in the morning, but for now there were no orders and no plans. He was hungry, so he headed for the mess hall. The name "mess hall" irritated him. It was a dumb name for a place to eat. It sounded more like a bathroom. On his way, he was stopped by two soldiers headed the opposite way.

"Lieutenant Heart, where are you going?" They questioned.

The question seemed friendly, so Todd responded, "to eat."

"You aren't going to the party?"

Todd wasn't sure what they were talking about, but he didn't want to show it.

"Maybe later. After I eat."

"Food is set up over there. I don't think they are even serving in the mess hall tonight," one of the soldiers stated.

Todd hated it when he didn't know what was going on.

"Right. Forgot. Let's go."

As they walked, the two soldiers kept looking Todd's way. It was driving him crazy. He couldn't stand it any more.

"Is there a problem?" he questioned.

One of the men spoke up, "No. No problem. We were talking about the mission before you joined us. It took some balls to jump in front of that barricade of Aldrich forces. Good thing General Ben Canaan saw that it was you."

Todd wasn't sure if the comment was a compliment or a rebuke.

Todd stayed neutral, "Ben Canaan knows what he's doing."

The other soldier spoke now, "Seems you do too. Did Benson beg?"

They had reached the party. An area had been setup outside with tables covered with barbecued steak and chicken as well as several sides. Many soldiers had already gathered. Music was blaring. Beer was flowing. A large bonfire had been built. The fierce soldiers of just a few hours ago had transformed into what looked like a group of college frat boys. The scene had diverted Todd's attention from the conversation with the two soldiers. He turned to answer now, but was cut off by shouts coming from a group of nearby men. They were headed for him and the other two. He assumed that they were friends of the two he was with. As they came closer though, they went straight for Todd. Caught off guard, they grabbed him and raised him into the air. They carried him towards the fire shouting as they went. Todd was fairly certain that they weren't going to throw him into the fire, so he relaxed a bit. The group carried him around the fire, and Todd could finally make out what they were chanting: "Victory."

After two rounds, they put him down. Man after man gave him a high five followed with various manly words of encouragement and praise. Todd was beginning to realize that his actions had not only brought down an evil man, but they had also won him the respect of his peers. In less than 48 hours he had gone from being the reckless, irresponsible Prince to a revered hero. The realization was both exhilarating and humbling. One act of valor had changed him. As he stood watching these men who had fought together with him and probably even defended his life as he moved forward, he gained an appreciation and respect for them that had not been there before. He had thought that he would go into this war, help win it, and then leave. Those plans were changing. He belonged here.

The men partied into the night. Some had had too much too drink and were passed out. Todd had allowed himself a couple of beers but no more. He was enjoying himself, but he couldn't forget that there had also been casualties that day. Newberry's death weighed heavily on him most of all. Todd looked around for Ben Canaan. He had seen him earlier, but he was nowhere to be found now. Todd pulled away from the group of soldiers he had been talking to, and went to look for the General.

One of the men called to Todd, "Hey, where you going? Tell us again what you said to Benson!"

Todd grinned and walked back to where the men where standing Todd started, "Once I had him on his knees I said..."

Todd once again recounted the story leaving out the detail about Becca and Ben Canaan as he had every time. When he finished the men slapped him on the back in camaraderie.

Todd walked away once more; this time the men did not call him back. He headed for Ben Canaan's quarters. He wondered if the General had heard any news about his father. As Todd approached he saw that the door was slightly ajar. He didn't want to invade his privacy but if the General was asleep he didn't want to wake him. Todd gently pushed the door open. Ben Canaan was sitting on the edge of his bed with his elbow on his knee and his head bowed, resting on his clinched fist. At first Todd was unsure what the General was doing but then he saw his lips silently moving. He was praying. The scene infuriated Todd, and he felt an immediate need to escape. Since his mother had died, Todd's attitude towards God was a constant battle. In Lionel, faith was constantly being shoved in his face, especially when he was in the palace, and it was a constant reminder that his own faith was questionable at best. He thought that being here, away from it all, would allow him a reprieve, but here was Ben Canaan bringing it to the forefront once again. Before he could retreat, General Ben Canaan looked up and spoke, "Is there something you need Lieutenant?"

"No." Todd's tone was indignant. The hero from moments before felt like a child that had just been caught doing something wrong.

Ben Canaan stood. He looked at Todd inquisitively.

"Debriefing for everyone should be over in a week. After that we will make arrangements for you to go back."

"Back where?" Todd questioned.

"To the palace." Ben Canaan growled.

"Is everyone going back?"

"No, they will be staying behind to help prepare for the next phase."

"Why?"

"Well, Zinn is still out there..."

"No, why am I going back?"

"I think that is the safest course of action at this point."

"I'm not going back until everyone else goes back."

"Todd, you've done well. You've defended your country but it's time for you to go back. Your father..."

"It's Lieutenant Heart. I more than earned that title today and you nor anyone else is going to strip me of it."

"Lieutenant..."

"No, I'm not done. This is bullshit! You have no grounds to send me back, do you?" Todd's last words were a challenge to Ben Canaan.

"Your return is not a punishment, Lt. Heart."

"Of course its a punishment! I'm being punished for being a Prince."

General Ben Canaan took a deep breath and sat back down on the bed. His chin rested on his intertwined hands and he sat silently for a moment scrutinizing Todd. Ben Canaan lifted his head and rested his hands on his knees.

"I speak with Commander West tomorrow and tell him that we intend to remain here while strategizing our next move. If he does not ask for your return then we'll let it be."

"And if he does?"

"Then I follow orders and so do you."

Todd stormed out. Todd knew that he should have waited for the General to dismiss him. He half hoped that Ben Canaan would stop him; he had a few more things he wanted to say. Todd was incensed. He had just brought down Lionel's biggest enemy and they wanted to send him to his room.

Todd didn't feel like partying anymore. He returned to the barracks and laid down. He knew he wouldn't be able to sleep.

Morning came and Todd returned to debriefing. He was finding that debriefing consisted of the same questions over and over again. The entire time he wondered if Ben Canaan had spoken with Chad. It irritated him that the decision rested in Chad's hands. He had not heard news of his father. Until now there had been enough action to keep his mind off of his father's condition. He felt somewhat guilty for not wanting to return to the palace, but he reasoned that there was nothing he could do if he was there anyway. Todd made a decision. If they did send him back, he was done. He would leave the palace for good. He had no doubt that he could make his own way.

As soon as debriefing was over, Todd debated whether or not he should seek out General Ben Canaan. He finally decided that if the General was going to send him home, then Todd wasn't going to make it easy on him. Todd headed off in the opposite direction of where he knew Ben Canaan was most likely to be.

Chapter 23

Noelle hurried to King Daren's office. The events of the last few days had caused quite a stir in the media. Reports were pouring out of Aldrich. Some were accurate, but most were sensational. Noelle would be meeting with the King to develop a press release and plan for questions. As she entered the vestibule leading to Daren's office, Shayla, his secretary greeted her.

"Ms. Rose, King Daren is waiting for you. You may go in."

Noelle thanked Shayla and proceeded to the office. Captain Woods stood outside the King's office. He nodded his head slightly in greeting, the stern expression never leaving his countenance. Noelle felt a sense of gratitude towards him for intervening when Commander Heart had assaulted Dawson.

She entered King Daren's office and waited for him to acknowledge her. He was reading something on his computer. He finished and looked up at her. She noted that he still appeared weary, but a hopeful look had taken the place of the forlorn one he had worn the past few months.

"Ms. Rose, according to the report I just read, our forces used King Benson's head in a game of football," Daren began.

Noelle smiled and replied, "Well, sir, that is what the press conference is for . . . to dispel some of the more melodramatic rumors."

"Yes. Have a seat, Ms. Rose." Daren ordered. "Commander West has been in contact with General Ben Canaan. This is what I want included in the press release."

As he spoke, Daren slid a piece of paper across the desk towards Noelle. King Daren had made sure that his palace was equipped with all of the latest technology. Each member of the council had multiple forms of electronic communication. However, the King still made a habit of writing down his thoughts as they came on various notebooks that he kept for such occasions. Noelle had once made the mistake of complaining that he did not send information electronically. She had been told that she was more than welcome to work somewhere else if she did not approve of the way things were handled in the palace. She had even been assured that a good reference would be provided. She never brought up the grievance again.

Noelle looked over the King's notes. King Daren had informed his Council Members of King Benson's demise and Prince Todd's involvement. Many of the council were still shocked that the prince had taken such a risk or even been allowed to. King Daren, however, had shown considerable admiration for his nephew's actions. Informing the public of Todd's involvement had been debated from both sides, but news reports coming out of Aldrich were accusing the prince of horrific atrocities. At this point, it would be best to set the record straight. The King's notes did just that.

"Sir, will Prince Todd be making a statement at any point?" Noelle questioned.

"General Ben Canaan is keeping the men at the base while they prepare for the next phase. I don't know when Todd will return. It won't be soon." Daren answered.

"I'm sure we don't want to make that public knowledge."

"No, we don't."

"Sir, is it wise for Prince Todd to remain so exposed?"

"He is surrounded by some of Lionel's finest. I have no concerns."

Daren's tone indicated that an argument would be futile, but Noelle was not one to let things go.

"Yes, sir. I understand that, but if they deploy again and Prince Todd is with them, will it not be dangerous for both him and those with him?"

Daren gave Noelle a warning look and answered, "Ms. Rose, I appreciate your concern. The matter is being taken care of."

"Yes, sir."

Daren's phone beeped followed by Shayla's voice, "Sir, Ms. Tracy is here to see you. Would you like me to send her in now or have her wait until you are finished with Ms. Rose?"

"Send her in." Daren's tone was flat.

"Yes, sir."

Daren turned his attention back to Noelle, "Ms. Rose, the press release you sent is acceptable. You can add my comments to it while I speak with Ms. Tracy. Stay here. I will look over the final release before you leave."

"Yes, sir."

Deanna appeared in the doorway.

"Ms. Rose, thank you. Ms. Tracy, have a seat."

Noelle moved to a small secondary desk that was in the office. Deanna did as the King had commanded.

"Ms. Tracy, what is it?" Daren questioned. Lately, visits from Deanna had been less than pleasant.

"Sir, as you know, funds have been quite strained lately. The attacks combined with the earthquake and now the military campaign against Aldrich have nearly drained our resources. And, it's not only the palace coffers that have been affected. The attacks and earthquake created a significant economic decline nationwide as well, Sir."

"Get to the point, Ms. Tracy."

"The point, Sir, is that we are broke. Unless a funding source is found or provided, we have reached our limits. Something has to give."

Daren had been the King of Lionel for twenty years. In those twenty years, his country had never experienced this type of economic difficulty. Daren was a frugal King, and he did not spend beyond his means. The country was based on a fair tax system where every citizen paid 10 percent of their income. There had always been more than enough to run the government, but the last few years had brought unforeseen calamities that had merged into the perfect economic storm.

Daren looked at Deanna, "Where can we pull from?"

Deanna sighed, "Sir, when I say that we are broke, I mean it. There are no resources left. I have been pulling from every possible direction over the past year, and I have been making it work. Doing so has left no funding for disasters or future military endeavors."

The king tensed just slightly at Deanna's last words. She seemed to notice and paused. Although the defeat of Benson had been a great victory, the knowledge that Zinn was still at large weighed heavily on everyone.

When Daren remained silent, Deanna continued, "I've funneled money into disaster relief over the past month, but the attacks and earthquake have affected jobs, building, and so many other areas. The amount coming in has declined and the amount going out has increased. In past years we would have had reserves to cover it, but not this time. The only short term solution I can suggest is to borrow from one of our allies, Sir."

"You know I won't do that."

"Sir, this is not the time to let pride dictate your actions. Your country is in need."

"Deanna, this is not a matter of pride!" Daren exclaimed. This had been a personal struggle for Daren and his tone was passionate as he continued. "As the King of Lionel, you know that I have done everything I could to honor God in all areas of my reign. Money has been no exception. I have been faithful to God, and He has been faithful to me and this country. I will not dishonor God by doubting him now. There must be something we haven't considered."

Noelle had been listening to the conversation between the King and his financial advisor. She had an idea that might help.

Noelle spoke up, "Sir, I have a suggestion."

Both Daren and Deanna seemed to have forgotten that she was in the room, and they both looked at her with dubious curiosity.

She continued, "Sir, you have shown great loyalty to the people of Lionel. It is time that they show their appreciation and loyalty to you as their King. Many may be suffering financial setbacks from the attacks and earthquakes, but I am sure that there are also many who are still flourishing. Ask them to help their fellow man. It would be an act of charity on their part. We would not be borrowing money, and it would give them the opportunity to share their blessings with those who have been less fortunate this past year."

It was Deanna who responded first, "Are you suggesting an additional tax on the people?"

Daren intervened, "Ms. Rose is suggesting that we give the people the opportunity to voluntarily help their fellow man. It would not be a tax, nor would it be mandatory. How are we going to make this happen?"

Noelle spoke up once more, "Sir, I also have an answer to that. The media is a powerful tool. Use it. We can set up a fund and then create public service announcements asking the people to donate. Media outlets could be asked to donate the time for the announcements. If they refuse, we'll pull their license."

Daren had been looking down as he listened to Noelle's ideas, but his head shot up at her last suggestion. He raised his eyebrows in question.

Noelle smiled and responded to his non-verbal inquiry, "Just making sure you were listening, Sir."

"I listen to everything, Ms. Rose. You and Deanna write up a proposal. Take it to Ian. Let him look over it and determine if there are any pitfalls or angles that have not been considered. Once he approves it, make it happen."

Daren addressed his two advisors, "Ms. Tracy, if there is nothing more, you may go. Ms. Rose, I need to speak with you."

Deanna rose to leave. Noelle waited for the King to continue.

When Deanna was out of earshot, Daren spoke, "Noelle, I am sure that the events of the past few months may have put a strain on your marriage. You and Mr. Moulder have been under a great deal of pressure. I want to reassure you that Dawson has been cleared of any involvement in the attacks. We will not be pursuing that angle any longer."

"Thank you, sir."

Daren noted that Noelle looked troubled, and he continued, "I realize it is difficult to separate your role as my advisor from your role as a wife. I want to thank you for handling your role as my advisor so well. Things will not always be so difficult."

Daren's phone rang. The ring-tone indicated that it was a direct call, and there were only a handful of people who had King Daren's direct number. Daren looked at the caller ID and sighed. He dismissed Noelle and picked up the receiver.

"Gavin." Daren's tone was dry.

"Daren. Congratulations. Expanding your territory, I see. I'm sure the rest of the world won't mourn the loss of Benson," Gavin sneered.

Daren ignored Gavin's accusation. "The days ahead will be difficult. I am sure that Trevor will have his share of troubles. I hope that he can count on you for your support."

"Of course. I have no issues with Trevor." Gavin sounded sincere, and it surprised Daren. Sincerity was not one of Gavin's characteristics.

Daren decided to push the envelope. "You have overcome your heritage, Gavin. Perhaps you can help Trevor do the same."

Gavin ignored the comment. "It seems that Gable has found a way to retain his power. Marriage to the Queen of Nivan assures him a spot in the ICP as well as making him an instant King."

Daren had heard of the union between Queen Leah and the former President of the Unified States, but he had not had time to give it much thought. Gable had proven himself to be a cunning creature, and Daren was sure that the marriage was not based on love.

"Right now, I still have other threats to occupy my time. As far as Gable is concerned, I'm sure it's love, Gavin." Daren quipped.

"And I am sure that we will both be keeping an eye on him." There was no humor in Gavin's tone.

Daren noted that Gavin had ignored the reference to Zinn. Gavin was likely to refrain from getting involved where Zinn was concerned, but Daren hoped that he would at least provide any information he may have been privy to. He wondered if Gavin had spoken to Queen Alyssa regarding the rumors that Zinn was in her country of Cashteh. Early in Gavin's reign, Mikasa had suffered domestic attacks on some of its landmarks. Gavin had since been very careful to avoid making any new enemies.

Daren gave a noncommittal response to Gavin's comment regarding Gable, "Indeed." He then changed the subject. "How are Megan and Silas doing?"

"They are fine." Gavin did not elaborate.

"Well, thank you for your call. Have a good day, Gavin."

"Daren."

At that, both men hung up. As usual, the conversation had gone well until it turned toward personal issues. For the millionth time, Daren questioned why his sister had married that man.

Chapter 24

Chad stepped out of the shower and began drying off. Before he could finish, the door opened and Ashley barged in. He instinctively covered himself. Ashley gave him her "seriously" one eyebrow raised look, and he felt rather foolish. She usually was not up this early. He had found that although he loved his wife dearly, her constant chatter in the mornings grated on his nerves, especially these days when his responsibilities had multiplied immensely.

"You are up early." Chad stated matter-of-factly.

He waited for her usual deluge of non-stop chatter, but her reply was unusually curt.

"I have a lot to do today."

She then began getting undressed to take her shower. Chad wanted to question her uncharacteristic behavior, but he knew that if he stayed in the room, neither of them would make it to work on time. He decided to wait until she was showered and fully dressed for further inquiry. Chad sat down to eat his breakfast. He thought about the day's events ahead of him. He then realized why Ashley was up so early. An unbidden pang of jealousy swept over him, and he quickly pushed it away. He then decided it might be best if he were gone when Ashley emerged from the bathroom. His realization had come too late though. She was headed his way. His plan was to kiss her goodbye and then leave, but pride overcame his will.

"Do you plan to call and congratulate him?" he questioned.

"What?"

Ashley was trying to feign ignorance, but Chad was not deceived. Every instinct was urging him to leave and let it go, but indignation held him back. Ashley had been busying herself with filling a pot with water. For all appearances, she was fully focused on her task, but when the water began overflowing, her ruse was foiled. She quickly turned off the water, poured out the excess and put the pot on the stove. When she headed for the refrigerator instead of giving him her attention, Chad's annoyance increased to aggravation.

"Ashley?" It was only her name, but the tone behind it spoke a thousand words.

"Do you think I should? I mean, it probably would be a good idea for someone from Lionel to show their support. Lance will most likely send something over, but a phone call might be good as well. Maybe I should ask Lance what he thinks. What do you think?"

If he didn't know her better, Chad would have thought Ashley to be one of the most cunning people he had ever met, but she was actually teeming with innocence. His accusation had inadvertently turned into a suggestion that she was seriously considering. If she did call Trevor to congratulate him on his coronation, it would be as a result of his own stupid pride. Chad sighed and shook his head. His aggravation was dissipating in the wake of his wife's unwavering ebullience. The water had begun boiling rapidly, and Ashley turned to take it off the stove. Immediately, the water calmed to a slow, steady boil. When she turned back towards him, Chad grabbed her and pulled her close.

He kissed her and then answered, "I think that a call from King Daren to another King would be most appropriate."

Ashley had thrown her arms around Chad's neck and was looking up at him smiling. She replied, "And this is why I married you. I love you."

At her comment, Chad lost all desire to go to work. He briefly considered dragging his wife back to the bedroom, but it was already late and he was the Commander. He kissed her once more.

"I love you too. Talk to you later?"

"Lunch?" Ashley looked hopeful.

"I will let you know. It's . . ."

"Busy." Ashley finished for him.

Their time together had certainly been reduced since he had become Commander. Chad felt guilty about that, but there was not much he could do. He gave Ashley an apologetic look and headed for work.

Chapter 25

Daren's children were ready and waiting, but his Queen was not. He walked to the bedroom once more to check on her progress. She was sitting in front of the mirror. Still. She looked beautiful to him even after fifteen years of marriage.

"Nicole, it's time to go." Daren insisted.

Nicole spoke to Daren's reflection.

"We will be on time. Don't rush me. I'm not going to let you be late for your birthday celebration."

Daren knew that pushing the issue would only delay them more. He left the room and rejoined the children in waiting.

In the past, the king's birthday had been a cause for celebration. No expenses were spared despite Daren's insistence on a low-key event. This year, however, there would be little celebration. Yes, Benson was dead, but after five months there were still no leads on Zinn's whereabouts. The economy was slowly recovering, but not enough to justify unnecessary expenses. This year Daren would celebrate his birthday with his family and council at a moderate dinner.

Nicole finally emerged from their room. Daren was sitting on the sofa with Emma on his lap. He gently pushed Emma off of his lap and stood.

Daren addressed his children, "Wait outside with Captain Woods for us."

Noah and Emma responded with "yes, sir," and Kiley rolled her eyes. Daren's attention was on Nicole, so he missed his daughter's less than respectful expression.

Once the children were gone, Daren wrapped his arms around his wife's waist and leaned in to kiss her. She truly was stunning, he thought. He knew that he had taken her for granted many times over the past month, but he also knew that her training had prepared her for the life of royalty. He took a moment to enjoy their brief time alone. She had chosen a shorter simple dress of mint green with black trim. Her hair was elegantly piled on top of her head with wavy, loose tendrils of blonde framing her face. Her skin was almost porcelain contrasting beautifully with her blue eyes. Black high heels finished off the look. It was a good look, Daren thought, although he had never seen her look anything else.

"Happy birthday, husband."

"Thank you. Just once I would like to enjoy my birthday, alone, in a room, with my wife. Let's get this dinner over with."

Daren kissed Nicole once more before they headed out.

Noah and Emma nearly bounced down the hall ahead of Daren and Nicole. Noah would pick Emma up and throw her over his shoulder. She would scream, and he would eventually set her down. Kiley sulked behind. Emma's screams were getting louder each time, but they were screams of joy. Daren found himself enjoying the sound of happiness. He only wished that Kiley could enjoy herself as well.

When they arrived at the dining hall, Nicole held everyone back while she fussed over Emma's clothes and hair.

Daren looked at his son, "Tuck your shirt in, Noah."

"Yes, sir."

As Noah fixed his shirt, Kiley spoke up, "If you hadn't run down the hall like an animal, it wouldn't have come untucked in the first place. You're acting like a child."

Noah simply laughed and moved threateningly towards his twin sister, "Are you jealous Kiley? Do you want me to throw you over my shoulder and spin you around? Come here! I can lift you."

Kiley backed away giving Noah her sternest look, "Don't you dare! Mom!"

Daren was the one who intervened, "Let's go. We ARE late." He shot an accusatory glance at Nicole. She just smiled.

"Dad saved you this time, but you're in for it after dinner," Noah threatened.

As Daren and his family entered the room, everyone rose to their feet. Originally this dinner was going to be with family only, but as most of the family were either absent or ill, council members and their spouses had been added to the guest list. Christopher had remained in a coma since his collapse. Although Chad seemed to be handling his new position fairly well, the Commander's absence was deeply felt. Todd was still away with General Ben Canaan. They had followed several leads in an attempt to find Zinn, but so far all had been dead ends. The high the entire country had felt at Benson's fall had long since diminished with the failure to locate Zinn. Kelly, since her father's illness, had practically locked herself away. Brandon was still away dealing with the disaster relief from the attacks. Daren took his seat and then everyone else sat.

Those who had arrived early or on time had been enjoying appetizers of tea smoked chicken, and grilled pear, brie and honey crostini. Once Alan saw that the King had arrived, he began bringing out Cesar salads. When all the salads had been delivered, Daren turned to Pastor Isaiah.

"Pastor, please bless this food for us." Daren requested.

Pastor Isaiah began, "Our Father, we thank you for the many blessings you have bestowed upon us. We thank you for another year of life for our King and ask that you continue to bless him, his family and his reign with goodness and mercy. We acknowledge your sovereignty and place our faith in your provision. We trust in your promise to give us hope and a future and ask that you give us strength during our times of trouble. Father, we ask you to bless this food that you have so graciously provided. We give you all honor, glory and power. We ask these things in Jesus name, Amen."

"Thank you, Pastor. Everyone, enjoy," Daren offered.

Noelle addressed the Queen, "Queen Nicole, Princess Ashley and I were just discussing the progress of the public announcements. Quite a bit of money has come in as a result of them."

Ashley interjected, "Yes, and Ms. Rose was just suggesting that we could do one together. What do you think Aunt Queen Nicole . . . or would it be Queen Aunt Nicole?" Ashley teasingly questioned.

"If you think it will inspire people to give more, then I am more than willing. God has been very faithful in blessing our efforts. Has there been any news from Prince Brandon on the progress of the relief efforts?" Nicole inquired.

It was Ian who answered her question, "Queen Nicole, the efforts are going well. Apparently there was a chasm created that is close to half a mile wide. It has cut off several crossroads, and they are working on getting that area functional again. As a result of the money donated through the announcements, a lot of machinery has been able to be brought in to move the earth and reposition things."

"That's good. I am glad that we have been able to do something to help," Nicole responded.

Various conversations continued around the table as they enjoyed their salads. When enough time had passed, Alan brought out the main course. It was Daren's favorite: spaghetti with browned butter and mizithra. It was not the healthiest meal, so Daren rarely allowed himself the pleasure of enjoying it.

Ashley had taken two bites of her dinner when she suddenly slammed down her fork and turned to Chad, "Where's my sister?" she demanded.

"Probably in her room," Chad answered.

"She should be here. Why isn't she here? She's family. Did anyone tell her about this? Did you?" Ashley continued.

"No, I believe the guest list was Ms. Corin's responsibility. Have you talked to Kelly recently?"

"Yes, a few days ago, on the phone. What about when you went to check on her? Did you tell her then? What did she say? Did she seem okay?"

"Ashley, if you are worried about her, you should go see her yourself. I am sure that she has told you the same thing she told me.

She's upset over your father's condition as well as the fact that Todd is still away."

"That's not a good enough reason to not come to a family dinner, especially this one."

"You will have to take that up with her." Chad responded.

Ashley sighed and returned to her meal. She was worried about Kelly, but there was not much to do about it right now. It would be rude and unacceptable to get up and leave, so she would have to wait until dinner was over to check on Kelly.

The sound of Trevor's name caught her attention. Ian and Lance were discussing King Daren's recent decision to rejoin the ICP. Chad started to say something to Ashley, but she shushed him.

Lance was talking, "The next meeting is in two weeks. I still haven't heard back from Councilor Hathaway regarding our request to rejoin."

Ian responded, "Does Trevor know that King Daren is rejoining in an effort to help him?"

"I've been in contact with him. His situation is difficult as it is without the added stress of other countries demanding retribution for his father's actions. He has already demonstrated evidence that he is not like his father, but still Benson raised him. I just hope that he doesn't tire of trying to do things differently and decide that his father's way was easier." Lance answered.

Ashley had been hoping that Lance would take her to the upcoming ICP meeting, and this was her chance to plead her case.

She spoke up, "I think Trevor just needs a little encouragement from those who support his efforts. We could take some time during the ICP meeting to talk with him about his options."

Lance turned his attention to her, "We?" he questioned.

Ashley gave him her most charming smile, "Two would be better than one, right?"

Lance looked towards the king to see if he had been listening, but the King's attention was focused intently elsewhere. Lance gave Ashley a non-committal, "Princess, we will talk about it," and then looked back at Daren to discern what had distracted him. Captain Woods was headed for the table. He approached Daren and then leaned down to whisper something to the king. Daren immediately stood.

The King looked at Sarah, Christopher's wife and addressed her flatly, "Sarah, come with me."

Without hesitation or question Sarah rose from the table and followed behind Daren who had already departed from the room. When she caught up with him, she gave him an entreating look. She did not want to disrespect the King by questioning him, but she was worried. This probably had to do with Christopher, and she didn't know if it was good or bad.

"Sarah, Christopher is awake. I don't know the details." Daren explained as he forged ahead.

The King had reassured her, and she chastised herself for allowing worry to overcome her. She had prayed for Christopher daily from the moment King Daren and Queen Nicole had asked her if she would consider marrying him. She had prayed for him hourly since his illness. God had given her a peace, and she had felt assurance that Christopher would recover, but even the devout Sarah experienced doubt sometimes. She silently raised a prayer now to God asking for forgiveness for her doubt and thanking Him for answering her prayers. She knew before they ever entered the clinic that Christopher was going to be okay.

Sarah glanced up at King Daren. His countenance was furrowed with apprehension. Even though it was not in her nature to address the king directly, Sarah felt compelled to reassure him.

"Sir, he will be okay." she modestly stated.

Her simple words stopped Daren in his tracks. He looked at this wisp of a girl with red hair and freckles who had endured a marriage with his brother. Here she was assuring him when she had just as much at stake. Her words and presence had a calming effect. He now realized that he had been ready to barge into the clinic with a barrage of questions for the doctor. This was not the time for that. Daren gave Sarah an uncharacteristic smile and continued for the clinic in a much better state of mind.

As they neared the door, Daren ushered Sarah through first. She immediately headed for Christopher's side. The doctor was with Christopher but stepped aside as Sarah entered. Daren entered the room but kept his distance. He had decided to play the part of observer until he better knew Christopher's condition. Dr. Xavier approached him.

"King Daren, Commander Heart awakened approximately 45 minutes ago. I waited to contact you to assure that his consciousness was permanent. His brain seems to be functioning normally, but he is weak and disoriented. I would recommend that he receive as little stimulation as possible for the time being," the doctor explained in a detached tone.

Daren took in what the doctor had said and then silently watched Sarah and Christopher. Christopher did look tired and weak. Daren wondered if he knew how long he had been out or remembered what had happened before his collapse. Daren waited a few moments before he addressed the doctor.

"Are we on the road to recovery or is there possibility of a relapse?" Daren questioned.

"Due to the nature of this illness, I would say that a full recovery will take time, but is more than plausible. Relapse is highly unlikely. Usually a patient will either die from the illness or overcome it. The commander has overcome it."

Tension that Daren had not realized had built up for months released. For the first time since the attacks, the earthquake, the economic strain, and Christopher's collapse, Daren allowed exhaustion to take over. His Commander, his protector, his brother and his best friend was alive and well. He had much to tell his brother, but it could wait. He determined that it would be best to allow Christopher a day of rest before announcing his recovery to everyone, but his plans were thwarted when he saw Ashley rushing through the doors of the clinic with Chad trailing behind. Daren quickly stepped outside Christopher's room to intercept them.

Daren positioned himself so that he was blocking the door. Hopefully Ashley had enough sense not to run him down and risk being tackled by Tyler. He wasn't so sure about that though.

Ashley exploded, "He's awake? Is he okay? Is he going to be okay? I want to see him. Why didn't you tell us?"

"He is okay."

Daren was both surprised and pleased when Ashley turned to Chad and threw her arms around him. He felt a strange reassurance that he had done the right thing in allowing them to marry. He did not want Ashley to follow in her mother's footsteps by seeking companionship elsewhere when Chad became too busy with the unending responsibilities that were a part of his position. He waited as they clung to each other. Ashley finally turned back to him. He could see the anticipation in her eyes, and he knew that asking her to wait until morning to see Christopher would be pointless.

He did warn her though, "Ashley, your father is still weak and disoriented. The doctor has warned against over stimulating him until he has regained some strength. Ashley, just . . . keep it calm."

Daren then stepped aside to let her and Chad pass. The room was rather small, but he followed them in. The doctor had stepped out. Ashley made her way to the side of the bed opposite of Sarah along with Chad. Daren joined Sarah. Ashley grabbed her father's arm.

"Dad, how are you feeling?" Ashley asked as calmly as possible.

"Like crap," Christopher answered.

His brother was certainly back, Daren mused.

Ashley responded, "Well I don't know why. You've been asleep for like six months! You should feel fully rested."

Daren shot Ashley a warning glance. He noticed that Chad had also grabbed her arm in an effort to restrain her.

Daren looked at Sarah and indicated for her to move aside, "May I?"

Sarah quickly moved out of the King's way.

Daren placed his hand on Christopher's forearm and addressed him, "It's good to have you back. Do what the doctor says. I need you fully recovered and I don't want your stubbornness impeding progress."

When Christopher made no response, Daren knew he really must feel like crap. Daren gave his arm a squeeze and exited the room.

All Daren wanted to do was go back to his room and sleep, but everyone at the dinner would be waiting to hear what the emergency was. Daren reluctantly made his way back to the dining hall. The look on everyone's face as he entered the room was somber, and Daren was grateful that he had encouraging news to share.

"Please, sit down," Daren commanded.

Daren remained standing as he addressed them.

"Commander Heart has regained consciousness. Doctor Xavier expects a full recovery in time. I am ordering that only family visit Christopher until the doctor feels that he can handle more. For now, Chad will continue in the position of Commander, but knowing Christopher, it will be a short-lived role. Circumstances are improving. Now, if money would just fall from the sky, our problems would all be solved. I thank you for joining me in my birthday celebration. God has given me quite an impressive gift today. I will not be staying for dessert, but I urge you to fully enjoy it before retiring. Noah, Kiley, Emma, you may stay if you wish. Nicole, we're going. Good night."

Nicole rose to join her husband. She noted that he looked both relieved and tired at the same time. She felt no need to question him further regarding Christopher. If he said Christopher would be fine, then he would. Daren never misled his family or council even if only to reassure them. He may not tell them everything if he felt it would spare them unnecessary anxiety, but he wouldn't tell them a lie.

His uncharacteristic quip had made her smile, and she questioned him on it now.

"You expect money to fall from the sky?"

"Why not. One should never limit God. Manna fell from the sky for the Israelites. Why could money not fall for the Lions?"

"I suppose you are right. As always."

"Of course I am. Nicole, I am going to sleep when we get to the room. You can give me my birthday gift in the morning."

Nicole knew that Daren must be completely exhausted. Her gift was one that only a wife could give her husband, and Daren never passed that up. Daren was true to his word. Within ten minutes of reaching their suite, he was in bed asleep. Nicole breathed a sigh of relief for her husband and thanked God for a reprieve.

Chapter 26

Ashley stayed with her father until he went to sleep. It had scared her and Sarah at first when he fell asleep, but the doctor had reassured them that he had not slipped back into a coma. Chad had left to go to his office. Ashley knew that he probably wanted to make sure everything was perfect before her father returned. With Christopher asleep, Ashley questioned Sarah if Kelly had been informed of their father's recovery. Sarah was not sure, so Ashley decided to find Kelly herself.

Ashley pushed the call button for Kelly's suite and waited. When Kelly didn't come, Ashley pushed it again. Still, no one answered. Ashley walked to the end of the hall and questioned the guard.

"Have you seen my sister, Kelly?"

Lieutenant Franklin responded, "No, ma'am. As far as I am aware, she's in her room. I've been here for 5 hours, and the person before didn't mention that she had left. Not that we'd think she did. I don't think she's left her room for months. We were getting worried about her until Commander West checked in."

Ashley sighed.

"Thank you, Lieutenant. Open her door, please."

"I don't know if I have permission to do that, ma'am."

"I am a princess. My husband is your Commander. My uncle is the King! Don't make me call them both just so that I can check on my sister!"

"Yes, Ma'am. You don't have to get all crazy about it. I was just trying to follow protocol. Probably get in trouble now."

"Just open the door."

As soon as Franklin had the door open, Ashley barged through. The room was dark. She found the light and turned it on. Ashley looked around. The room was spotless. Usually her sister was a bit of a slob. Clothes would lay wherever she took them off. Empty and half-filled glasses would be found where Kelly last used them. Neatness was not Kelly's strong suit. Not finding her sister in the common area of the suite, Ashley headed for Kelly's bedroom. When she reached it, she found the door locked. Ashley was getting slightly annoyed with her sister at this point, but she was also a bit worried.

She knocked on the bedroom door and called, "Kelly, are you in there? Kelly, open the door."

Ashley thought she heard movement, but the door remained closed.

She continued, "Kelly, dad is conscious. He's going to recover. You need to go see him. Kelly, open the door!" Ashley waited. "Kelly, I swear I will go get Chad to tear this door down if you don't open it right now! Are you okay? Kelly!"

The door opened and Ashley found herself staring at a ghost. Kelly's complexion had lost its zest. She looked almost ashen, and there were dark circles under her eyes either from crying or lack of sleep. Even more alarming though was the perfectly rounded belly bump Kelly was trying in vain to hide with a laundry basket she was holding. Ashley grabbed the basket from Kelly and threw it on the floor.

"Kelly, what is that?"

When Kelly stood motionless and silent, Ashley continued with concern in her voice, "Are you pregnant?"

"It would seem so," Kelly uttered.

"How?"

"How do you think, Ashley?"

"Who did this to you?"

"It wasn't like that. We . . . love each other."

"Love? How long have you been in here? Who is it? Does he know?"

"Yes, love. I don't know what else to say, Ashley."

"Well, you could start by explaining how this happened. Dad's going to kill you! Does Chad know about this?"

"I had sex with a man, Ashley! That's how this happens, and no, of course Chad doesn't know."

"So, nobody knows about this?"

"Well, you do now."

"Kelly, what have you done? Are you going to marry him? Who is it?"

Kelly just shook her head, and it infuriated Ashley.

"What do you mean, no? No, you're not going to marry him? You really don't have much of a choice, Kelly. WHO is it?"

When Kelly refused to answer, Ashley went back into the hallway and summoned Lieutenant Franklin.

"Tell Chad that I need him here, now."

Franklin gave Ashley a questioning look but didn't argue.

He spoke into his earpiece. "Commander West, Princess Ashley is requesting your presence in hallway H, suite 211."

Ashley couldn't hear Chad's response, but she heard Lieutenant Franklin say, "I don't think so, sir. She seems rather distraught."

"Just tell him to get down here!" Ashley nearly yelled and then darted back to Kelly's room.

Chad was halfway down the hall when he heard Ashley's frantic voice.

He picked up his pace and entered the room just as Ashley said, "If this is about love, then why aren't you marrying this guy? Why won't you tell me who he is?"

The cause of Ashley's panic was immediately obvious. He felt guilty, but all Chad could think about was the fact that Commander Heart's daughter, the King's niece, was pregnant, and it had happened while he was in charge. This was a situation that no amount of training had prepared him for. Unsure of what to do, Chad waited for Kelly to respond to Ashley's question.

Kelly remained silent, and Ashley turned on him.

"You checked on her just days ago! Did you not see that she was pregnant? You need to find out who did this!"

Chad looked to Kelly and inquired, "Are you pregnant?"

Out of the corner of his eye, he saw Ashley's eyes nearly pop out of her head. Before Ashley could say anything, Chad continued,

"Obviously you are. Who is the father? When did this happen?"

Ashley chimed in, "How far along are you?"

Kelly finally responded, "I don't know. Probably six or seven."

Chad actually felt a modicum of relief. If Kelly was six months pregnant, then she became pregnant before Christopher's illness. He then felt guilty for focusing so much on his own dilemma rather than on Kelly.

"Kelly, we need to know who the father is. Did I hear right that you love him?" Chad questioned.

"Yes, I do."

"Then a marriage will be arranged and all will be well."

"Is that before or after Dad kills the guy, Chad?" The comment came from Ashley.

"I'm sure that your father will be angry at first, but he will eventually come around."

"Really? You think so? This is going to throw him back into a coma!" Ashley spurted.

"That's a bit extreme, Ashley. Kelly, who is it?"

"I don't know," Kelly replied.

Ashley exploded all over again, "What do you mean you don't know? Is there more than one possibility?"

"NO! I do know. I just . . . "

"Just what?" Ashley asked.

"I just don't want to tell anyone," Kelly stammered.

Chad intervened, "Kelly, you will have to tell someone at some point. For right now, you should see the doctor. Your father is in the clinic though, and I don't think it would be good for him to see you like this right now. I'll go down and make sure the curtains are drawn to his room so that you can come down, or I will see if it is better for Dr. Riverdale to come here."

"I don't want to see a doctor."

"Well, that's just tough," Ashley responded for Chad.

Chad left happy to have a mission that took him away from Kelly and Ashley. He knew that his next stop would have to be King Daren's suite. He considered waiting until morning to inform the King rather than risk waking him, but felt that Daren would want to know immediately.

Lieutenant Kraft was stationed outside the King's door. Chad approached him.

"Has King Daren retired for the night?" Chad inquired.

"Yes, sir. I believe so."

Chad was hoping that the answer would be no. Nevertheless, Chad pushed the call button for the King's suite. As he waited for someone to answer, Chad could see that Lieutenant Kraft looked perplexed. If the King was angry at being awakened, both Chad and Kraft might be paying for it tomorrow.

It was Queen Nicole who came to the door. Chad was caught off guard and took too long to speak to her.

She raised an eyebrow and questioned, "Commander West, I trust you have a good reason for being here at this time of night on Daren's birthday."

"Yes, ma'am. There's been a . . . development that requires his attention."

"Is someone's life at stake?"

If Christopher found out that someone had impregnated his daughter, there might be, Chad thought.

"No, ma'am. Not at the moment."

"Has someone been injured? Are we under attack? Has there been a natural disaster?"

"No, ma'am, not exactly, but it is something that King Daren should be informed about."

"Will telling him tonight rather than tomorrow change the circumstances?" Nicole continued.

"No, ma'am. Probably not." Chad was beginning to feel a bit foolish in the wake of the Queen's interrogation.

"Commander West, King Daren is asleep. Unless this is an emergency that needs to be dealt with immediately, I feel it is best not to wake him. I will take responsibility for that decision. Good night, Chad."

With that, Queen Nicole shut the door.

Chad was exhausted. Since he had left the King's suite, he had gone to check on Ashley and Kelly in the clinic, waited while the doctor finished the exam, and then escorted Kelly back to her suite. It was nearly 3:00 in the morning, which meant he might get 3 hours of sleep if he was lucky. After delivering Kelly to her room, Chad had sent Ashley back to their suite while he stopped to talk with Lieutenant Franklin. The lieutenant seemed to have no useful information regarding Kelly.

Chad entered his suite fully prepared to strip to his boxers and fall into bed. Ashley had other plans.

As soon as he came through the door, she broke into a diatribe.

"How did nobody know about this? How is it that my sister, a princess in the palace, can be six months pregnant, and nobody knows about it?"

"Ashley, everyone just assumed that she was upset over the attacks, your father, and Todd. She's always kept to herself, and under extreme circumstances, it was not farfetched for her to withdraw even more."

"Is that your excuse? And you, of all people, to assume that she's just hiding because of the events that have taken place! I don't understand, Chad. I thought you checked on her!"

"I did, and she told me what I just told you. Exactly what, Ashley, would ever give me the idea that she might be pregnant? She obviously hid it well when I went to see her."

"You're the Commander. Shouldn't you be able to pick up on things like this? Shouldn't you know when someone is trying to hide something?"

Ashley's words wounded Chad's pride, but he was determined not to respond in anger. He had every right to. He had never expected to get married and then be handed the role of Commander less than a month later. He was doing everything he could to keep it all together.
However, he also knew that Ashley was upset about her sister, and he just happened to be the one she was taking it out on. They both needed sleep, and that would be his current goal.

"Ashley, I know you are upset about Kelly. I am sorry that this happened. Fighting about it right now is not productive. We both need some sleep. Tomorrow is going to be a long day."

"My sister is pregnant, Chad. We don't know who the father is, and she's seventeen years old. By law, Chad, she will have to marry this guy!" Ashley paused and a look of dread appeared on her face, "Unless he's married! Chad, what if he's married? What if that's why she doesn't want to tell us? Don't tell me to go to sleep!"

Every scenario had already raced through Chad's mind. One of Lionel's virtues was its strong commitment to the sanctity of marriage. Though some would consider their laws and policies antiquated, Lionel remained a leader in two-parent homes, a nearly non-existent STD rate, extremely low crime rates and a superior education system. That was not to say that there was not the occasional scandal, even in the palace, but the laws were clear, and King Daren had a history of making an example of anyone who neglected them. Once the father was discovered, he would have to marry Kelly. If he was already married, as Ashley had suggested, then the man's wife would have the option of forgiving him or allowing his execution. It greatly concerned Chad that Kelly refused to reveal the father. It meant that she had something to hide. Beyond the harsh laws regarding matters such as this, there was also Commander Heart to worry about. He was very protective and demanding where his children were concerned, and Chad felt a brief moment of pity for the man who had dared dishonor the Commander's daughter.

Chad tried to reassure Ashley. "We will find out who the father is, Ashley. Believe me. It's done though, and it can't be taken back. No amount of fretting or fighting is going to change that. I am sure she will need your support over the next few days. Come and lay down with me."

Ashley threw her hands in the air.

"I can't believe you're so calm about this! I can't sleep right now! My dad is going to lose it. He's had enough to deal with - everything with my mom, my brother, and now this. And you want me to sleep? My sister is not ready to be a mother!"

Ashley had been busying herself with putting away dishes. As she spoke her last sentence, she slammed both of her hands down on the counter. Chad came from behind and put his arms around her in a protective gesture. He could feel that her body was full of tension, but as he rubbed her arms she seemed to relax somewhat against him. After a few minutes, he turned her so that she was facing him.

"It's going to be okay. It will be hard, but it will be okay," Chad soothed.

Chad didn't feel as confident as he portrayed, but Ashley needed him to be strong, so he was. As Ashley's eyes teared up, Chad pulled her closer and just held her.

Chapter 27

Daren waited outside the room while the doctor finished his check-up on Christopher. He knew Christopher was feeling better because he was arguing with the doctor about something. Daren considered what a good fit Dr. Xavier was for the palace. The man had virtually no personality to speak of, but he also had no problem handling the more difficult members of the palace, including Daren himself.

The doctor exited the room. When he saw Daren waiting, he stopped.

"King Daren, Commander Heart is rapidly recovering. I would release him today if I thought he'd follow orders once he was back to his suite. He won't, so he is staying here."

"Thank you. Is he well enough to handle distressing news?" Daren inquired.

"Princess Kelly's pregnancy? There's no danger of Commander Heart relapsing. The news may raise his blood pressure, but I see no reason to withhold the information."

Three days ago, Daren had been looking forward to having a conversation with his brother after so many months. Now, he was dreading it. Daren entered Christopher's room and pulled the doctor's stool over to the side of the bed. He sat down. Sarah had brought Christopher sweatpants and a t-shirt to put on. Christopher was sitting up in bed wearing them. Daren could see that the illness had taken its toll on Christopher's body. He had lost much of his muscle tone, and the clothes hung loosely. The sight was disturbing to Daren and reminded him of pictures he had seen of prisoners of war. Christopher had always been strong. Daren couldn't help but think that the strength of all of Lionel was faltering and Christopher was a symbol. Financial failure mixed with the attacks and failure to find Zinn had left the spirit of his country emaciated as well.

"Finally found some time in your busy schedule to come see me?" Christopher groused.

"Well, it's nice of you to finally wake up."

"Hmph."

144

"You just couldn't get the flu like a normal person? Had to get meningitis?"

"I'm surprised that you managed to function without me."

Daren ignored the comment. He was not going to admit that he had been worried and had needed his brother on more than one occasion over the past six months.

"We have six months to catch up on. Let's get started," Daren stated. "I know you are aware that Chad and Ashley are still married although your untimely illness has certainly put an unexpected strain on their marriage. Chad has done well overall."

"Of course he has. He was well-trained."

"And your son has become a national hero."

"When will he return?"

"He's on his way back. He will be here in a few days."

"It doesn't take a few days to get here from the border of Aldrich."

"No, but he and Ben Canaan were making a stop on the way."

"Where?"

"General Perelli's."

"Hmm."

Sarah had told Christopher about Todd's actions in Aldrich. For the first time in his life, Christopher had felt proud of his son. He hoped that Todd would continue to make him proud and spending time with men such as Ben Canaan and Perelli was definitely a good path for him.

For the next hour, Christopher and Daren talked business. Christopher had missed a lot of important events, and he needed to be brought up to speed in order to do his job. The point finally came where Daren knew that he could no longer stall the inevitable.

"Christopher, was Kelly dating before you became ill?"

"There was someone she wanted to date, but she didn't."

"Who?"

"Wade Dupree. He was severely injured in the attacks. She went to see him in the hospital. Why are you asking?"

"Was there anybody else that you are aware of?"

"No. Why? What's going on?"

Daren took a deep breath and leaned forward, "Christopher, Kelly is about six and a half months pregnant."

It took a moment for Daren's words to sink in, but Daren knew the moment that they did. Christopher's face turned a deep crimson. He threw his legs over the bed and stood up.

"Where is she?!" he bellowed.

"Sit down."

"You just told me that my daughter is pregnant. I'm not sitting down."

As he spoke, Christopher had been pulling at the IV in his arm. Tyler was right outside the door, and Daren could call him in at any moment, but for now he thought the best plan of action was to keep the atmosphere as calm as possible. Daren remained in a seated position as he tried to reason with his brother.

"Christopher, sit down. There is nothing you can do about it right now."

Daren knew what Christopher was feeling. He had wanted to rip someone's head off himself when Chad had first told him.

Daren continued, "Besides, we need information from Kelly. I need you to talk to her and try to find out who the father is. You need to be calm when you do. She's not talking to anyone else."

Daren himself had briefly tried to talk to her, but her stubbornness had begun to aggravate him. He knew she had been through quite a bit of turmoil lately, so he had tried to be gentler with her. He had decided to leave before he lost his cool.

Christopher was still standing, but he had stopped pulling on the IV. He stood motionless for some moments and then stumbled back towards the bed. He was still weak. The news and his subsequent reaction had exhausted him. Daren saw him stagger and jumped up to help him. Christopher allowed him.

Back in bed, Christopher looked Daren's way. He breathed a hefty sigh and asked, "Does no one know who she was seeing?"

Daren had remained standing after assisting Christopher.

"Dawson has gone through hours of footage. There's nothing. At least nothing that we can find, and I don't understand why Kelly is refusing to reveal the father. It's not making me very happy."

There were only a few reasons that Daren could think of that would cause Kelly to be tight-lipped about the identity of the father. He was married. He held a high-ranking or respected position, which he would certainly lose possibly along with his life. Or he was somehow an enemy of Lionel. The more Daren thought about it, the more he wanted answers. The fact that the father was not stepping forward himself made Daren even angrier. When they did find out his identity, he might not be long for this world.

Christopher knew that Daren's last statement held a masked threat. Daren did not like deceit or dishonesty, and Kelly's lack of cooperation would be seen as such. Although he was angry over what Kelly had done, Christopher loved his daughter, and he knew that it would be in her best interest to cooperate.

"Have her brought to me. I'll talk to her."

"That's probably a good idea. Maybe you should rest a little more, and I'll have her brought later. We will talk again tomorrow."

Christopher nodded in agreement. Daren turned and left.

Chapter 28

Her father had returned, and that meant that Todd was also somewhere in the palace. After greeting her father, Becca had made her way to the dining hall hoping that Todd might happen to be there. She couldn't wait to see him. The entire country was heralding him as a hero. She had nearly idolized him even before he went away, but now that he had taken out the man responsible for her mother's death, Todd was her own personal hero.

She was disappointed when she reached the dining hall. Todd was nowhere in sight. She wasn't really hungry, but there was a chance that if she hung around long enough, he would eventually show up. She walked towards the serving area.

Todd's head was about ready to pop off his shoulders. Everywhere he went in the palace, people were congratulating him, giving him high fives, patting him on the back and shaking his hand as though he were a celebrity. He was a celebrity. He always had been, but now he had done something that was making people take notice of him for more than just his heritage. And, to top it all off, he had a pretty girl on his arm. He was at the height of his glory.

He was taking Hannah to the dining hall where she would wait for him while he went to visit his father. They entered the hall together. Todd reveled in the fact that every single person's head turned as he passed by. He lifted his head, stuck out his chin and walked tall. When they reached the serving area, Todd stopped and turned to Hannah.

"Sorry, we don't have any pretzels, but you can take what you want," Todd explained. "Just find a seat in this area when . . . "

Todd had stopped mid-sentence. A mass of strawberry blonde curls had caught his attention. Becca had her back to him and was talking with Ms. Hembrooke, the palace teacher.

"Hey, it's Becca! Come here. You've got to meet her. You can eat with her," Todd said as he practically dragged Hannah along.

Todd came up behind Becca and lightly tugged on one of her ringlets. "Hey weed girl."

At the sound of Todd's voice, Becca's heart had skipped a beat. A broad smile covered her face as she turned to greet him.

She didn't say anything, and neither did Todd for quite some time. His jaw almost dropped as he stared at her.

It was Hannah who broke the silence, "Oh my gosh, Becca Ben Canaan? Of course that makes sense. General Ben Canaan is here. You would be too. Duh. Oh my gosh. It's so good to see you!"

Hannah threw her arms around Becca to hug her.

"You look great, Becca. Wow. Todd is going to talk to his father. Wanna grab some lunch and catch up?"

Becca knew from Todd's letter that he had met Hannah and was interested in her. Becca didn't know that Hannah was coming to the palace with him. Becca tried hard not to feel jealousy towards Hannah. She had known her most of her life, and they had been friends when their fathers worked together. Hannah was good.

Todd found his voice, "Becca, you've changed." His tone held disbelief.

Becca smiled and first answered Hannah, "Of course. I'd like to eat lunch." She then looked to Todd, "What do you mean?"

"You're just . . . different. What'd you do? Eat fertilizer?" Todd was trying to come across as indifferent to cover the odd frustration he was feeling. Becca was definitely taller. She must be wearing different make-up, Todd thought. Her body had curves, rather generous curves. Todd tried not to stare at the curves. After all, this was weed girl, General Ben Canaan's daughter.

"No," Becca responded.

"I am so hungry," Hannah interjected. "Come on, Becca. This food looks delicious."

Hannah ushered Becca away leaving Todd standing alone. He watched them for a moment and then became aware that there were still other people around. He remembered that he needed to go see his dad, and he left.

****

Todd had been looking forward to seeing Becca and introducing her to Hannah, but things had not gone as planned. First of all, he did not realize that Hannah and Becca already knew each other. It made perfect sense, and it irritated him that he hadn't put that together. Secondly, Becca had changed. He had only been gone six months, but it was like she was a completely different person. He was not prepared for that, and he didn't like it. He couldn't quite describe it. She was grown up or something, but that description seemed childish. He started to wonder if there were other changes. Was Becca dating someone? Probably not. She would have asked her father, and he wasn't available. But then what if this new Becca wouldn't ask. Why did he even care? The whole situation was frustrating him. Todd had unconsciously been making his way toward the palace clinic. As he neared it, the air became more sterile as he breathed it in. The smell of alcohol and disinfectant shocked his senses back to his current mission, and he put thoughts of Becca aside in anticipation of seeing his father.

Christopher was sitting up in bed eating when Todd entered, and for the second time today, Todd found himself completely caught off guard. His dad looked dreadful. Todd really hadn't thought too much about this moment. In fact, he had spent the last six months trying to think about anything except his father. The sight of Christopher's weakened form brought the reality of his father's condition crashing down on him.

Todd couldn't speak. Guilt and something more were overwhelming him. It was almost a feeling of embarrassment at seeing his father in this condition. Todd, who had taken on Benson and his forces face to face now wanted to run from the room like a little child who had seen something he shouldn't.

Christopher spoke, "Son, I'm glad you're home."

Todd was surprised at the sound of his father's voice. While his body seemed weakened, his voice still held its customary strength and confidence. It helped Todd overcome some of the awkwardness he was feeling, and he stepped closer to the bed. For several moments, both father and son silently stared at one another.

Christopher spoke again, "I'm proud of you, son. You did well."

"I didn't get kicked out," Todd retorted and then immediately felt stupid for saying it.

"No, you didn't, but you did prove yourself a man."

"Well, I would've been here, but I was kinda busy."

Christopher recognized the guilt in Todd's response. "Son, I was in a coma, and it is good to know that while I was laying here useless, my son was carrying on my legacy."

Todd held back the smile that was threatening to form. "Well, somebody in this family had to do something useful."

"Benson's defeat is a great victory - both for Lionel and Raxx."

Although his father's words were meant as a compliment, they were also a reminder that there was still another victory that was needed. All intelligence suggested that Zinn was still on the run, but Todd wondered how long it would take him to regroup and retaliate again. The sooner they could eliminate him, the better. His entire unit had been chomping at the bits to find and take Zinn out, but their enthusiasm had dwindled as week after week and eventually month after month had passed.

Christopher's next words brought Todd back to the moment, "You've heard about your sister?"

"Ashley?" Todd raised an eyebrow. "What? Is she already over that loser?"

Christopher chose to ignore Todd's disrespect towards Chad. "No, not Ashley. Kelly."

Todd was confused and immediately concerned. Had his father found out about Kelly's relationship with Newberry? He hadn't planned on being able to discuss Newberry's death with his father, but if he already knew then it would be a relief to Todd. Still, Todd was careful.

"What about Kelly? What did ugly do now?" Todd and Kelly had playfully insulted each other with the nicknames "ugly" and "stupid" since they were old to enough understand the meanings of the words.

Todd was totally unprepared for Christopher's response.

"Your sister is pregnant."

Todd stammered, "She's pregnant? Who?"

"She didn't tell you?" Christopher knew that Kelly rarely kept secrets from Todd.

"I haven't been here, so no."

"You were here when it happened."

"What's that supposed to mean?"

Christopher was feeling confident that Todd was as clueless as he was as to the identity of the father. Normally, Christopher would not have shared information so easily with Todd, but for some reason, Todd's actions in Aldrich had changed his perception of his son's ability to handle things. "Kelly is almost 7 months pregnant. She won't tell us who the father is, and no one has stepped forward."

For the first time, things were going well with his father and for the first time, Todd didn't want to do anything to jeopardize his relationship with his father. The news about Kelly frustrated and saddened him. He was fairly certain he knew who was responsible and should tell his father, but Kelly was his twin sister and they had always stuck together. He needed to talk to her first, so for now, Todd ignored the news his father had just shared.

"You know you look terrible. You should probably do something about that. I've gotta go."

Before Christopher had a chance to respond, Todd was gone. He made a brief stop before making his way to Kelly's room.

Chapter 29

Todd's talk with Kelly had been brief. He had confirmed that Newberry was indeed the father. She had agreed to tell their father about Newberry once the baby was born, and he had agreed to keep it a secret giving her time to grieve. He had then sat awkwardly as Kelly blubbered over the letters from Newberry that he had brought her. Todd was relieved when a call from General Ben Canaan gave him an excuse to depart.

Todd wanted to find Becca. Well, he wanted to find Hannah who was with Becca. He wanted to find them both. Todd found the nearest security guard and demanded Hannah's location.

Lieutenant Franklin rambled excitedly as he tried to locate her. "Well, I don't know who Hannah Perelli is, but I will in just a moment when I pull up her picture and this thing tells me where she's at."

Todd took an interest in the device that Franklin was using. He had never seen one before, but he guessed it was a part of the new security system that Mr. Moulder had been working on. He was as anxious as Franklin to see it at work.

They waited a while. Todd looked from the device to Franklin. The Lieutenant's expression never changed. He wore a perpetual smile that was offset by an outdated afro that he refused to get rid of. Looking at him no one would ever guess that he was the best shot in the palace. A picture finally popped up. It was a picture of Deanna Tracy, the King's financial advisor.

"I don't think that's Hannah Perelli. Not unless Ms. Tracy changed her name, but I haven't heard anything about that. This thing doesn't seem to be working right. Guess we'll have to rely on some good ol' fashioned . . . "

Todd interrupted, "Could you just hurry up and find her?"

"I'm working on it. I can talk and function at the same time. By the way, heard you gave Benson a whooping. Nice job. Just give me a minute here." Franklin now spoke into his earpiece, "This is Lieutenant Franklin. I need a location on a Hannah Perelli."

Todd paced as he waited.

"It seems your Miss Perelli is at the pool," Franklin responded after a moment.

Todd left without giving Franklin a chance to say anything more. A smile crossed his lips. If the ladies were at the pool, that most likely meant bikinis. He picked up his pace.

Hannah was laying on one of the chairs in the sun. Todd noted that she did have on a bright pink bikini that she looked quite hot in. Her skin was tan all over and her legs looked even longer when they were bare. He looked around for Becca. He had seen her in a bikini several times, but that was before. He was curious to see if she looked as different with her clothes off as she did with them on. It was purely curiosity of course. He was disappointed. Becca was nowhere to be seen.

Todd walked to Hannah and questioned her, "Where's Becca?"

Hannah was listening to music and had had her eyes closed. She hadn't heard Todd approach, and when he spoke, it startled her. She thought he sounded irritated, but then she was learning that he often sounded that way.

She removed her ear buds and looked up at him, "Well, hello to you too. Did you see your father?"

"Yes. Where's Becca?"

"Well, it seems you have a one track mind. If you must know, some guy came by and she took off with him. He was kinda cute. I'm pretty sure he might be related to you. I think I've seen him in pictures before, but there are so many in your family, I can't keep track of them all. Anyway, she showed me here because I said I would like to lay out, and then she left."

"How long ago was that? I thought she was going to stay with you."

"Todd, it's fine. You don't have to worry about me. I could lay out here for hours soaking up the sun and listening to music. I'm not hard to please. So, should I go in and get a shower? What's the plan?"

"Yeah, go take a shower." Todd walked with Hannah as she headed to her room.

When they arrived, Todd turned to Hannah and spoke, "I'll be back in about an hour. See you then."

"Sounds good. Looking forward to it."

As soon as Hannah's door shut, Todd set out on a hunt for Becca. He couldn't imagine who she was hanging out with. Becca didn't hang out with people and especially not with any of his family members. Hannah must have gotten it wrong. Maybe it was Dr. Xavier. Becca sometimes went down to the clinic to work with him. His looks could be easily be mistaken for royalty, Todd thought. With that in mind, Todd changed his course for the clinic. He could have stopped and asked security to locate her, but for some reason, he didn't want to. It was none of their business.

On his way to the clinic, Todd passed by one of the sitting

rooms. Becca was sitting on a couch alone with her back to the hallway. He entered the room to find Wesley, his cousin, sitting on the floor in front of Becca. Wesley had several books and papers spread out in front of him. It looked like he was working on some sort of project.

Todd ignored Wesley and addressed Becca, "What are you doing?"

Todd's tone was accusatory.

Becca looked up at him. Todd thought she looked concerned and he regretted his tone.

She answered, "We are working on a project. It's due next Tuesday."

"Becca, it's Saturday. Come on." As he spoke, Todd picked up Becca's books and put them in her bag. She had a notebook and papers on her lap. Todd grabbed them as well and stuffed them into the bag.

Becca protested, "Todd, I was working on that. I had it organized. Let me . . . "

Becca's plea disintegrated as she looked up at Todd. He was standing just above her looking down. He was staring at her. She suddenly felt self-conscious. She squirmed on the couch. She wanted to move, but he blocked any decent movement she might make. The moment lasted for only a few seconds, but to Becca it seemed like decades.

Todd moved away and growled, "Fine, get your stuff together. Let's go."

Becca had on a shirt that she had worn with him a million times before, but now she filled it out and from the angle he was standing, he could see, well, definitely more than anyone should see. She certainly had not had those when he left.

Todd suddenly felt the need to leave. Becca was fumbling around getting the rest of her stuff together while apologizing to his stupid cousin for having to leave. She was taking too long.

"Don't apologize to him. You were supposed to be with Hannah."

Todd realized that once again, his words were an accusation. He didn't care this time. He reasoned that he had left Hannah in Becca's care, and there was no good reason for her to be hanging out with Wesley instead, especially not with that shirt on. Plus, he had been gone a long time. Becca was his friend, not Wesley's, and they had a lot to talk about.

Becca had finally gotten her junk in the bag and was standing waiting. Todd looked at her and felt a pang of guilt. She looked like a wide-eyed deer staring at the end of a gun. He was the one holding the gun. He felt like a bully picking on the sweetest girl on the playground.

Todd grabbed her bag from her and tried to temper his previous outburst, "Becca, it's Saturday. It's time to have some fun."

His words had the intended effect. Becca's smile returned as she followed him out the door. They were walking side by side. Todd stopped and turned towards her. He pulled one of her curls. Her hair had always been so soft and springy, and he had made a constant habit of playing with it.

"Your hair is long."

"I probably should get it cut soon."

"No, don't." Todd felt foolish. Why did he care if she cut her hair or not. "I mean, do whatever you want. It just . . . looks nice. So, I noticed that there's still a major weed problem around here. I'm gone for six months and everything grows like crazy."

At his last comment, Todd had unintentionally glanced down at Becca's breasts. Realizing it, he quickly averted his gaze. Hopefully Becca hadn't noticed. She was still smiling so probably not. Todd turned away and started walking again.

Becca spoke up, "Thank you. Maybe I'll keep it long. Do you plan on pulling weeds now that you're back?"

"Where do you think we're going?" Todd had a playful look.

Becca was finding it difficult to talk to Todd. He seemed to constantly switch from being irritated to playful with her, and she wasn't sure if something was wrong or not. She had imagined many times what she would say to him when he returned. He had shared so much with her about his travels and the war in the letters he had sent. Some of it had been very personal, and she was excited that he had opened up to her so much. Now that he was back though, there was this unexplained awkwardness between them.

"Will Hannah be joining us?" Becca joked back.

"She's taking a shower." Once more Todd sounded irritated.

"Oh, okay."

Todd stopped walking again. He didn't know why he was having so much trouble talking to Becca. He gave himself a good mental kick in the butt and gathered his wits.

"So, Weed Girl, did you pass chemistry with an A or an A+?"

"Just an A. Couldn't pull the plus." Todd noted the disappointment in her voice.

He dramatically stopped and turned so that he was face to face with her. "Woah, is that the first time ever?"

"Maybe." She wouldn't meet his gaze and Todd found her embarrassment amusing.

"Did you cry?" he teased even more.

"Maybe."

"Seriously?" Instinctively he again reached out and pulled on one of her curls.

The gesture made her smile and she looked up at him with a slight smile. "It ruined my perfect record."

"Is this why you have the nerd tutoring you now?"

"What?" There was confusion on her face.

"Wesley. The big geek. The one that I'm pretty sure was adopted."

"You shouldn't talk about your cousin that way." They had continued on their journey and were now heading outside.

Todd opened the door for Becca as he replied, "He's not my cousin. Definitely adopted."

"Todd. He's a nice guy. And he's really smart."

"Nice and smart? Yeah, that's what I want a chick to say about me."

"He's not bad looking either."

Todd tried to sound unconcerned but his tone suggested otherwise. "Seriously? You sound like you are actually interested in him."

Becca noted the concern and looked at Todd questioningly. "Maybe."

"Maybe what?"

"I might be interested."

Todd tried to determine if Becca was just playing with him. She had her flippant moments, but they were few and far between. She wasn't looking directly at him, but she didn't have that cute little smirk she always wore when she teased him either. She was serious.

"Let me give you a visual Becca. A date with Wesley is sitting in side by side rocking chairs reading books."

"Not every date."

"Um, yes Becca, every . . . Wait, are you actually dating him?" Todd had stopped once more in his tracks, but this time the drama was not feigned.

"Well, not right now, but we have."

Todd relaxed as he remembered that this was Wesley they were talking about. "Oh, this is going to be good. Tell me about your date. Details, lots of details, Becca."

Todd was actually frustrating Becca now, and she finally made eye contact with him. Todd was looking at her with one eyebrow raised, and he was barely holding back his laughter. It should have angered her even more, but his sparkly blue eyes that were regarding her with great interest melted away any frustration she had. His jawline angled down towards his perfectly rounded chin. He had full lips that were pursed together in an effort to suppress his amusement. His dirty blonde hair had grown out a little while he had been gone and was tousled on top of his head. She inadvertently let her eyes move down his body. He was tall, but not quite as tall as his father. He had filled out some. He had always been in good shape, but the intense training he had received in preparation for war had toned him even more. She suddenly had a longing to see him with his shirt off. She chastised herself for such a thought and focused her attention back on his face. The amusement had disappeared from his eyes and mouth, and he was regarding her with a look that she did not recognize.

Unnerved by the look, she became defensive. "Does the thought that I have actually dated someone amuse you?"

They were moving into dangerous waters, and Todd was determined to keep the mood light. "Um, no Becca, the thought that Wesley has actually dated someone amuses me. And the possibility that you actually enjoyed dating him astounds me. You can do much better, Becca. You've been locked up in the palace too long if you think a date with Wesley is enjoyable."

"Well, I did enjoy it, and I think it's rude for you to criticize." Becca sounded serious.

"Woah, weed girl! Did you just speak your mind?" Todd was actually quite impressed.

"That's not my name, and yes, I did."

"Good job, Miss Rebecca Ben Canaan." Apparently the changes in Becca were not just physical. He liked this slightly more assertive version.

"Let's not talk about this anymore."

"I'm just saying that you shouldn't set your standards so low, Becca."

"Let's just drop it, okay?" A look of sadness or disappointment clouded over Becca's face. Todd wasn't sure why. Becca continued, "Listen Todd, I know you are with Hannah now, so I probably won't get a chance to talk to you too much and especially not alone. I just want to say thank you. I know everyone sees you as a hero, but what you did is especially heroic to me. So, thank you."

Becca's gratitude humbled Todd. "I just did what should have been done a long time ago."

"I'm sure there are a lot of people who are grateful."

Todd wondered how many others like Becca and Ben Canaan had been victims of Benson's cruelty. His brief moment of heroism paled in comparison to the pensive agony apparent in Becca's eyes at the mention of Benson. "Yeah, probably."

Something else Becca had just said bothered Todd, and he felt it was a good time to change the subject. "What does Hannah have to do with us talking?"

"Well, you will probably be spending most of your time with her."

Todd was feeling annoyed that Hannah had become a part of this conversation. For some reason he was feeling caged, and he didn't like it. He knew that no matter what happened, he didn't want anything to jeopardize his relationship with Becca.

"You and Hannah are friends, right? We can all hang out. So, did you kiss him?"

Becca sighed. "It's impossible for you to let this go, isn't it?"

"Pretty much so. Yeah. I suppose he could have read how to do it in a book. So, which is better Becca? Text book kissing or real kissing?"

Becca shook her head in exasperation. "I wouldn't know."

"You wouldn't know? Why? Never experienced a real kiss?"

"What time is it?"

"Trying to change the subject? What, do you have a date with the dork tonight?"

Becca ignored the question. Todd had looked at his watch when Becca asked. He hadn't realized so much time had passed. It had been almost an hour and a half since he had left Hannah. He wanted to talk to Becca longer, but he knew Hannah was waiting. He felt torn.

"Becca, Hannah went back to her room to get ready for dinner. Let me walk you back to your suite and we'll come by to get you in 30 minutes," Todd instructed as he repositioned Becca's bag on his shoulder.

"For what?" Becca questioned.

"For dinner. You can make it up to Hannah for dumping her this afternoon." Todd stated.

"Okay. I hope she's not upset about this afternoon. I explained to her why I had to go."

Todd and Becca were now back inside and almost to Becca's room. Todd had taken Becca's concern as a statement and didn't feel the need to respond. For a short while, they walked in silence. Todd felt a heaviness that he couldn't quite explain. Maybe he was just finally coming down off of the high from the war. They had told him that he might experience depression eventually, but he had shrugged it off as beneath him. Maybe he was just tired. It had been a long day. They reached Becca's suite. Todd wondered if the General was there, and decided he didn't want to encounter him if he was. Again, Todd didn't quite know why he felt that way.

Todd handed Becca her bag "I'll see you in thirty minutes."

Chapter 30

Todd had been a little concerned how dinner would go, but Hannah's incessant chatter had assured that there were no uncomfortable moments. In fact Hannah had not seemed at all bothered when he told her that Becca would be joining them. Todd tried to focus on what Hannah was saying, but his attention seemed to constantly turn to Becca. She was wearing a sleeveless pink flowered top with a white skirt. The top must have been new because it certainly fit her better than the one she had had on earlier. When they had been walking to the dining hall, Todd couldn't help but notice the nice curve of her calves in the sandaled heels she was wearing. Hannah looked nice too of course, but Todd reasoned that it was the drastic changes in Becca that kept him so enamored with her. The shock of it all would eventually wear off, and they could go back to normal.

They were halfway through their meal when King Daren and his family entered the dining hall. Todd noted that Prince Noah had grown a bit taller since he had left. The kid was practically all arms and legs. Noah looked Todd's way and caught him staring at him. Todd nodded to Noah.

Noah elbowed his father and then said something to him. King Daren then looked Todd's way. The King motioned for his family to continue to the royal dining area and then headed directly for Todd's table with Noah following behind. Todd stood and waited for the King to reach him. Hannah remained oblivious to the situation and had continued jabbering on until Todd stood. She looked up at him.

"Are you going somewhere?"

Todd didn't bother to explain. He just looked at the two girls and ordered, "Stand up. Both of you, stand up."

Becca immediately followed his directions, but Hannah hesitated. Before he could say anything more to her, the King had reached the table. Hannah suddenly realized why Todd was standing and jumped up.

King Daren addressed Todd, "Lieutenant Heart. Todd. Good job."

Todd was waiting for more, but the King just stood there apparently waiting for a response. Todd looked around the room. Everyone was staring at him.

"You're welcome, Sir."

Daren grinned at his nephew's pompous reply and then turned his attention to Becca who was trembling in his presence. He couldn't recall a time when he had given her reason to fear him so much, but he reasoned that her experience in Aldrich with Benson had given her cause to fear any King.

Daren addressed Becca, "Miss Ben Canaan, I'm sure your father was happy to see you."

Becca's eyes were wide as she responded, "Thank you, I mean, yes Sir, he was. Thank you."

Noah had practically been dancing behind Daren. He stepped forward and looked at Todd expectantly as he asked, "What was Aldrich like? Did you really kill King Benson all by yourself?"

Todd could tell that the spoiled little prince was in awe of him. He decided to play it up, "Well, Aldrich was dark and dirty. Extremely creepy. You should have seen Benson's face right before I . . ."

Daren intervened, "Lieutenant Heart, who is this young lady?"

Todd was confused by the King's question at first. King Daren obviously knew who Becca was. He had just addressed her. Then Todd felt rather foolish as he realized he had forgotten Hannah was there as well. Todd turned to Hannah and ushered her forward.

"King Daren, this Hannah Perelli, General Perelli's daughter, Sir."

Daren noted the change in Todd as he switched from speaking to Noah to addressing his King. The military training and most likely Todd's experiences in Aldrich had changed his nephew. The arrogance was still there, but there was also an obvious respect present as well. Daren extended his hand to Hannah.

"Miss Perelli. Your father is held in the highest regard here. It's nice to meet you."

"Thank you, King Daren. My father has the utmost respect for you as well. It is an honor to be able to spend time in the palace. Thank you."

Daren addressed all three, "Enjoy your meal. Good evening."

As soon as Daren was out of earshot, Todd turned to Becca.

"He's not going to attack you, Becca. What is wrong with you?"

Becca breathed. Todd surmised that she had been holding her breath during their entire encounter with Daren. Becca looked at him.

"Nothing."

"Whatever. Let's finish our dinner."

Todd waited for both girls to sit and then sat down himself. Hannah immediately started gushing. Todd half-heartedly listened to her while scanning the dining hall. Noelle Moulder walked in. Todd looked around for Dawson, but didn't see him. Noelle got her food and sat down with Deanna. The dining hall was not very busy. It seemed that most of the palace residents were dining in. Todd was hoping that Chad and Ashley would show up. He was looking forward to an encounter with Chad. It probably was killing Chad that the entire country considered Todd a hero, and Todd fully intended to rub it in as much he could.

To Todd's disappointment, Ian was the next person to walk through the door. At first Todd ignored him turning his attention back to Hannah, but then he noted that Ian's walk was purposeful, and he was headed for the royal dining area. Todd knew that Ian would not interrupt Daren during dinner with his family unless it was urgent. Todd's curiosity piqued. This had to be about Zinn. As a member of the royal family, he had access to the royal dining area. He excused himself and followed Ian.

Daren saw Ian approaching. He stopped eating and waited. He doubted he would be able to finish the meal. It was never good when one of his council members interrupted dinner. A hundred dire possibilities had raced through Daren's mind before Ian ever reached the table.

Ian immediately addressed the King, "Sir, I apologize for interrupting your dinner, but there's been an unexpected development."

"Get to the point, Ian. What's happened now?"

Daren pushed his chair away from the table as he spoke. He didn't stand, but his hands tightened on the arms of the chair as he waited for the inevitable bad news.

"Daren, all of our financial problems have just been solved."

Daren stood and anger flashed in his countenance.

"What have you done?" Daren demanded.

"Sir, I haven't done anything . . . " Ian started.

"Then who? I made it quite clear that I will not accept charity from another country!"

"No, sir, you don't understand. There are diamonds. They found diamonds in the crevices caused by the earthquake. Some of the land is owned privately, but much of it is protected and therefore belongs to you, to all of Lionel."

Daren sat down. Todd had never seen Daren look dumbfounded, but that was the only way to describe the expression on his face. The king sat completely still for several moments.

Daren finally looked up at Ian and questioned, "Is there at least enough to get Lionel back on its feet?"

"Sir, from what they are telling me, there is enough to at least relieve the necessity to go into debt. It won't allow for expanded spending, but with the money from the ad campaigns and the diamonds, it will be enough to provide for our immediate needs."

Daren stood once more. He looked around the room and then back at Ian.

"He continues to provide, Ian. Our faithfulness has been rewarded."

Todd stood by shocked as his uncle briefly embraced Ian in a man hug.

"Ian, call a council meeting. Immediately."

As Ian left the room to follow the King's orders, Daren turned to Nicole. Taking her hand, he pulled her up, threw his arms around her and kissed her. Todd suddenly felt uncomfortable and turned to leave. He felt somewhat guilty over the disappointment that had flooded over him that the news had not been about Zinn. He hadn't fully realized the extent of the financial crisis Lionel must be in. He knew he should be happy about the discovery, but he was still being ruled by revenge. He wouldn't be happy until Zinn was found and taken out just as Benson had been.

Todd headed back to his table. Both Hannah and Becca were still there, and that annoyed him. Hannah was still chattering away.

Todd interrupted her, "Let's go, Hannah. It's late. I'll walk you back to your room." He then looked at Becca, "Good night Becca. See you later."

Todd thought he noted a brief look of disappointment on Becca's face, but it was quickly replaced with her usual accommodating smile.

"Good night Hannah. It was good to spend some time with you. Good night Todd. I'm glad you are back."

"Thanks. Hannah, let's go." Todd demanded.

"Just a minute," Hannah retorted. "I have to say goodbye to my girl, Becca."

Hannah gave Becca a hug, "Good night. It was good to see you too. We'll have to get in some more pool time tomorrow. I'll call you around 9, okay?"

Becca nodded in agreement as Todd guided Hannah away.

All the way to the room, Hannah never stopped talking. She only stopped once they were at her door.

Todd turned to her, "Do you hear that?"

"What?"

"Shhh, listen."

They both remained silent as Hannah tried to hear whatever it was Todd was talking about.

She couldn't contain herself anymore, "Todd, what exactly am I listening for?"

"Silence. It was actually quiet for a few moments."

Hannah playfully whacked Todd on the shoulder.

"Are you trying to say I talk too much?"

"Me? No. Of course not. I just think you don't fully comprehend the value of a moment of silence."

Hannah moved to whack Todd again, but this time he grabbed her hand before it hit its mark. Taking his gesture as an invitation, Hannah grasped his hand and moved in closer.

"I can appreciate silence," Hannah whispered.

She then moved in to kiss him. Her body was warm and soft. Her lips were smooth, and her perfume was almost intoxicating. Todd kissed her back impulsively. He was certainly enjoying the kiss, but something didn't feel right. He lingered a few moments more before pulling away. Hannah was smiling. Todd didn't know what to do. Hannah took his hesitation as an opportunity and moved in once more. Their lips had barely touched this time when Todd gently pushed her away.

"I should go." Todd stated. "Good night."

Todd pushed the button to open Hannah's door and ushered her in. Before she could speak, he shut the door and left.

Chapter 31

Daren sat looking at his council members. He couldn't remember the last time he had seen any one of them smile, and now they were all joyful and ecstatic over the news of the diamonds. Christopher had managed to make it to the meeting, and even he had an optimistic look.

Prince Brandon was the one who had made the call to Ian. Brandon had left Pilnez immediately following the call and was now at the palace in route to the council meeting room. As soon as he arrived, they would begin working out details, but for now Daren let his council enjoy the moment.

Daren noted that Deanna was wiping her eyes with a tissue. He knew she had been working nonstop for quite a while now to keep things running. She would still have a lot of work to do, but hopefully it would be less stressful and more enjoyable.

The warning light on Daren's console lit up indicating someone was at the door. Daren opened up communications.

"King Daren, Prince Brandon has arrived." announced Captain Woods.

"Let him in," Daren ordered.

When Brandon walked in, Daren hardly recognized him. The look of mischief that he always wore was gone. He looked more man than boy; even his clothing suggested maturity. He was wearing a black suit with a cream colored shirt that was unbuttoned at the top. Daren wondered if he had underestimated his brother; perhaps he should have given him more responsibility sooner. Either way, Daren was thrilled that Brandon was finally stepping up.

Daren stood and greeted Brandon. He then quickly filled him in on what they already knew and asked if Brandon had any further details.

Brandon spoke to the room, "The first diamonds were found by a farmer who was cleaning up his fields from the damage of the earthquake. One of the smaller fissures had broken through part of his land. It had filled with water and debris. The farmer wanted to have the water and soil tested for pollutants. He started digging up the soil in and around the fissure. He found the first three diamonds. News spread quickly and others started searching. Our focus had been on decontamination within living areas, so not much work had actually been done within the fissures. When I heard about the farmer, I put together a team of men to explore the conservation areas that had been affected. The team came back the same day. They had explored only a 50 square foot portion and found more diamonds. Based on what they found, we are going to continue to excavate the entire area."

The room grew silent as Brandon's last words sunk in.

Daren stood, "It is important at this time to acknowledge God's grace. He has provided both through the generosity of our citizens and now by turning tragedy into triumph. Let us not make the mistake of failing to give Him the glory. It is now time for us to be still and know that he is God. Tomorrow will be a day of fasting and prayer for the entire country. We will set aside a week for feasting, celebration and thanksgiving to commemorate this time of blessing. Alan, make plans and then meet with Ian to determine the dates."

Daren assigned responsibilities for preparation to each of his advisors. He then turned to Brandon.

"Brandon, stay here for the next few days. You and I will discuss this and then you will go back to Pilnez to oversee the mining process. I am also giving you the authority to appoint someone to take over the relief process. Contact Christopher directly with any security needs you may have." Daren then addressed his council, "Before we dismiss, are there any other items we need to discuss?"

Lance spoke up, "Perhaps we could work on making Aldrich our ally rather than our enemy. Trevor is the king now, and although I wouldn't trust him any farther than I can throw him, we certainly have more influence with him than we ever did with his father."

Noelle chimed in, "What are you suggesting, Mr. Sterling? Are we to give handouts to Aldrich? Won't that make us look like we regret attacking them? We will end up appearing weak."

Brandon was still in the room and decided to add his two cents worth, "Since when do we bribe our enemies? I'm gone for a few months and our values go to hell?"

Lance responded, "It is not uncommon for us to assist our allies. We have done so many times in the past. I'm not suggesting that we simply hand him cash, but rather that we identify some of the needs he may have in establishing his kingship and then assist in whatever subtle ways we can. Actually, our involvement would need to be kept to a minimum and done as delicately as possible. There are still many in Aldrich who have been brainwashed to loathe Lionel. They would not take well to a King who openly befriends Lionel."

Alan commented, "Some might oppose an alliance between Aldrich and Lionel on principle, but I guarantee that most would be easily swayed if it somehow benefitted them. Most people's loyalties are tied directly to the thickness of their wallets and the amount of prestige they can gain. Warren Benson was an evil man who made many enemies. I would deduce that most of Aldrich was happy to see him go. Whatever assistance we do give Aldrich will not only build an alliance, but more importantly will potentially help those who have been oppressed for far too long. If it is seen as bribery or a handout doesn't matter. The question rather should be - what is the right thing to do?"

Daren spoke up, "We need to find out what Trevor needs. Although God has blessed u in supplying our needs, we still need to be good stewards of our finances. We may be able to assist in ways other than monetary support. Lance, do you have any suggestions?"

"I could only conjecture, Sir. The best strategy might be to just ask him," Lance replied.

"Does Trevor even know what he needs? I am sure that he was not fully prepared for this turn of events. He might just be treading water at this point," Ian stated.

"We could send someone as an ambassador. They would need to be trained in logistics and be knowledgeable about Aldrich. Perhaps through discussions with Trevor, the ambassador could get a grasp on what Trevor's needs are and which ones we can help meet," Lance suggested.

Daren questioned, "Do you really think Trevor will be receptive to a representative from Lionel?"

"All we can do is suggest it to him and let him take the lead from there. It would have to be someone that he perceives as non-threatening."

"Who do you suggest?" asked Daren.

"Well, it shouldn't be anyone directly tied to the palace. I may need a little time to compile a list. Sebastian Taylor may be an option," Lance offered.

Noelle broke in, "Trevor seemed pretty cozy with Princess Ashley during his visit. She's being trained for this type of thing. Why don't you send her? I doubt Trevor will mind having her visit."

Christopher hadn't said much, but at Noelle's suggestion, he suddenly came alive. "My daughter is not going to be used as a pawn. It would be completely asinine to send her into a country that we just conquered. Have you forgotten that it was Ashley's brother who took out Trevor's father? How receptive is he going to be to any member of this family?"

Daren looked from Christopher to Lance and ordered, "Lance, give Trevor a call. Make the suggestion that Ashley go there. See how he responds. That will be our answer. If he seems receptive, then she goes. And Christopher, we can discuss this in private. We have a celebration to prepare for. Good evening. Alan, I need to speak with you before you go."

As the rest of the council members made their way back to work, King Daren and Alan discussed plans for the celebration. As the palace relations advisor, much of the preparation would fall on Alan. Daren noticed that Chad was still lingering in the hallway.

"Commander West, is there something you need?" Daren questioned.

"Yes, sir. I will wait until you are finished."

"This may take a while Commander. Speak your mind."

"Yes, sir. Sir, I understand the reasoning for possibly sending Ashley to Aldrich, and if you truly feel that it will benefit Lionel, then I trust your judgment. However, I would like to request that I accompany her if she goes."

"Chad, I don't see any reason why you shouldn't go."

"Thank you, sir."

Chad didn't leave, and it took Daren a moment to realize why. Now that Christopher had recovered, Chad was technically no longer the Commander.

"You are dismissed."

Chapter 32

After leaving Hannah's room, Todd had decided that he needed to take a walk. It seemed that news of the diamond fields discovery had spread rapidly throughout the palace. Everywhere he turned was crowded with people talking about the discovery. He finally decided to go outside. What the heck was wrong with him? He was a national hero. He had come home with a beautiful girl on his arm. His father could have died, but didn't. On the other hand, his sister was pregnant with a dead man's baby, and his other sister was married to a wannabe. And Becca, Becca was "dating" his stupid cousin. Gosh, she looked good. How could someone change so much in such little time. Thoughts of Becca made him wonder what she was doing. He felt bad that he had left her after dinner. Then again, why should he feel bad? It's not like Becca didn't know where she was going. She was a grown woman, fully grown woman, after all. And why the heck did he not enjoy kissing Hannah? Well, he kind of enjoyed it, but it just seemed wrong. He then wondered what it would be like to kiss Becca. Ugh, Wesley was her first kiss. Disgusting. He was probably feeling guilty because if he had been here, then Becca and Wesley would never have been an issue, and he could have saved her from that disaster. He needed to see her. Maybe talking to her would help.

Todd walked in circles for probably half an hour more before finally heading to Becca's room. Hoping that the General was not back yet, he pushed the door pager. He waited several seconds, but no one answered. He pushed it again. This time he heard a crashing sound followed by an "ouch!" Then the door opened.

Becca stood before him. She had on her pajamas: pink pajama pants that tied at the waist with a white tank top that showed off all of her assets.

"Todd? Is something wrong?" Becca asked. "Todd?"

"Becca, I just wanted to tell you good night."

"Oh, okay. Good night."

Todd had gathered his wits. "What was that sound? Are you okay?"

"Yes, I'm fine, but I'm not sure about the lamp."

Todd pushed past Becca into the suite. A lamp was on the floor. The shade was crushed and the bulb broken. Todd picked up the lamp and set it on the table.

"Becca, were you angry with the lamp? Did it do something to you?"

"It failed to turn on when I needed light and then it impeded my pathway to the door."

"It seems the General's daughter has anger management issues. Did you get hurt?"

"No. Only my pride a little."

Todd wanted to stay in the room with Becca, but he knew that would be unwise. He walked back to the door and and leaned on the frame with one arm.

"It's really good to see you," Todd stated.

"You too. I missed you. You're the best friend I have here. I got all your e-mails."

"Yeah, me too. Thanks for keeping me up to date on everything here."

Todd reached for one of Becca's curls. She moved closer.

"I missed these curls. None of the guys have any like this." Todd joked.

Becca smiled.

"Are you happy that you went?" She questioned.

"I am. It's where I needed to be."

Becca smiled again. She was so beautiful. Todd found himself leaning forward involuntarily. He touched her face. It was soft. He slid his fingers to the back of her neck and pulled her forward gently. Without hesitation he leaned down and kissed her.

Everything in Todd's world suddenly seemed to come into focus. His heart was racing, and a feeling of euphoria swept over him. No anger, no sadness, no joy, no passion of any kind had ever come close to the feeling he was experiencing. Becca's body against his, her lips pressed to his, the rapt synchronization of the beating of their hearts together felt like home. There was a comfort in this moment, and somehow, surprisingly, he knew instinctively that Becca reciprocated these feelings. She had been his closest friend, but he had never until now seen how much more she could be. The realization terrified him as he realized how far this could go if he let it.

Todd reluctantly broke off the kiss and gently moved Becca to a less enticing position. One hand remained on her waist while the other stroked her cheek. Feeling that words would taint the moment, Todd simply stared at Becca with a newfound awareness. At first Becca seemed to be sharing the feeling, but then without warning, she pulled away. Her face became a mixture of embarrassment and fear. Not understanding her reaction, Todd's impulse was to reassure her, but before he could speak, the cause of her anxiety became quite clear.

From behind Todd, General Ben Canaan addressed his daughter, "Becca."

Although the General had not raised his voice as he spoke her name, Todd could sense in his tone a mixture of anger and confusion. They were still in the doorway of the suite, and Todd had been leaning back against the frame. He now stood to his full height but did not turn around. He longed to hold onto this moment, and to turn and face Ben Canaan would be giving it up.

Becca seemed frozen. She remained silent.

Ben Canaan continued, "Becca, go inside."

Todd's desire for revenge against King Benson had been strong, but it paled in comparison to the desire he felt right now. Becca had reacted to the General's command, but with determination, Todd turned towards the General placing himself next to Becca and taking her hand. Todd thought the General's head was going to pop off. Then Becca abandoned him. Giving Todd an apologetic look, she slipped her hand out of his and went inside closing the door behind.

Todd knew that the General was overly protective of his daughter. However, there really was no reason for the General to be upset about what had just happened. Todd was, after all, a prince and a national hero. Besides, he and the General had spent some quality time together lately and had an understanding, reasoned Todd. They would simply have a man to man talk.

"What the hell do you think you are doing?" Boomed Ben Canaan.

Apparently, things were not going to go as smoothly as Todd had hoped. He wasn't sure how to respond to the General's question.

In response to Todd's hesitation, General Ben Canaan continued, "I don't care who you are or what you've done, I will not stand by and allow you to take advantage of my daughter, or of General Perelli's daughter, for that matter."

Todd had completely forgotten about Hannah in light of the events with Becca. It was quite obvious though that the General however, had knowledge of his recent tryst with Hannah. "Crap," Todd thought.

"I'm not taking advantage of Becca. This is different." Todd argued. The General's accusation had flustered Todd, and both his tone and stance became defensive giving him an air of arrogance rather than his intended sincerity.

Misinterpreting the Prince's intention, Caleb let loose, "I understand that you are on top of the world right now, Todd. The whole country is singing your praises, and I am sure that you think you can have anything you want. Well, son, pride comes before a fall, and if you so much as look at Becca again, I don't care whose son or nephew you are, so help me, I will make sure she is the LAST girl whose heart you break!"

"Come on . . . I can't believe this. Hannah kissed ME! It's different with Becca." Todd was emphatic.

"You're damn right, it's different. Becca is MY daughter, and whatever happened here tonight is over."

General Ben Canaan started for the door, but Todd blocked his way. "It's not over. It's just begun. You're not going to stop us, and I wouldn't hurt Becca. She's my best friend."

"Lieutenant Heart, get out of my way!"

Todd didn't move.

"I just gave you an order, Lieutenant."

"Really? That's your way of dealing with this? You're just going to pull rank on me? Well, I have rank too, and right now . . . "

Todd stopped. A momentary look of defeat and pain had flashed across the General's face. It was gone just as quickly, but it had been there. The look threw Todd for just a moment, but he continued.

"If I want to date Becca, I will, and no one is going to stop me."

Todd was done. The General could try to stop him, but it would be futile. Feeling he had made his intentions clear, Todd stormed away.

Chapter 33

For probably the hundredth time, Chad had come into the Commander's office. He was like a mother hen, Christopher thought, and it was about to drive him crazy. He listened half-heartedly as Chad explained to him yet another insignificant decision he had made during his brief stint as Commander. If Chad was ever going to make it as a Commander in the future, confidence was definitely an issue.

"Captain West, unless I question you directly about something that happened while I was away, I don't want to hear about it. It's pointless to appoint a standing Commander if it means I have to waste time listening to him second-guess every decision he made upon my return. So, shut up, and get out of my office."

At least his son-in-law was smart enough not to argue.

As Chad turned to leave, Christopher's secretary, Lieutenant Bailey, paged him, "Sir, General Ben Canaan is here to see you."

Christopher's mood instantly lightened. He had been looking forward to hearing Caleb's account of the Aldrich mission.

"Send him in."

Christopher stood as his top General and friend entered the room. The men shook hands and then Christopher invited Caleb to sit.

Christopher spoke first, "It's good to see you Caleb. I want to thank you for keeping an eye on my son. I know you've been debriefed on the mission, but I'd still like to hear about it first person."

"Commander, I will certainly give you an account, but I'm actually here for another, somewhat related reason."

"What is it, Caleb?"

"Well, sir, I am concerned about Todd and how he's handling his fame."

"Caleb, my son is not a stranger to superfluous attention." Christopher's tone was a dismissal of Caleb's concern.

"No, Christopher, but he's never dealt with this kind of attention before. He's gone from being directionless and irresponsible to national hero in less than two months time. I'm worried that he's letting it go to his head."

"Caleb, you know well that members of my family are not necessarily known for their subtlety. Is there something specific that concerns you?"

"It's just a lot for a young man to take in, and he may be overstepping his bounds and abusing his power for selfish gain."

This made Christopher bristle. "General Ben Canaan, what exactly are you accusing my son of?"

Caleb looked uncomfortable, but he continued, "It seems that Todd . . . well, I'm not sure how to say this delicately, Christopher. . . "

"You're not one to worry about delicacies, Caleb."

"Sir, your son is playing both Hannah and Becca with no regard for the consequences. When I confronted him about it, he insisted that he would do as he pleased."

"Playing?"

"Yes, playing. Becca and Hannah both deserve better, and I won't stand by while Todd sows his oats by leading them on. It will only end in heartache for both of them. It's not right, Christopher. I know he's your son, and I know he's a Prince, but that doesn't give him the right . . ."

"Caleb, stop now." Christopher's tone was controlled but firm. "What has Todd done to make you think he is playing anyone?"

"In the space of less than an hour last night, your son felt compelled to give both girls a long kiss goodnight."

Christopher exhaled audibly. He had only been back at his desk for two days, and his body was still weak from the illness. He knew that the only reason Caleb cared about Todd's exploits was because Becca was involved. This would be tricky.

"Caleb, I am sure that Todd has no intentions of hurting Becca, but you have to understand that she's not a child anymore. She will have many experiences, and heartache will most likely be one of them. I am sure they will work it out."

"Christopher, I know you've been out of commission for a while now, but dismissing an obvious issue is not a solution. I will not allow your son to take advantage of my daughter!" Caleb was emphatic.

Christopher saw that his attempt to pacify Caleb had fallen flat. He empathized with the General, but Caleb was over-reacting. Additionally, Caleb's allusion to Christopher's recovery was a low blow.

"Caleb, I can think of much worse things than Todd and Becca getting together. I will talk to Todd about his intentions. They have been friends for quite some time now; I will make sure Todd understands the value of a lasting and true friendship."

Christopher's words seemed to reassure the General. Caleb mumbled unintelligibly and stood. Christopher, disappointed that their conversation had not been more amenable, quickly dismissed the General.

Caleb's reaction to a possible relationship between Todd and Becca had disappointed Christopher and injured his pride a little. He was Caleb's Commander, but he also considered Caleb a friend. A friend that he had hoped would consider his son a suitable match for Becca. It was clear to Christopher that Rebecca Ben Canaan would be good for his son. Her calm and gentle nature was the perfect contrast to Todd's strong-willed spirit. With a little more maturity, he felt that Becca could be the stabilizing factor that Todd needed. Considering it now, Christopher realized that she had already had quite an impact on Todd just as his friend. He hoped that Todd's interest in Becca was sincere.

Christopher pushed the intercom button, "Lieutenant Bailey, find out where my son is."

"Yes, sir."

"Also, bring up Hannah Perelli's security information."

"Yes, sir. Prince Todd is in your suite, Sir. Would you like to see him?"

"Yes, but I'll go to him. Do you have Hannah's information yet?"

"Sending it to your computer screen now, sir."

Background information and a picture appeared on Christopher's screen. The young woman in the picture was quite attractive. Christopher took a moment to scan through the information. It included family details, school records and extra-curricular activities. Hannah seemed well rounded, but Christopher already knew that Perelli would have high expectations for his daughter. She looked a little bit older than Becca, but according to the record, they were just a few months apart in age. The challenge now would be to talk to his son without starting a war.

Christopher rose from his desk and made his way out of the office.

"Bailey, reschedule any appointments I have for the next two hours. And unless Zinn himself shows up, don't bother me."

"Yes, sir. What about King Daren?"

"What about King Daren?" Christopher didn't wait to hear Bailey's reply.

Christopher entered the suite that he and Sarah still shared with Todd when he was home. Sarah was sitting on the sofa holding Austin. Todd was on the floor with David changing his diaper.

The sight threw Christopher off guard. Something was definitely going on with Todd. His son did not change diapers. This might be even more difficult than Christopher had anticipated.

"We have a changing table, Todd."

"Yeah, I know." Todd's tone was dismissive.

"Why are you on the floor?"

Todd didn't bother with a response. Instead, he picked up the dirty diaper he had just removed and chucked it at his father. Christopher caught it mid-air and cringed at the smell.

"Thanks, Todd. We need to talk."

"Seriously? You can't handle a dirty diaper?"

"I've handled plenty of dirty diapers, including yours. Caleb came to see me. It seems I'm still cleaning up your messes."

"You know what? I'm sick of this shit." Todd got up and started for the door.

Christopher blocked his way. He wasn't sure why he had provoked Todd; that hadn't been his intention. He held up his hands in a gesture of surrender.

"Todd, just stop. I want to talk to you about what happened last night."

"Not sure what you want to talk about. I'm pretty sure you know everything or at least think you do."

"That's why I'm here, son - to hear your side of things."

"Why? Have I done something wrong? What are you going to do dad? Ground me?"

Christopher had no idea how to handle this Todd. Todd's childish stubbornness still lingered, but he was a man now. Christopher decided to be direct.

"What are your intentions, Todd?"

"My intentions? I intend to walk out that door, get on my motorcycle and go for a long ride."

"And what about Becca and Hannah?"

"I don't think both of them will fit on the motorcycle with me." Todd snarked.

"Look Todd, I understand that you are pretty sure of yourself right now, and you have a right to be. You've done well. But son . . ."

Todd cut his father off, "Why does everyone keep saying that? You have no idea what I'm thinking, or feeling for that matter."

"Alright then, tell me." Christopher's tone held invitation rather than its usual accusation.

Todd relaxed. "Ben Canaan is overreacting."

"Becca is his world, Todd. He doesn't want her to get hurt."

Todd bristled once more. "That's not going to happen. Neither of you get it."

"You brought Hannah here."

"That's before I saw Becca."

Christopher could tell that his son was genuinely conflicted. Still, he questioned, "Were you comparing kisses?"

Christopher noted that the conversation was uncomfortable for Todd. Todd had been averting his gaze, but at Christopher's last question, Todd looked directly at his father before replying.

"No." Todd's answer was both sincere and adamant.

"Then I'll ask again. What are your intentions?"

Todd shook his head and looked up at the ceiling. "Hannah needs to go home."

Christopher felt relief. "Then you need to tell her before this gets out of hand."

"I wasn't trying to . . ." Todd's voiced trailed off. Christopher understood. He felt sympathy for his son. Letting a woman down was not an easy task. Killing Benson would pale in comparison.

"The longer you draw this out, the worse it will be." Christopher stated.

"Yeah. Are you going to move?"

Christopher realized he was still blocking the door. He moved aside.

"I could have gotten past you if I'd wanted to," Todd remarked as he exited.

At first it frustrated Todd that Caleb was accusing him of inappropriate behavior with Becca and Hannah. Todd had never intended for things to work out the way they had, and looking at it from Ben Canaan's perspective, Todd could, perhaps, understand the General's concern. Caleb had come to respect Todd on the battlefield, but when it came to Becca, Todd realized that the general still saw him as the bratty, spoiled teenager who had been sentenced to pull weeds as punishment under Caleb's supervision. Todd might even have to admit to himself that he had come across that way when speaking to Ben Canaan.

Todd hoped that Caleb would come to accept his interest in Becca as genuine, and he also hoped that Caleb's disapproval would not spill over into their work relationship. Todd was enjoying serving under Ben Canaan. Caleb had treated him with respect and given him the opportunity to prove himself. Todd still wanted to go after Zinn, and he wanted to be on Caleb's team. Todd had to figure out how to fix this.

Chapter 34

Todd decided to take the advice of his father. As soon as he left the suite, he set out on a mission to find Hannah. He was informed by one of the security guards that she was in the concert hall.

Todd headed to the concert hall expecting to find Hannah practicing her violin. Instead, he was surprised to find her sitting at the piano with Wesley standing behind her leaning into her and turning pages as she attempted to play. The sight infuriated Todd. Was his cousin an idiot? First Becca and now Hannah! Todd lost control.

"What do you think you're doing?" roared Todd.

Neither Hannah nor Wesley had noticed Todd until he spoke. Wesley now looked at Todd with a clueless expression. Hannah looked like she wanted to get up but was blocked by Wesley.

"Get away from her!" Todd yelled as he lunged towards Wesley.

Wesley, finally realizing the danger he was in, dodged Todd's attack and ran to the other side of the piano. What followed was a humorous game of cat and mouse in which Todd chased Wesley around the piano several times before finally grabbing his shirt. Wesley lost his balance and fell into the piano bench hitting the piano keys as he went down. The sound from the piano came across as a mournful wail matching Wesley's strained cries of help. Todd was startled back to reality. He was hovering over Wesley, one hand holding onto his shirt, and one fist in the air, ready to smash his cousin's face in. He stopped. Wesley had stopped yelling, but there was still screeching. He looked up to see Hannah flapping her arms and squawking like a peacock. Todd immediately felt like a fool. He had come here to try to make things right. Instead he was acting like a jealous idiot.

"Hannah, stop! This is just stupid." Todd stood pulling Wesley up with him. "Get out of here." The command was directed at Wesley who made no hesitation to leave.

Todd ignored him and directed his attention to Hannah. "Hannah, you need to go home."

Hannah was indignant. "Why? Because I asked Wesley to teach me to play the piano? What were you thinking, Todd? I tried to find you this morning, but you seemed to have disappeared. So, instead of just sitting in my room, I decided to do something with my time. Wesley is a great . . . "

"Just stop. This has nothing to do with Wesley."

"Really Todd? Is that why you just chased him around the piano like a raving lunatic?"

"Lunatic?" The word angered Todd until he realized that he probably did look like a raving lunatic. His own behavior frustrated him.

Todd continued, "I'm sorry, Hannah. This isn't working out. I'll arrange for someone to take you home."

Hannah looked confused and Todd somewhat regretted his brusqueness with her. The whole stupid incident with Wesley had screwed things up. He tried again.

"Look, it's just not meant to be. It's not you."

"Seriously? Are you about to give me the 'it's not you, it's me speech?' You know what Todd, save your breath. We barely know each other. It's not like I'm going to be heartbroken. It's been great getting to come here. I had fun. Not many people get to experience this, so, thank you. I hope we can remain friends, and yes, I just took your line."

Todd smiled.

"What?" Hannah inquired.

"That was easier than I thought."

Hannah gave Todd a playful shove. "Oh, come on, Todd. It's pretty obvious that we wouldn't work out. I'm fairly certain there's someone around here who's much better for you."

"What's that supposed to mean?"

"Let's just say that the moment you saw Becca, I pretty much became chopped liver."

Although it bothered Todd that Hannah had noticed his interest in Becca, he appreciated her understanding. "Liver is disgusting. You're better than liver." Todd mumbled.

"Wow, thanks Todd. Do I at least get a limo to ride home in?"

"Sure." Todd had handled the situation with Hannah. He could now focus all his attention on Becca. He told Hannah goodbye and then headed for the clinic where he knew Becca would be with Dr. Xavier.

There were no patients in the clinic. Becca sat at a desk reading a book. She was unaware of Todd's presence, so he took the opportunity to watch her. He still couldn't get over how much she had changed physically. The before war Becca had been his best friend. She would still be that friend, but now she would be more, and it would be perfect. He moved closer to where she was sitting. She looked up. As soon as she saw him, she jumped up knocking over the chair she had been sitting in. She looked down at the chair as if it had offended her and then moved to pick it up.

"Don't. I'll take care of it." Todd walked behind the desk and straightened the offending chair. Rather than move from behind the desk to let Todd in, Becca had stepped to the side and was now trapped by two walls, a desk and Todd. She tried to move past him to get out of the way, and in doing so knocked off a stapler, a box of paper clips and the tape dispenser. Before she could do more damage, Todd grabbed her by the shoulders and moved her out of the way avoiding any other obstacles. Just touching her for that brief moment sent shockwaves through his body. He tugged on a curl.

"Becca, I was coming here to take you somewhere, not to pick up after you."

"Where are we going?"

"Nowhere now. You made a mess." Todd teased.

Becca had seemed momentarily paralyzed after Todd moved her out of the way, but she had since regained composure. She leaned down to help pick up the paperclips. As she did so, her shirt gaped giving Todd a glimpse of the pink bra she was wearing. Although it was tempting to enjoy the view, Todd had too much respect for Becca to do so. He reached down to pull her up.

"Becca, I've got it." Todd's response was curt and it startled Becca. He tempered his tone trying to be more playful, "I enjoy crawling around on the floor."

Becca was biting her lower lip, "Sorry." She gave Todd a doe-eyed look.

Todd found the last paper clip and stood up. "Let's go."

"I can't."

"Why not?"

"I'm working."

"Where's Xavier?"

"In his office."

Todd strode towards the closed door of the Doctor's office, opened it and leaned in.

"Dr. Xavier, Becca is leaving." Todd then shut the door and guided Becca out of the clinic.

Becca was dazed, but found her voice, "Todd, I can't just . . . You can't . . . "

"Yes, Becca, I can. Let's go."

Todd grabbed Becca's hand and led her to the palace garage. He walked to a cabinet and pulled out a helmet. He then strode back to Becca.

"We're going to have to do something about these curls. Do you have a rubber band?"

"Todd, I can't use a rubber band for my hair. It would ruin it."

"Oh, don't girls usually pull back their hair with one of those rubber band things?"

"It's not really a rubber band."

Todd was getting impatient. He wanted to get going. "Okay, Becca, I'm a guy. I don't know the technical term for the rubber band hair thingy. The point is, do you have something for your hair?"

"No."

"Hold your hair back."

Becca held her hair while Todd gently fitted the helmet onto her head. He then walked over to his motorcycle and guided it out.

"Get on."

Becca gave Todd a questioning look, but didn't argue. As she positioned herself behind him, Todd found himself second-guessing this idea. He needed to get moving - fast.

"Where's your helmet," Becca questioned.

"Don't need one. Put your shield down and hold on."

The hills leading down from the palace were tricky, but Todd maneuvered them with ease. He stopped at the checkpoint. He could tell the guards were uneasy about letting him pass, but none of them dared stop him. Then they were free. Todd turned towards the road leading away from the city and took off. Becca had started off with her hands resting on Todd's shoulders for balance. She now had both arms wrapped tightly around his waist, but she wasn't complaining.

After half an hour of hard riding, Todd pulled over to give Becca a break and make sure she was okay. He also wanted her to see the view. The path he had taken had led them deeper into the mountains. The outlook gave them a view of a waterfall in the distance. Todd steadied the motorcycle while helping Becca off. He then lowered the kickstand and dismounted.

Becca had already removed her helmet. Todd reached to pull on a curl, but ended up with a handful of tangled hair.

"Becca, there's a problem."

Becca looked concerned, "What?"

He pulled her hair to the front to show her. It moved as a single mass. Even with her hair in a complete mess, Becca was still stunning. Todd just stared.

Becca smiled. "Conditioner will solve it."

"What?"

"The hair problem - conditioner will take care of it."

"Oh, right. Do you like it?"

"My hair?"

"No, Becca, the motorcycle."

Becca smiled again, and once more Todd marveled at how amazing she was. He didn't want to change anything about her. She was perfect. Her smile made his whole world stop.

"It's exciting. A little scary."

"Scary?" Todd inquired.

"There's nothing to protect you. If you hit something or something hit you, there's nothing. I do like it though."

Todd took Becca's hand and led her to the lookout. He watched her as she took in the view. He had come here many times over the past year. It was a place that gave him peace and helped him gain focus. He wanted Becca to be here with him, and now that she was, everything seemed to be falling into place.

"Becca, Hannah is leaving tomorrow."

Becca turned to him but didn't speak.

Todd continued, "I don't know what your father told you, but things are over with Hannah. They never really got started."

"I told him you wouldn't do that."

"Becca, I want to be clear. I did kiss Hannah. Well, she kissed me . . . and I didn't stop it. But it didn't feel right. I wanted to talk to you about it. That's why I came to your suite. And you, Becca, you've changed so much. I didn't realize before how much . . . Alright, look, I want to be with you."

"Me too."

"You want to be with yourself?"

Becca looked genuinely frustrated and it amused Todd as she tried to explain, "No, I mean I want to be with you too."

"Well, I'm glad we got that straightened out."

Todd stepped closer to Becca and leaned in to kiss her. The kiss was both gentle and passionate yet brief. Todd took Becca's hand and they stood silently taking in the view. When a few minutes had passed, Todd turned back to Becca.

"Ready to go? Do you feel like you could ride for a couple more hours?" he asked.

"Yes, but I'm a little hungry."

"We'll stop somewhere."

Fifteen minutes later, Todd pulled off the road into the dirt parking lot of a building that looked like a rustic log cabin. There was a large porch at the front of the building with wooden tables made from the trunk of large trees. Each table had the rings of the wood indicating the age of the tree from which it had been cut. The chairs were treated stumps of wood with a lacquer finish. Inside the restaurant, the decor was similar with large windows open onto the porch. Todd guided Becca inside and found a table with two stumps near one of the windows.

"I'd pull out your chair for you, but I don't think they move."

As they sat down, a waitress dressed in jeans, a white t-shirt and red apron emerged from the kitchen with water, chips and salsa.

"Welcome. Glad you stopped by. You picked the best seat in the house. Good job young man. I brought you out some water, but I can get you something else if you'd like."

Todd spoke, "Water is fine. We'll also take two #5 combos."

"That's a lot of food. This one doesn't look like she can eat that much. I'm sure you'll need some to go boxes."

"If there are any leftovers, I'll take care of it."

"Yes, of course. You need to eat good to feed those muscles. I'll put that order right in for you. We have specials on Margaritas right now if you're interested."

"No, thank you."

Except for the occasional check from the waitress, Todd and Becca enjoyed their meal with no interruptions. No one knew who they were or cared. Todd cherished every moment. It was so good to just talk

180

to Becca. As he listened to her dreams of becoming a doctor and her plans to go to college in less than six months, Todd began mapping out his own plan for their future together. And once more, Todd felt like he was home. Alone with Becca, there was no restlessness, no pressure, and no sadness. He felt like a fool for not realizing how much she meant to him sooner.

Becca had eaten more than either he or the waitress expected, but their lunch was nearing its end. The waitress checked on them one last time with a promise to bring the check. As she walked away, Todd came to an embarrassing realization. He had no money. When he had whisked Becca away from the palace, he wasn't planning on stopping for food. While Todd was contemplating what to do, the waitress returned with the check and placed it on the table.

"I'll take that when you're ready. No hurry. The two of you can sit there and enjoy yourselves as long as you like. It's so refreshing to see two young people in love. You two are just adorable."

She turned to walk away, but Todd stopped her, "Excuse me, there's a problem."

"Oh? Did I ring something up wrong?"

"No. I forgot my money. We left the p . . . We left. I can bring it to you tomorrow."

"Why don't I just have the manager come over."

Todd noted that the waitress had suddenly lost her friendly demeanor. He looked at Becca apologetically. She looked terrified. It slightly amused him. He briefly considered teasing her about spending the night in jail, but thought better of it. The waitress was talking to a man who had been sitting in a corner of the restaurant drinking what was probably coke and watching the TV that was positioned above the bar. The man got up and headed their way.

Todd stood as he approached. Hoping to gain the upper hand, Todd spoke first, "Sir, I apologize, but I left without my money. I'll bring it in first thing tomorrow."

"Son, I don't intend to be rude, but if I made that a policy then I'd be broke. I don't doubt your intentions, but I don't know you. Surely there's someone who could bring you the money? Or perhaps one of you could remain here while the other goes to get it?"

That's not going to happen, thought Todd.

"I could ask my uncle to bring it," offered Todd. He cringed as he said it. He hated using the royalty card, but it was all he had at the moment.

"Well, go ahead and give him a call."

"I don't have a phone."

"Stacey, let this young man use the phone."

"Look, I'm not going to call my uncle. My name is Todd Heart. King Daren is my uncle. I'm good for my word. I'll pay you in the morning, and if an earthquake hits and I don't make it, you can bill the palace." Todd was growing annoyed, but he knew he couldn't really blame the owner. Most people in Lionel were trustworthy, but there were no guarantees.

Todd was impressed with the manager's response.

"Prince Heart, I did not recognize you. I am honored that you would patronize our little establishment, and I will respect your anonymity. There's no need to bring the money back. I hope you enjoyed your meal and I apologize for inconveniencing you."

"Thank you sir, but I do pay my debts." Todd turned to Becca, "Becca, are you ready?"

As soon as they were outside, Todd questioned Becca, "What did you think was going to happen?"

Becca seemed to be searching for words, so Todd filled the silence.

"Becca, did you think they were going to throw us in jail?"

Apparently this was an easier question for her.

"Maybe."

"Really?"

"Well, you couldn't pay."

"Becca, if anyone ever tried to throw either of us in jail, I guarantee there would be hell to pay."

"I suppose."

"I know. We need to get back to the palace."

Todd took his time on the way back. He would have liked to stay out longer, but it would be dark in a few hours, and he wasn't going to keep Becca out past dark.

They entered the palace checkpoint and headed for the garage. Inside the garage, Todd maneuvered to his space. Ben Canaan was standing in it. Todd briefly contemplated turning around and speeding out, but practical wisdom overcame childish impulse. The general stood by as Todd helped Becca off the bike and took her helmet. As soon as she was free of it, her father addressed her.

"Rebecca Ben Canaan, go to your room."

Becca started to go, but Todd grabbed her arm to stop her.

"Becca, before you go I want you to hear what I say to your father." Todd then addressed the general, "Sir, I respect your daughter. I'm not going to hurt her, and I am going to date her."

"You claim you respect my daughter, but you just get up and take her out of the palace without telling anyone where you are going and leaving no way to contact you!?"

"She was with me. She was safe."

"I don't think you understand Todd. To respect my daughter is to respect me as her father as well. What you just did is the epitome of disrespect. It was selfish, careless and thoughtless. Did you even take one moment to consider the effect your actions would have? You care about her? Tell me then, Todd, how would you feel if someone did the exact same thing tomorrow. Only this time you don't know where she is, what she's doing, when she's coming back, or if she's coming back. We are still at war, Todd. A war in which our enemy is targeting members of the royal family. You do not deserve to date my daughter. She deserves more than someone who only cares about his own selfish desires. She's not safe with you."

Todd needed a moment to gather his thoughts. He knew Ben Canaan was right. Taking Becca out of the palace was dangerous and foolish. He was still holding Becca's helmet. He walked to the cabinet and very deliberately placed it on the rack. He then turned back to Ben Canaan.

"I'm sorry." Todd didn't know what else to say. He doubted his apology would do any good, but it was sincere.

Ben Canaan deflated somewhat. He had been ready for a fight that didn't happen. He now looked a little lost to Todd.

Instead of responding to Todd, Caleb addressed his daughter, "Becca, let's go."

Todd didn't protest. He tried to give Becca a reassuring look before she left. Todd was now determined to find a way to prove himself to the general.

Chapter 35

Chad had awakened and showered. As he walked out of the bathroom, he noted that Ashley still had not budged from the middle of the bed where she had planted herself at precisely 2:00am that morning. He wondered how much of her long, auburn hair he had inhaled during the course of the night. He walked towards the closet to take out his clothes, but was halted by the sound of the door pager to the suite. Chad grabbed the pajama pants he had thrown on the end of the bed and put them on as he headed to the door.

Dawson had recently installed a panel that allowed Chad to see who was outside. Chad pushed the button to bring the image up on the screen and was shocked to see King Daren standing outside his door. Chad was torn between the decision of making the King wait while he changed or greeting him in his pajamas. Taking a deep breath, he opened the door.

It was difficult for Chad not to immediately excuse himself to go change, but protocol demanded that he wait for the King to speak first.

"Chad, Mr. Sterling received a phone call from King Trevor this morning. I need to speak with you and Ashley."

"Yes sir. I will get her up. I will go get her," Chad stumbled.

"Take your time." Daren offered.

"Y.. yes, sir. Thank you, sir. We'll be right out."

As he waited, the King walked around the suite. He found it interesting to look at the decor that Chad and Ashley had chosen. He noted that the centerpiece on the mantel in the sitting area was a crystal vase that once belonged to Ashley's mother, Belle. Daren's own father, the previous King had given it to Christopher and Belle on their wedding day. It had originally belonged to Daren's grandmother. Daren had foreseen that he may have to wait for Chad and Ashley, so he was not put out by the wait at all. Besides, if Chad did not change out of his paisley pajamas, Daren wasn't sure he could keep a straight face.

Daren went to the kitchen area and helped himself to a glass of orange juice. He and his youngest daughter, Emma, had already joined in their usual morning cereal ritual. When Emma was around four years old, she would wake up every morning when she heard the door to Daren and Nicole's room open as Daren headed to his office. She would run out of her room and cling to him not wanting him to leave. After several weeks of dealing with her tears and trying everything he could think of, he finally found a solution by accident. One morning, he got up much earlier than usual in hopes that he could slip out unnoticed, but as soon as his door opened, Emma came springing out of her room. Since he had more time than usual, he decided to try to distract her with food. He poured her some cereal and handed it to her. She looked at it, looked at him and then got up and walked over to the counter. She was barely tall enough to reach the top of it and her little hand kept barely missing the cereal box. He remembered being flustered at the time, but he asked her what she wanted. She insisted that he eat cereal with her. That's how the ritual began. As long as they ate together, she seemed to be content with letting him go to work. This had been four years ago, and he now looked forward to the time he had with her in the mornings.

The door to Chad and Ashley's bedroom opened breaking Daren out of his reverie. Ashley emerged in jeans and a t-shirt. Her hair was a mess, but she had tried to tame it by pulling it back with a hair tie. Chad came behind her looking much more put together now in his uniform, but still slightly unnerved. Ashley, on the other hand, bounced over to him without a qualm.

"King Daren, Chad said you heard from Trevor?"

"Lance spoke with him early this morning. He is open to allowing you to come to Aldrich as an ambassador."

"When do we go?" Ashley questioned.

Daren noted the excitement that danced in Ashley's eyes. Daren knew that Ashley was ill prepared for the possible dangers she would face in Aldrich.

Daren took a fatherly tone as he spoke, "Ashley, you have never been to Aldrich. Benson may be dead, but his influence still lingers. That much evil doesn't just go away easily. Not only will you be in danger simply because of your gender, but anyone who may still hold a grudge over Benson's death could see you as a means for revenge."

"Chad will be there, and I really think that Trevor will want to strengthen ties with Lionel. He will make sure we are safe."

The fact that Chad would accompany her did put many of Daren's fears at ease, but still there was no certainty.

"If you think you can be ready, then you and Chad will leave next week after you have undergone preparation."

Daren noted that the expressions on Chad and Ashley's faces were polar opposites. Chad's jaw was set and his expression serious and contemplative. Ashley was smiling from ear to ear, and her excitement was palpable.

The King once again addressed the newly married couple, "This undertaking is going to be challenging for both of you for different reasons, and the whole world will be watching. I am expecting you to uphold your own dignity and honor as well as that of Lionel. You will be there to support each other. Ashley, Chad is well trained and knowledgeable about many things. He is also your husband. More than ever, listen to him while you are over there. He will have your best interest at heart. Chad, be vigilant. Aldrich is the opposite of Lionel in every possible aspect. Ashley has a mission, but safety takes priority. You will both need to speak with Mr. Sterling to work out the details."

"Yes, sir," Chad agreed.

With a nod, the King exited the suite.

Chad turned to Ashley. He appreciated what King Daren had said and felt it opened the door for a serious conversation about this trip. Before he could get a word out, Ashley chirped, "What should I wear over there? Will it be the same temperature as here?"

Chad sighed, "I am sure you will figure it out, Ashley. Talk to Lance. I need to get to work before your father shows up at the door next."

If Ashley had noticed the slight annoyance in Chad's tone, she showed no indication. She took off towards their room on an obvious mission. Chad rubbed his temples, took a deep breath and headed out.

Chapter 36

It had been a week since Chad and Ashley had been told they were going to Aldrich. Chad had tried on several occasions to talk privately with Ashley about the trip to Aldrich, but her preparations on diplomatic aspects combined with his usual responsibilities as well as security preparations for the trip left little time alone. Ashley had allowed herself to be compromised with Trevor within the walls of Lionel's palace. He hoped she would be more restrained when they reached Aldrich.

Even this morning they had gone their separate ways as soon as they awakened. Ashley had last minute business with Lance, and Christopher wanted to drill Chad once more on security protocol. Chad was actually looking forward to the four-hour plane ride.

At exactly 35 minutes before they were scheduled to depart, Chad made his way to the airstrip. Chad arrived at the plane and stood outside waiting for Ashley to arrive.

The pilot hailed him on the radio.

"This is Commander West," Chad responded.

"Sir, are you ready to board?"

"I'm waiting for Princess Ashley."

"Sir, she's on the plane."

Chad didn't bother to respond. He felt momentarily embarrassed and frustrated, but quickly chastised himself. He realized that he had been snapping at his wife quite a bit lately, and he had no good reason other than his own anxiety over this trip.

Chad boarded the plane to find Ashley engrossed in a document that she had up on her handheld. The plane took off and within minutes, all hope of any conversation with Ashley was quashed. She was sound asleep, handheld still in her lap. Chad gently removed the handheld and covered her with a blanket.

Ashley awakened to the sound of the pilot's voice informing them that the plane would be landing in 20 minutes. Immediate panic set in as she dove into her grooming ritual. When she was finished, Chad made sure to provide the appropriate compliments on her beauty.

The plane landed, and as they neared the hanger, Chad looked out the window to see rows of armed guards lining the building. The palace in Aldrich did not have its own airstrip, so they would be transported by car from this point. Chad looked out at the armed guards very aware that some of these men might have been involved in combat with Lionel forces only months before. Hopefully, none of them had a grudge to grind.

They had come to Aldrich with a small security detail of only four highly trained special forces. However, Lionel still had a contingency of soldiers that had remained in Aldrich following the war. Chad was also aware that there would be satellites trained on their every move as they navigated the country and a father who would have an army ready if he perceived his daughter to be in any kind of danger at any time.

The drive to the palace was long and rough, and with every mile, Chad grew more and more anxious. He glanced at Ashley and thought that even she looked somewhat subdued. The countryside around the airport had been flat and nondescript, but as they neared the city, it seemed to loom in front of them like a rusty brown monster. At every turn, more armed guards patrolled the streets. There was an occasional pedestrian who always seemed to be hurrying to safety even though there was no immediate sign of danger. On some corners, small groups of men huddled outside establishments that had blacked out windows and bouncers at the doors. Chad made a point to take in every detail of the streets they travelled and down one alley he noted at least 12 - 15 scantily clad women lingering along the walls. Instinctively, he wrapped his arm around Ashley and pulled her close.

They finally reached the palace, which was surrounded by a medieval looking moat with a huge iron gate blocking the entrance. The gate opened as they approached, and the car proceeded across the seemingly ancient bridge passing over the moat. Chad looked ahead to see Trevor Benson himself awaiting their arrival. The car stopped a respectable distance away from the new King, and the driver opened the door for Ashley. Chad was pleased to see that Ashley waited until he came to her side to exit the car. Two of the Aldrich armed guards joined the four Lionel guards as they approached Trevor. When they were within 20 feet of the King, the two guards fully prostrated themselves before him. Ashley had entwined her arm with Chad's, and he felt her hesitate at the guards' actions. He continued forward, leading her with him.

As they approached Trevor, Chad noted that all of his attention was on Ashley. Trevor took a step toward her and reached for her free hand. Without acknowledging Chad, he lifted her hand and kissed it.

Without letting go, he addressed Ashley, "Welcome to Aldrich, Princess Ashley. I am pleased that you came. Rise."

Although he had not taken his eyes off of Ashley, his last command had been apparently directed at the guards who had remained recumbent on the ground. At his command, they rose to their feet.

For the first time, Trevor broke his attention away from Ashley and seemed to take in his surroundings. He then continued, "We should go inside."

Chad thought he noted a brief look of concern flash across the King's face, and he wondered if Trevor feared for his own safety in this unstable kingdom. As Trevor spoke, he had turned slightly to the side and was now offering his arm to Ashley. She gave Chad an apologetic look as she disengaged herself and joined Trevor. Chad followed behind as they made their way into the palace.

The palace in Lionel had been constructed by King Daren's great-great-grandfather and was designed to exploit space and light at every turn possible. King Daren's father had continued adding to the palace updating the decor to both reflect the history of Lionel and the continued progression of the nation. King Daren's contributions had been minimal but were mostly focused on technological enhancements to the palace. The palace in Aldrich reminded Chad of the ancient structures he had read about in what was termed the medieval history of the world. Since the Great War, few structures remained from that time period. Most had been destroyed by nuclear explosions while many others were demolished in natural disasters that occurred as a result of the worldwide nuclear assault. This palace had been built after the war, but it could have easily fit into that medieval time. Chad recalled some of the horrors that had transpired during those dark ages when men had seemingly found pleasure in finding ways to torture and torment their fellow man. If this palace was built to intimidate and replicate the oppression of that time, it had succeeded. They had entered the palace through a side entrance and passed through several long, dark hallways. They now emerged into a larger room, which looked to be the main entrance to the palace. Two large staircases wound up the sides of the room to a second floor. They stopped.

For the first time, Trevor acknowledged Chad's presence, but still did not address him directly. Instead he spoke to one of the guards who had been following their procession.

"Take him to his room," he ordered.

The guard stepped forward and motioned for Chad to follow.

Chad spoke up, "Thank you for your hospitality, King Trevor, but I am sure that Ashley would like to settle into our room as well before diving into business."

Despite the numerous hours of preparation with Lance, Ashley found herself rattled by her surroundings. During the long walk to this point, she had been having an internal conversation with herself. She knew she had to get over the cultural shock and focus on the mission. Having Chad here made it more difficult in some ways. He insisted on protecting her which she loved about him, but right now she needed to feel independent. As much as she knew it would hurt Chad, getting some time alone with Trevor was the best strategy for diplomacy. Trevor would most likely open up to her if she could create that comfortable repertoire they shared with one another. Chad's presence would only create tension and impede progress. She had also noticed the look of displeasure that had darkened Trevor's face at Chad's suggestion.

She pulled away from Trevor and walked over to Chad.

Giving Chad a look of confidence and hopefully assurance, Ashley spoke, "Our time here is short. Do you mind getting things settled while King Trevor and I begin working? We have a lot to accomplish. I will join you for dinner later." Turning to Trevor, she continued, "Maybe we can all have dinner together. Will Kendra join us?"

Trevor answered, "Perhaps. We will discuss plans later. Come."

Ashley once again gave Chad an apologetic look and followed Trevor who had walked away following his one word command.

Chad motioned for the security detail to follow Ashley and then requested to be shown to his room.

Ashley had caught up to Trevor, and he once again offered his arm. They walked in silence until Ashley finally broke it, "Aldrich finally has a good king."

Instead of responding to her comment, Trevor turned and addressed the men who were still following, "You are not needed. Princess Ashley will be safe with me."

Ashley could see the struggle on their faces, but it was obvious that Trevor was not going to communicate as long as they were present. She spoke up to reassure them, "King Trevor and I have much to discuss. I will contact you if I need you."

Lieutenant Kraft spoke, "We are to stay with you at all times, Princess Ashley."

"Well, I don't think we will all fit into the office together comfortably. King Trevor, will you allow them to secure the area where we will be and then wait outside?"

Anger filled Trevor's voice as he replied, "I have given my assurances that you will be safe, Ashley. It is enough."

"I will be okay, Lieutenant." Ashley turned and began walking hoping that her escort would remain behind. She wasn't afraid to be alone with Trevor, but Daren's words of warning about other possible dangers did linger in her mind. To her relief, her escort followed.

Ashley realized that any trace of the Trevor she had once known was gone within the walls of this prison. She wasn't sure if she could once again reach that Trevor, but she knew she had to try and getting him alone was the first step. They came to a door and stopped. The hallway they had entered to get here was empty. This somewhat relieved Ashley as every person they had passed along the way had prostrated themselves at the sight of their King. The gesture made her uncomfortable each time. Trevor opened the door and motioned for her to enter.

It was a rather spacious office and the decor contrasted with that of the rest of the palace. A small window occupied one wall of the office and unlike the few windows she had seen, the drapes were open allowing a feeble ray of light to shine into the room. The office was sparse but somewhat welcoming compared to the rest of the palace.

"Is this your office?" Ashley questioned.

"It is."

"Did you take it over when you became King?"

"I took the office of King, but no, I am not fond of my father's former office. It remains unoccupied."

"New King, new ways, new office?"

"Perhaps."

Ashley had smiled when she commented, and Trevor seemed to be relaxing somewhat. Although he had not offered, Ashley seated herself on the couch that lined the wall beneath the window. It was set to the side and did not necessarily allow for easy conversation with whoever may be sitting at the desk. She wondered if anyone ever sat in the King of Aldrich's presence. She was amused as she watched Trevor's reaction. He seemed a bit confused for a moment. He stood statuesque in the center of the room halfway between the door and the desk. Although he was not close to her at the moment, his height and build even from a distance made it seem as if he was looming over her. After giving her a long, piercing stare, his marble facade finally broke. One side of his lip raised in smirk, and he strolled over to join her on the sofa.

"Has anyone ever sat on this couch?" She questioned.

"Yes, but he is no longer with us."

Ashley had diverted her attention to the rest of the room as she asked the question, but Trevor's answer was so solemn that she had to look back at him to discover whether or not he was serious. The smirk was still there, and she took it as a sign that he was teasing her. Hopefully.

"Trevor, with you as the King, our countries can finally be allies. I am sorry that you lost your father, but I am excited about your future."

"And what is that future, Ashley? An occupied Aldrich?" The question was sincere and Ashley did not sense any malice in it.

"The only reason Lionel troops are still here is to ensure your safety and make sure the country remains stable as power is transferred. If you want them to leave, I can relay your wishes to King Daren."

"I will inform King Daren when I am ready for them to leave."

"That will work too. Trevor, you have never been an enemy. No one holds you responsible for what your father did."

"Do Chad and your brother share your sentiments?"

"That's a personal matter. I am here for political matters. How can Lionel help you?"

"You think I need help?"

Ashley was finding it extremely difficult to read Trevor. She wasn't sure whether she should respond to him in earnest or try to keep the conversation light. They had been and were still friends, but her role here now added a whole new dimension to their relationship. She knew that more than anything, she wanted to nurture his trust.

"Well, that's what I am trying to find out. Can we help you?"

Trevor stood and walked towards the desk. With his back to her, he responded, "I will need the support of the ICP. King Daren may no longer be a voting member, but he still has influence. Not everyone in Aldrich supports me as the King, but if they know the world is behind me, they will capitulate."

Trevor had just given her more than she expected and she could tell it hurt his pride to do so. She would try to bolster it.

"You are the rightful King, Trevor. There should be no question. King Daren has already recognized you and he will do everything in his power to support you."

"That is the problem Ashley. The people of Raxx have been brainwashed to loathe Lionel. Many see my cooperation with Lionel as treason or weakness. They may happily support a more suitable replacement for my father if the opportunity arose. Has Zinn been located?"

"They are working on that."

"Friendship with Lionel could also be a detriment to Aldrich."

"Well, you see where being enemies with Lionel got your father."

Trevor rejoined her on the sofa. "I need people I can trust. People who I can be assured will support me when I do things differently than my father did."

The conversation was becoming very hopeful. Ashley was delighted to hear that Trevor did not plan to continue his father's tyranny. In mindless exhilaration, she blurted out, "That is why I am here Trevor. I will help you."

"You will agree to stay?"

"What? Stay? Yes, I will be here for three days."

"Upon my visit to Lionel, you informed me that you plan to take over Mr. Sterling's job, correct?"

"Well, yes, eventually."

"I can guarantee that Lance Sterling will not go quickly. Remain in Lionel and be a second-rate assistant to the King's advisor for an indefinite time period or come here and be the second most powerful person in Aldrich."

Although the offer certainly appealed to Ashley's ego, this was not the direction she wanted the conversation to go. She made a feeble attempt to redirect.

"A woman second in command? Isn't that unthinkable in Aldrich?"

Ashley's comment had been made in jest, but it did not have the intended effect on Trevor. His countenance again darkened as he replied.

"As I said, I do not plan to do things the same as my father did."

"That's good." Ashley sought to lighten the mood again. "When are we eating dinner?"

"I will have food brought to us when you are ready."

"Then Chad and Kendra will be joining us here?"

Trevor gave Ashley a threatening look, but she was determined to keep her resolve. She stared back at him refusing to give in. He stood once more and stepped towards her. For a passing moment, she found herself frightened of him, but then he turned and once again walked to his desk. This time however, he took a seat and lifted the receiver of the telephone. The person on the other end was instructed to make preparations for dinner at 8:00pm and to inform both Queen Kendra and Lieutenant West that they were to attend.

Ashley was not sure if Trevor and herself were included in the plans, and she wanted clarification.

"Trevor, thank you. It will be good to see Kendra," Ashley forced out.

Trevor had quickly recovered from his obvious anger over her insistence that they have dinner with their spouses, and quipped back, "Will Chad enjoy seeing Kendra as well?"

Ashley knew Trevor was trying to rattle her, and she wasn't going to take the bait. Kendra was Queen Nicole's niece, and she and Chad had had a very volatile relationship when she lived in the palace at Lionel. It had ended badly, and Ashley was fairly certain that Chad had never looked back.

"Maybe. I don't know," she replied non-commitally.

For the next four hours, Ashley and Trevor talked. Some of it was political; some of it was personal. Ashley felt that Trevor was being open with her much of the time, but she could tell that there was a wall there that had not been there in the past. She knew that their relationship would change, but she wished that he could fully trust her. He did not bring up the idea of her coming to Aldrich again, and she was glad. The time for dinner came. Trevor summoned someone to take Ashley to her room. A man named Raymond appeared seconds later. Ashley noted that when he approached Trevor, he only bowed at the waist rather than fully prostrating himself. She made a mental note to question Trevor about it later. As she and Raymond neared the end of the hall, Lieutenant Kraft and the other three were waiting. Kraft gave her yet another look of disapproval and then took his place behind her.

After passing through two hallways, Lieutenant Kraft apparently could contain himself no longer.

"We were ordered to stay with you at all times, Princess Ashley."

Raymond seemed unaffected by the Lieutenant's outburst and continued on without acknowledgment.

"Get over it, Log. Nothing happened."

"It could have, and we still have two more days here."

Ashley gave a sigh of frustration. Hopefully Raymond would go away once they reached the suite, and she could talk sensibly to

Lieutenant Kraft. Once they reached the room, Raymond seemed uninterested in loitering any longer than necessary. When she thought he was out of earshot, she turned on Kraft.

"What was I supposed to do, Log?" Ashley questioned cocking her head to the right, "Trevor is the king, and we are his guests. If we defy his orders from the start, it doesn't leave room for much progress. Whether you like it or not, he is also my friend. He would not allow harm to come to me."

"Lionel still has enemies here, and one man cannot guarantee your safety."

"Fine, Log. You win, but it doesn't change anything, and if this mission fails because of your stubbornness, I'll never speak to you again!"

Ashley opened the door and entered making sure to slam it shut behind her. She and Logan Kraft had a long history with one another. He had been assigned to her as security when she went away to college. This was just one more disagreement amongst many that they had had. Still, she trusted him completely and knew his concern was sincere. She was finding it very difficult to balance all the men in her life.

Chad was sitting in a chair in the room when she entered and raised an eyebrow at her slamming of the door. Immediately she regretted her last action. Chad would expect an explanation or worse, he would assume that things had gone badly with Trevor.

She decided blatant honesty was best, "Look, Trevor would not allow the security detail into the administrative area of the palace. They were fairly close by at all times, and I was perfectly safe, but they weren't happy about it. Log just threw a fit."

"As he should," Chad responded.

"I figured you would take his side." Ashley countered preparing herself for a fight with Chad.

"Do you need to change?" he questioned.

"What?"

"Your clothes, Ashley. Are you going to change for dinner, or are you ready?"

"Oh. Give me just a minute. . . Are you okay?"

"Yes. Why?"

"No reason."

Chad was well aware of the situation and didn't like it, but knew there was not much he could do. When Lieutenant Kraft had contacted him earlier about it, he had just instructed him to remain vigilant. The fact was that if anything happened to Ashley while they were here, there would be no more Aldrich to speak of. It was the only reassurance he had. Hopefully the next two days would go quickly.

When Ashley emerged from the bathroom, Chad noted that she was stunning in the dress she had chosen, and Chad wasn't sure he liked that fact right now. Trevor did not need further encouragement.

"Does this look okay?" Ashley questioned.

"There's a piece in the back that seems to be pooching out," Chad lied.

"I don't believe you."

Chad just shook his head side to side. "You always look beautiful, Ashley. Ready?"

Chapter 37

The dining hall consisted of one long dark wooden table with heavy chairs lining each side. Trevor sat at one of the ends of the table with Kendra to his left. Ashley was to his right with Chad next to her. The room was consistent with the drab bleakness of the rest of the palace. Two large, antique looking chandeliers hung above either end of the table. Dark red velvet covered serving tables lined the walls to the sides of the dining table. Raymond had arrived at their room at 7:55pm to escort them to the dining hall. When they arrived, Trevor was waiting for them, but Kendra arrived almost fifteen minutes late. Having Trevor and Chad in the same room had created an air of awkward tension, but Kendra's arrival added an icy edginess.

Once the proper greetings had been made, they all sat down to dinner. The conversation had been trivial for the most part, but it was Kendra who turned the tide.

"I see you finally bagged a princess, Chad."

Chad had been about to take a bite of the roasted duck when the comment came. He now sat motionless, fork in mid-air. After a few moments, he set the fork deliberately on his plate, naked duck flesh still speared unceremoniously.

Ashley spoke, "That was rather blunt. Was that an underhanded way of congratulating us, Kendra?"

"No. He has always wanted to bag a Princess; he did try with me, first."

Chad still sat stunned by the original comment.

Ashley tried to redirect the conversation, "Roasted duck. We don't have roasted duck too often in Lionel. It's very . . . different."

Trevor spoke, "It is fresh. It was shot down this morning by one of our expert archers."

"Perfectly good duck wasted on a peasant," Kendra commented.

"Well, Kendra, as I recall, you were rejected by this perfectly good peasant," interjected Ashley.

Chad felt like he should say or do something before all hell broke loose, but he couldn't formulate any words to deal with this situation. No training had prepared him for the inevitable catfight that was about to take place. For once, he was relieved that Trevor still found Ashley desirable. Otherwise, she might end up in an Aldrich prison before this was over.

Kendra wouldn't back down, "I rejected him. That's why he went crawling to second best when I was done with him."

"Enough." Trevor's voice was barely audible, but its tone was lethal. "Princess Ashley and Commander Heart are guests here. They will be respected."

Ashley noted that it was the first time Trevor had ever used Chad's appropriate title. She also noted that the darkness she had witnessed within Trevor on multiple brief occasions had surfaced more strongly than she had ever seen before. His lips were pressed purposefully together and fire burned rather than flashed in his eyes. Kendra, oblivious to the storm that was raging, stood and looked at him in defiance.

"Well, Trevor, you are a king now, and perhaps you should be more discerning in your choice of guests."

"Sit down," Trevor commanded.

"I've lost my appetite."

Ashley was getting angry. Kendra was a spoiled, selfish witch. Trevor needed a wife who would support and help him right now, and Kendra was anything but that. The disrespect she was showing him was unacceptable, and it saddened Ashley that Trevor would not have the support of a loving and understanding wife.

Kendra left the room. Awkward silence followed.

Chad broke the silence, "I see that not much has changed with Kendra. It takes an extremely brave and strong individual to deal with her. Your resolve is to be admired, your majesty."

"Queen Kendra, Lieutenant West," corrected Trevor.

Ashley saw Chad's jaw clench, but he held his frustration in check.

"Of course. My apologies."

The remainder of dinner passed quickly. Chad and Ashley returned to their room after Ashley agreed to meet again with Trevor at 9:00am the next morning.

As soon as the door shut, Ashley turned on Chad.

"Seriously? Did that just happen?"

"It's Kendra. It shouldn't be surprising."

"Really? You seemed a bit surprised. Stunned. Paralyzed."

"I didn't want to provoke the situation."

"Chicken. Or should I say 'roasted duck'. Oh, and 'your majesty?' Really? Suck-up."

Ashley was enjoying teasing Chad about the night's events. She loved her so serious husband, but she was determined to get him to lighten up.

"A humiliated king can be a dangerous affair."

Ashley exhaled and planted herself directly in front of Chad. She placed both hands on his shoulders and stood on tip-toe so that she was eye to eye with him.

"Is it true?" she asked.

Chad looked lost. "Yes, Ashley, when a King is humiliated . . ."

Ashley put her hand over Chad's mouth.

"That's not what I'm talking about," she clarified.

Chad mumbled a muffled, "What?" beneath her hand.

"Are you really a princess hunter? Is that why you married me?"

A slight grin finally escaped Chad's mouth as he wrapped his arms around Ashley and carried her to the bed. The thought of what they were about to do in Trevor's palace gave him a smug contentment.

"I heard princesses are the best," he replied.

"Oh, we are."

****

The next day with Trevor was productive only in the sense that Ashley was able to get Trevor to relax as they conversed about everything from their initial meeting years before to the current living members of his family. Very little was mentioned regarding his role as king or his country's needs. As Trevor was describing his younger brother Cameron, the seemingly ever-present Raymond appeared at the door to Trevor's office. Trevor motioned him in. Raymond entered and postured himself in a half-bow waiting for Trevor to address him. Ashley had noted that while most of Trevor's subjects fully prostrated themselves, a few seemed to be spared that humiliating display of submission. Raymond was one of those.

Trevor spoke, "What is it, Raymond?"

Raymond rose and addressed his king, "Your majesty, Mr. Baczewski is here to see you. He scheduled an appointment several weeks ago."

Trevor sighed, "Send him in, but tell him to make it brief."

"Yes, your majesty."

Raymond departed and only seconds later, a man probably in his mid-twenties walked in escorting a young woman of about the same age. Ashley noted from the way they were dressed that they were probably wealthy and high standing. Both walked towards Trevor, stopped nearly fifteen feet away and prostrated themselves.

Trevor addressed them, "Rise."

Both stood. When Trevor remained silent, the man looked somewhat uncomfortable. The woman stood tall but kept her head down with her gaze never leaving the floor. Even Ashley was feeling tense and hoped that Trevor would speak. She was tempted to say something herself, but knew that would be completely against Aldrich protocol.

"Mr. Baczewski, what is your request?" Trevor inquired.

The man stepped forward slightly as he answered, "Your majesty, this is my fiancé, Nadia Jirasek. We are to be married in three weeks."

The man had paused. Trevor looked somewhat displeased at the man's intrusion.

"Congratulations. Is that all?"

A look of confusion crossed Mr. Baczewski's face as he replied, "No, your majesty. As is the custom, I am offering Nadia for your pleasure prior to our marriage. I will return for her in a week's time."

Trevor took a deep breath and glanced at Ashley. Ashley waited apprehensively for Trevor's response. The girl was very attractive, and the offer seemed commonplace to both the man and woman. Nadia had shown no signs of surprise nor repulsion to the suggestion.

Trevor stood and walked to the front of his desk. He offered his hand to Mr. Baczewski.

As the two shook hands, Trevor spoke, "You may return for Miss Jirasek in three days, Mr. Baczewski. You may leave."

Baczewski left and his fiancé remained still staring at the floor.

Trevor now moved to stand in front of her and addressed her, "Nadia, Raymond will escort you to a room."

The girl now looked up at the king and Ashley saw that there was fear in her eyes. Ashley wanted to stop Trevor. This was not the way to overcome his father's legacy. Strangely, Trevor must have sensed her frustration. He turned to look at her, and his expression held a silent warning. Ashley remained silent, but she was seething inside.

Trevor walked back to his desk and summoned Raymond.

When Raymond entered, Trevor ordered, "Take her to a room."

As soon as Raymond and Nadia departed, Ashley spoke up, "What will Kendra think about this?"

Trevor looked completely unaffected by the whole situation, which infuriated Ashley even more. Still, she had to remember that her visit here was for diplomacy.

"There are certain customs here that I know are frowned upon in Lionel. Kendra is well aware of those customs."

Ashley tried to restrain herself, but couldn't resist commenting, "I thought you were planning to change some of those customs."

"I am. Miss Jirasek is simply a guest here for the next few days. Nothing more."

"Why would you even give the appearance of . . ." Ashley started.

Trevor cut her off. "The changes have to come slowly, Ashley. I already have opposition. I don't have the luxury of entire loyalty."

Ashley argued, "It will be harder to change in the future if you allow . . ."

Again, Trevor cut her short. "This is not your concern. It has nothing to do with Lionel."

Trevor's countenance suggested that further conversation regarding the matter was futile. Although Ashley wanted to say more, she restrained herself. It took some time, but she eventually was able to get their conversation back on track.

By day three, the conversation started moving in the direction Ashley needed it to. Ashley had met Trevor early that day, and they were enjoying a breakfast of sliced meats and freshly baked bread in his office. She had been watching Trevor and noted that this was the first time that he seemed completely relaxed. In all their other times together, it took time for him to get to this point. Today, however, was different. Ashley took advantage of the opportunity.

"Trevor, what can Lionel do to make this transition easier for you?" She questioned.

Trevor looked thoughtful. Ashley waited for him to formulate a response, being careful not to pressure him.

"I know King Daren has petitioned to rejoin the ICP as a voting member," Trevor stated.

"Yes, he has, and once he's accepted, he fully intends to use his influence to support you."

"That will be a change. Lionel supporting Aldrich at the ICP." Trevor grinned ironically. "Daren has allies in the ICP already. Some pressure on them to support me as well would be beneficial."

"I don't see that as a problem. As long as you remain dedicated to changing Aldrich for the better and ridding it of your father's influence, I think the majority of the world would support you." Ashley smiled reassuringly.

Trevor's brow creased. "Your faith, Ashley, in the goodness of mankind is somewhat naive."

Ashley felt chided, but she wasn't going to let Trevor know he had affected her. "And your faith in mankind has been tainted by the evil of your father. Not everyone is like him."

"No, but the majority of people have their own interests at heart. As long as it serves them in some way to support Aldrich, then yes, I am sure they will. As soon as that support becomes sacrificial in any way to them, they will scatter like flies leaving Aldrich to the mercy of blood-thirsty, power hungry predators. I can assure you, Ashley, Lionel is not much different when all is said and done." Trevor stated this matter-of-factly. There was no anger or malice in his voice but rather a defeated acceptance of the inevitable.

"Then we will just have to make sure that they do have a valuable interest in Aldrich," Ashley offered.

"How do you propose we do that?" There was challenge in Trevor's voice. He leaned back in his chair.

Ashley thought for a moment. "Well, what does Aldrich have to offer? Most countries are likely to support another country that is giving them something they need. What does Aldrich have that others might need or even want?"

"We have several manufacturing plants that were shut down over the years as more and more countries set embargoes against us. If those embargoes were lifted and some start-up funding provided, perhaps we could reopen the plants," Trevor suggested.

"Well, I can't promise anything right now, but that seems fair. I am here to find out what you need so I can take it back to the council. Anything else?"

"You."

Ashley shook her head and grinned. "I'm not going to take that back to the council."

"They sent you here to me now. I think our time has been beneficial. Just think of what we could accomplish if we had more time," Trevor tempted in his usual mesmerizing monotone.

Ashley knew that she had influence over Trevor. It was not a vain perception but rather a basic understanding. If there was some way to work with Trevor without emotions getting in the way, they could truly do great things together for Aldrich. He had behaved himself these past few days for the most part; maybe it was possible.

Trevor's voice interrupted her thoughts, "You are thinking about it. You know how influential you could be here, Ashley. Much more so than if you remain Sterling's gopher."

Trevor was manipulating her, and she knew it. "I will speak to the council about sending someone to assist you," she suggested.

She immediately realized her mistake. Trevor stood and the stone wall was back in place. She wasn't going to get much more out of him right now. The breakfast tray was nearly empty and both had had their fill. It was a good time for a break.

Ashley suggested just that. "Why don't you think about what else Lionel could do to help, and we can regroup in a few hours."

"Very well. Return here in two hours." His tone was dismissive and Ashley hoped that two hours would be enough time for him to stop sulking.

****

Ashley awakened refreshed, ready to leave. The last two days with Trevor had been very productive overall, and she felt that her time here was well spent. She would be meeting with Trevor one last time before heading back to Lionel at 11:00am. It was 7:00am.

Showered and dressed, Ashley walked out of the bathroom. Chad was still in bed, but was awake. As soon as he saw her, he spoke up, "Ashley, did you know. . ."

"Chad, if you ask me if I know something one more time, I'm going to throw your handheld out the window so that you can no longer sit here and read useless information all day long."

Ashley then kissed him and left.

Log was waiting outside the door as usual. He was still sulking over their disagreement days earlier and the fact that nothing had changed where security was concerned.

As they made their way to Trevor's office, Ashley once more pondered the fact that Trevor had to live in this dungeon. He had grown up here as well, and she wondered what horrors a small boy had encountered or imagined in these long, dark, foreboding hallways.

Trevor was sitting at his desk when she entered. Raymond was standing before him. She had discovered upon asking Trevor that Raymond was the palace director under Warren Benson and had retained the position upon Trevor's succession. She also learned that Trevor relied on him for nearly everything. The fact that he had worked for Benson made her wary of him. The moment Trevor saw Ashley, he dismissed Raymond.

Trevor stood and greeted Ashley with a kiss on the cheek.

"Your presence here has been a great comfort, Ashley." His frustration from the morning before had long dissipated.

"I am happy that you allowed me to come."

"You are welcome any time."

"Thank you."

"Have you given further consideration to my offer?"

His offer was tempting but implausible. Still, Trevor was persistent.

"Trevor, you know that is impractical. I am married, and I do not think Chad would join me here."

"You could arrange to visit one another. I am sure that his duties prevent him from spending much time with you as it is. It would not be a loss."

"Trevor, it's just not . . ."

"I need you."

"Trevor . . ."

"I don't know who I can trust here. There's no one."

His words tore at her heart just as they were intended. "There's Kendra. In time, maybe she would . . ."

"Ashley, you are 100x the woman Kendra is. I need someone who has my best interests and that of Aldrich at heart, not selfish ambition. With you here these past few days, I have hope that I can make Aldrich better, but I cannot do it alone."

"I will speak with King Daren and see if there is anyone he would recommend."

Trevor moved closer to Ashley as he spoke the next words. "I do not want just anyone, Ashley. You are my muse and my inspiration. Just think of what we could do for Aldrich together. The whole world would take notice."

His closeness and the desperation of his tone bewildered her. "Maybe. Maybe I will see if there is anything I can do."

"And I know Ashley, that when you want something, you find a way to make it happen. It is that determination and drive that make you so compelling."

"Is there anything else we need to discuss before I go?" Ashley tried to redirect the conversation.

"I should have never let you go."

The comment and the passion with which he said it, startled and strangely frightened Ashley. As he gazed at her, she felt as though tiny daggers were being aimed at her heart. Instinctively she stepped back and away from him. Her retreat was met with a flash of anger which just as quickly fled.

"I do not intend to make you uncomfortable, Ashley. I simply do not wish to see you go so soon."

"I need to go so that I can help you. King Daren needs to know what we have discussed."

"I understand. I only wish that I had your promise that you will return."

"I'm sure that there will be future visits. Thank you for your hospitality."

"You are most welcome."

"Well, goodbye then."

Trevor stood gazing at her for a few moments before returning to his desk. He pushed a button and then addressed Ashley one last time, "Raymond will see you out."

Chapter 38

Dawson Moulder entered Chad's office and took a seat in one of the chairs facing Chad's desk. He rested his elbows on his legs and leaned forward. The office itself was not extremely spacious, but Chad's desk was rather large. It was made of oak and curved so that Chad could make use of three sides. However, most of the desk was immaculately clean with only a small stack of folders and his computer taking up space on the desk. Glass plated oak bookshelves lined the walls behind Dawson. The space between the black leather chair in which Dawson sat and the front of Chad's desk was minimal causing a rather cramped space for Dawson's long legs.

"What did you need?" Dawson inquired.

"Commander Heart wants me to have the same security access in this office as he does in his office," Chad explained.

"I can do that."

"Thank you."

Dawson picked up his tablet from the chair beside him where he had placed it and set to work. He could have returned to his office to do the work, but he and Chad had not had much opportunity to talk lately, so he remained.

"How did things go in Aldrich?" Dawson asked.

"Just great," Chad replied. They had been back for two days.

"How did she do?"

"Great. She loved it."

"You didn't."

"No, I didn't, but she was determined to go. She insists that it was a success. I don't know why it couldn't have been accomplished with a phone call."

"Well, Chad we both married women that have a mind of their own. Has King Trevor seduced her yet?"

Chad glared at Dawson.

"She might be going back," Chad stated.

Dawson had been looking down at his tablet as they talked, but at Chad's comment his head jerked up.

"What?"

Chad looked perplexed and Dawson immediately felt pity for him.

"Trevor has invited her to work as his advisor," Chad explained.

"I'm sure that's not going to happen."

Chad shook his head. "The council is seriously considering it. They've decided to put it to a vote."

Dawson sat back in his chair, a look of disbelief on his face.

"Check your access," Dawson instructed. "Don't worry Chad. If he messes with Ashley, I can hack into his systems and wreak havoc."

"How do I check access?" Chad questioned.

"You're pathetic, man," Dawson admonished as he remotely accessed Chad's computer.

"I feel violated," Chad complained.

"As you should. It's not my fault I have skills."

"Too bad you don't have them on the courts."

"I'm pretty sure I won the last time."

"I don't think so."

"We can do a rematch any time. The newlywed excuse is getting old."

"Are you actually going to show me how to do this, or am I going to have to call you every time I need to access the system?" asked Chad.

Before Dawson could answer, the phone rang. Chad picked it up.

"This is Commander West."

Dawson waited as Chad spoke briefly with the person on the line. As soon as he hung up, Chad stood up. He seemed excited.

Chad looked at Dawson, "We found him," he announced.

"Zinn?"

Chad nodded an affirmative. "I have to go."

An emergency council meeting had been called. Zinn was hiding in the small country of Platinum. A satellite manned by the country of Eden had picked up images that indicated a possible location. The intel had been shared with Lionel and a recon team had confirmed. Christopher was to assemble a strike team immediately. The border country of Eden had agreed to allow Lionel troops passage across the border into Platinum. As soon as a team was ready, they would go. King Daren was concerned that Eden may have shared the information with other interested parties, so Ian was given the responsibility of contacting King Ethan in Raxx to inform him of the plan. As Zinn was responsible for the bombing that had injured Ethan's wife, Ethan had equal interest in Zinn's annihilation.

****

Todd sat in the belly of the military transport cargo plane next to General Ben Canaan. It had been an easy decision to send Ben Canaan's unit on the mission. It would give them the satisfaction of finishing what they had started with Benson. The engines of the plane were a constant roar making conversation difficult if not impossible.

The men had been instructed to try to rest as much as possible during the long plane ride. Once on the ground, there would be no time to relax. They didn't want to risk the possibility of Zinn changing location before they could get to him.

The plane landed in Eden near the border of Platinum and the men disembarked. Most of the soldiers were the same ones who had stormed the palace in Raxx. There were a few new faces, and Todd was reminded of the losses they had suffered. Particularly, Newberry. A pang of guilt gripped his heart at the thought. He had failed his sister.

Ben Canaan was barking orders. The border was only 30 minutes away, and Zinn was located within sixty miles of the border. Queen Esther had agreed to provide ground transportation for the team. A representative from the Queen greeted them and led them to a nearby hangar. Inside the hangar were thirty-four motorcycles. Todd would be right at home.

As well trained as they were, it was evident that some of the men had never been on a bike. Those who were more experienced attempted to do a brief overview without wounding any pride. They took off, engines howling in the early morning mist. Four miles out from Zinn's hideout, the men discarded their motorcycles and continued on foot. As the sun came up, steam rose in the hot humidity of the day. It reminded Todd of the heat in Aldrich nearly ten months before. He hoped this mission would be as auspicious as that one had been. There were woods surrounding the abandoned warehouses providing the perfect cover. Intel showed a total of four entrances to the building. Half of the team would enter through the front doors of the building and flush Zinn and his men out the back where the rest of the team would be waiting to gun them down. If the intel was accurate, it was a fool-proof plan. Both Ben Canaan and Todd would be a part of the outside team. Everyone was in place. Caleb gave the signal for the men to infiltrate. Outside, shouts and gunshots could be heard coming from the inside. Todd's adrenaline was pumping hard. He was geared and ready for the first man to come running through the door. The anticipation of not knowing when that would happen was both frustrating and exhilarating. The shouts and gunshots were getting closer. Todd braced himself and raised his gun.

Suddenly, without warning, a missile whizzed by his head and slammed into the wall of the warehouse. Once the smoke had cleared, a gaping hole was left. Confusion followed as men rushed out of the exits and the hole that had been created. Todd and the others began shooting, but everything was chaotic. Todd looked back to where the missile had originated and saw soldiers pouring out of the woods. He wasn't sure which way to shoot. Heat signatures had indicated that Zinn and all of his men were inside except for the few patrols they had taken out quietly when they arrived. Either Zinn had a larger number of men than they anticipated or something wasn't right.

Todd scanned the area for Caleb. He had positioned himself behind some debris from the wall and was shooting left and right. One of his bullets found the chest of a man who had emerged from the woods. Todd stopped firing. Something definitely was not right. Some of the men had drawn closer, and Todd could see an insignia on their uniforms. It was that of Raxx. Immediately Todd started yelling to the other team members to take cover and stop firing. Zinn's men were in the mix, but it would be reckless and inexcusable to accidentally shoot down any more Raxx soldiers. Todd looked back towards Ben Canaan. He too had stopped firing and must be aware of the situation. He started yelling to his men as well. Todd then looked around for whoever was in charge of the Raxx troops. When he thought he had located him, Todd left his post and headed his way. Todd was able to get fairly close to the man before he saw Todd. He pointed his gun towards Todd, but then recognition dawned on his face. He too started yelling at his own men to stand down.

Todd looked back towards the warehouse and saw six of Zinn's men covering one of the exits. He headed for the exit. Sure enough, Zinn emerged. His black hair and pale skin blended with that of his men, but Zinn stood taller than the others sporting a sculptured mustache and thin lined beard. As soon as he was clear, Zinn and his men started running towards the wall that bordered one side of the warehouse. Caleb saw it too and went after him. Todd rushed behind. Zinn and his men reached the wall. Five of them turned and spewed gunfire towards any would be assailants as Zinn and one other scaled the wall. Todd and Caleb dove for cover. From his position, Caleb fired a shot and clipped the man on the wall with Zinn. As soon as Zinn was over, the rest of the men followed. Caleb and Todd continued pursuit. Caleb reached the wall first and jumped up and over. Todd was only seconds behind. When he hit the other side, he landed next to Ben Canaan.

Caleb was still on the ground holding his leg, which was twisted unnaturally. As soon as he saw Todd, he yelled, "Go, go, go!!!"

Todd hesitated. Caleb yelled again, and Todd took off. As he reached the edge of the woods, gunfire erupted hitting the trees around him. Todd took cover behind one and waited until it stopped. Taking a deep breath, he stepped from behind the tree and quickly scanned the brush. He saw one of Zinn's men reloading. Todd pointed his gun and fired. The bullet found its mark in the center of the man's forehead. Todd continued on quite pleased with himself. He recognized the man as Zinn's right hand.

Todd was running as fast as he could. He finally caught a glimpse of someone ahead. As he drew closer, he realized it was Zinn himself. He pushed himself even harder. He was succeeding in closing the gap between them when he slammed into the ground. His gun went flying and his body was buried in mud. Mud was in his eyes as he scrambled for the gun on his hands and knees. From out of nowhere, someone kicked him in the gut. Todd tried to stand, but was halted by the feeling of something hard being pressed against his head. Todd turned his head to the side to try to see his attacker. It was Zinn. Todd's heart skipped a beat.

Zinn spoke in a heavy accent, "The hero prince of Lionel. You will die in the mud like the pig you are."

He pulled the trigger. Todd heard a click and he felt moist warmness trickle down his leg as he realized his bladder had failed. His eyes were closed, and all he could hear was a thumping sound. It took him a moment to realize it was the sound of his own heart. If his heart was beating, then he was still alive. He opened his eyes. Zinn had fled. Todd jumped to his feet, cursed at the air, grabbed his gun and pursued. Zinn's men had doubled back for him. Todd stopped in his tracks. They fired towards him haphazardly. It was then that Todd heard the rumble. A train was coming. Todd watched helplessly as Zinn and his men jumped on it. The mission had failed.

Still covered in mud, Todd trudged back towards the warehouse. Halfway back, he ran into some of his other unit members.

He was angry, and he let loose, "Where the hell were you?"

One brave soul spoke up, "Are you okay Lieutenant?"

"Do I look f******* okay? Zinn is gone. Don't waste your time looking for him. Where's the general?"

Although many of these men outranked Todd, they all now deferred to him.

Someone else spoke up, "They are carrying him back to the drop-off site on a stretcher, sir."

"And where the hell is the commander of the Raxx forces?"

"I don't know, sir."

They had started walking back to the warehouse with Todd as they talked. When they reached it, Todd separated from them. He needed a moment alone before he ripped someone's head off. This had been a complete disaster, and he wanted to know who was to blame. Once he had cooled off, he set out in search of the Raxx commander. No Raxx forces were anywhere to be found. They had apparently high-tailed it out of there.

Todd watched from a distance as the wounded were rounded up and makeshift stretchers were made to carry them to the drop-off point. It occurred to him now that the motorcycles although fast were not the most practical form of transportation for the wounded. He cursed once more. This entire mission was a debacle. His father would be enraged.

Somehow they had managed to make it back across the Eden border. The wounded were attended to before being loaded onto the plane. All those who could still walk, plodded onto the plane behind. The ride home was somber, a sharp contrast to the ride from Aldrich months before. Todd had hoped to have an opportunity to talk to Ben

Canaan, but they had given him a sedative for the extreme pain he was in. Todd sat silently wishing the ride would end.

Chapter 39

The plane landed. Almost 32 hours had passed since they left Lionel for Platinum.   Exhaustion had set in, but Todd was chomping at the bits to get off the plane and find his father. Christopher was waiting on the ground. Todd made a beeline for him.

As Todd neared, Christopher raised his hand to grip Todd's shoulder in a gesture of reassurance. Todd slammed his hand away. Todd's clothes were still covered in mud. He had scrapes and bruises up and down his arms and on his forehead. His eyes had a look of rage as he addressed his father.

"What the hell was that, Dad? A suicide mission?"

Christopher had heard bits and pieces of what had happened, but he was hoping to get a better picture once he spoke with Caleb and Todd. Caleb was still sedated, and Todd was obviously in no mental condition to talk reasonably.

"Things didn't go as planned," Christopher explained.

"The hell they didn't. You nearly lost 34 of your best men, Dad. And the worst part is that Zinn got a good laugh at our stupidity."

"Todd. . ."

"No, I'm not done. Maybe you do need to step down and let someone else take over because you obviously aren't doing your job! You sent men over to be gunned down by our supposed allies."

Christopher and Todd began walking to the palace. As they made their way to the suite, Christopher allowed Todd to rant, but once they reached the suite, it was time to cut it off. His son needed rest.

Before opening the door, Christopher turned and addressed his son, "Sarah and the boys are sleeping, Todd. Get some rest, and we will discuss this tomorrow."

Christopher opened the door and entered before Todd could protest.

It was 4:30am. Todd awoke in a cold sweat. He could still feel the barrel of the gun against his head. His mud soaked clothes laid on the floor where he had stripped them off, and he had not bothered to take a shower before collapsing into bed, naked and spent. Sleep had come easier than expected, but it had been a fitful sleep. Every muscle in his body ached and his head was throbbing. He rolled over and sat on the edge of the bed with his head in his hands. Pieces of mud fell to the ground. The mud brought remembrance, and he picked up his shoe and chucked it across the room slamming it into the wall. Knowing that further sleep was futile, Todd headed for the shower.

For a long time, Todd stood with his hands against the wall leaning forward to allow the water to pour over his entire body washing away the remnants of failure. By the time he stepped out of the shower, it was 5:15. He knew his father would be awake.

He pulled on fatigue bottoms and a t-shirt and headed out. His father was not in the suite, so he headed for his office. If he was not there, Todd would wait. He was still angry, but the rage had subsided for the most part.

Christopher was sitting at his desk when Todd entered unannounced. He invited his son to sit down.

"Todd, I know you are rightfully upset about what happened, but General Ben Canaan will be undergoing immediate surgery on his leg, and I need a firsthand account of events."

"What the hell was Raxx doing there?"

"I don't know. Lance will be in contact with Ethan for more information."

"You don't know? We gunned down some of their men," Todd exclaimed. "No one knew what was happening, so we were firing at anyone who wasn't with us."

"Damn it." Christopher had not been aware that his own men had fired on the Raxx soldiers. This definitely complicated things even further. "Why the hell would Ethan send men in when he knew we were going in?" The question was more to himself, but Todd didn't realize that.

"You're asking me? Seriously? We walked into a death trap! I still don't know how everyone made it out alive. And, motorcycles? Who the hell gives you motorcycles for a mission like that? We had to f****** strap injured men to the back of the damn things to get back!"

"I am sure that Queen Esther had good intentions."

"Good intentions, my ass."

"Enough of the language, Todd."

"I just had a f****** gun stuck to my head, and you are criticizing my language?"

Again, Christopher was caught off guard. This was yet another detail of the mission that he was unaware of. However, before he was able to question Todd further, King Daren stormed into the office.

"Give me an explanation, now," Daren demanded.

Christopher was still getting his head around the information that Todd had just shared with him and did not immediately respond.

Todd piped in, "Obviously no one around here knows what the hell they are doing."

Daren threw Todd a warning look and addressed Christopher once more.

"I just got off the phone with Ethan, Christopher. He informed me that some of his men were fatally shot by our men! What the hell happened out there?"

"Language." Todd uttered the word with a cocky smirk at his father.

Both King Daren and Christopher gave Todd a look of warning.

Todd continued, "We shot them because we didn't know who the hell they were. As far as I am aware, we were never told in the briefing to watch out for unexpected visitors. I mean, once they shot the rpg past our heads, all bets were off."

Daren turned his anger on Todd, "Your impulsiveness has left us in a compromising position."

Todd stood and faced off with the king.

"My impulsiveness? If someone is firing at me, I fire back. It's called self-preservation. They shot at us too. We're just better. 34 good men went in there trusting that their king and commander had their backs only to be ambushed by f****** allies."

Christopher could tell by the look on Daren's face that Todd had crossed a line. No matter how justified his son's anger was, Daren was the king and demanded respect. Todd had come so far, and Christopher didn't want one event to ruin that.

He tried to intervene, "Daren, Ethan knew we would be there. If he sent in troops anyway, that's on him."

Silence followed Christopher's comment.

Ignoring Christopher, Daren spoke to Todd, "Lieutenant Heart, if you are unhappy with the way things are being handled, then perhaps you have gotten yourself in over your head. I would be more than willing to grant you a discharge."

Todd put his hands on his hips and drew in a breath that expanded his chest before speaking. "I took out Lionel's number one enemy. I just went on suicide mission and survived managing to bring back every member of my unit alive, and you expect me to beg you for a discharge? Somebody needs to be discharged, but it's certainly not me."

Christopher started to speak, but Daren held up his hand. Daren's commander obeyed his silent command.

As Daren spoke, he widened his legs and his stance was unyielding, "This country has flourished for quite some time without you, Todd. And although what you did was commendable, and yes, perhaps heroic, even you are expendable. I do not care how valuable you think you are, I will not have a man in my military who does not respect me."

Christopher expected Daren to dismiss Todd following his rebuke, but he did not. The king sat down. Todd was still standing. Daren's reprimand had subdued Todd. Todd realized that his anger was unproductive and he now had an intense desire to effectively communicate what had transpired. He hoped that Daren would still give him the opportunity. When no one dismissed him, Todd sat back down.

Daren questioned Christopher, "What exactly did Ian say to Ethan?"

"How would I know?"

Daren gave Christopher a frustrated look and ordered, "Call him."

After several minutes of yelling, it had been ascertained that Ian dropped the ball. Ethan had not been contacted. Daren accused Christopher of not following through, and Christopher questioned if he needed to babysit all of Daren's advisors to make sure they did their job. As the two men argued back and forth, Todd picked up on things he had never noticed before. He had always thought his father to have an uncontrollable temper, but he saw now that although his father spoke his mind to the king, there were unspoken warning signals from Daren that Christopher skillfully navigated with surprising control.

Daren wanted details. It was now Todd's turn to speak. Christopher invited him into the conversation, "Todd, tell us what happened from the beginning."

Todd recounted all of the events leading up to his encounter with Zinn. He then hesitated. A latent fear gripped him. What if his father and the king found his actions to be cowardly? He had run the scene through his mind over and over again, but he didn't know what he could have done differently. Taking a deep breath, he continued his story, "I pursued him. I had almost caught up to him when I tripped. It was muddy. I couldn't see. Zinn must have doubled back to where I was. He tried to kill me, but I guess he was out of ammo."

Christopher remembered what Todd had said earlier and put it all together.

Todd finished, "By the time I got up, Zinn and his men had jumped a train. I lost them."

The look on Daren's face as he listened to Todd had been intense. Growing up in the palace as a member of the royal family, Todd had had several encounters with Daren. Daren was his uncle and a man, but for the first time today, Todd really understood that Daren was his king.

Daren waited to make sure Todd was finished; he thanked him and then turned to Christopher, "I will deal with Ethan. Find Zinn. I do not care what it takes, find him and eliminate him. I will not allow him to harm my family any longer."

Daren rose and left.

Christopher saw that his son was still exhausted. "Todd, get some rest. You might want to let Becca know that her father is okay."

Todd was spent. So much had happened, and he needed some time to himself to make sense of it all. He called Becca to let her know about Ben Canaan and reassured her as best he could that all would be well. Normally, he would have gone to see her, but she was in class and he was exhausted. He went to his room and passed out.

Chapter 40

The next morning, Todd again rolled out of bed early. His alarm clock had been set for 6am, but it was only 4. Sleep had once more been fitful with images rotating through his mind of him holding a gun to Benson's head contrasted with those of a gun being held against his own head. He felt the need to clear his head. His whole body was still screaming with soreness from the events two days before and lack of sleep, but still he knew that a good run would do him good. He threw on the same fatigues and t-shirt from the day before and headed out.

It was still dark out as Todd made his way towards the path that ran through the forest around the palace and Todd willed himself against the shadows that seemed to creep around him in the moonlight. Soon, the sun came up and with it; Todd finished off his run and headed back to the palace. He now felt bad about not going to see Becca the day before, so he decided to take a shower and then find her.

By the time he was finished with his shower, Todd had changed his plans somewhat. There were still unspoken words between himself and Ben Canaan, and after what had happened with Zinn, he needed to set things right. He and the general had worked together in acquiescent silence over the past few weeks, but Todd knew that Ben Canaan was still miffed about what had happened with Becca.

Christopher had insisted that General Ben Canaan be treated by Dr. Xavier, so Todd made his way to the palace clinic. Ben Canaan was sitting up in one of the clinic beds with his leg held in some kind of brace that looked like a torture device. Deanna Tracy, the King's financial advisor, was sitting in a chair next to the bed.

When she saw Todd, she stood and excused herself. "Prince Todd, be careful. He's a bit of bear this morning." She smiled at Ben Canaan, touched his arm and left.

Caleb just grunted.

As soon as she left, Ben Canaan growled at Todd, "Where's your father?"

Todd shrugged. "I don't know."

"You tell him he needs to get his sorry ass down here and explain what the hell happened out there," Caleb demanded.

Todd understood the general's frustration. It mirrored his own from the day before. He grabbed the doctor's rolling stool and pulled it next to Caleb's bed as he took a seat.

"I already gave both my father and King Daren a piece of my mind. Freakin' suicide mission."

Todd took a few moments to recount the information he had learned regarding what happened. General Ben Canaan had a disgusted scowl on his face when Todd finished. Based on explicatives used at various points, Todd surmised that Ian Garrett should be thankful the General was temporarily out of commission.

"I'll let the Commander know you want to talk to him," Todd promised.

Caleb grunted in agreement.

Battle talk was easy. Now it was time to move on to the difficult conversation. Todd had trouble knowing where to begin.

Todd looked down at the General's leg. "What is this? Some kind of torture device or something? That come from Aldrich?"

Ben Canaan made an effort to move his leg and grimaced in pain. "Caught my damn leg on that wall jumping over."

"Yeah, I know. I saw. I was pretty impressed you made it over the wall at all."

Caleb looked like he wanted to strangle Todd. Todd rolled slightly away from the bed.

Taking a deep breath, Todd dove in, "Sir, I'd like to ask your permission to take Becca to the celebration tomorrow."

Caleb gave a harumph in reply. Todd waited, but Caleb remained silent.

"Was that a yes?" Todd finally questioned.

"I thought you did what you wanted and damn the consequences," Ben Canaan accused.

"Is that what you really think?" Todd knew this wasn't going to be easy, but he had hoped for the best. Apparently, Caleb was not quite ready to forgive.

"What am I supposed to think, Todd? After Aldrich, you paraded around here like a peacock in mating season."

"Sir, I wasn't . . ." Todd started but was cut off by Caleb.

"You made it very clear, Todd, that you are a prince, and you get and do what you want. You used Hannah. You put Becca in danger, and disrespected me as her father. You've had weeks to talk to me about this, but you only come crawling in here when you want something." Ben Canaan was nearly roaring now.

Todd exhaled in frustration. "Sir, I apologize. I'm sorry for what happened before. I'm trying to make it right. What do I need to do to prove myself?"

Caleb's tone was tempered as he replied, "It's going to take time, Todd. I don't think it's a good idea for Becca to go with you to the celebration at this point."

After several moments of silence, Todd responded, "Fine. I hope your leg heals quickly."

Todd stood up to leave, but he looked Ben Canaan in the eyes as he spoke, "You know, I really do care about Becca. I would never intentionally put her in harm's way or hurt her."

Caleb made no reply, so Todd turned and walked towards the door. Just as he was about to exit, the General spoke, "Todd, stop. Becca is all I have, and I have done everything in my power to protect her. She can go with you to the celebration, but if you do hurt her, I won't care who you are."

Todd held back a smile and instead gave Caleb his sincerest look. "Thank you, sir." Then, before the general could change his mind, Todd made a beeline for Becca.

Chapter 41

As guests arrived at Lionel palace they were mesmerized by millions of tiny white lights adorning the palace courtyard. The lights were meant to symbolize both the discovery of the diamonds and the end of dark times for the country. Hearts had been somewhat heavy since Zinn had evaded capture, and Daren hoped that this celebration would lift the spirits of his people. Each guest emerged from their vehicle in their finest attire. Ladies wore floor length ball gowns and the men were in tuxedos. The excitement inside the palace rivaled that of the guests who had begun to make their way through the palace security check point. The gala was an integral part of the weeklong celebration. It had been four months since the discovery of the diamond mines.

Mr. Dawson Moulder had finally managed to get all palace security systems up and running. Christopher had put Captain Teresa Walters in charge of arranging security for this event. This made the most sense as Teresa's husband Alan would be organizing the event and they could collaborate together. Teresa had nearly driven Dawson crazy with concerns about the new system. Although it had taken Dawson months longer than he anticipated to get the systems online, he was confident in his work.

Once through the security checkpoint guests were regaled with the sounds of piano music provided by Prince Wesley, himself. Hors d'oeuvres were provided in the rotunda where Wesley played. Guests then entered the grand ballroom where the rest of the evening's festivities would take place.

It was seven o'clock and Todd made his way through the crowd and headed to Becca's suite to escort her to the gala. He had promised to come for her at 7:15. It was now 7:10 so he waited outside the door knowing she would not be ready. He checked his own appearance in a mirror that was hung in the hallway. He hated wearing a tuxedo. He felt like he looked about six years old in it. It was time. He punched the door pager. Ben Canaan was on duty this evening so he knew Becca would be the one to open the door. The door opened and Becca stood before him in a light pink ball gown. Todd smiled. She was beautiful.

Although Todd had grown up in the palace, he had always felt uncomfortable at events like this, but this time he was excited. Becca would be by his side. Becca's hair was pulled up and back away from her face, but a few of her curls framed her face. Todd reached forward and pulled on one of the curls. Becca didn't chastise him for messing up her hair, but rather gave him a shy, demure smile. Although Becca lived in the palace with her father, she had never attended the official events of the palace. For the most part, Becca was timid and kept to herself. Todd knew from their discussions that Becca was both terrified and excited about going to the gala. After this, the world would know that they were together.

Todd offered Becca his arm, "Dr. Ben Canaan?"

"Todd, I'm not a doctor yet."

"That's good because all the guys would be lining up at your door to be your patient. You look beautiful. We may need to rethink this doctor thing."

Becca just smiled and shook her head.

"Are you ready to dance?"

A brief look of terror swept over Becca's face.

"I don't plan on dancing." Becca stated.

"Oh, you are going to dance."

"I can't."

"How can you live in a palace and not know how to dance?"

"I don't know. I just don't." Becca sounded hurt.

"You're a closet dancer, aren't you?"

"A what?"

"You wait for your dad to leave, and then blare the music and dance all over the suite."

"No."

"Well, we are going to dance, and you are going to like it." Todd's tone was playful yet determined.

They were now standing just outside the ballroom. Todd thought he could hear Becca's heart beating. He was amused at her trepidation. As they entered together, cameras flashed almost immediately. Normally, the media was not permitted to take pictures or film within the palace, but because of the nature of this particular celebration, King Daren had allowed both within a set time frame. Although he would never admit it, Todd was happy that his father had suggested Becca speak with both Dr. Hill and Ms. Rose to prepare her for the onslaught of media she would face now, but especially when she went away to the university in a few months. He glanced over at her. She held onto his arm with an iron grip, but otherwise she seemed composed. Todd had never felt so proud.

Todd saw his sister across the room and headed that way. As he got closer, he saw that Ashley did not seem to be enjoying herself. It was highly unusual for his sister to be in a room full of people and not be happy. She was staring at something across the room. He followed her gaze and it landed on Chad.

Reaching her, he inquired, "What's your problem?"

Ashley glared at him initially, but then seemed to relax.

"Nothing. It's just . . . the biggest event of the decade, and I can't even enjoy it."

"Do I need to take care of someone for you?"

"No, not yet."

"I guess ugly and uglier won't be here tonight."

Ashley smacked her brother. "You're so mean. Jonathan is absolutely adorable."

"Of course, he's my nephew."

"You need to go see Kelly again. She still thinks you are upset with her."

"I am."

"Todd."

Ashley seemed to suddenly become aware that Becca was attached to Todd's arm. "Becca, I'm sorry. It's good to see you. I love your dress. It's beautiful. Todd actually doesn't look so bad with you by his side." She grinned.

"Well, I least I have somebody by my side." Todd retorted.

"You two should go dance. Go, go."

"Did you hear that, Becca? That's an order from the princess that we go dance."

Todd grinned at the terror that once again flashed across Becca's face as he pulled her to the dance floor. His strategy was to draw her into a conversation to distract her from the actual dancing.

"Every weekend." Todd stated.

Becca looked at him questioningly. As he spoke, he had placed her hand on his shoulder. His right hand rested on her waist, and their other hands were entwined to the side in a classic dance pose.

"The first six weekends will be spent taking dance lessons," Todd continued.

Becca had actually relaxed into dancing a bit, but at his mention of lessons, she tensed up again.

"I don't need to learn to dance." She stated.

"Mmm, if you are marrying a prince, you definitely need to know how to dance."

No formal proposal had been made, but Todd had laid out their future together in his head. Over the past couple of months he had designed a master plan and timeline for Becca and himself. Her insistence on going away to the university had initially put a damper on his plans, but he had made adjustments that they both could agree on. Becca rarely contradicted him, but she had remained adamant about her education. When it came down to it, although it would keep them apart more than he wished, he had to admit that it was not only her beauty that drew him to her, but she was one of the most brilliant women he knew.

Common sense was a bit of a struggle for her, but her lack of it provided constant amusement and entertainment for him. He was also reminded of her clumsiness as she stepped on his shoe for the fourteenth time. He stopped dancing and drew her close.

He looked intently at her as he spoke, "I love you, Becca Ben Canaan."

Becca's eyes lit up as he reached up and touched her cheek. Somewhere close by a flash went off. It annoyed Todd, but he wasn't going to let it ruin the moment. Becca would be leaving soon, and he was determined to enjoy every minute he had left with her here, and she needed to know beyond a shadow of a doubt how he felt before she left.

"I will be there every weekend." Todd had emphasized the "will" this time.

"I'll have something to look forward to every week then."

Becca had not spoken the words, but Todd knew that she felt the same.

****

If Chad's plan was to ignore her the entire evening, it was not going to succeed. Ashley had had enough. He could claim that it was work keeping him occupied all he wanted, but she knew better. Sulking in the corner had not had the desired effect, so she put a new plan into motion. Chad was still across the room, and he was engaged in a conversation with Alan Walters. She stood up and walked purposefully to them.

"Excuse me Mr. Walters, but Captain West needs to dance with his wife."

She thought she recognized reproach in the look that Alan gave her, but she didn't allow it to impact her. She knew that Alan and her father did not approve of the council's decision to send her to Aldrich as Trevor's advisor, but she also knew that his disapproval was out of concern, not malice. Every other council member had voted to send her. Alan and Chad shared common ground on the matter, and it was the reason that Chad had been avoiding her.

Alan returned to work giving her and Chad a chance to talk.

Chad spoke, "Ashley, I have to work. I can't dance."

"Then I'll just go ask my father to relieve you for the rest of the night."

"He's not going to do that."

"We'll see." Ashley turned to find her father.

As expected, Chad grabbed her arm and pulled her back.

"You can't keep doing that." Chad complained.

Ashley ignored the complaint. "Is this how it's going to be for the next three weeks?"

"This is not the place, Ashley." Chad looked around to see if anyone was listening. He placed his hand on her arm as he spoke.

221

Ashley jerked away. "Then where is the place, Chad, because you don't talk to me even in our suite."

Chad sighed. "I do talk. You don't listen."

"The way you are acting makes me want to leave sooner."

"Then go. I am sure Trevor will welcome you with open arms."

"You are really going to waste our time together acting this way? This is supposed to be a celebration. We should be dancing. God has given us much to be thankful for, and all you can do is brood." Ashley knew her comment would convict Chad.

Chad was struggling. The truth was that he understood the importance of taking advantage of this opportunity with Aldrich. The two countries had been enemies for decades, and this opening was monumental. He just wished that there was someone else who could go. Still, he did not understand how King Daren and the council had determined it morally acceptable to send his wife far away to live in a palace with her former fiancé who was obviously still obsessed with her. Some on the council had seen this as an open door provided by God. Chad wrestled with the idea that God would open such a tempting door.

Ashley continued, "I am going to Aldrich, Chad. You need to accept that. You can either make me never want to come back or make me long to come back. Let's have some fun while I'm still here. Dance with me, please!"

Chad relented. He allowed Ashley to guide him to the dance floor. She threw her arms around his neck and moved close. He held her tightly as they danced. He did not want her to go with friction between them. He did not want her to go at all. She was right on one thing though, he needed to make sure she would be unbearably homesick while in Aldrich.

As the song ended, Ashley looked Chad in the eye, "Isn't this much better?"

"I love you Ashley. I don't want to share you, and I don't want to worry about you."

"It's work, Chad. Nothing more."

"It's Aldrich, and its Trevor."

"You worry too much." She tilted her head to the side studying him. "Someday I hope our son has your eyes."

Chad wrapped his arm around the back of her head and gently pulled her close. Leaning his head down, he kissed the top of her head. Several clicks were heard as cameras captured the moment.

Dinner was served, and at 9:00pm, King Daren strode to the middle of the ballroom. He would address the guests of the gala while simultaneously addressing the nation through the hoards of media that were present.

He began, "We are a blessed nation. We must continue to follow and serve our God and always remember to offer thanksgiving to Him for all He has done and all that he is doing. Our country has suffered much in the past few years, and there will no doubt be trials to come.

God tries us; He tests our faith and as we endure, he lavishes his grace and mercy upon us. We have come through the fire, and now we stand in a time of abundant blessing. Throughout history, Kings and nations have endured trials. In Psalm 66, King David wrote:

'Praise our God, all peoples, let the sound of his praise be heard; He has preserved our lives and kept our feet from slipping. For you, God, tested us; you refined us like silver. You brought us into prison and laid burdens on our backs. You let people ride over our heads; we went through fire and water, but you brought us to a place of abundance.'

We will continue to praise God through whatever comes, and will give Him thanks for his provisions. We have had four days of celebration. We have dined together, danced together and rejoiced together. We have allowed ourselves lavish enjoyment. I call upon our country now to look to the future. It is easy when things are going well to neglect the One who provides. I encourage you to take the next few days to take the time to fast and pray for God's guidance for our country and for our leaders. We must ask God to search our hearts. We will continue our celebration this evening. Thank you."

Members of the media had been instructed to leave following the King's address. Taking advantage of the distraction, Alan made his way to King Daren.

The king had returned to his table and was sitting with his family. Alan approached and addressed Daren, "King Daren."

Daren looked up, eyebrows raised in question. Alan continued, "Sir, I wanted to take the opportunity to commend you on an excellent address. Our country is truly blessed to have a righteous king."

Daren stood. As he shook Alan's hand, he commented, "Thank you. I appreciate your encouragement."

Alan gave a dignified nod. "Sir."

Alan returned to work. Daren scanned the room. Everyone seemed to be enjoying the evening, and it pleased him. He knew that life in the palace could be stressful, especially on married couples, and he hoped that times such as this gave them opportunity to reconnect. His eyes rested on Todd and Becca. Todd had followed palace protocol and come to him requesting permission to date Miss Ben Canaan. Daren had inquired of Christopher who seemed uncommonly thrilled by the idea. He had readily given his permission. Apparently things were going well. Daren decided to take a moment to speak to the young couple.

As he approached them, Todd was immediately aware of his presence. Becca had her back to him and was unaware. As he came closer, Todd placed his hand on Becca's elbow and turned her to the king.

Daren stopped in front of them.

"Todd. Rebecca. I hope you are enjoying the evening."

Todd replied, "Yes, sir."

Todd looked at Becca. Her face was as white as a daisy, and her eyes were huge. No sound escaped her lips. Todd squeezed her elbow slightly to no avail. She remained frozen.

Daren could see that his presence was having a paralyzing effect on the young girl. He tried to remember if he had ever spoken to her before, but at that moment he could not recall any occasion. He felt somewhat guilty over the realization. At the same time, he hoped that if she were going to be a part of the family, that she would be able to overcome her seeming terror of him.

From behind him, Daren heard his name. He turned. Governors Gibson and Erikson stepped forward to shake the king's hand.

Governor Gibson spoke, "King Daren, that was an excellent speech. It is comforting to know that our country is no longer under financial strain."

"Thank you, Governor Gibson."

Todd noted that the vultures were already circling.

Daren turned his attention back to Todd and Becca in dismissal of the governors.

"Tonight is quite significant for the two of you. Your presence here together is an announcement to the world of your relationship. Todd, you represent this family, and many eyes have been and will continue to be on you. I trust that you will uphold our values."

"I understand, sir."

"You are doing well, son. I am pleased with your choices. Keep it up."

"Yes, sir."

Daren turned slightly to confront Becca, "Miss Ben Canaan, I understand you will be studying medicine at the university soon. Doctor Xavier is quite impressed with your potential."

Becca stood completely dazed.

When she didn't respond, Daren turned back to Todd, "Todd, you can tell her what I said later when she recovers."

Todd smiled knowingly and Daren returned to his table.

Once Daren had departed, Todd gently grabbed Becca's chin and turned her towards him.

"Becca? Are you there? Hello?"

"Um, yes."

"Does my uncle scare you?"

"He's the king."

"He's my uncle. He's not going to bite . . . much."

"Okay."

Todd just shook his head. They would definitely have to work on this. He guided her once more to the dance floor. Still in apparent shock, she did not protest this time.

Three hours later the celebration ended.

Chapter 42

Although the gala had been only two weeks ago, it seemed like a distant memory. It was a week before Ashley was scheduled to leave for Aldrich. Chad continued to dissuade her from going, but his overall attitude had improved considerably since the gala. Ashley had been working with Lance to prepare for the past few weeks, but this week she was only working half of each day. She was in her suite getting things ready when Chad entered. It was 1:00pm. She assumed he was on a lunch break.

He stopped just inches in front of her. He placed a hand on her shoulder as he spoke, "Ashley, I still do not want you to go to Aldrich. I think it is a foolish idea. However, if you still insist on going, then I am going to insist that you take some precautions."

Ashley huffed, "I am, Chad."

"All you have done is prepare for the political aspect of the trip. Aldrich is still not safe. What have you done to prepare for that?"

"Log will be with me."

"He was not with you the whole time before."

"Everything's going to be fine. Stop worrying about it."

Chad grabbed her arm and twisted it around so that she was pinned in an immovable position.

"What are you doing, Chad?"

She struggled for freedom to no avail.

"Chad, let go." Ashley yelled.

Chad kept his hold. "Is that what you would say to an attacker, Ashley? I doubt they would comply."

"Just stop it. This isn't fair. I wasn't expecting you to do that."

"You are right, Ashley. I am sure that an attacker would warn you first."

"I hate you."

"Good. Do something about it."

Ashley struggled some more, but it was useless. She was getting angry. She tried to play dirty but the way Chad was holding her prohibited almost any movement.

"I said let me go," she demanded.

"I will, as soon as you promise to listen to me."

"I always listen to you."

"That's debatable," Chad countered as he released her. "You are only working half days with Lance right now. I want you spend the other half learning some self-defense tactics."

"From whom?"

"Me."

"Right. When are you going to have time to do that?"

"Every day from noon till midnight."

"Twelve hours?" Ashley was incredulous.

"I am sure we can make time for some other things in the schedule as well."

Ashley ignored the insinuation. She was still frustrated at his attack and doubtful that he would have time for her. "You don't have to work? How did you manage that?"

"I spoke with King Daren."

"Really?"

"Yes, Ashley. I won't see you for quite some time once you are over there. I think the request was reasonable."

Chad grabbed her again and explained, "There is a way to get out of this, Ashley. You just have to know the right moves."

For four days now, Chad and Ashley had practiced self-defense 4 hours daily. Her departure was just days away. Chad had taught her numerous tactics for multiple situations. Normally she would arrive at their suite first and he would then meet her there. Today, he made it a point to arrive before her. Unsuspecting, Ashley opened the door and strolled into the room. Chad assaulted her from behind a retaining wall that separated the kitchen area from the living room. She was caught off guard, and he managed to knock her down and pin her to the floor.

Completely unnerved, Ashley screamed at him, "Are you crazy? Get off of me!"

Chad did not comply. There was irritation in his voice as he spoke, "Ashley, you have to be vigilant at all times."

"I'm in Lionel in my own suite in a palace surrounded by men that both my father and husband command. I should be safe."

"That's what I'm afraid of, Ashley. You have felt safe your entire life, and you won't know how to handle it when you are not!"

"Stop it. Just stop it Chad. I will be fine. No one is going to be jumping out at me from around corners, and if they do, Log will bash their heads into the concrete."

He continued to pin her down as they glared at one another.

Ashley continued, "You are obsessing over this. This is crazy."

Chad cooled a bit as he said, "I'm sorry, Ashley. I just want to know that you will be okay. If you are caught off guard and end up in a position such as . . ."

Chad's voice had broken as he spoke. Ashley felt somewhat convicted at the pain she saw in his eyes. She knew he loved her and was trying to help, but he really was obsessive.

"I love you, Chad. I'm not trying to torture you despite what you may think. Now, show me how to get out of this."

"I . . . I can't." Chad rolled to the side

"Oh, come on Chad. We finally get to the fun part, and you are going to bail out?"

"This isn't fun and games, Ashley. Do you understand what a man could do to you?" Chad's tone was serious.

Ashley tried to calm him. "I do, but it is going to be okay, Chad. I promise."

Chapter 43

It had been three weeks since Todd had returned. The first two weeks Todd had gone to his father's office daily to find out if there were any new leads. By the third week, the high from the mission had worn off and Todd had returned to a routine. Most of his time was spent continually training. Over the past six months he had gotten to know many of the men in the military, and he was becoming well-known and liked. It was Thursday. Tomorrow he would make his way to the university to spend the weekend with Becca. The university had guesthouses, and he had reserved one for himself for the entire year so that he could come and go as he pleased.

Becca was doing well. She was enjoying her classes, and was on track to finish in accordance with Todd's plan. They talked daily. She had come home for a few days after her father's surgery. It had been difficult to convince her that Ben Canaan was perfectly capable of recovering without her constant nurture.

Todd's biggest problem over the past few weeks had been finding things to do to keep him occupied at night. His room was still in his father's suite, and although Sarah was sickeningly nice, he didn't care to spend all his time with his step-mom and half-brothers. Tonight he had decided to watch a movie. The palace had a small movie theater that residents could use at will. The theater consisted of a large screen with surround sound and about fifty roomy leather reclining seats. Todd sat in the dark in the middle of the theater with a bag of pretzels and a coke. As he crunched on a pretzel, he wished Becca was there with him, but knew that the crunching would have driven her crazy. He crunched even louder. The movie was a love story that took place during the Third World War. Many movies had been made about the war and natural disasters that had changed history as they knew it. Todd had seen most of them, but he particularly liked the fact that the director of this one paid attention to the details of battle strategy. Just as a nuclear bomb was about to explode in what used to be North America, Todd's phone buzzed. He was about to dismiss the call when he saw that it was Hannah. That was odd. One good thing that had come of the fiasco with

Hannah was that she and Becca had reunited and were now sharing a room together at the university.

Todd answered, "Pretzel girl?" Even though their brief relationship had not worked out, they had remained friends and he had retained his nickname for her.

"Todd?"

"Why are you calling me?" Todd questioned.

"It's Becca."

Todd stood up, "What about Becca?" There was urgency in his voice.

"She won't stop shaking."

Something was wrong with Becca. Todd left the theater and was headed for the garage. "Shaking? What do you mean, shaking? Is she having some kind of seizure? Is there a doctor?"

"No, she's not sick. We watched a movie."

Todd waited for Hannah to continue, but the girl who usually couldn't shut up wasn't talking. He got annoyed, "Hannah, you're not making sense. What is wrong with Becca?"

Todd reached the garage and climbed into his black sport utility truck. He pealed out.

Hannah was trying to explain, "The movie freaked her out."

"What did you watch," Todd asked. Maybe this wasn't as serious as Hannah was making it. She could be overly dramatic at times.

"It was some movie about a serial killer in a place called Texas. It was really old. This freak was killing everyone with a chainsaw."

"You let Becca watch that?"

"We didn't know what it was. Some guys brought it over to the dorm. We were watching it in our room."

"Some guys?"

"Look, are you coming or not?"

"I'm on my way, but I don't understand what is wrong with Becca."

Hannah nearly screeched, "I don't know either. That's why I called you!"

"I'm on my way." Todd hung up. He couldn't take any more of Hannah. It didn't sound like Becca was dying, but if she needed him, then he would be there.

Todd maneuvered into the no parking zone directly in front of Becca's dorm. He rushed inside. He was opening the door to her hallway when a female voice questioned, "Where are you going?"

Todd appreciated the fact that men were not allowed in the girl's hallways after 9:00pm, but this was different. Not wanting to waste time, he turned to the girl who was standing with her hands on her hips trying to look official.

"I'm going to see Becca Ben Canaan."

"You're a guy."

"Good job. I'm also Todd Heart. Todd pointed to a magazine that was laying on a table. His face covered the front of it.

The girl looked at the magazine, looked at him, looked back at the magazine and then said, "Oh."

She then walked away. Todd opened the door and continued to Becca's room. He didn't bother to knock but barged in unannounced.

He saw Hannah first, "Why is your door unlocked?"

He scanned the room for Becca. His question was forgotten when he saw her balled up on the floor in front of the sofa. He immediately went to her and knelt beside her.

Putting his arms around her, he pulled her to him. "Becca?" She didn't respond. "Becca? Becca, are you alright?"

Her breathing was irregular as though she were having a panic attack. She was shaking as Hannah had said, and she had a vacant stare on her face. She wouldn't even look at him, and it frightened Todd.

He pushed her away a little so that he could grasp her shoulders. He shook her gently, "Becca, look at me." He shook harder and raised his voice. This time it was a command, "Becca, look at me."

Slowly, she began to come out of her stupor. She looked at Todd and recognition flashed across her face. She clung to him and began to sob. Todd held her until the crying subsided.

He pushed her back again and lifted her chin so that she was looking at him, "Becca, what happened?"

"I'm sorry."

"Ok, what's wrong?"

"I'm sorry."

"Becca, for what?"

"I shouldn't have watched it."

"Probably not. Let's go home." Todd hoped that he could make some sense of this on the way home.

Todd took her to the car and drove off. After he felt that he had given her enough time, Todd questioned, "Becca, what exactly happened back there?"

Becca seemed to struggle for words. "My mother. He did those . . ." Her voice trailed off.

"The bastard is dead Becca. He can't hurt anyone anymore."

Once Todd had proven to Ben Canaan that he was serious about Becca, Caleb had shared with him that Becca had witnessed the rape and murder of her own mother by King Warren Benson. Caleb had also explained that Becca still suffered trauma from the event. This was the first time Todd had witnessed it. He only wished he had tortured the bastard before disposing of him.

By the time they reached the palace, Becca seemed to have recovered. He had decided that she needed a weeklong break from school. Becca was smart enough to do the work remotely, and she would be just fine.

Todd jumped out of the SUT and circled around to open the door for Becca. He helped her out.

Todd looked at her as she stood in front of him. Despite the fact that she had been crying her eyes out, she was still beautiful. He felt an intense desire to protect her, "Becca, I'll take care of you. You have nothing to be afraid of. I will never let anyone hurt you."

"I'm sorry you had to drive all the way."

Todd sighed, "For you, Becca, I would drive to the moon." It sounded funny to Todd even as he said it, and he gave Becca a lopsided grin.

She smiled back. He reached for her curls and tugged. "I have missed you so much."

"Me too."

"I've missed you more."

Becca just smiled. Todd had been tense since the moment Hannah told him something was wrong with Becca. Standing with Becca now and watching her smile, made him relax. He couldn't help but think again how perfect she was and how perfect they were together. He reached out and pulled her to him.

She tilted her head upward and he bent his to meet her lips. After a long kiss, Todd looked at Becca once more.

"I love you, Becca Ben Canaan," he stated.

"I love you, Lieutenant, Prince Todd Heart."

It was late, so Todd escorted Becca to her room.

****

Becca had protested at first when Todd informed her the next day that she would not be going back to school for a week, but Todd had won the battle. Four days had passed, and Todd was considering finding a way to keep her away from school permanently. His father had warned him early on that if he held Becca back from the goals she had set, that there could come a time that she would resent him for it. Christopher had also hinted that Todd may have opportunities for advancement in the military, and some time without distraction might be good for him.

They had planned to go swimming today. Todd was still getting up early to train, so he had planned to meet Becca at the pool at 10:00am. He was running late. When he reached the pool, Becca was already there. She was lying on a lounge chair next to the pool wearing sunglasses and an orange bikini. The fleeting thought that this could be a bad idea crossed his mind, but he quickly dismissed it. He was going to enjoy himself.

He dived into the pool and swam across to where she was. She lifted her head to look at him.

"Come on." He splashed water in her direction.

She stood up and entered the pool from the steps. They had only been in the pool about fifteen minutes when Todd's phone buzzed. The only person that mattered was with him, so he ignored it. Becca gave him a questioning look, but he shrugged his shoulders and rolled his eyes dismissing it.

Ten minutes later, Lieutenant Franklin showed up. He walked to the side of the pool and wearing a huge smile addressed Todd.

"Lieutenant Heart, you've been paged."

"Really?"

"Yes, sir. I was ordered by Commander Heart to fetch you."

"To 'fetch' me?"

"Yes, sir. He wants to see you immediately."

Todd looked at Becca and ordered, "Stay here. I will be back."

He then swam to the side of the pool. He lifted himself out of the water and turned to sit on the side of the pool. He splashed some water at Becca with his foot before standing up and leaving.

Todd arrived at his father's office with a towel wrapped around his waist over his bathing suit. His top was bare. He was slightly embarrassed when he saw King Daren sitting in the office with Christopher.

"Umm, family gathering?" Todd asked.

Neither king nor commander seemed amused. The atmosphere in the room was tense and Todd wondered if he had done something wrong.

"I'm just going to go change."

Christopher nodded approval and Todd headed to the gear room, which was close by. He knew that if he was in some sort of trouble, then keeping them waiting any longer was unwise. He hurriedly put on fatigues and shoes and returned to the office. Christopher ordered him to shut the door and sit down.

Todd sat down and waited. In the silence, his concern grew. He started running everything through his mind, trying to figure out if there was something he'd missed. By the looks on their faces, he even wondered if they were going to disown him from the family. He smirked a little at that thought.

Christopher was the first to speak. "Todd, Zinn apparently has a personal vendetta against you."

"He should. I took out his right hand man," Todd bragged.

"Well, he is willing to pay a substantial amount of money to have you killed."

"How much?"

"There's a bounty of $30 million set on your head."

"Sweet. This is great. This could make it easier to find him."

Neither man spoke, and they both still had solemn looks on their faces.

Todd inquired, "Anything else?"

Christopher continued, "Todd, this means that anyone close to you could be in danger. It is not past reasoning that Zinn would even pay more to see you suffer loss. You will be safe in the palace. I have already contacted the forces commander in Aldrich to be extra vigilant in case anyone goes after Ashley."

Todd gave that thought, "We should send more security. Or, maybe she should just come back now."

"I have taken action to ensure her safety," Christopher assured him. "Todd, you need to consider what to do about Becca."

"She's fine. She's here."

"Yes, but she goes back to the university on Monday."

"She'll just stay here until it's settled."

Christopher had been leaning back in his chair, but he now sat forward and gave his son a pointed look, "Son, it took six months to find Zinn the first time. He will be even more vigilant now that he knows we are actively hunting him. We may not find him for months or even years. Is Becca willing to postpone her plans inevitably?"

"It doesn't matter. It's what she will have to do."

Christopher looked at Daren. He seemed to be searching for words, so Todd decided to help him out.

"What exactly are you asking me to do?" he questioned.

"Todd, we have talked about this before. I still feel it is important that Becca pursues her own goals. It's a mistake I made with your mother, and I don't want you to have to deal with the same mistakes I made. I have no doubt that Becca will stay here if you ask her to, but if you love her, son, then you have to let her become who she is meant to be."

Disbelief was on Todd's face. "What are you saying?"

"The only way to ensure Becca's safety AND allow her to continue with her plans is to break things off for a while, Todd." Christopher saw the defiance in Todd's eyes. He waited for a response.

"Seriously?"

Christopher knew that Todd was resistant, but he continued anyway, "When you break it off, you can't tell her why. It has to be convincing. Anyone watching her needs to believe that she has no connection to you anymore."

Todd shook his head, "This is crazy!"

Daren interjected "Todd, Becca is going to school. She needs to be safe. Take care of it." Daren rose to leave. As he walked to the door, he squeezed Todd's shoulder and stated, "I want Zinn just as badly as you do."

Todd looked at his dad. There was pain in his eyes. "So I'm just supposed to go down there and lie and say, 'I hate you Becca. I never want to see you again.'?"

"You have power, and you have fame, Todd. Now comes the very hard responsibility. It is never easy, but the way you handle it will determine who you become."

Todd had had enough. He needed time to think. Without another word, he got up and left.

Upon leaving his father's office, Todd had spent the last three hours on the outdoor training courses. Although he had resigned himself to breaking up with Becca, he was still angry over it. He reasoned that it would be best to get it over with as quickly as possible. Otherwise, he may not have the strength to go through with it. Becca would be here for three more days, and her father would be able to comfort her. He knew she had probably waited for him at the pool for hours before finally giving up. That was good. Maybe she would be mad at him. He had left his phone at the pool, and he was counting on Becca to bring it to him later. He had decided that he would go to the dining hall and await her arrival. It would be the hardest thing he had ever done.

Todd had been sitting for almost half an hour. He ate slowly trying to make it last in hopes that Becca would show up soon. Alan had passed by numerous times apparently concerned that Todd was not enjoying his dinner. Todd had finally told him not to bother him anymore. He felt guilty. After another ten minutes, Becca appeared at the entrance to the dining hall.

She looked his way, and he quickly glanced back down at his plate. From the corner of his eye, he could see her coming towards him. She arrived at the table.

"Are you okay?"

Any other woman would have yelled at him for abandoning her at the pool. He briefly wished she was like them.

"I'm fine," he answered while shoving food into his mouth.

Becca sat down across from him.

He looked up and tried to scowl at her, "What do you want?"

"What happened to you today?" she asked.

"I got called into work." Todd kept his head down as he answered unable to look her in the eye.

"Oh. You just sort of disappeared."

"Well, I couldn't call you because you have my phone." He took an accusatory tone and immediately felt like a complete jerk.

"Right. Sorry. Here." She held out his phone.

He grabbed it.

She gave him a confused look. "Todd, is something wrong?"

"Maybe you should go back to school tomorrow."

"Okay, why?" Becca looked confused.

"I don't think this is working." Todd made an effort to sound firm, but inside he was crumbling.

"What do you mean?"

"This, Becca. Us. It's not working." Todd had noted the hurt in her voice, and he wanted more than anything to reassure her, but knew he couldn't.

"Todd, what happened? Things were fine earlier today."

"That's just it, Becca. You always think things are just fine. . . Well, they aren't."

"Then let's talk about it. What needs to change?"

Todd had hoped that he could just end things quickly and neatly with Becca, but she was as much in love with him as he was with her. Becca had a stubbornness about her when it came to the people she loved, and it tortured Todd that he would have to get mean with her to make this happen.

"I need a change." He looked at her now in an attempt to drive his point home. The hurt look on her face tore at him.

"Okay, Todd, I don't know what happened today, but please talk to me."

Todd raised his voice, "I am talking to you! What more do I have to say? I can't come running to you, Becca, every time you have an issue. This isn't working, and I'm done! It's over, so get over it."

Todd glanced at Becca. All the color had drained from her face, and she sat paralyzed. His impulse was to go to her and comfort her. It took every bit of resolve he had to stand up, throw his fork on the table and walk out. Every eye in the dining hall followed him as he left. He wanted to shout at them to go comfort Becca and stop looking at him.

Once out of the dining hall, Todd went directly to the suite. He hoped it would be empty, but when he opened the door, his father was sitting on the sofa with Sarah. It was an unusual sight. For a moment, Todd just stood staring at them. He felt out of control. He walked to his room without acknowledging his father or Sarah. He started to lay down, but he weight of what had just happened crashed down on him, and he felt sick. He barely made it to the toilet before he threw up.

After a few moments had passed, Christopher entered the bathroom. Todd was sitting on the side of the bathtub. He was no longer throwing up, but he still felt ill.

He looked up at his father, "Get out!"

Christopher took a deep breath and walked towards Todd. Todd picked up a towel and chocked it at his father.

"I said, get out!"

Christopher caught the towel in mid-air and threw it into a corner. He then sat down next to Todd.

"Todd, I'm proud of you."

"Leave me alone."

"No. I won't. I have made a lot of mistakes, Todd. One of those is that I have greatly underestimated my own son."

Todd briefly looked at his father, but then returned to staring at the floor.

Christopher continued, "I know what it is like to lose. . . Todd, this isn't the end for you and Becca. You are sacrificing for her, and some day she will understand that."

A few moments passed before Todd spoke, "Why?"

Christopher understood the question. It was the same question that had haunted him for years. His family had suffered immensely. He had suffered. Now his son was suffering. The question agonized him, and it tormented him even more that he had no answers for his son.

"I don't know."

Todd looked at his father with a look of disgust, but then he saw that the pain on his father's face mirrored his own. Anger had been an easy emotion for Christopher, and it was the only passion his children had seen from him, even when their mother had died. Todd was beginning to understand that that anger masked pain.

It was too much for Todd. He didn't want to see it. Not now. He wanted to run, but exhaustion held him in place. With his elbows resting on his knees, he rested his head in his hands and gave way to the sobs that began to wrack his body. His father, the formidable commander, simply sat next to him with his own tears staining his face. It was a moment that neither of them would ever mention again but that they would share for a lifetime.

Chapter 44

Ashley was giddy with excitement. She had accompanied Trevor to the ICP meeting, and Chad would be arriving soon. It had been nearly three months since she had seen her husband. She stood in the rotunda of the ICP building. Every time the door opened, she stood on tiptoe to see who was coming through. Finally, it was Lance that she saw first. She made her way to him looking past him for signs of Chad.

"Am I not good enough, Princess?" Lance teased.

"You are perfect, Lance," she said as she hugged him.

Lance smiled. "He's in the third car. He will be coming in after King Daren."

"Who?" Ashley joked.

Lance smiled as he offered her his arm. She took it and continued her vigil.

King Daren, Queen Nicole, and Prince Noah arrived. This was an important meeting for both Lionel and Aldrich. Prince Noah's coming of age gave Lionel the opportunity to rejoin as a voting member of the ICP, and this would be Noah's introduction to the world.

Daren addressed Ashley, "Princess Ashley, you look well. Chad is in the car behind us."

"Thank you, King Daren. I am well, and Chad needs to pick up the pace."

"I assure you. He is just as . . . giddy as you are."

"Ahh, he wants to see me." She acknowledged the queen and prince, "Queen Nicole, Prince Noah, how are you?"

Nicole spoke, "We are well, thank you."

Ashley looked once more at Noah. Her eyes travelled upward. "You've grown. What are they feeding you?"

Noah smiled.

Suddenly Ashley's eyes lit up. She disengaged herself from Lance and hurried to the doors. Chad had finally arrived. As soon as he was clear of the people around him, Ashley threw her arms around his neck. From afar, Daren watched as Chad closed his eyes and buried his face in the top of her head. He still struggled with the decision to keep the two apart.

Ashley looked up at Chad. She reached up and kissed him.

"Did you bring them?" she questioned.

"Was I supposed to bring something?"

"Um, yes." She was adamant.

"Are you referring to these?" Chad held out a small box that he had somehow concealed within his tuxedo.

She grabbed the box and opened it. Inside were 10 perfectly shaped Alan's special cookies. Ashley looked to see if anyone was watching and then stuffed a cookie in her mouth. Chad just shook his head at her.

"Do you want me to hold onto them for you?" he offered.

"Can I trust you?"

"Yes. I've missed you."

"I miss you too."

"You could come home with us tomorrow."

"Ashley." It was Trevor's voice. There was a dark possession in his tone.

Ashley stepped away from Chad and faced Trevor.

"Yes?" Ashley's voice held slight agitation. She had been looking forward to seeing Chad and she did not want their time together to end so quickly.

"The meeting is starting. Join me," Trevor commanded as he offered his arm.

Ashley looked at Chad and then boldly turned to Trevor, "I will be there momentarily. Save me a seat, please."

Trevor did not look pleased, but he capitulated. Deliberately, he turned and walked away. Ashley turned back to Chad.

"I want my husband to escort me."

Chad smiled. It was good to see his wife.

Ashley entered the assembly room and took her seat next to Trevor. She had helped him write the speech that he would give to the assembly at some point this evening. She thought it was good, and she was anxious to see the reactions to it. Everything was going well. Trevor had been very accepting of assistance from Lionel and the start of an amiable alliance had begun.

As Daren was rejoining the ICP and wanted to have voting powers immediately, his reentry was at the top of the docket. Councilor Hathaway invited Daren to stand and speak. Daren stated his reasons for wishing to rejoin and then introduced Noah to the world. Ashley felt a sense of pride in her country as the room erupted in applause. Now that Noah had grown quite a bit, it was obvious that he was going to at least look the part of a king. She had also been around him enough to know that he would have the heart of a king.

The formality of voting on Daren's reentry commenced. Whereas there would have been concern over the votes at one time, Daren now had enough support within the ICP that it was a nonissue. Lance had spent months pouring over the guidelines and procedures of the ICP looking for a loophole, and now within minutes, Lionel was once more a voting member.

As King Daren and Prince Noah sat down, Daren took a moment to acknowledge his foreign affairs advisor. He leaned across Nicole to speak to him, "Well done, Lance. This is a result of your hard work."

"Thank you, sir." It was always good to be back in the king's good graces.

Lance passed the agenda to Daren. There was only one other item that Daren was interested in at this meeting. He scanned the list. At the very bottom, he found what he was looking for. Since Aldrich had recently been defeated in war and it now had a new king, the ICP reserved the right to review the situation and determine if there was any breach of ethics on either side. Daren didn't really care what the council decided where he was concerned. Lionel was in a good place. God's blessing was upon them, and Daren was not going to worry about the works of men. He was, however, very interested in what Trevor would have to say. Although Ashley had continuously assured Lance that Trevor was taking his country in a new direction, Daren wanted to hear it from the king's mouth.

As Trevor would not be speaking for quite some time, Daren took the opportunity to show his son around the ICP.

He nudged Noah with his arm, "Let's go."

Noah looked at him questioningly.

"Get up." Daren quietly ordered.

Noah obeyed. Outside, Daren found that he was not the only world leader who was "skipping" the meeting. Ethan was speaking with Queen Esther. Daren approached them.

"Ethan. Queen Esther." Daren greeted.

"Daren." Ethan returned.

"King Daren. Always a pleasure. Prince Noah, I remember when you were born. You have become quite a handsome young man," Queen Esther commented in a thick accent.

"Thank you, Queen Esther," Noah answered.

Daren spoke, "Queen Esther, it is always good to see you."

"Thank you, King Daren. If you will excuse me."

Daren nodded and then addressed his brother-in-law, "Ethan, I sincerely hope that our miscommunication in Platinum has not jeopardized our friendship."

Ethan nodded, "I concede that it was a lack of communication on both of our parts. I believe that we still share the same goal."

"That's good to hear, Ethan. How is Brooke?" Daren inquired.

"She has fully recovered physically. It was very traumatic."

"I understand. We almost had him." Daren had intended the comment as a reassurance, but realized it may have been taken as a reprimand. If Ethan's men had not shown up, they probably would have succeeded.

Daren tried to assuage the unintended wound, "We will get him. He will pay for what he's done."

"Thank you, Daren. Please tell Nicole that I would like to speak with her before she leaves."

Daren nodded in agreement.

Ethan looked to Noah, "Prince Noah, congratulations. I am surprised that Kiley did not join you."

Daren was taken aback by the comment. He and Nicole had aggressively discussed the possibility of Kiley taking the throne of Raxx once she was of age, and it was now apparent that Nicole had shared with her brother. Daren chose to save the fight for another day.

Noah had looked to his father for an answer, but seeing that his father remained silent, he spoke, "She wanted to come, but dad said no."

"I see." Ethan commented.

"Well, Ethan, if you don't mind, I am giving Noah a tour of the building."

"Of course, Daren. It has been a pleasure."

Daren enjoyed showing his son around. Noah asked good questions and took note of the things he should. Daren was proud of him. Once again, he felt blessed. He reflected on the numerous times that he had felt that he was being tried and tested and how Pastor Isaiah had continuously encouraged him to call upon God and trust Him.

Daren and Noah had returned to the ICP meeting after several hours. It seemed that Noah was as anxious to hear Trevor's speech as Daren was. He had asked about it several times during their tour. It was finally time for Trevor to address the ICP. It was now late into the night. At 1:15am, Trevor was given the floor.

As Ashley sat and listened, she subconsciously mouthed the words along with him. At one point she caught herself and looked around self-consciously. Trevor was almost to the end of the speech, and he now broached the topic that interested Daren.

Trevor's voice was strong and unwavering as he addressed the members of the ICP. " . . . Although Lionel and Aldrich have been enemies for centuries, we look to a new dawn of understanding and cooperation. My father committed atrocities. I am not my father. My desire is for Aldrich to progress: economically, industrially, and politically. It will only be with the support of strong allies and the ICP that we will accomplish this. I ask that the ICP recognize my right as king and that the country of Aldrich be pardoned for any iniquities committed prior to my reign. I thank you for your time."

It was over. Daren left the assembly room feeling tired yet relieved. His mind was going in a hundred directions, but his thoughts were hopeful. Never before had Lionel been in such a strong position. As the king, he had gained allies and defeated enemies. It had not been easy and Daren had certainly stumbled, but they had come through a season of mourning into a season of rejoicing. As Daren watched his son, he prayed that the season would be a long one.

Daren was pulled from his thoughts by a female voice. "Brother?"

Daren turned to see Megan standing nearby with Gavin. He hugged his sister and then shook the hand of the King of Mikasa. She looked happier now. He hoped that she and Gavin had worked out their troubles.

Gavin spoke, "King Daren, it seems that Lionel is doing well."

"It is," Daren agreed.

"It would seem that only one enemy has eluded you. Zinn?"

"Yes, he has, but we will find him." Daren's tone was confident.

Daren had stepped away from the rest of his entourage to speak with Gavin and Megan. He now excused himself and rejoined his family. He noted that Chad looked somewhat anxious.

Daren addressed Chad, "Captain West, we will be leaving at 11:00am in the morning. What you do with your time between now and then is solely your choice. Make good use of it."

Chad was a bit embarrassed at the king's uncharacteristic innuendo. He excused himself and set off to find his wife. Country leaders were given accommodations within the ICP building itself. Their representatives and guests stayed at nearby hotels. Chad hoped that Ashley had not yet left for the hotel. He walked through the crowds searching for her auburn hair. He tried calling her, but was sent to voicemail. He finally saw her standing with a group of people. As he drew closer, he realized that some of the group members were the leaders of other countries. He immediately felt out of place. He stood back waiting for her to finish.

Ashley was engrossed in conversation, but when she saw Chad, her eyes lit up and her smile glowed. Everyone in the group turned to see the source of her happiness. Chad looked like a lost puppy. Ashley excused herself and went to him. She didn't bother introducing him as she had seen the red hue flash across his face at the unwanted attention.

She took his arm as they walked outside. They were finally alone.

Chad spoke, "Where is Trevor?"

"I don't know. I don't really care right now."

It was enough. Chad relaxed.

"This is where it all began," Ashley commented.

Chad was confused. "Where what began?"

"Seriously? Let me help you remember." Ashley continued in a low voice trying to emulate Chad, "Here, Ashley. Let me save you and direct you to your room. I'm so smart. I know everything about the ICP building! Oh, you're thirsty? Let me get you a Pepsi! Oh, there's something in your hair. Let me use that to my advantage to kiss you."

She threw her arms around him and reached up for a real kiss.

When it was over, she backed away and smiled, "This time you don't have to worry about my father killing you."

Chad was actually laughing. It was really more of a chuckle, but it was happy.

"I love you, Captain Chad West."

"I love you, Ashley."

"I know."

DEDICATION

First of all, we give thanks to God with the desire that our story and characters will bring glory to His name.

To our moms who let us play with Barbie dolls late into the night thus spurring on our imaginations and creativity! And to our husbands who continued that tradition. Oh, wait, I don't think our husbands knew. Still, thank you dears for sleeping many nights without us as we worked on our book.

To our dads (one who is now in heaven), who are just awesome fathers who will probably never read this book but gave their support anyway.

Madison and Maybree, thank you for your persistent encouragement. To my oldest daughter Mikayla, the best guinea pig reader we could have asked for.

Lastly, for helping us survive long days and late nights, thank you to: homemade chocolate chip cookies, pretzels, sweet tea, Coca-Cola, Chick-fil-a, NutThins and Mexican food.

Bye! . . . for now. :)